THE SAD TALE
OF THE BROTHERS
GROSSBART

Manfried awoke at dawn, his brother snoring beside him. The ashes were cold, indicating his slovenly brother had packed it in hours before. Cursing, he moved behind his brother and knelt down, putting his lips beside Hegel's ear.

"Up!" Manfried hollered, startling both brother and horse awake.

"Eh?!" Hegel rolled away and scrambled to his feet, peering about blearily.

"Sleepin on watch." Manfried shook his head. "Shameful."

"Who's sleepin on watch? I woke you last, you bastard!"

"Liar, you dozed off your first turn at it."

"I kicked you, you miserable goat!"

"When?"

"When I was done lookin out!"

"Hmmm." Manfried chewed his beard, dimly recollecting a foot to his side in the depths of slumber. "Well, I suppose it's no fault a either a us, then."

"No fault? You sayin you didn't get up at all? What the Hell, brother, that's your fault clean and simple."

"Should a made sure I was up," Manfried grumbled, then brightened. "Fuck it all, Hegel, what're we on about? There's loot waitin just down the hill!"

THE SAD TALE
OF THE BROTHERS
GROSSBART

JESSE BULLINGTON

www.orbitbooks.net

ORBIT

First published in Great Britain in 2009 by Orbit
Reprinted 2009

Copyright © 2009 by Jesse Bullington

Excerpt from *Mr Shivers* by Robert Jackson Bennett
Copyright © 2010 by Robert Jackson Bennett

The moral right of the author has been asserted.

A CIP catalogue record for this book
is available from the British Library.

ISBN 978-1-84149-783-9

Printed and bound in Great Britain by
Clays Ltd, St Ives plc

Papers used by Orbit are natural, renewable and
recyclable products sourced from well-managed forests and certified
in accordance with the rules of the Forest Stewardship Council.

Mixed Sources
Product group from well-managed
forests and other controlled sources
www.fsc.org   Cert no. SGS-COC-004081
© 1996 Forest Stewardship Council

FSC

Orbit
An imprint of
Little, Brown Book Group
100 Victoria Embankment
London EC4Y 0DY

An Hachette UK Company
www.hachette.co.uk

www.orbitbooks.net

Dedicated to

Raechel	*David*
Molly	*Travis*
John	*Jonathan*

Preface

The story of the Brothers Grossbart does not begin with the discovery of the illuminated pages comprising *Die Tragödie der Brüder Große Bärte* tucked inside a half-copied Bible in a German monastery five hundred years ago, nor does it end with the incineration of those irreplaceable artifacts during the firebombing of Dresden last century. Even the myriad oral accounts that were eventually transcribed into the aforementioned codex by an unremembered monk hardly constitute a true starting point, and, as the recent resurgence in scholarship testifies, the chronicle of the Grossbarts has not yet concluded. The pan-cultural perseverance of these medieval tales makes the lack of a definitive modern translation even more puzzling, with the only texts available to the contemporary reader being the handful of remaining nineteenth-century reprints of the original documents and the mercifully out-of-print verse translations of Trevor Caleb Walker. That Walker was a better scholar than a poet is nowhere more evident than in that vanity edition, and thus came the impetus to retell *Die Tragödie* in a manner that would transmit the story as it would have been appreciated by its original audience.

The distinction here between stories and story represents what is, presumably, a first in the field—rather than treating *Die Tragödie* as a collection of independent fragments, comparable to the contemporaneous *Romance of Reynard*, I have focused on the quest continuously reiterated by the Grossbarts themselves in order to cobble together a cohesive and linear narrative. A benefit of transforming the work into a single account is the inclusion of previously unlinked stories, divergences that illuminate aspects of the greater narrative even if they at first seem quite disparate save for their era and locale. Another consequence of this approach is that small leaps occasionally occur in the journey as overly repetitious adventures are elided.

Scholars curious as to whether this humble author sides with the apologists Dunn and Ardanuy or the revisionists Rahimi and Tanzer will be disappointed—this tale is intended for those members of the public having no previous acquaintance with the Grossbarts, and is thus unadorned with academic grandstanding. For this reason, and to avoid unduly distracting the average reader, the following pages lack annotation, with the most popular interpretation of any given incident defaulted to when variations arise. As has already been stated, the adventures of the Grossbarts are often remarkably similar save for locale— reflecting regional differences on the part of the original storytellers—and so marking up these deviations would defeat the entire purpose of the project, which is to convey the tale as it would have come across in its original form. After all, the average German serf would be no more aware that his Dutch neighbors blamed his region for spawning the Grossbarts than the merchant of Dordrecht would be that down in Bad Endorf the Germans insisted his town was where the twins were born.

This is indicative of the gulf separating contemporary readers from the original audience, an audience alien almost to the point of incomprehensibility. Those first storytellers and listeners might, for example, have taken the fantastic and violent elements much more seriously with only hearth or campfire to stave off the perilous night. The fourteenth century, wherein the tales were both told and set, was, as Barbara Tuchman opens her history of that era, a "violent, tormented, bewildered, suffering and disintegrating age, a time, as many thought, of Satan triumphant."

Yet it was no arbitrary decision that led Tuchman to title that work *A Distant Mirror*. Tragedies and atrocities may seem inherently worse when appraised from long after they occurred, but despite all we have accomplished wars rage, righteous uprisings are viciously suppressed, religious persecution thrives, famine and plague decimate the innocent. This is not to excuse or apologize for any cruelties peppering the following pages, but simply to provide a lens, should the reader require one, through which to view them.

We will never know if the Grossbarts were heroes or villains, for as Margaret Atwood observes in her novel *The Handmaid's Tale*, "We may call Eurydice forth from the world of the dead, but we cannot make her answer; and when we turn to look at her we glimpse her only for a moment, before she slips from our grasp and flees." That the Grossbarts themselves would take umbrage at both being associated with the witchery of Orpheus' quest to the underworld and this particular account of their deeds seems probable, but whether their medieval audience would approve remains forever unknowable. This tale is exhumed for our enlightenment, and while I have done some tailoring for our modern sensibilities their spirit remains just that, and as such, unquenchable. "As all historians know," Atwood concludes that selfsame quote, "the past is a great darkness, and filled with echoes. Voices may reach us from it; but what they say to us is imbued with the obscurity of the matrix out of which they come; and, try as we may, we cannot always decipher them precisely in the clearer light of our own day." With that wisdom in mind, let us cock our ears and squint our eyes toward the Brothers Grossbart and a beginning in Bad Endorf.

I
The First Blasphemy

To claim that the Brothers Grossbart were cruel and selfish brigands is to slander even the nastiest highwayman, and to say they were murderous swine is an insult to even the filthiest boar. They were Grossbarts through and true, and in many lands such a title still carries serious weight. While not as repugnant as their father nor as cunning as his, horrible though both men were, the Brothers proved worse. Blood can go bad in a single generation or it can be distilled down through the ages into something truly wicked, which was the case with those abominable twins, Hegel and Manfried.

Both were average of height but scrawny of trunk. Manfried possessed disproportionately large ears, while Hegel's nose dwarfed many a turnip in size and knobbiness. Hegel's copper hair and bushy eyebrows contrasted the matted silver of his brother's crown, and both were pockmarked and gaunt of cheek. They had each seen only twenty-five years but possessed beards of such noteworthy length that from even a short distance they were often mistaken for old men. Whose was longest proved a constant bone of contention between the two.

Before being caught and hanged in some dismal village far to the north, their father passed on the family trade; assuming the burglarizing of graveyards can be considered a gainful occupation.

Long before their granddad's time the name Grossbart was synonymous with skulduggery of the shadiest sort, but only as cemeteries grew into something more than potter's fields did the family truly find its calling. Their father abandoned them to their mother when they were barely old enough to raise a prybar and went in search of his fortune, just as his father had disappeared when he was but a fledgling sneak-thief.

The elder Grossbart is rumored to have died wealthier than a king in the desert country to the south, where the tombs surpass the grandest castle of the Holy Roman Empire in both size and affluence. That is what the younger told his sons, but it is doubtful there was even the most shriveled kernel of truth in his ramblings. The Brothers firmly believed their dad had joined their grandfather in Gyptland, leaving them to rot with their alcoholic and abusive mother. Had they known he actually wound up as crow-bait without a coin in his coffer it is doubtful they would have altered the track of their lives, although they may have cursed his name less—or more, it is difficult to say.

An uncle of dubious legitimacy and motivation rescued them from their demented mother and took them under his wing during their formative man-boy years. Whatever his relation to the lads, his beard was undeniably long, and he was as fervent as any Grossbart before him to crack open crypts and pilfer what sullen rewards they offered. After a number of too-close shaves with local authorities he absconded in the night with all their possessions, leaving the destitute Brothers to wander back to their mother, intent on stealing whatever the wizened old drunk had not lost or spent over the intervening years.

The shack where they were born had aged worse than they, the mossy roof having joined the floor while they were ransacking churchyards along the Danube with their uncle. The moldy structure housed only a badger, which the Grossbarts dined on after suffering only mild injures from the sleepy beast's claws. Inquiring at the manor house's stable, they learned their mother had expired over the winter and lay with all the rest in the barrow at the end of town. Spitting on the mound in the torrential rain, the Brothers Grossbart vowed they would rest in the grand tombs of the Infidel or not at all.

Possessing only their wide-brimmed hats, rank clothes, and tools, but cheered by the pauper's grave in which their miserable matriarch rotted, they made ready to journey south. Such an expedition required more supplies than a pair of prybars and a small piece of metal that might have once been a coin, so they set off to settle an old score. The mud pulled at their shoes in a vain attempt to slow their malicious course.

The yeoman Heinrich had grown turnips a short distance outside the town's wall his entire life, the hard lot of his station compounded by the difficult crop and the substandard hedge around his field. When they were boys the Brothers often purloined the unripe vegetation until the night Heinrich lay in wait for them. Not content to use a switch or his hands, the rightly furious farmer thrashed them both with his shovel. Manfried's smashed-in nose never returned to its normal shape and Hegel's indented left buttock forever bore the shame of the spade.

Ever since the boys had disappeared Heinrich had enjoyed fertility both in his soil and the bed he shared with his wife and children. Two young daughters joined their elder sister and brother, the aging farmer looking forward to having more hands to put to use. Heinrich even saved enough to purchase a healthy horse to replace their nag, and had almost reimbursed his friend Egon for the cart he had built them.

The Brothers Grossbart tramped across the field toward the dark house, the rain blotting out whatever moonlight hid above the clouds. Their eyes had long grown accustomed to the night, however, and they could see that the farmer now had a small barn beside his home. They spit simultaneously on his door, and exchanging grins, set to beating the wood.

"Fire!" yelled Manfried.

"Fire!" repeated Hegel.

"Town's aflame, Heinrich!"

"Heinrich, bring able hands!"

In his haste to lend aid to his neighbors Heinrich stumbled out of bed without appreciating the drumming of rain upon his roof and flung open the door. The sputtering rushlight in his hand illuminated not concerned citizens but the scar-cratered visages of the Brothers Grossbart. Heinrich recognized them at once, and with a yelp dropped his light and made to slam the door.

The Grossbarts were too quick and dragged him into the rain. The farmer struck at Hegel but Manfried kicked the back of Heinrich's knee before Heinrich landed a blow. Heinrich twisted as he fell and attempted to snatch Manfried when Hegel delivered a sound punch to the yeoman's neck. Heinrich thrashed in the mud while the two worked him over, but just as he despaired, bleeding from mouth and nose, his wife Gertie emerged from the house with their woodax.

If Manfried's nose had not been so flat the blade would have cleaved it open as she slipped in the mire. Hegel tackled her, the two rolling in the mud while her husband groaned and Manfried retrieved the ax. Gertie bit Hegel's face and clawed his ear but then Hegel saw his brother raise the ax and he rolled free as the blade plummeted into her back. Through the muddy film coating his face Heinrich watched his wife kick and piss herself, the rain slowing to a drizzle as she bled out in the muck.

Neither brother had ever killed a person before, but neither felt the slightest remorse for the heinous crime. Heinrich crawled to Gertie, Hegel went to the barn, and Manfried entered the house of children's tears. Hegel latched up the horse, threw Heinrich's shovel and a convenient sack of turnips into the bed of the cart, and led it around front.

Inside the darkened house Heinrich's eldest daughter lunged at Manfried with a knife but he intercepted her charge with the ax. Despite his charitable decision to knock her with the blunt end of the ax head, the metal crumpled in her skull and she collapsed. The two babes cried in the bed, the only son cowering by his fallen sister. Spying a hog-fat tallow beside the small stack of rushlights, Manfried tucked the rare candle into his pocket and lit one of the lard-coated reeds on the hearth coals, inspecting the interior.

Stripping the blankets off the bed and babes, he tossed the rushlights, the few knives he found, and the tubers roasting on the hearth into the pilfered cloth and tied the bundle with cord. He blew out the rushlight, pocketed it, and stepped over the weeping lad. The horse and cart waited, but his brother and Heinrich were nowhere to be seen.

Manfried tossed the blankets into the cart and peered about, his eyes rapidly readjusting to the drizzly night. He saw Heinrich fifty paces off, slipping as he ran from the silently pursuing Hegel. Hegel dived at his quarry's legs and missed, falling on his face in the mud as Heinrich broke away toward town.

Cupping his hands, Manfried bellowed, "Got the young ones here, Heinrich! Come on back! You run and they's dead!"

Heinrich continued a few paces before slowing to a walk on the periphery of Manfried's vision. Hegel righted himself and scowled at the farmer but knew better than to risk spooking him with further pursuit. Hurrying back to his brother, Hegel muttered in Manfried's cavernous ear as Heinrich trudged back toward the farm.

"Gotta be consequences," Hegel murmured. "Gotta be."

"He'd have the whole town on us," his brother agreed. "Just not right, after his wife tried to murder us." Manfried touched his long-healed nose.

"We was just settlin accounts, no call for her bringin axes into it." Hegel rubbed his scarred posterior.

Heinrich approached the Brothers, only registering their words on an instinctual level. Every good farmer loves his son even more than his wife, and he knew the Grossbarts would slaughter young Brennen without hesitation. Heinrich broke into a maniacal grin, thinking of how on the morrow the town would rally around his loss, track these dogs down, and hang them from the gibbet.

The yeoman gave Hegel the hard-eye but Hegel gave it right back, then the Grossbart punched Heinrich in the nose. The farmer's head swam as he felt himself trussed up like a rebellious sow, the rope biting his ankles and wrists. Heinrich dimly saw Manfried go back into the house, then snapped fully awake when the doorway lit up. Manfried had shifted some of the coals onto the straw bed, the cries of the little girls amplifying as the whole cot ignited. Manfried reappeared with the near-catatonic Brennen in one hand and a turnip in the other.

"Didn't have to be this way," said Manfried. "You's forced our hands."

"Did us wrong twice over," Hegel concurred.

"Please." Heinrich's bloodshot eyes shifted wildly between the doorway and his son. "I'm sorry, lads, honest. Let him free, and spare the little ones." The babes screeched all the louder. "In God's name, have mercy!"

"Mercy's a proper virtue," said Hegel, rubbing the wooden image of the Virgin he had retrieved from a cord around Gertie's neck. "Show'em mercy, brother."

"Sound words indeed," Manfried conceded, setting the boy gently on his heels facing his father.

"Yes," Heinrich gasped, tears eroding the mud on the proud farmer's cheeks, "the girls, please, let them go!"

"They's already on their way," said Manfried, watching smoke curl out of the roof as he slit the boy's throat. If Hegel found this judgment harsh he did not say. Night robbed the blood of its sacramental coloring, black liquid spurting onto Heinrich's face. Brennen pitched forward, confused eyes breaking his father's heart, lips moving soundlessly in the mud.

"Bless Mary," Hegel intoned, kissing the pinched necklace.

"And bless us, too," Manfried finished, taking a bite from the warm tuber.

The babes in the burning house had gone silent when the Grossbarts pulled out of the yard, Hegel atop the horse and Manfried settling into the cart. They had shoved a turnip into Heinrich's mouth, depriving him of even his prayers. Turning onto the path leading south into the mountains, the rain had stopped as the Brothers casually made their escape.

II
Bastards at Large

Dawn found the smoldering carcass of Heinrich's house sending plumes of smoke heavenward, summoning the village's able-bodied men. An hour later most had regained the nerve they had lost at seeing the carnage. Despite his protests Heinrich went into the village to warm his bones and belly if not his soul while the half dozen men who comprised the local jury rode south. They had borrowed horses of varying worth and food to last two days, and the manor lord's assistant Gunter fetched his three best hounds. Gunter also convinced his lord of the necessity of borrowing several crossbows and a sword, and the others gathered any weapons they could lay their hands on, though all agreed the fugitives should be brought back alive so Heinrich could watch them hang.

Gunter knew well the Grossbart name, and cursed himself for not suspecting trouble when they had arrived at the manor house the night before. He comforted himself with the knowledge that no good man could predict such evil. Still, he had a wife and three sons of his own, and although he did not count Heinrich amongst his closest friends no man deserved such a loss. He would send his boys to help Heinrich next planting but knew it was a piss-poor substitute for one's own kin.

They rode as fast as the nags allowed, making good time over field and foothill. The wind chilled the jury but the sun burned off the dismal clouds and dried the mud, where the cart tracks collaborated with the dogs to assure them of their course. Even if the killers fled without resting Gunter knew they could still be overtaken by sundown. He prayed they would surrender at seeing the superior force but he doubted it. These were Grossbarts, after all.

Being Grossbarts, Hegel and Manfried knew better than to stop, instead driving the horse close to breaking before stopping near dawn. Even had they wanted to continue the trail disappeared among the dark trees and remained invisible until cockcrow. They had reached the thick forest that separated the mountains proper from the rolling hills of their childhood home, and Manfried found a stream to water the frothy horse. He wiped it down while his brother slept and generously offered it a turnip. Turning its long nose up, it instead munched what grass grew on the edge of the wood before also closing its eyes.

Manfried roused them both after the sun appeared, and his brother hitched the horse while he whittled a beard comb from an alder branch. Soon they were winding up a rocky path ill-suited for a farmer's cart. Each tugged and scratched his beard as they slowly proceeded, both minds occupied on a single matter.

"Chance they went east," Hegel said after a few hours.

"Nah," Manfried said, stopping the cart to remove a fallen branch from the trail. "They'll figure us to cut south, what with the scarcity a other towns round here."

"So they must be comin on now," grunted Hegel.

"If that bastard didn't get freed earlier, suppose someone must a found'em by now. Probably hollered all night. Had I cut his throat, too, he couldn't a yelled for help."

"Yeah, but then there'd be no one left to learn the lesson, and he had a fat turnip to chew through."

"True enough," Manfried conceded.

"So they's definitely on to us."

"Yeah," said Manfried, "and with just horses, they'll catch us by shut-in."

"If not fore that." Hegel spit on their panting horse.

"Shouldn't a bothered with the cart," said Manfried.

"You wanna carry them extra blankets? All a them turnips? No thank you. Cart's only thing good bout a horse. Can pull a cart." Hegel could never articulate exactly why, but he had always distrusted quadrupeds. Too many legs, he figured.

"Yeah, and what do you think we's gonna be eatin when we run out a turnips?"

"True words, true words."

The Brothers shared a laugh, then Manfried turned serious again. "So we got the vantage if we use it, cause we's ahead and they's behind. What say we run this cart a bit ahead, lash the horse to a tree and cut back through the wood? Get the pounce on'em."

"Nah, not sharp enough. Up through them trees I spied where the trail starts switchin up the face. We wait up there. High ground, brother, only boon we's gonna get."

"Catch as catch can, I suppose. Think I'll carve us some spears." Manfried hopped from the cart and walked beside them, peering through the thickets for suitable boughs. The treacherous path advised against speed, allowing Manfried to easily keep pace. After heaping several long branches in the cart, he resumed his seat and set to task.

Gunter stopped the jury where the path began arcing back and forth up the mountainside, only transient hunters and their more sensible game preventing the trail from being swallowed entirely by the wilds. Even with the prodigious trees to shield them from an avalanche the reduced visibility allowed their quarry any number of ambush spots. The dogs sat as far from the horses as their tethers allowed, and he dismounted to water them.

The dusk hour would give the jury just enough time and light to reach the pass. With a heavy sigh Gunter freed the hounds from their leashes and watched them dash excitedly up the trail. He had hoped to overtake the murderers before they reached the switchbacks, but the jury had ridden slowly through the forest lest the Grossbarts had broken from the trail. While they might have plunged down the opposite slope rather than lying in wait along the way, Gunter doubted it. They were ruthless, and the only advantage save numbers the townsfolk possessed was a few more hours of sleep the night before.

"Quick as you can," Gunter called, "but leave a few horse-lengths twixt you and the man ahead."

The thick forest had yielded to scree and hardy pines that seemingly grew directly from the rock. The setting sun shone on the trail that within the week would be salted with snow, and each man carried a heavy fear along with his weapon. Gunter led, his nephew Kurt close behind, then Egon the carpenter, with the farmers Bertram, Hans, and Helmut following after. The dogs bayed as they charged ahead, Gunter following them with his eyes for three bends in the road before they ascended out of view.

The steepest point of the trail lay near the top, before the incline evened out at the pass. At the last switchback Manfried waited with a large pile of rocks and his spears, a wizened tree and a small boulder providing cover. Brown grass coated the mountainside wherever the scree and rock shelves did not, and on the path halfway down to the next bend Hegel finished his work with the shovel and prybar. He had forced up rocks and dug the hard dirt beneath to provide as many horse-breaking holes as time afforded, and now scurried to conceal them with the dead grass. The hounds rushing up the trail below him were too winded to bark but Hegel sensed their presence all the same.

Hegel despised dogs more than all other four-legged beasts combined and hefted his shovel. Seeing their prey, the hounds fell upon him. The shovel caught the lead animal in the brow and sent it rolling to the side but before he could swing again the other two leaped. One snapped past his flailing arms and landed behind him, the last latching on to his ankle. Unbalanced, he drove the shovelhead into the neck of the dog on his leg, cracking its spine. The mortal blow did not detach the cur, however, its teeth embedded in his flesh.

Manfried chewed his lip, eyes darting between his brother and the horsemen he saw riding up the switchbacks below. Hegel spun as the dog behind him jumped, parrying it with the haft of his tool but losing his balance; he fell. At seeing Hegel stumble on the dead dog fastened to his leg Manfried slid down the side of the slope. The beast Hegel had first laid out regained its feet as Manfried jumped down to the trail, prybar in hand.

Manfried heard the riders but the horizontal Hegel heard only the growling of the dog attacking his face. Hegel jerked back so it merely tore at his ear and scalp, and as a testament to his utter hatred of the creature, he clamped both arms around its torso and bit into the mangy fur of its throat. The confused hound yelped and struggled to get away but he pulled it closer, chewing through its coat and into the meat. Gagging on muddy, stinking dog, he opened his mouth wider and got his teeth around the veins.

In his descent Manfried had wrapped a swath of blanket around his lower left arm, and easily coaxed his wounded foe into biting. He cooed to the beast until it lunged at his waving appendage, and no sooner did it bite than he brained it with his prybar. Tucking the weapon into his belt, he hefted the hound's shuddering corpse and rushed to the edge of the trail. Recognizing Gunter on the trail below, he hurled the dead dog at him and dashed back up the trail to his roost.

"Move your legs, brother!" Manfried wheezed.

Hegel had broken the jaw of the murdered cur on his ankle, and the throat-bitten hound rapidly bled out on the ground beside it. Hearing hooves, he limped as quickly as he could after his brother. Having chosen their ambush location for its sheer walls and steep ascent, Hegel had no hope of reaching the switchback Manfried rounded before the horsemen caught him. He threw himself behind a boulder just as Gunter appeared around the bend below.

Gunter's favorite bitch had nearly knocked him from his horse, and had his steed been fresh it surely would have bolted in fear. His tunic slick with dog blood and his shoulder bruising, he kicked the horse and called to his men, "We're on them, lads!"

Seeing the next piece of trail empty save for another of his fallen hounds and several boulders, Gunter pushed his mount harder up the incline. The surefooted stallion avoided the holes Hegel had excavated and clipped past the crouched Grossbart, reaching the next bend. From the edge of his eye Gunter caught sight of Hegel but before he could double back the murderers made their move.

Following his uncle, Kurt noticed Hegel just as the shovel dug into his hip bone and sent him toppling. The startled horse reared back, stepped into a hole and, snapping its fetlock, fell onto Kurt before he could blink. The horse pinned him, crushing his legs as it frantically rolled and kicked. Hegel saw another rider rounding the bend below and scampered around the fallen, crazed horse to relieve the trapped rider of his crossbow, which had skittered out of reach. Not that Kurt noticed, having had the wind knocked from him, his legs broken, and a horse mashing his lower half into pulp against the stony path.

The crossbow Gunter aimed at Hegel fell clattering on the

stones when a rock hurled by the hidden Manfried collided with his temple. Blood running into his eye, Gunter quickly dismounted the nervous horse and put it between himself and his unseen attacker. He snatched up the crossbow as another stone hit his horse hard enough to make it lunge up the trail, and Gunter dropped the reins lest he be dragged after. Loading another quarrel, Gunter squinted his good eye and made out Manfried through the deepening dusk.

Egon stopped his horse at the curve, shocked to see Kurt's horse thrashing on top of the boy, a dark figure creeping over him. Unsure how to proceed and armed with only an ax, he dismounted and tied his horse to a stunted tree. Bertram rode past the confused carpenter, driving his horse as close to a gallop as the steep trail allowed. Unlike the others, he had served on several such juries and had no doubts as to an appropriate action: he saw a Grossbart, and he would ride that Grossbart down.

Hegel hefted Kurt's crossbow, miraculously intact but unloaded. Bertram bore toward him and Hegel waited, muscles tensed. When horse and rider had almost reached him he dived backward between the flailing legs of Kurt's felled horse and rolled across the trail. Bertram spurred his horse to leap over its crippled kin, but the confused beast instead angled to pass beside it. The narrow edge of the trail gave way under hoof, man and horse giving the illusion of riding straight down the mountainside before they began tumbling over each other to the trail below.

Manfried knew Gunter had the drop on him but took the risk and burst from behind the scraggly bush, intercepting the spooked horse and poking its nose with a spear. It reared and bolted back down the trail. The horse between them, both men launched their missiles. Both hit their marks with surprising accuracy—Manfried toppled as the bolt connected with his head, and the confused horse went berserk as the thrown rock smashed into its bouncing scrotum. Gunter tried to evade the wild horse but as it skidded around the switchback it knocked him over the edge.

Hegel grinned as Bertram rode off the sheer side with a final shout, then his smile turned south as hard hoofbeats charged down behind him. He drew himself into a ball, Gunter's unmanned horse on top of him. Unlike Bertram's steed, this horse leaped over the thrashing beast blocking the trail and rushed toward the other three men. In landing, its rear hoof crushed Kurt's chest, bloody foam erupting from his mouth and nose.

Hans and Helmut watched dumbstruck as first Bertram's and then Gunter's horses undid their riders, the latter beast tearing past them as it fled down the trail. They wisely tied their horses to the same tree as Egon's, and the three men warily advanced on Hegel. Seeing they lacked bows, Hegel maneuvered around Kurt's horse and searched the dead man for bolts. A feather protruded from under the animal's side, and rubbing his bloody hands together, he knelt beside Kurt and tried to extract the buried quiver.

"You breathin, brother?" Hegel called, looking over his shoulder to ensure the three men were not sneaking too quickly upon him.

"Strong as faith!" Manfried shouted, finally cutting the arrowhead free from the bolt skewering his right ear. His cheek and scalp were raw from the shaft, the quarrel having stopped only at the feather. With the head gone he pulled the missile out of the bloody mess of an ear and got to his feet.

Gunter groaned, pulling himself back up to the trail with his only good arm. The left had snapped on a rock as he rolled down the sheer slope, but he had snatched a branch with his right before momentum sent him hurtling all the way to the foothills. Prior to his horse running him from the road he had watched Manfried take a bolt to the face and could not understand how the man still drew breath.

"Surrender your arms!" Hans barked at Hegel's back.

"You've nowhere to run," Helmut seconded with considerably less certainty in his voice.

"Neither do you," Hegel snarled, jamming his feet on the crosspiece of his weapon and yanking the string back. Notching a liberated bolt into the arbalest, Hegel spun to his feet. The three men were only a few steps away, but all halted at the fearsome sight of Hegel, blood dripping from his mouth and beard. Each assumed that the Grossbart had feasted upon Kurt, and Egon whimpered.

The men faced each other, and Egon surreptitiously began walking backward. Hans and Helmut shared a glance that Hegel recognized at once, but before either could move he shot Hans in the groin. Helmut rushed him with an ax but Hegel hurled the crossbow at the man's legs and tripped him. Withdrawing his prybar and charging down the trail, Hegel stopped short as Helmut got to one knee and brandished the ax. He shakily got to his feet, Hegel taking another cautious step forward.

"My ax has blood on it, how bout yours?" Manfried asked from just behind Hegel. He sidestepped the fallen horse and hefted the weapon Gertie had ambushed him with the night before. Standing beside his brother, each Grossbart looked more sinister and dangerous than he did alone.

"Don't stand to reason, try and kill us both." Hegel nodded at Hans, who twitched on the ground, gasping and clutching the bolt in his crotch. "Want what he got? Said he did, seems to have changed his mind."

"Got no need to truck with you," Manfried said, and both Grossbarts stepped forward. "Got no qualms for killin you, neither."

Already frightened, and remembering the devastation he had witnessed at the farmhouse that morning, Helmut relaxed his grip on the ax. Hans moaned beside him and Helmut tightened again, thinking better than to trust Grossbarts. A shadow moved behind the Brothers, and Helmut grinned despite himself.

Hegel felt the danger in his bones and spun around just as the returned Gunter clumsily brought his sword across. The killing blow instead slashed open Hegel's lip and cheek, and the Grossbart furiously lashed out with his prybar. Hegel caught Gunter in his broken arm, sending the man wailing to his knees.

Manfried and Helmut never unlocked their eyes and both attacked. Helmut swung down and Manfried swung sideways yet their ax heads met each other instead of meat. Pain reverberated through Helmut's hand and elbows yet the stout serf held his weapon, whereas Manfried's went skittering over the rocks and the Grossbart dropped to one knee from the force of the collision.

Helmut swung again but Manfried pounced, driving his shoulder into the man before the blade fell. They rolled over each other down the trail, the ax handle between them. Sliding to a halt, the farmer overpowered Manfried and pressed the wooden haft down against his neck. Manfried groped at his belt for a knife but Helmut got a knee on the Grossbart's elbow and pinned him down. The wooden handle dug into Manfried's throat, ripping his beard and swelling his eyes, his windpipe near collapse.

Gurgling under the ax, his vision shimmering, Manfried pawed the road with his free hand and unearthed a decent stone. This he smashed into Helmut's ear with the hidden strength of a snared weasel. Helmut blinked, the rock connected a second time, and then he slumped forward.

Jerking his other arm loose, Manfried rooted it under the ax handle, finally allowing air back into his body. He continued to smash Helmut's head from underneath until the skull cracked and bone and juices flowed out all over him. Finally Manfried rolled Helmut over and got awkwardly to his feet, only to sit back down on the warm corpse.

Hegel had finished Gunter with a single blow to the temple,

loosening the man's brains. He rushed to his brother's aid but Hans still had a touch of fight left and snatched Hegel's wounded ankle when he ran past. Hegel quickly regained his balance, and forgetting his brother being choked just behind him, proceeded to kick the life out of the farmer, centering most of his blows on the shaft protruding from Hans's groin.

"Fled," Manfried gasped behind him, bringing Hegel back to his senses.

"Eh?" Hegel grunted.

"Other. Fuck. Ran. Off." Manfried had difficulty getting more than a word out between breaths, and motioned down the trail. "Horses. Too. Bastard."

Squinting, Hegel dimly made out the curve in the path where the three men had tethered their horses. Worried the Grossbarts were demons and in fear of his soul as well as his life, Egon had still possessed enough sense to release the other horses and send them ahead down the trail. Looking back at Manfried, Hegel saw a wide, purple stripe swelling on his brother's neck.

"That all they gave you? A little necklace for your trouble?" Hegel thrust out his bloody leg. "Sides my face gettin carved, I been dog-et and road-kissed whiles you was sittin pretty up the bend."

"What's. That?" Manfried cocked his punctured, torn ear. "Can't. Hear. So. Good."

Both laughed heartily, which caused Hegel's wounded cheek to split and dribble. Kurt's crippled horse stared dejectedly at them until Hegel used his prybar to seal the deal and Manfried's ax unfettered it of enough meat to feed a dozen lesser men. In a rare show of generosity, the Brothers elected to allow the wolves and crows first pilfer of the other corpses, and the two staggered up through the pass, night dropping over them like the shadow of an enormous vulture.

III
Night in the Mountains

Starting a fire in the dark on a windy mountain pass might daunt most, but to the Grossbarts it proved of little difficulty. While Manfried swore at the kindling Hegel gathered more wood, and when he made water he caught it in their dented cooking pot. He daubed his torn cheek and lip with his urine, wincing and adding more curses to the obstinate fire. Eventually the twigs caught, and by the growing light Hegel cut strips of cloth from the rattiest blanket and handed the pot to his brother.

Manfried remembered a barber mentioning horse piss was superior to that of a man and patiently waited over an hour until he heard the telltale sound and hurried to catch the precious stream. They knew only a little about the concept that melancholic, sanguine, choleric, and phlegmatic humours coursed through their bodies and determined their health, the Brothers instead sticking to simple quackery. The horse meat cooked slowly over the fresh coals, and Manfried set the pot beside it to heat the liquid. Hegel saw what his brother intended and cackled scornfully.

"Thinkin a Hamlin?" Hegel asked.

"Thinkin how fell that piss a yours stinks," said Manfried, using a rag to apply the hot urine to his mangled ear.

"Shouldn't use nuthin what comes from a beast," said Hegel, taking a bite of meat.

"Yeah, cept the flesh you's chewin, and that hide slung on your back." Manfried snorted.

"It's different. Beast gotta be dead to eat or wear it."

"What bout feathers?" Manfried said after a pause.

"Feathers?"

"Feathers."

"What're you on bout?" Hegel scowled.

"Use feathers for arrows and combs and such, and the bird ain't gotta be dead to take'em."

"Course *that* don't count," Hegel guffawed. "Birds ain't beasts."

"Well...I suppose they's a touch different."

"Course they is. How many birds you see crawlin like a beast? Completely different. Same for fish. I'll wrap some fish skin on me if I's cut up, no question."

Manfried nodded, not convinced but knowing the conversation could progress no further. The twins agreed on most matters, but even after all these years he could not fathom his brother's distrust of four-legged creatures. Hegel certainly felt no aversion to eating or riding upon them, on the contrary, he took a pleasure from such things that Manfried correctly chalked up as sadistic. Dousing his ear in horse piss, Manfried splashed some on his sore neck for good measure.

Hegel felt splendid aside from his plethora of wounds. Chewing his dinner, he withdrew the murdered Gertie's necklace from under his tunic and held it to the light. The rough carving would only be recognizable for what it represented by a truly devout individual, so crude and indistinct were Her angles. He rubbed the lump of the Virgin's breasts with his thumb, and contemplated what it meant to be merciful.

Watching his brother, Manfried felt a twinge of jealousy. He considered himself far more pious than his brother, who had only taken to praising Her name after Manfried explained Her worth. Still, he reckoned, true mercy would be to allow his brother to keep his trophy rather than claiming it for himself. Even if he had been the one to slay the filthy heretic who originally wore it, his brother clearly took succor from Her. Inspiration arrived like a stinging gnat, and Manfried took one of the unused spears from the cart, broke the shaft, and began carving his own Virgin. His would be a more faithful representation, one with a larger chest and belly.

Eventually Hegel stretched out beside the fire and went to sleep, his brother standing watch. Manfried ate slowly, consuming several pounds of horse as the night wore on. He reflected on the fine meal, thinking with a satisfied smile that the days of rotting oats and badger meat were behind them. He knew the mountains could not stretch forever, and beyond them lay the sea, and passage to where their granddad's wealth waited. After a spell he roused his brother to stand guard, and lay down on the patch of warm earth Hegel vacated. Manfried imagined the stars to be jewels shining in the depths of a long-sealed crypt and, drifting off, he almost glimpsed himself prying open the lid of night and stuffing his pocket with the glittering gems.

Heaping wood on the blaze and wrapping himself in another blanket, Hegel sat on a rock and wolfed down more meat. Splashing some water in the pot, he burned himself getting a bit of ash into it and scrubbed out the horse piss. He then filled it halfway with the last of their water, adding turnip pieces and hunks of meat. The stew simmered under Hegel's watchful eye, the Grossbart also reflecting on their situation. He knew in his heart that for the first time in their lives they were truly on the road to riches.

While his brother dreamed of gold and sand and the Virgin, Hegel put his mind to their immediate wealth. Down the trail several dead horses waited for an industrious soul to turn them into headcheese, steaks, and pudding, to say nothing of the ligaments he could use to tie his shoes and the hide to be tanned for cloaks. Bones could be carved into fishhooks, a dried tail used to whip their carthorse. His mind turned over the possibilities when he remembered that there were dead men there as well.

Rather than feeling remorse at the blood they had spilled, Hegel groaned at their laziness in not searching the corpses immediately. In his mind each possessed pouches stuffed with coins, pouches that even now beasts dumbly bit off and swallowed or carried home to their nests. New shoes and hose dragged into dens, rings and bracelets rolling into rat holes. He took several steps down the trail, but without a sliver of moon he doubted even his keen eyes and sure feet could navigate the treacherous path. Instead he sat away from the fire, ears pricked for the sound of movement from the mountainside below. After hours of this futile exercise, he gently kicked his brother awake and lay back down.

Manfried awoke at dawn, his brother snoring beside him. The ashes were cold, indicating his slovenly brother had packed it in hours before. Cursing, he moved behind his brother and knelt down, putting his lips beside Hegel's ear.

"Up!" Manfried hollered, startling both brother and horse awake.

"Eh?!" Hegel rolled away and scrambled to his feet, peering about blearily.

"Sleepin on watch." Manfried shook his head. "Shameful."

"Who's sleepin on watch? I woke you last, you bastard!"

"Liar, you dozed off your first turn at it."

"I kicked you, you miserable goat!"

"When?"

"When I was done lookin out!"

"Hmmm." Manfried chewed his beard, dimly recollecting a foot to his side in the depths of slumber. "Well, I suppose it's no fault a either a us, then."

"No fault? You sayin you didn't get up at all? What the Hell, brother, that's your fault clean and simple."

"Should a made sure I was up," Manfried grumbled, then brightened. "Fuck it all, Hegel, what're we on about? There's loot waitin just down the hill!"

Snatching seared pieces of meat, the two raced down the trail to the scene of the slaughter. Any nocturnal scavengers had left the bear's share for the Brothers, who meticulously piled anything of worth in the middle of the trail. After a brief council, they plodded down the switchbacks to where Bertram had come to rest after his horse rode off the side of the sheer path. Defying the odds the hardy man still lived, although his splintered spine prevented him from moving anything more than his lips.

"Gross," he mumbled through the wreckage of his face. "Gross bar."

"Yeah," Hegel allowed, "that's us."

"Tough, ain't you?" Manfried was impressed.

"Bass," the man wheezed. "Bass. Bass."

"What's that?" Hegel scowled, smelling a slander on the wind.

"Turds," came out as a gurgle, Manfried experimentally pressing on Bertram's chest with his heel. "Bastards."

"Now, that's hardly fair." Hegel squatted in the dust. "We both recollect our father's face, even if our mother didn't."

"He's past pain, brother," said Manfried, sliding off Bertram's boot and poking his toes with a knife. "Look, he ain't even flinchin."

"Kill," Bertram gasped. "Kill. Ill!"

"Who, you or us?" Hegel grinned and turned to his brother. "Tore up to death and still talkin vengeance! Not a bad sort, not at all."

"Mercy, then?" Manfried asked. "I was dealin with old Cunter, so's I didn't see. Say his horse took'em over?"

"Yeah, the one we seen on the slope above, all busted up." Hegel looked Bertram in his unswollen eye. "That's you served proper for puttin faith in a beast. Should a dismounted, might a stood a chance."

Bertram tried to spit but only drooled blood.

"Seen'em before?" Manfried asked, still absently cutting into Bertram's foot.

"Can't say that I recall'em from our small times." Hegel scratched his beard. "On account a his cowardice in bringin a horse to a man-fight, I's a mind to leave'em for the birds."

"He didn't run, though," Manfried countered, having taken a shine to the man's perseverance. "Didn't cut out on his fellows like that other fuckscum. Didn't try to get all dishonest with a bow, neither, and lived all night in the cold."

"Still, brother, a horse? He meant to ride me down. Just think, Manfried, me, kilt by a goddamn horse!"

"A test, then," said Manfried. He set down his knife and joined his brother in squatting by Bertram's head. "You want mercy, coward?"

"Hell," Bertram belched. "Die. Gross."

"See?" Manfried smiled triumphantly at his brother. "Only a coward asks for mercy, even if it's offered."

"Pigshit," said Hegel. "Only a mecky coward would lie on his ass while someone tickled his toes with a blade."

"Assholes," Bertram managed.

"Clear as day, he's too broke to move anythin else. Watch." Manfried prodded Bertram's lips with his finger, and despite his agony the man snapped his teeth, desperate for even a drop of Grossbart blood.

"Well, alright," Hegel relented, and smashed in Bertram's skull with a rock.

They had little to show for their toil except for boots to replace their worn, pointed turnshoes, and actual weapons. Hegel claimed Gunter's sword and Hans's pick, while Hegel took Bertram's mace and Helmut's ax, leaving the one used on Heinrich's wife in the road as a warning to any who came after. The few salvageable bolts they shoved into makeshift quivers; cudgels, dull knives, and several choice round stones were tossed in with the rest of their gear.

The clothing had suffered worse than the men who wore it, and not a corpse present had either coinage or jewelry. Bertram they covered in scree but the rest were unanimously judged to be cowards and thus crowfeed. Daylight showed the impracticality of attempting to maneuver the cart down the opposite slope, the trail diminishing to the point that even getting the horse down would prove daunting. The Grossbarts had faith, though, and loaded up the animal Manfried named "Horse" and Hegel dubbed "Stupid."

Hegel applied ax to cart, further burdening the workhorse-turned-pack mule with all the firewood he could cram into the folds of blanket lashed onto its back. Then they started off, Manfried leading Horse down the mountainside. Although the path showed no signs of usage, they remained convinced it would soon join a wider road leading all the way through the mountains. They were wrong, of course, but did not learn this for some time. By noon they reached a wooded valley, and after plodding though the shade they climbed another rise and came to an even steeper pass late in the afternoon.

In the failing light they decided to camp at the bottom of the slope. Providence offered them a clearing split by a small stream, and they gathered wood to conserve the cart pieces for leaner times. Hegel unwrapped the horse head he had severed that morning and set to carving and stewing it for headcheese. Manfried caught frogs in the brook, but mid-autumn in the lowlands was early winter in the mountains, and the few specimens he found were sluggish and small. The chill brought on by night forced them close to the fire, but the Grossbarts' morale rose with the stars as they discussed the days and weeks to come. One of the dead horses had yielded a cask full of rank beer and they shared it happily, laughing and swearing late into the dark. The cold ensured that one always stood watch to stoke the fire, and shortly before dawn they loaded up Horse, came out of the trees, and went up the next incline.

This pass came even higher, and after struggling upward for the better part of the morning they were afforded an unbroken view of pristine peaks before them and the foothills behind. Their exuberance dampened several hours later when they came down into an alpine meadow where the trail faded into the grass and could not be found again. The mount they had descended met another across the field, jabbing skyward high as the sun. After much cursing and accusations, they decided to continue on a roughly southern course, for somewhere beyond lay a wide and worn road leading all the way to the sea-lands. Another argument ended with the conclusion that a slower road with the option of horse meat down the path was superior to the instant gratification a quicker, more direct approach might yield.

Hegel laughed triumphantly each time Stupid slid on the rocks, but Manfried cooed to Horse and encouraged him to double his efforts. Eventually they crested the obstacle and were rewarded with an even more precarious descent to the next meadow. Here they dropped down exhausted, and did not rise until shadows coated the vale. Hegel assaulted the only tree to be found with an ax while Manfried kindled a fire and wiped down Horse.

The headcheese had grown ripe in Hegel's pack, and they feasted on horsesteaks and brains as they debated theology. The stars shone and the wind blew, the Brothers enrapt in their discussion of Mary and Her ponce of a son. Hegel could not fathom how such a wonderful maiden had borne such a pusillanimous boy.

"Seems simple," Manfried theorized. "After all, Ma was shit as shit can be, yet we's immaculate."

"True words." Hegel nodded. "But it's natural for fine crops to spring from mecky earth, so we's not so much a anomaly as a rare, decent woman birthin heel stead a hero."

"He took his lumps, though. Didn't squeal none."

"So what? Not puttin up a fuss when you's gettin stuck up on a cross don't seem honest to me. He could a kicked one a them, at the very goddamn least."

"I's not quarrelin that point."

"Only cause you can't, you contrary cunt. Suppose you could go on about it bein braver to let'em torture you to death but we both know that don't wash."

"Is damn strange, though. Seems someone must a closed their ears at some point in the tale and got it all crooked when it came out again. She's the bride a the Lord, yet She's a virgin. A virgin what gets with foal. Then She gives birth to Her husband."

Hegel chortled. "Guess he got in there after all!"

"Watch your blasphemous tongue," snapped Manfried, tugging his beard. "Had you the sense to listen you'd hear how I got it all figured."

"Oh you do, huh?"

"Damn right. See, one thinks She can't be a virgin, cause virgins can't have babes or they ain't virgin. The Lord's pole is pole nonetheless, Hell, if anythin, it's the biggest pole to ever poke fold."

Hegel unbunged the cask, reckoning they needed some sacramental beverage if they were to truly unravel the mystery.

"But She's definitely a virgin, I mean, just look at Her." Manfried held up the Virgin he had recently carved. All day he had waited for an excuse to show up his brother's necklace.

"No question," Hegel agreed, trading the beer for a better look at his brother's handiwork.

"So here's what I think. The Lord comes pokin his thing round Mary, bein all sweet and tryin to get him some a Her sweetness. And She straight denies him the privilege."

"Why'd She do that?"

"To stay pure. Lord or man, She knew to stay holier than the rest She'd have to be virgin for all time, else She'd be just another mecky sinner."

Hegel stared at the statue, contemplating this.

"So the Lord's mad, real mad, as the Lord's wont to do. So he sticks it to Her anyway." Manfried belched.

"No!"

"Yes!"

"But couldn't he, I dunno, make Her want to?"

"He tried! Everythin's got limits, brother, and even the Lord can't make a girl *want* to spread for him, even if he can force Her."

"Poor Mary."

"Don't pity Her, cause She got Her revenge. Made sure the Lord's son was the snivelingist, cuntiest, most craven coward in a thousand years."

Enlightenment misted Hegel's eyes. "She done that for *vengeance*?"

"Worst fate imaginable, havin a son like that. And that's why She's holy, brother. Out a all the folk the Lord tested and punished, She's the only one who got him back, and worse than he got Her. That's why She intercedes on our behalf, cause She loves thems what stand up to the Lord more than those kneelin to'em."

"I understand *that*. But why's She still called the Virgin?"

"Well Hell, everyone knows rape ain't the same."

"It ain't?"

"Nah, you gotta want it. It's fuckin spiritual."

Hegel ruminated only a moment before his mind convinced his mouth that his brother was indeed in the wrong: "Nah."

"Nah?"

"Nah."

"Explain your fuckin *nah* or stand and deliver, you mouthy bastard!"

"Rape," Hegel cleared his throat, "is the forcible takin a one's purity through brute effort. Or in simpler speak for simpler ears, *only* a virgin can be raped, and she ain't virgin once she's had the business."

"Seein's how I happen to be dealin with a hollowhead, I's prepared to overlook your disparagin view a my ears. As for rape bein constrained to those what still got their chaste goin on, let lone possible only on such, may I ask by whose oafish, misshapen mouth you gained this wisdom?"

"Jurgen was sayin—"

"Ah! Illumi-fuckin-nation! The same Jurgen what was so fond a tellin you the evils a liberatin the dead a their unused valuables, that ill-learned asshole?"

"Now Jurgen weren't half bad!"

"Correct again, that sister-fuckin thief was all bad. Can't trust a man what cleans his dirty junk in his ma's mouth, regardless how fit she might appear to the unrelated eye."

"That's damn conjecture and you know it!"

"Jecture or no, don't lend'em weight as a reliable font a knowledge." Manfried adopted the northern accent of the accused incest practitioner: "*Only virgins kin git rapt. Gittin rapt means you ain't virgin nah more.* Ashes to assholes that filth told you fuckin your own kin weren't no sin, neither, eh?"

"No," Hegel lied, and poorly at that.

"Well, who you trust is up to you," Manfried sighed, "some forsaken degenerate or your own blood, sayin naught a the fuckin Virgin."

"You know it ain't like that, brother!"

"Then why's we still talkin, eh?"

That was good enough for the both of them, and they bedded down for the night. A howling wolf somewhere deep in the mountains reminded them of the prudence of keeping watch and they passed another night in shifts. The sun found them where it had left them—mildly lost in the Alps.

Picking their way up and down the range for several days brought them no closer to the southern road, and after a minor squabble over whose sense of direction surpassed the other's, they traveled southwest over the spines of great peaks, skirting their stony brows and plodding onward, always in search of the next pass. The weather grew meaner by the day, the winds slashing ever deeper through their coats. The grassy meadows diminished in size and frequency while the glaciers increased, and each night the baying of wolves seemed closer. The meat had run out and the turnips were growing scant, and while Manfried's logic had thus far prevailed, they both appraised Horse hungrily by starlight.

After a week they clambered to the summit of a boulder field and surveyed a forest sprouting between two monstrous ridges. They scrambled down the scree, dragging the weary Horse behind them. Firewood, fresh water, protection from the wind, and hopefully meat awaited them. Birds circled the thick pines, and the shady Brothers were cheered to enter shadows after being exposed to the open sky for days on end. The silence of tombs enveloped them, and the naïve Brothers prayed they might even stumble upon an overgrown churchyard. The Virgin had delivered them into such a fine sanctuary the idea did not seem beyond reason.

"Mark me well," Hegel cautioned, "them hill-dogs we's been hearin is probably laid up somewhere in here."

"Stands to reason," Manfried agreed, scampering around the thick bushes that choked the wood. "Wolf meat's better than none, though."

A brook could be heard deeper in the copse, and when they finally found it among the twisted trunks they made camp nearby. Stretching out on the moss and drinking their fill, they realized they had burned most of their daylight; night comes on fearful quick in the mountains. They collected a huge pile of fallen limbs and underbrush but found no evidence of any animal they might catch for dinner. Hegel made a stew out of the last few turnips while his brother set snares along the stream, and even when the wind rocked the trees and howled through the crags above they remained comfortable.

"You want to sit first?" Manfried asked, pulling his blankets tight.

"Guess so." Hegel set both crossbows beside the fire. They had salvaged only a dozen bolts, one of these having been removed from Hans's groin. Hegel looked forward to trying out the heavy sword and pick, his brother curling up beside Bertram's mace and his ax leaned against a tree. After Manfried began snoring, Hegel swigged the last bit of gutrot.

Night wore slowly under the trees, the canopy blotting out any stars or moonshine. The large fire provided ample light though, and nothing stirred in the wood. Just as Hegel felt his lids droop and reckoned he should wake his brother, a peculiar feeling crept over him.

In the course of their nefarious adventures neither Grossbart was a stranger to being hunted, yet time and again Hegel felt some inkling of when their pursuers drew close, and always knew when they were being watched. He kept such things to himself save when the situation necessitated it, and years earlier his uncle had declared him to possess the Witches' Sight after Hegel suddenly urged they take cover just before a search party rounded the path they had walked. Hegel resented the term as any good Christian would, but his hunches always proved right.

The familiar raising of his hackles told him eyes watched from somewhere beyond the fire, and given the unbroken silence their owner must be soft of sole indeed. A more cautious and clever man might have feigned sleep to lure out the voyeur or slowly reached for a weapon. Such intelligent action would have meant disaster for both Grossbarts, so it is fortunate Hegel instead leaped to his feet as he notched a quarrel, shouting at the top of his lungs.

"Come out, you bastards!"

Manfried rolled out of his blankets and gained his feet, mace and ax at the ready.

"Got guests?" Manfried blinked his eyes, peering into the night.

"Don't know," Hegel shouted even louder. "Guests show themselves, honest-like! Only fools and fiends cower in the dark!"

A deep laugh rolled out of the blackness, and to Hegel's shock it came from just behind him. He twisted around, crossbow leveled, but found no target. He aimed at where he thought the laughter emanated from but held his finger, wanting to make sure.

"Come over by the fire," Hegel called a bit more softly. Manfried moved closer to his brother, squinting into the moonless forest.

"No thank you," a voice growled from the dark, seeming to come from a throat choked with gravel. "Unless you care to douse that fire."

Another chuckle that chilled the guts of both Brothers. They were accustomed to being the sinister voice in the night, and did not care to be on the receiving end of such a discourse. Manfried attempted to wrest control of the situation.

Taking a step forward, Manfried intoned, "May all those who love their salvation say evermore Mary is great!"

Another genuine belly laugh, and after a pause, that voice: "My mistress is far closer than that slattern, dwelling as she does in this very wood!"

"Fire your bow," Manfried hissed.

Hands shaking, Hegel fired toward the voice. There was a skittering in the underbrush while Hegel clumsily reloaded, Manfried cocking his ear to pin down where the man was moving. Readied, Hegel raised the weapon but the silence persisted, only their breathing and the wind disturbing the stillness. Then they heard a swishing, like a switch being swung back and forth. Now the man must be even closer, somewhere just beyond the glow of the fire.

"Not Christian," the man complained. "Come into my house and try to murder me."

"See, it ain't like that," Hegel explained. "My finger slipped."

The chortling bothered them more than the voice, and the faint whipping noise did not help.

"Slipped, did it? Oh, then it's alright. After all, travelers in the night are right to be cautious, especially so deep in the wood, so far in the mountains. Never know who's out there, prowling the night."

"Right enough," Manfried answered, sorely aware he did not need to yell to be heard.

"It's been an awful long time," said the man, "since we've had any visitors who'd talk to us."

"That a fact?" Hegel swallowed, still trying to pinpoint the man's location.

"Most just scream like children and run. Rather, they try to run." Neither Grossbart found this warranted even a chuckle, let alone the drawn-out laugh that shook their nerves.

"We's talkin," Manfried pointed out. "Ain't gonna run. Anyone runs, reckon it'll be you."

Hegel could not return his brother's weak smile. "Yeah, uh, that's how it is, friend."

"Oh, I think I could make you run," the voice growled. "Yes, I wager you'd run if you weren't too scared to do nothing but mess your drawers and pray. All it'd take is me taking a few more steps toward that fire. Still want me to come into the light? Fair's fair, here I come."

"Nah, that's alright," Hegel quickly interjected. "You's fine where you's at, and we's fine where we's at, no sense in, uh, no sense in—"

"Forcin us to kill you," Manfried finished, but the words almost stuck in his craw. He was no superstitious bumpkin but he knew dark things move at night, especially in the wilds where men rarely journey. Still, no sense in getting all frazzled. Sweat poured down his face despite the frigid night air. The chortling coming from the dark twisted his bowels, and his whole body shook with nervous excitement.

"Can't have that," the unseen interloper managed through his mirth. "My goodness, no."

"Knew he was bluffin," Manfried muttered, mouth dry and brow damp.

"Can't have *you* killing *me*, that wouldn't do at all. Have to put food on the board, yes?" the man rasped, only now his voice came from above them, drifting down out of the thick pine boughs. Manfried felt nauseous and light-headed, even his over-sized ears failing to detect the movement in the dark.

"Yeah." Hegel tried to keep his voice from quavering but he felt ill and weird. The Witches' Sight—if that was truly what he possessed instead of mundane intuition—wracked his body with chills, every scrap of his skin itching to dash off into the night away from this clearly Mary-forsaken wood.

"So we's decided," Hegel finally said.

"Yes we are," the voice almost whispered from the trees.

"You stay where you's at and we stay where we's at," Hegel confirmed.

"Yes."

"Good." Hegel felt relieved.

"Until morning."

"Til mornin?" Manfried bit his lip.

"When I fall upon you and eat you both alive."

For the first time in their lives the Grossbarts were dumb-struck.

"You'll scream then," he continued, his voice rising with the wind. "You'll beg and cry and I'll suck the marrow from your bones before you expire. You'll feel bits of you sliding into my belly still attached, and I'll wear your skins when the weather turns."

"Uh," Hegel managed, looking like an occupant of the crypts from which they made their living.

Manfried could not even get that much out, eyes like saucers. His lips moved in prayer but no sound emerged. His faith that whoever waited outside their vision posed no serious hazard to them had dissipated. He wanted to spit in the face of whoever lurked in the trees, to say something so insulting it would make even his brother blush. What finally came out mirrored Hegel's statement:

"Uh."

Laughter rained down on them with such heartiness that pine needles accompanied it. The Brothers had subconsciously drawn so close that when their shoulders brushed they both jumped. No further sound came from the darkness, save the swishing both found familiar yet neither could place.

"Fire's low," Hegel whispered, the shadows lengthening on their periphery.

"So put wood on," Manfried snapped. Neither had taken his eyes off the overhanging branches since the laughter had trailed off on the wind. They were uncertain whether moments or hours had passed, scanning the trees for movement. Hegel cracked first but used his feet to kick limbs onto the blaze, unwilling to set down his crossbow for even an instant.

"Watch my ass," Manfried said, and retrieved the other arbalest. Stringing it, he rejoined his brother's vigil. "Got an idea. Need to shoot soon as you see'em." Manfried had lapsed into a guttural vernacular that only his brother could decipher. Their uncle grew furious whenever the Brothers adopted it, paranoid they were plotting against him. His suspicions were only occasionally justified.

"No need to say it twice," Hegel replied in the same.

"Gotta stoke these flames, shine some light on matters," Manfried announced to the wood, back in his regular Germanic mode of speech.

Dumping more branches on what quickly grew into a bonfire, Manfried suddenly leaped to his feet and hurled a flaming brand into the limbs overhead. Hegel stood ready but saw only the thick boughs of the pines. When the branch plummeted back down they avoided being singed by the hair of their beards.

"Damn," they both said, Hegel looking right, Manfried looking left.

"Suppose he's a ghost?" Hegel asked in their unique tongue.

"More likely a cannibal tryin to put the spook on us," Manfried replied in kind.

"What's a cannibal do all the way out here?"

"What you think he does? Eats people, told us himself."

"Awful strange, be smart enough to talk but dumb enough to eat other folk stead a proper beasts. All they's good for." Hegel glanced at Stupid, who had calmed after the voice departed and stood dozing near the fire.

"Them crumbs you find in church is all cannibals, and they's liable to talk you to death in the bargain."

"What crumbs? What church?" asked Hegel.

"All a them. That's what they eat, say it's the body a Mary's babe, and the wine's his blood."

"Oh, that rot again. Recollect that time we stole all a that hard bread and wine? That make us cannibals?"

"Hell no! Need a priest to turn it to flesh and blood."

"Witchery," Hegel judged it.

"It surely is. That's how you know a man's pure or not. Honest man don't eat nobody else. Specially not no kin a Mary, I don't care how much a bitchswine he is."

"So you think whoever's out there's just a heretic?" Hegel felt relieved.

"Yeah, nuthin more nor less." Manfried was not the least bit sure but it would not do to frighten his brother with speculation. "Besides, if he was somethin more than moonfruit what's stoppin him from rushin us right now? Or earlier when I was asleep?"

"True words. Means to put the rattle on us, so's we stay up all night and is half-strong come cockcrow."

"Exactly." Manfried heartened at Hegel's sound point. "Any fool'll tell you night's when there's real nastiness afoot. Nuthin I ever heard a prefers day to night cept ordinary people. So you get some rest, and I'll stand guard."

"I won't hear it, brother, my watch had only begun when I roused you. I'll stay up, you take in some shut-eye."

"Nonsense. I can see from here your eyes are saggin and you's got that tremor on your lip you always get when you's tuckered."

Hegel tried unsuccessfully to get a gander at his own mouth but his bulbous nose blotted out all but his lower beard. He reluctantly lay down, too out of sorts to argue anymore. He still felt hot and cold all over but could no longer be sure if this came from being watched or from exhaustion. He pretended to sleep for several hours, always keeping one eye half-cocked on the trees. He then switched places with Manfried, who did the same even less convincingly. Only Horse got any rest that night, and an hour before dawn both Grossbarts squatted beside the fire, crossbows ready, too tired to speak and without even a turnip to gnaw.

IV
A Lamentable Loss

The dawn light grew with agonizing slowness, and when Horse whinnied the Brothers both spun around. In the dimness nothing stirred save Stupid, who stomped and pulled at his tether, eyes swelling at something behind them. Then they heard the swishing, and slowly turned to face the enemy.

He perched on a low-hanging branch a few dozen paces away, smiling mischievously. Guessing from his sparse and wispy hair he held over fifty years on his wrinkled crown, but his teeth and eyes appeared hard and sharp. His face, however, did not hold their attention.

Under his chin any semblance of humanity was absent, his body instead akin to those of the panthers and leopards that stalk desolate regions. His mottled pelt bristled, various hues contrasting splotches of naked skin. The swish-swish-swishing came from the balding tail whipping behind him of its own accord. His front paws dangled over the branch, hooked claws lazily extending and retracting.

The Grossbarts had prepared themselves for anything; unfortunately, their concept of anything failed to include a hog-sized cat with the head of an old man. Horse whinnied but no other sound disturbed the morning, the monster and the men watching each other while light drifted down through the branches.

With an air of finality the beast rose on its haunches, its four legs balanced on the limb.

"Uhhh . . ." Hegel dumbly leveled his crossbow at it.

Manfried stared, transfixed.

They would fire their crossbows simultaneously, Hegel imagined, each quarrel embedding in one of the creature's eyes. It would fall dead from the tree, snapping its neck for good measure when it hit the ground. The cunningly wrought animal-skin cloak would be dislodged, revealing what had to be a wizened but decidedly human body underneath. Hegel swallowed, and put the plan into action.

Hegel fired his weapon but shook too badly to properly aim and his quarrel shot past the monster into the forest. Manfried reflexively pulled his trigger but did not raise the bow, the bolt kicking up dirt at their feet. The old man's grin widened and he stepped forward along the branch.

Their only chance lay in battling the creature on the ground. If they held their nerve they might accomplish together what would be impossible for a solitary man. If they hesitated in their course both would die, and neither doubted it to be less than the worst end conceivable. Their options stolen, they must fight.

They ran. Screaming. In opposite directions.

Manfried's mind burned with the single purpose of finding an end to the forest. Being fleeter of foot than Hegel, he would have lost him in his mad flight even if Hegel had not dashed the other way. Manfried could see the trees and brush and now the stream but the mill wheel of his mind had ceased turning; he had become a beast himself, intent on escape at any cost.

Rather than being attacked or hearing sounds of pursuit, it was the sudden realization that he was alone that brought each Grossbart back to true consciousness. They had broken for a time but now understood that they were separated and hunted. Hegel did not pause in his flight but cut sharply left, and noticing he had dropped his crossbow, drew his sword. Manfried jumped over the stream and stopped cold, bile creeping up his throat. He slowly turned to see what followed.

Nothing but the breeze ruffling the treetops. The gurgling water blunted his hearing, his chest hurt horribly, and breathing only made it worse. He still clutched his crossbow but the quarrels were back at camp. The ax had slipped out of its belt loop but Mary be praised, the mace had not. He shakily withdrew it, and spun around to face the thing that had creeped behind him. Again only the thick forest greeted him, and he went weak in the knees, keeping his feet by leaning against a mossy trunk.

Manfried had to find his brother. They had played into the Devil's hands, and if he did not find his brother soon they would both be undone. To call out might summon that thing instead of Hegel, though.

Something splashed in the water, making Manfried hop into the air. He twirled around until he became dizzy, desperate to prevent being taken unawares. Only when he felt confident in his solitude did he peer into the stream.

Squatting, Manfried lifted the metal scrap from the water. His trembling turned into violent spasms as he realized it was part of Horse's bridle. A scratching came from over his shoulder, and slowly turning, he saw it.

It climbed slowly down the tree he had leaned on moments ago. It went straight down the sheer trunk, digging its talons through the bark and into the wood. It took its time, smiling at Manfried.

Manfried made to run but slipped on the moss and tumbled from the bank. He yelled his loudest, splashing in the water until he gained the opposite side. It crouched across the stream from him, tail swaying.

"Hegel!" echoed through the trees and that Grossbart stopped, trying to determine where it came from. Either his brother lay close by or the nature of the wood amplified his voice. When no other sound followed save that of the nearby brook he again charged into the underbrush, intuition his only guide.

It bounded over the water at Manfried. Blabbering prayers to Mary, he swung with his mace and grazed its scalp but it went low, knocking his legs out from under him. Fortunately its mouth held human teeth, the bite to his thigh only tearing his hose and bruising the skin before it jumped away, avoiding another clumsy swing of the mace.

Pouncing onto a nearby boulder, it watched Manfried attempt to gain his feet. The bite had not damaged him but when it retreated it had kicked his calf with a rear paw. Blood welled out when he tried to stand, but he managed to get to his knees and heft his mace. He screamed wordlessly at it, and it descended upon him again.

His mace smashed into its shoulder, sending it rolling away in a blur of lashing claws. He found the strength to stand but knew at his best he could not have outrun it and his left leg throbbed miserably. It scrambled upright and charged but stopped short of striking range and then began circling him, growling low in its throat.

It moved quickly behind him, and with his wound he could not fully turn before it rushed in. It went for his hamstrings but Hegel burst from the trees, startling both of them. Manfried tripped over its back but avoided the claws. It dodged Hegel's sword and leaped back across the creek, disappearing into the forest.

"Get up," Hegel hissed, helping his brother rise.

Manfried swallowed, unable to speak.

"Can you run?"

Manfried shook his head, gesturing to his bloody leg.

Hegel cursed, peering around.

"Wrap it up," Manfried finally croaked.

"What?"

"My leg. Tie it off, and I can run."

Hegel gave the wood a final going over and knelt down. Three nasty cuts marred the sullied hose covering his brother's hairy calf and, wiping the blood away, Hegel tore his shirt and bound the wounds. That damnable laughter came again, and to their dismay it emanated from the thicket behind them. Hegel felt confident that if they broke the treeline they stood an honest chance to get away, depriving it of any cover to ambush them. He scampered along the creek, Manfried close at his heels despite the pain each step brought.

They darted under branches and scrambled through brushwood, but within minutes they both realized the hopelessness of their plight. The creature waited on a stump just downstream, making no attempt to hide. Realizing the futility of an action and altering said action are two entirely different matters, however, and the Grossbarts plunged off into the forest anew, away from their stalker.

Wheezing and wide-eyed, they stumbled over rocks that hid beneath the loam. A thick grove of yews covered a steep decline, and before one brother could caution the other they both slid down the embankment. They caught themselves midway down on slick branches, but before they regained their balance the thing had appeared between them in the mossy tangle of tree limbs.

Hegel almost dived down the slope but paused, more from fear of later facing their adversary alone than from true courage. Manfried held on to a bough ten feet up the hill, the lattice of branches allowing the creature to advance above him. A tapered limb sagged under its weight just above Manfried. Instead of jumping up to meet his end the Grossbart leaped toward a lower tree. He slid past it and his brother, who now hurried after, the trees shaking around them.

At the bottom Manfried scrambled up but his brother crashed

into him, both of them wet with dirt and bruised with rock. They seemed to dance a few steps, arms wrapped around each other to keep from falling. The trees overhead swayed and the creature lunged.

The Grossbarts shoved themselves apart, making it land between rather than atop them. Even disoriented, exhausted, and terrified, the Brothers excelled at this sort of scrape. Operating purely on instinct, they fell on the beast before it could get out from between the two. Manfried embedded the flanged mace in its haunches and Hegel brought his blade across its face, slicing into the bridge of its nose and eyes. It swiped Hegel's arm in the process but he held his sword even though it suddenly felt a hundreds pounds heavier.

It blindly tried to run but Manfried's mace moored it, and it kicked at him with its hind legs. He let go of his weapon to avoid the claws, but as it skittered away into the hollow Hegel pounced, aiming for his brother's weapon protruding from its back. The sword ricocheted off the head of the mace even as that weapon came loose from its flesh, and Hegel's blade cleaved into the creature's raised spine.

Toppling forward, it let out a distinctly human scream. Hegel stared in shock, the thing pulling itself forward with its front legs despite the wreckage of its haunches and the wound to its face. Manfried appeared beside him, hefting a large rock he had unearthed. A delighted grin appearing from under his beard, he slammed it into the monster's wispy pate. It went still, shitting itself all over their boots. They beamed at each other, then each grabbed a back leg and dragged it out of the thicket.

A loud crack came from behind them but after the initial fear they understood thunder to be the culprit. Snow lightly filtered through the canopy as they pulled the dead thing into a small clearing. Manfried retrieved his mace and kissed its gory head. Hegel's numb right arm dripped even after he clumsily bound it.

They both poked at the corpse, their earlier jubilation now darkened by the sheer nastiness of the thing.

"Four legs," Hegel mumbled, "four goddamn legs."

"Stands to reason," said Manfried, not needing to elaborate.

After a period of quiet observation Manfried turned and vomited. His brother moved to heckle him but something in the corner of his eye stopped him dead. He turned back, his hackles rising.

"Mary's Teats!" Hegel barked, pawing his brother's back as he drew his sword. "It's movin!"

Manfried looked up, tried to say something, and vomited again. The sticky fluid had not finished coming up before he stumbled toward the thing, fumbling with his mace. True enough, its flank rose and fell, and one paw began digging into the dirt.

Manfried rolled the thing onto its stomach with his weapon. The shallow wounds on its back were far less severe then they definitely had been when they had dragged it out of the brush. Seeing this, Hegel went berserk. He hacked the crushed head free and kicked it away from the bleeding stump, then stomped at its cranium until the pulpy chunk bore no vestiges of humanity.

Occupied with his task, Hegel did not see what happened to the corpse. Manfried could not open his mouth, hypnotized by the sight. Steam pored from the mutilated remains, its legs pulling inward, its back arching. In moments the skin holding it together melted off into a greasy pool, taking all color with it. The musculature and bones remained but these were sallow and pasty as a grub. Its hair came loose and floated in the pool save for a wide flap of pelt running from shoulders to haunches, resting on the gruesome lump like an ill-fitting cloak. This scrap retained its odd coloration, shining black and gray, red and blond.

Finally tearing himself away from splattering brains, Hegel took one look at the mess in front of Manfried and dropped his sword.

"What in Hell did you *do*?" Hegel was more than a little impressed.

"Power a prayer." Manfried shuddered.

"I, uh, didn't mean to. Didn't mean to—" Hegel swallowed. "Didn't mean to take Her, uh, Bosom in vain."

Manfried waved it off, eyes locked on the pelt. Something about it intrigued him, maybe the way the different hues played off each other. Hegel watched his brother, apprehensive that a reference to the Virgin's chest failed to get a response, regardless of extenuating circumstances.

Hegel narrowed his eyes, steeling himself for the coming blasphemy. "Mary's Wet Ass."

"Uh huh." Manfried leaned out to touch it, to see if it felt as warm and dry as he suspected.

"Stay away from that!" Hegel barked, grabbing his brother's wrist.

Manfried shoved him away, suddenly light-headed. "What're you on bout?"

"What am I— No, what're you on bout? Why you want to touch that nasty thing?" Hegel could not articulate why the idea bothered him, but it did.

"Dunno." Manfried grumbled, standing up slowly. "Looked nice."

"Nice? Nice! It's a rotten old skin from some demon and you think it's pretty?!"

"Suppose it *is* a demon-skin," Manfried admitted, still staring at it. "Guess I probably shouldn't lay hands on it."

"Damn right," Hegel huffed, secretly relieved Manfried had not picked up on his defamation of the Virgin.

"We can't just leave it here," said Manfried, "some heretic might find it and put it to evil use."

"What use?"

"I ain't no heretic so I couldn't say. But they'd find a use for it, rest assured. So we should probably take it with us."

"What fresh Hell is this? We's not takin that mangy hide no place. It stays where it lays."

Manfried worried his lip. "Can't have that. Maybe we oughta bury it?"

"Sound enough, though I reckon the fire would suit it better."

"That'd mean touchin it, though, to carry it back to camp," Manfried pointed out.

"Could carry it on a stick."

"Stick might break and it'd land on your hand."

"You's keen on just that a minute ago."

Manfried grunted, still curious whether it would feel soft or bristly.

"We can start a blaze here, burn it up," Hegel suggested.

"Might not burn."

"What?!"

"Think bout it. Demons crawl up out a Hell, so stands to reason their skins don't burn. Otherwise they'd never get out a Hell in the first place."

"If it's a demon," said Hegel.

"What else you think it is?"

"Seems more like the thing that Viktor in Ostereich was talkin bout. Lou Garou, or some such," Hegel ruminated.

"Lou Garou?"

"Yeah, them folks what turn into wolves."

"That demon look like a wolf to you?"

"No need to condescend," said Hegel. "Chance Old Scratch tricked him, turned'em into somethin else. Sides, look at his bones, more like a man than a cat's or a demon's."

"Or a wolf's."

"Well, I never heard a no demon preferred daylight to moonshine."

"Manticore," whispered Manfried, his eyes widening.

"How's that?"

"Goddamn, brother, we killed us a manticore!" Manfried clapped Hegel's shoulder. "Heard mention a them from Adrian."

"Which Adrian? Huge Adrian?"

"Nah, Stout Adrian. Yeoman we camped with two summers back what had a predilection for sheep."

"Huge Adrian had a taste for bleaters, too, if I recall. Reckon they's kin?"

"Possible," said Manfried. "Regardless, *Stout* Adrian was sayin his da's da's uncle's cousin or some such went off to Arabland in his younger days, and there was thick with manticores."

Hegel scowled. "Mean there's more a them things where we's for?"

"Yeah, but we's in practice now."

"Why don't I recollect him talkin bout'em?"

"Probably drunk. I think he said they's poisonous, too."

They both took a step back from the corpse.

"Manticore skin burn?" Hegel asked.

"Dunno. Best bury it rather than takin a chance. If it's poison-pelted it might let off vapors if we try, kill us dead."

They dug a shallow pit and peeled the hide from the remains with a branch. Hegel dropped the stick in with it and refilled the hole. Manfried had surreptitiously gone to a large pine and carved their sign into the trunk with his dagger: a crude G, the only character the illiterate Brothers knew. If they ever came back through these parts he wanted to be able to dig it up and see if it kept its luster underground.

Tamping the rocky earth, Hegel gave a final scowl to the decapitated skeleton and began trudging in what he hoped was the direction of their camp. Manfried hurried after, giving the tree a final jab for good measure. Hegel had seen Manfried's endeavor, however, and several times he feigned urinating to creep off and mark other large pines in a similar fashion. He had no intention of ever coming this way again, but one could not be overly cautious when a soul was in danger. Hegel had long ago realized his brother occasionally became fixated on things he ought not to.

Eventually they found the stream again, the winter-dust thickening along its banks, and from there picked their way back to Manfried's ditched crossbow. After pawing through the undergrowth for an hour they discovered his ax, and from there the camp quickly came into sight. Horse lay gutted, his corpse still warm and his head mangled. Their belongings were scattered all over the ground, and the monster had taken the time to piss on their blankets, the ammonia stink turning their raw stomachs.

Still badly shaken, the Grossbarts rekindled the embers and sat in the falling snow, oblivious to the storm-grumbles and how cold the air had turned. Hegel wasted no time in cutting into Stupid's legs and heaping spits with the fresh meat. He avoided any areas where claw marks rent the skin, greatly displeased that the creature had attacked the head. He had looked forward to more headcheese but would be damned before he would risk being poisoned.

Manfried helped his brother skin Horse, pitching the wide flaps of hide upright to cure beside the fire. They had already burned the tainted blankets, only one of them spared a soiling. The meat went down far better than turnips, and the two soon felt rejuvenated.

The flurries and impotent thunder abated and the light faded, leaving them damp and dark. Neither had the strength to tend the coals throughout the night, let alone keep watch, but the bitter cold forced Hegel awake several times to blearily rekindle the fire. He sat up and began eating before cockcrow, mulling over the previous day. Be it shapechanger, demon, or manticore, they had definitely smote it back to Hell. When the snow began floating down again and the haze of morning arrived, he went to wake his brother, meaning to have a word with him about the propriety of leaving some things alone. Manfried would not stir, despite Hegel's mounting efforts. He would not awaken at all, for his arrow-punctured ear had reopened and turned sour, infecting him with a mortal fever.

V

The Other Cheek

"Death," said the priest, "is not the end, Heinrich. You know this."

"Do I?" Heinrich flexed his toes in the too-tight turnshoes Egon had given him. The dry clothes were of course appreciated after a night in the wet mud choking on a turnip, but the carpenter had obviously failed to deliver the two things Heinrich truly wanted. That the rest of the jury had not returned hardly surprised the yeoman, having experienced firsthand what the Grossbarts were capable of.

"Outliving one's family is the greatest test of our faith. While this is your supreme loss, it is hardly your first," the priest said gently. "The stillborn child and the other—"

"Two were stillborn, Father." Heinrich glowered at the man. "And what of Gertie and Brennen and my three girls? Been too long since we all seen you. What if—" Heinrich choked on the words and the thought of damnation.

"Heinrich," said the priest. "We've been through this. It's not as if your wife or children committed the sort of sins that would require my intercession!"

"What did you say?" Heinrich felt chills spiraling up his legs into his bowels. "Sins requiring intercession?"

"I said, it's not as if they committed the sort of wickedness that might damn a soul were it not absolved by a priest. We all have our little foibles but the good Lord has— What are you doing?" The priest blinked at Heinrich, who had jumped to his feet. The grieving turnip farmer went straight to Egon's table and snatched up a knife. The priest would have called Egon and his wife back inside the carpenter's hovel but Heinrich had turned back around.

"Absolution. Penance. Forgiveness." Heinrich shook the knife at the priest, his voice cracking. "You saying there's a way?"

"A way? Heinrich, the knife—"

"Oh." Heinrich crouched and cut into his soiled leather hose heaped near the door, gritting his teeth at the exertion but watching the priest intently. "If they get to one of yours and confess and do the work, they'll be forgiven. Is that what you're saying to me?"

"Ah," said the priest. "Well..."

"That's it, isn't it?" Heinrich stood, wrapping the blade in a strip of leather cut from his hose and dropping the knife into the single pocket of his tunic. "I'm off then, Father."

"What?" the priest nervously backed toward the door as Heinrich advanced. "Where are you—"

"Think I'll forget? Think I'll forgive?" Heinrich glared at the priest, whose back now met the wooden door. "Excuse me, there's work to be done."

Sliding out of the way, the priest waited a beat until Heinrich had flung open the door and stepped out into the daylight before following. The priest knew something had changed inside the farmer and suspected that unless he acted quickly sin might well beget sin. Egon's eldest son bumped into the priest as he went outside and he saw Egon arguing with Heinrich in the yard, several other villagers approaching from their respective homes near the manor house.

"What's he on about?" the lad asked. "He looks worse than he did the day after they—"

"Hush, boy," said the priest, emboldened by the sun and the witnesses. "Ho, Heinrich, be still!"

Heinrich and Egon both turned to the priest, a small crowd quickly forming. Among them were the kin of those jury members the Grossbarts had murdered on the mountainside. The priest and the farmer squared off on either side of the group, and the priest sensed his chance to shame the man into obedience.

"I know what you are plotting." The priest addressed the village as much as he did Heinrich. "You wish justice! Don't we all? But you risk your soul by attempting to do the Lord's work for Him!"

"And you don't try and do the Lord's work every day?" said Heinrich, earning gasps from more than one neighbor. "I aim to do one thing, and that's catch the Grossbarts before they can get to a priest and wash themselves clean. There's no place in Heaven for such as them, and I'm but an instrument of God."

"You?! Heinrich, you are incensed with grief and rage and pride, and it is a terrible sin to call yourself such! Let the Lord work His own justice and risk not your soul!"

"I'll need your help." Heinrich turned from the priest to the blanched faces surrounding him. "I've no horse nor blankets nor food nor weapons—they took everything. But I swear I won't rest until I've sent them to their master. Hannah, your Gunter—"

"My Gunter," spit the snotty-faced widow, "died because of you!"

"Me?" Heinrich felt as though the woman had punched him in the stomach. "No, I—"

"Cried and begged and wailed, wanting your wrongs righted! You'd trusted to the Lord he'd not have gone off with the rest and been murdered by those devils!"

"Hannah," Heinrich pleaded. "I wanted to go with them! I know their ways more than any here and I could have…" He trailed off seeing the cold eyes of his neighbors, faces set, cheeks puffy. Lowering his head farther, Heinrich nearly choked on the "Please."

None spoke, several turning back to their homes.

"Better go," Egon hissed, and Heinrich blinked away the tears, trying to fathom how they were blaming him instead of the wicked Grossbarts. "I understand even if they don't. I'll ride you out as far as I can, aye?"

"I'll buy her," Heinrich said as they turned away from the silent condemnation of the town. "My whole field's yours. You know it's more than fair."

"I'm sorry, Heinrich." Egon stopped and stared at the dirt after they rounded his hut to where the nag stood tethered. "You know's well as any that we've got a sight fewer horses than we did a few days ago, so I won't be the only one needin this girl. But while they was..." Egon paused, cleared his throat, and wiped his eyes at the horrid memory before he was able to finish. "While those Brothers was doing their work I cut Hans and Helmut's horses loose, so perchance we'll come across'em on the road."

Heinrich nodded, understanding too well the man's reluctance to sell the animal with planting just a winter away.

"And if we don't come across them horses," Egon continued, "well, I'll take you clear down to the highway they're probably makin for. Gain some ground, as they cut into the mountains on the old hunting trail, try and shortcut it. But I know that little path don't go nowhere so it'll add days if not weeks fore they get over to the real road. Assuming they're going south, of course."

Neither had anything more to say on the matter, Heinrich still trying to understand how any could fault him for everything that had transpired over the past several days. Heinrich climbed onto the horse behind his last friend and they rode back around the house toward the southern road. Egon's son intercepted them with a sack of turnips and then they were off, but Heinrich failed to thank him properly. All the man could think of was the impossibility of catching the damned Brothers without a steed of his own.

VI
The Teeth of a Donated Horse

Manfried sweated and shuddered in his nightmares, his mind sensing his impending death and providing appropriate visions. The manticore stalked him through tightening caverns, his brother, his faith, and his weapons all missing. The pearls of the desert would remain buried and only his beard would grow in the grave.

Hegel nearly dropped his sick brother a dozen times that day, sliding on moss and rot as he staggered through the dim forest. Clearly the miasma found in low-lying regions had affected Manfried, Hegel assumed, refusing to allow the possibility of manticore venom. The solution lay in reaching higher ground where the wind prevented the pestilential vapors from gathering.

Both had nearly expired from the plague when they were ten years old and Hegel knew the cure as well as the symptoms—since Manfried had yet to sprout the buboes, clean wind and prayer might save him. Their mother had known, which is surely why she delivered them into a decayed lean-to high in the hills and abandoned them when their humours became disturbed so long ago.

Hegel dragged Stupid's hardened skin behind them by its former owner's tether, but with his brother's dead weight on his shoulders Hegel had to leave most of the meat behind. He wheezed his way up the creek, reckoning it to be the surest path to higher ground. Pausing only when it was necessitated by exhaustion, Hegel trudged onward, his injured right arm dripping more than sweat from his exertions. Midday never came in that dismal wood, evening following directly after morning. The snow fell steadier than before, and his brother's damp body pressing against his back gave Hegel a stubborn cough.

With the light almost gone and the forest even thicker, Hegel laid his dying brother on the ground and collapsed beside him, hacking up phlegm. He pinched Manfried's nose and poured water down his throat and unsuccessfully attempted to force him to swallow some horse meat Hegel had chew-softened. He gathered wood but his numb fingers hampered his ability, and he glumly realized the smoke leaving his mouth with each breath would probably exceed what he could coax from the damp branches. Returning to his equally snow-brushed brother, Hegel began to pray.

The pitiful fire he managed hissed and popped, and no matter how hard Hegel blew the thick pieces would not catch and the thickening snow sizzled as it smothered. As he looked up to curse the heavens, his sharp eyes caught a hint of red in the forest. Holding his breath, terrified it was only his own paltry fire reflecting off a wet leaf, he stood and stared. He took several weak-kneed steps forward, squinting. His wide grin split his cheek anew, blood dribbling into his beard.

Hurriedly gathering their scant provisions and hoisting his brother, Hegel plowed through the underbrush, blind but for the white cloud of snow around him and the distant beacon. He broke into a clearing and stumbled onward, free of the limbs and roots that impeded his progress. Now he could make out the roof and walls, and the single window glowing through the white and black night. He had feared it to be fairyfire or worse, but Mary be praised, a cabin emerged from the snow and darkness.

Without setting down his brother he slapped the flimsy door with his good hand, bellowing out:

"Open up! Ill man out here, open up! Open up in the name a Mary and all the saints!"

Nothing. No sound at all, save the Brothers' labored breathing. Manfried moaned in his sleep, and Hegel banged again.

"Open up or I'll knock it down," Hegel roared. "Give us our sanctuary or by Mary's Will I'll take it!"

A shuffling came toward the door. A voice, faint enough to be almost drowned out by Manfried's whimpering, floated through. Hegel could not say if it belonged to man or woman, child or parent.

"Your word first," flitted out. "You'll do no evil, lest your soul be blackened for all time."

Impatient beyond reckoning, Hegel yelled even louder. "Course I ain't evil! Open up!"

"And you'll try no mischief, nor do no harm?"

"There'll be mischief plenty if you don't let us in!"

"Your word."

"My word, yes, and my brother's, and Mary's, and her moon-fruit boy's if you open up!"

"What was that about the Christ?"

"What? Nuthin!"

"Calm yourself, and remember your word," and wood slid on wood, and the door pushed out. Blinded by the glare, Hegel stumbled inside, knocking over a small table. Stamping his feet, Hegel set Manfried on the ground. A smell of spoiled milk and sour sweat filled the thick, greasy air of the hut. The door closed behind them and the board slid back in place. Hegel whirled to confront the person who had possibly murdered his brother by forcing him to wait out in the snow on the verge of death.

The oldest person Hegel had ever seen stared back at him, a woman sixty years old if she was a day. He could be sure of her sex only by her lack of beard, her taut yet cracked face offering no other markers. Bald save for specters of white hair and swathed in rags, her bulbous body contrasted her emaciated countenance. The manticore-slayer and dog-breaker Hegel took a step back from the fearsome crone.

She grinned, black-toothed and scab-gummed. "Welcome, welcome."

"Uh, thank you," said Hegel.

"Hard night for traveling?" Her eyes shone in the firelight.

"Had worse. My brother's in a bad way, though."

"So I see." Yet she did not remove her eyes from Hegel.

"Caught'em a touch a the pest out in the wood." Hegel's body hummed, either from the change in climate or her presence, he could not be sure which.

"Oh did he? Found a pest in the forest?" she asked.

"No, er, *the* pestilence. You know, buboes?"

"He's got the black bulges, does he?"

"Not yet, he—" Hegel stopped short when the woman darted out a hand and poked his wounded face. He snatched for his sword, but the look in her eye held it in its sheath. He stared aghast as she licked the blood from her finger, appraisingly.

"Not out there," she muttered, "no, no, caught a different case of death, I'd wager."

"He ain't dead yet," said Hegel, turning to Manfried.

The walls of the cramped interior bulged with cluttered shelves containing bottles, jars, and heaps of bones and feathers, and from the ceiling hung a hundred different bundles of drying plants and strips of cloth. The firepit in the rear filled the room with a pungent, piney haze that masked the sickly smell of the crone, a small, snowmelt-dripping hole in the roof failing to accommodate all the smoke. An empty chair sat before the firepit and one corner held a heap of rags, the other a small woodpile.

Hegel dragged his brother onto the hearthstones. Manfried had grown pale but his skin burned, his body wracked with spasms. The crone leaned over them both, clucking softly.

"Caught a case right enough, a case of the comeuppance!" she jeered.

Hegel's hand again reached for his sword but her tongue intercepted him.

"Calm, calm, Grossbart, remember your promise."

"Slag," Hegel hissed, "you watch yourself."

She cackled in a manner only the elderly can master.

"Wait a tic." Hegel swallowed, neck-hairs reaching for the roof. "How'd you know our name?"

"You look like long-beards to me," she replied. "Don't you call a thing by what it most resembles? Call a dog a dog, a beast a beast, eh?"

"Suppose so," Hegel allowed, not convinced.

"Your brother's dying," she said, her voice lacking the solemnity Hegel felt the situation deserved.

"Maybe he is, maybe he ain't. You don't look like no barber, so maybe you should mind your mouth."

"Well, Grossbart," she said, "'tis true I'm no barber—I'm better than one. Barber couldn't do anything for that man, just put him on the cart for the crows. *I* might help him, if I was so inclined."

Hegel stepped toward her, dried belladonna brushing his hair. "If I was you, I'd incline myself with the quickness."

"Menacing words, menacing eyes."

"You—"

"Careful. I'll mend your brother, and you besides, if you do as I say."

"What we got that you want?"

"Oh, nothing special, nothing unique. Just that thing all men got, the tail we feeble women lack."

It took a moment for her meaning to sink in, but when it did Hegel recoiled. "I couldn't give you that even if I was a mind to."

"No? Even for your brother?"

Hegel chewed his lip, considered slaying the woman, thought better of it, spit twice and said, "See, I's chaste—"

"Even better!"

"I wouldn't know how—"

"I can teach you, it's simply done."

"I—"

"You?"

"After you fix'em up."

She brayed again. "Think I trust you, Grossbart? Think I don't know what you're thinking? Don't worry, it'll be done soon, and might not be as bad as you think."

"I doubt that. What guarantee I got you can even heal'em?"

"Guarantee's my oath, just like yours. I can sweeten his wounds, same as I can make it sweet for you." She lasciviously hiked her rags up around her thighs, revealing complicated networks of veins bulging under the pruned skin. Hegel smelled a stronger, acidic scent overpowering the burning wood and felt his horse meat rise in his throat but choked it down.

"Like I said," he managed through his disgust, "I would if I could, but I can't, and that's all there is to it."

She had turned and rooted through an array of jars on a shelf, her backside thrown out toward him. She turned back triumphantly with a dusty vessel, its rag stopper half-rotten. Withdrawing the rag she offered it to Hegel.

"Knock this into that gut of yours." Her eyes glittered.

"Give me your word it ain't poison."

"Given, given," she replied dismissively.

"What is it?"

"Something good. Something that'll make you able. Hell, it'll make you eager."

He stared hard into the bottle, his intuition goading him to cast it in the fire and run her through regardless of Manfried's condition. He had no doubt his brother's soul would make it to Heaven, it was his own body he felt concern for. In the end his pride would not allow him to walk a coward's road, and so with a prayer to Mary he downed the contents, the stuff filling his mouth with the taste of putrid mushrooms.

The room spun and the bottle broke on the stones, a yellow mist clouding his vision. Hegel turned to his hostess to inform her that no way no how would a little fungus water make him willing when his breath caught in his throat and tremors radiated outward from his groin. She reclined in the chair but had set one foot on an upended bucket, the firelight illuminating a thigh the color of goat cream. The pouty turn of her thin lips, the vulnerable want in her milky eyes, the gnarly fingers now snaking between her legs, the reedy sigh as she pushed her bottom forward on the chair to meet her digits—Hegel felt an almost-pain in his breeches, and his hands dropped to his waist to relieve the source of his discomfort.

The crone appeared no different from before Hegel had taken the draught, but he no longer remembered such simple things as his faith's prohibition of carnal pleasures or his society's scorn and disgust for women more than a decade into puberty. He simply saw her for the beauty she was, albeit a beauty of remarkably advanced years. Dropping to his knees in a show of contrition, Hegel crawled toward his host, who spread her legs farther on the chair to accommodate her guest. A pleasant chevre odor wafting from between her curd-textured, indigo-marbled thighs tickled the bulbous nose that soon tickled her mound, and his left hand hoisted her rags out of the way while its twin fumbled with his belt.

Cold as her outer skin felt, Hegel's tongue nearly stuck to her frigid folds and the white wisps drifting from his full mouth mingled with the pale cloud itching his nostrils. She patiently coached him until he set off a trembling gush, refreshing, brisk wetness cooling his hot throat even as she squirmed off of the chair and pushed him onto his back. Tasting herself in his kiss, she settled onto his trowel and he worked her furrow, his rough hands surprisingly gentle as she guided his fingers from breasts to mouth to rear and back again.

"What's your name?" Hegel gasped, desperate to know before he lost himself. He knew something important was brewing and somehow he had to find out before the end. "Please?"

"Call me Mary." She grinned, popping his index finger back into her mouth as she ground against him.

Hegel spent himself quickly but she kept moving after he had stopped, and before he could protest or lose his firmness his prune-skinned paramour utilized tactics that would make the most weathered whore in the Holy Roman Empire scratch her head in wonder, and soon she reached another occasion. Freshly invigorated, Hegel would not let her rest and greedily set to bouncing her again. Eyes locked on a fetching little liver spot just beneath the folds of her jowly neck, Hegel had no way of anticipating how suddenly the potion would fade and his old convictions would return.

He pulled her closer, their tongues intertwining up until the climactic moment. Then she broke the kiss, a cord of saliva bridging their panting mouths, and his perception of the heavenly Mary vanished, replaced with an odious witch.

Withered breasts swaying pendulously, her tongue flicked over her few teeth and severed their drool-bond. He shriveled even as he came inside her cold clamminess, screaming in terror at the realization he had been bewitched and wrenching away from her headfirst into the tipped table. He blacked out and vomited simultaneously, her cruel laughter following him into nightmares that stood no chance of besting his first sexual encounter.

Hegel kept consciousness at bay as best he could but eventually the room came back into focus. Sitting up, he spied the hag crouched over his brother, and getting to his feet, he silently drew his sword. Witch, he thought, witch, witch, witch.

Without turning she said, "He'll die awful soon if I don't finish my work."

Teeth gritted, Hegel closed his eyes and did not move for a long time. Finally he snapped, "If he's not fit awful soon I'll open you up."

"Fair's fair."

"You's a witch."

"Perceptive."

"Devil worshipper."

She turned, a rust-colored needle in hand. "Not what you called me earlier."

"You tricked me."

"You agreed to the price, Grossbart. From the goodness of my soul I fixed it sweet for you, so you had as fine a time as I, and now you're acting a right child." She batted her eyes at him.

"Witch."

"Got some quim-juice drying in your womb-broom." She motioned to his beard.

"Witch!"

"Oh, horse apples. You're no monk yourself, lover."

"Call me that again and all a us'll be in Hell fore this night's out."

"Tempting, tempting. Now put that thing away, you insatiable letch." She went back to stitching Manfried.

Hegel felt the draft on his nether regions and, blushing, sheathed both of his tools. He collapsed into the chair, his stomach contorting painfully from her words and his memory. Blinking at the window, he realized daylight had come and the snow had departed. He stood and went outside to loosen up his stomach.

Coming in after doing his business, he joined the witch at his brother's side. Manfried breathed easier, and his brow felt neither scalding nor frigid to the touch. She had cropped most of his right ear, the severed, blackened pieces drying on the hearth. Poultices were bound to his leg and ear, and his chest rose and fell rhythmically.

"That all needs doin?" Hegel asked.

"You took longer than he, but the beard should cover any scars."

"Eh?" Hegel touched his face, surprised to feel the crust of some ointment smeared on his wounded cheek and underneath that the bumps of stitches. The whole side of his face was numb and, continuing his inspection, he felt ointment on his dog-bitten ear and scalp, and more stitches on his manticore-clawed arm and hound-gnawed leg.

"When did you do all that, then?"

"Last night. Had to open up the old bite on your ankle and get the nasty out, would've turned in another week and rotted off."

"Eh," Hegel said in lieu of thanks. He was not going to thank that witch for nothing. "Simple as that, then? Sew us up like we was ripped tunics? What kind a witchery's this?"

"Hegel," Manfried groaned in his sleep, slapping the floor.

"Right here, brother," Hegel said, forgetting his line of questioning.

Manfried opened one bloodshot eye and grabbed his brother's hand. "Manticore," he hissed, and passed out again.

"What's that he said?" the witch asked from behind Hegel.

"Never you mind."

"Fair's fair. Eat some of this." She set a bowl of stew beside Hegel.

"Ain't eatin nuthin you's touched, witch. Probably poison."

"Hush. You've already et the foulest thing in this house." She cackled and sat down in the chair.

Hegel reluctantly devoured the food. Between mouthfuls he would glance from witch to Manfried and back again. Finally he asked, "How long til he can get up?"

"My ways are better than a barber's, as I've told you. He should be fit by tomorrow, and if not, then the next."

"Eh." Hegel did not relish spending another moment in her company, let alone another night. The day passed excruciatingly slowly, and with darkness the snow returned. He went out to the side of the shack and fetched enough wood to replenish the pile, and at one point Manfried sat up, guzzled four bowls of stew, and promptly went back to sleep without a word.

"Fancy something sweet to warm yourself?" the witch asked coyly, night settling onto the mountains.

"Shut that loaded trap fore I spring it," Hegel retorted, trying to bully her into silence.

"Oh, I see how your dirty mind works. No, no, sorry dear, no more of that for you. Got me all tuckered and puckered."

"I said—" but he saw the bottle she offered and suspended judgment for the briefest of intervals. He sniffed the mouth suspiciously, relief and joy coursing through him as the familiar scent of mead wafted out. "Better not have mixed none a that other in here, or I'll cut off your head and burn it, witch."

"Promise?"

"Promise."

"Drink."

Crossing himself, Hegel took a small pull, then a larger one. It tasted slightly stronger than other honey brews he had sampled and he greedily drank more. Out of a sense of fairness he pinched Manfried's nose and poured a bit down his brother's throat. That the ill Grossbart did not gag from this liquid intru-

sion is testament to his quality. Hegel pretended not to notice the
witch staring at him but his nerves would not let him relax.

"What?" Hegel eventually snarled, trying his damnedest to
be intimidating.

"If I tell you something, will you give your word to keep sword
in place?"

"Ain't promisin you nuthin."

"Very well."

Time wore on, and the more Hegel drank the more his curiosity gnawed at him like a rat at a grain sack. He fidgeted and
scratched. He checked on his brother until Manfried managed
a few obscenities and clumsily struck at him. He went out and
pissed, stared at the snow, and came back inside to fidget some
more. Eventually:

"What are you on bout, then?"

"You'll keep your hands to yourself?"

"Only if you do the same," Hegel snorted.

"Fair's fair. Your word, then?"

After a small pause, "My word."

The witch began talking and did not stop for what seemed
ages. Hegel settled in by the fire, pleased the witch had abandoned her foul innuendos for the time. The warm, well-fed, and
drunk graverobber listened to her tale, perking up at times, at
others nearly dozing. Manfried stirred occasionally, catching
enough with his good ear to color his dreams.

VII
A Cautionary Yarn, Spun for Fathers and Daughters Alike

The old woman's shadow appeared distended and ghoulish to Nicolette, but the crone herself possessed a bit of those qualities to begin with. Turnips, the girl thought, looking at the woman's knobby fingers bridged in her lap. The fire was warm and Nicolette was not, however, so she scooted closer to the hearth and its proprietor. The wind blew in through the hovel's window without even a scrap of cheesecloth to keep it at bay. Nicolette shivered, but the old woman leaned back in her chair, savoring the draft.

The hut was small but the door had a slat latching it shut and the window rested just below the ceiling, allowing Nicolette to feel far securer than she had but minutes before. Few people enjoy being lost in the wood at night, and those who do one had best avoid. Being out of the dark forest had calmed her heart, although her host unnerved her.

Who would want to spend their days and nights so achingly far from other people? Overwhelmed with joy at spying a dim light through the trees, the girl had considered the question only in passing. For an instant she had even let herself believe it was her home despite the older, larger trees and other differences in the nightscape.

The sun had rested squarely over her father's cabin when their sole pig had jerked forward, pulling the tether from her hands and rushing off into the forest. The first hour she spent chiding herself for not minding her charge better, the second for not minding her path better as she attempted to find a familiar marker. Her growing anxiety was given brief respite when she spotted the errant swine across a patch of frozen bog, but after her quarry again escaped into the underbrush Nicolette became distraught. Fear overrode her embarrassment, and she began calling out as dusk slunk through the branches.

When the sun fully departed and the forest came alive with noises she valiantly held in her tears. Her father had told her if she was old enough to wed she was too old to cry, and while no suitors had tramped along the muddy path to their cabin in pursuit of her hand, she maintained caring for a husband could be no more difficult or desirable than tending a pig or a father. Nevertheless, the girl sniffled as she groped her way among the cold bark pillars looming around her.

Then the glow in the distance, and Nicolette ran as fast as she could given the abundance of roots and trunks rearing out of the dark at her calloused feet. Approaching the crooked hut she slowed, relief becoming tinged with her earlier fear of the dark wood. Her father had cautioned her about charcoal burners— their filthy lifestyles, deceptive charms, and rapacious hunger for pretty young girls. She paused at the door, uncertainty seizing up her arms and legs, when she felt the sudden and powerful sensation of being watched. She turned slowly, and saw nothing but night in an unfamiliar part of the vast forest.

A twig snapped in the blackness, and Nicolette was crying and banging on the door with both hands. The old woman let her in, slipped the board back into place, and brought the girl to her meager firepit. Minutes later the lass had calmed down, gotten the numbness out of her feet, and taken in both surroundings and savior.

She felt she should explain her predicament, but her host seemed disinterested. Glancing around the cramped interior, she saw a small table and a few ledges cluttered with drying plants and earthen pots. A large stack of firewood filled one corner beside the hearth and a bitter-smelling heap of rags occupied the other. A pinestraw mat and the chair were the only other furnishings. Drawing her arms around her legs, Nicolette sighed in a bid to draw the old woman's attention away from the smoldering logs.

In response the woman began to sing quietly, rubbing her chin with her tuberish fingers. Nicolette peered up at her, teeth on lip. Considering the shadows of the flames, the run-down state of the shack and its owner, and now her rasping unfamiliar words in a strange melody, the old woman appeared positively witchy.

Something landed on the roof, dust snowing down on them. Nicolette yelped, staring up as the boughs of the ceiling sank down ominously over the door, then sprang back up as others sank down closer to the small hole where the smoke escaped. The wood squeaked, the depression moving over their heads. Nicolette remembered to breathe but could not move, entranced by the shifting ceiling. She shook with such violence her vision blurred, but her eyes snapped back into focus as the old woman leaped at her. With surprising alacrity the crone snatched a clump of Nicolette's hair and plucked out a half dozen cinnamon strands.

The old woman grinned at the wincing girl, showing her few remaining blackened teeth. She rose and shuffled to the window, holding Nicolette's hair before her like a charm. Raising her hand to the hole into the wilds, the old woman offered up the hair. With all the slowness of dawn's arrival on a winter morn, something between a hand and a paw reached down out of the night and carefully extracted the long wisps, then disappeared back up out of the window.

The song trailed off, the old woman laboriously returning to the fire. Resuming her seat, she looked directly at Nicolette for the first time. The girl now looked years younger, her face the milky yellow of fresh cream. A small puddle pooled around her, seeping between the flat hearthstones. She opened and closed her mouth three times as tears mixed with her other fluids on the floor before she squinted her eyes shut and squeaked, "What is it?"

Had Nicolette opened her eyes she would not have cared one bit for the scowl on the crone's withered face.

"What it's become only the wolves and night-birds know," the old woman croaked, shifting closer in her seat to the petrified girl, "but it used to be my husband."

Nicolette nodded in the way she might politely accept a stale bit of cheese she did not actually want, and then was sick all over herself. She next became conscious of the old woman soothing her blubbering, stubby digits caressing her cheeks and hair. She recoiled, suddenly aware of her nakedness. The old woman stood and turned, fetching a bowl and a knife from the table. Taking Nicolette's soiled woolen dress from beside her chair, she cut into it with disturbing passion. The girl crawled away toward the corner, but the groaning of the roof stopped her.

"Here now," the old woman cooed, stooping over her with a dripping scrap of dress. Nicolette gaped upward as the crone wiped her clean, and while her heart still pounded with such intensity it hurt, she calmed enough to realize the old woman lingered over her delicate parts. The seemingly decrepit host licked her lips while she dipped the rag back into the bowl, squeezing Nicolette's budding chest as she wiped away the bits of mushroom the girl had found in the forest.

Nicolette wanted to spit but dared not move, instead shuddering passively under the old woman's strokes. The girl's upper half clean, the rag dipped below her navel, the aged eyes reflecting firelight. Strange and terrible as the night had grown, Nicolette refused to consent to its becoming any worse. Having reached her limit, the young woman crossed her legs and backed away.

The old woman's yellowish eyes flickered, and with that same disarming quickness she upended the bowl, dousing the girl's lap. Water sizzled on the stones and the two women stared at each other, the elder bemused, the younger defiant. The utter bizarreness of the day and night had sapped Nicolette of her usual resilience and strength, but no longer. Then the old woman leaned in, again singing that foreign song, and a faint scratching came from above. The girl slumped forward, drawing her knees up to her chest; the old woman once more clutched Nicolette's tresses and used the knife to clip a small lock.

Again she went to the window, and again held up her tribute. Again Nicolette stared entranced at the bestial appendage and again she felt her stomach cramp and her eyes water. Again the crone resumed her seat, trailing off as the thing on the roof shifted about.

The old woman grinned at Nicolette, motioning her closer. The girl shifted, more to draw nearer the fire than the crone. She hated the old woman, she hated the miserable, cold shack, she hated the moonless wood outside, she hated her nakedness and fear, and she especially hated whatever had crept out of her nightmares and onto the roof. She hated her cleverness, which forbade her from pretending everything was an awful dream from which she would soon awake, thus ending the pain in her stomach and chest. And she hated that blasted pig.

"He eats children," the crone hissed, instantly regaining Nicolette's attention. "Every little shred. Toenails and teeth, bones and fat, lips and assholes. Gobbles them all up. Does it slow, so they scream while he eats and maybe does other things to them. In here you can hear them wailing some nights, out there in the dark."

Drinking in the girl's bulging eyes and shallow breaths, the old woman adopted a matronly tone. "Don't you worry, child, I know his corrupt ways well. The hair's his favorite, he eats it last, often leaving naught but the scalp for his next night's breakfast. He keeps them in the trees but I see them swaying, and when the moon is bright I watch from the window, yes I do, see him sucking and chewing on them like they was dipped in honey."

Despite the gentler tone of voice Nicolette's stomach contracted and she gagged at what the woman described, instantly knowing it to be true.

"But," the old woman hurried, whispering, "there are ways to keep him up there instead of in here until morning. Always flees at cockcrow, slinking back to his lair until shut-in. If we occupy his attentions until dawn, you can steal home before next gloaming."

Nicolette forgot her embarrassment and threw herself at the old woman's plump legs, chest heaving with dry, soundless sobs. The crone smiled and began her song, gently taking her knife to a thin plait of hair. And this is the story every child knows, wherein the old woman slowly snips the girl's hair and slips it to the beast, keeping it sated until the morn. Then the girl picks her way home through the wood, bald as a babe but none the worse for her ordeal. Her relieved father draws a warm bath and no longer works her so hard, and perhaps she even finds the errant shoat along the way. The following afternoon a handsome hunter arrives, having just slain a terrible monster in the forest, and before her hair has grown to her shoulders she is a happy wife and expectant mother.

Only the most ignorant or optimistic child could believe this is how the tale ends. As to what truly transpired that night in the wood so heartbreakingly far from home, a reexamination is in order. If Nicolette is to arrive home intact, the old woman must be true of word and purpose, and even the aforementioned ignorant child may wonder why any good-hearted person would dwell in the black belly of a monster-ridden forest, listening at night to children being killed and eaten. While the duller young listeners might be satisfied to hear that the crone had grown too old to make the journey back to civilization, those shrewd of wit will hasten to counter with examples of the old woman's unnatural vigor. The truth, which should have been painfully obvious from the beginning, is that the old woman was an abominable witch who savored the flesh of children and ate them every chance she got.

Ah, the quick-witted will say, then perhaps the beast is actually kind and innocent but stays on the roof, afraid of the witch. He has fallen in love with Nicolette, and sniffs her hair longingly, slowly gathering the courage to confront the crone and rescue the maiden. After he defeats the evil hag Nicolette will love him despite his appearance, so he will be restored to human shape and everything will be daisies and buttercups for the happy couple.

Such preposterous rot demonstrates that the only thing more foolish than a too-stupid child is a too-smart one. A sharp child might invent such fallacious fantasies, questioning the motives of a deadly menace, whereas the dullard sees a beast with jagged maw agape and acknowledges it for the obvious danger it is. The fiend upon the roof surpassed even the witch in its malevolent hunger for human meat, as the slower children will have known from the start.

Together the two had eaten many children, but more often fed on hunters, charcoal burners, and anyone else unlucky enough to wander into that accursed part of the wood. Both preferred their meat fresh, although the wife favored her supper cooked a little bit more than the dripping stuff her husband craved. Nicolette had stumbled into a grimmer predicament than she could have imagined in her most loathsome fever dream, and worse still, she did not even know it.

Desperation often overrules intellect, which is why Nicolette believed the hag. The old woman sang every so often, passing up more and more of the lady-child's locks, until all that remained in the bowl was a small pile of hairs the witch had shaved. Utterly bald, Nicolette shivered all the more, several rivulets of blood trickling behind her ears from where the blade had pressed too firmly. Unlike in the children's tale, hours still stretched before daybreak, the old woman having passed up the hair far too quickly.

"Now," the witch said, "let's do the rest." The docile young woman allowed the crone to shave what few hairs grew on her arms and under them, then blushed as the blade worked its way up her legs. Nicks bled onto the stones, Nicolette silently crying until only the small thatch between her hips remained. The song was sung and the offering offered.

Nicolette watched the hirsute claw raise the bowl, then return it to the waiting witch. The lass's anxiety had transformed to suspicion during the preceding hour, a careful consideration of how fast her hair disappeared contradicting the old woman's proposal. The crone grew cheerier the less hair remained, not a comforting sign. The girl's father often scolded her for being too clever, and while he was correct, this too-cleverness alerted Nicolette to her mounting peril. Furthermore, she marked that every time the witch sang the beast came to the window, and while the words still made no sense at all, she repeated them over and over in her mind until she knew them by heart.

The old woman returned, her song finished, and squatted before the musing girl. "Spread those pretty legs," she leered, "and lets have that last little bit."

Nicolette knew that with all her hair gone she would have nothing to ward off the crone's husband, so the crafty girl shuddered and motioned to the fire.

"I'm so cold," she said, chattering her teeth. "May I put on more wood first?"

"Very well," said the witch, running pale tongue over shriveled lips. She had grown ravenous while shaving the girl, the way a fat farmer will when plucking a chicken. Retrieving a log from the stack, Nicolette noted the worn ax resting against it. As she tossed the wood into the hearth she saw something that made her heart plummet into her bowels. She could not be sure, so she grabbed another log, slyly poking the blaze before the wood slipped from her fingers.

Nicolette had never seen a human skull before but recognized it at once, despite its being blackened, cracked, and coated in ash. She also noticed how small it looked, and knew instantly the old woman had tricked her, and was likely a witch as well as a murderous cannibal. She yelped when she felt a poke to her side, and tried to mask her rekindled terror.

"Come now," the witch cooed, "that little patch should hold him until dawn."

"But," Nicolette began, her fear turning her cleverness as sharp as the traps her father used to catch rabbits, "my father has said nobody may ever touch me there save myself or my husband, when I get one."

The hag cackled at that, and made to pounce on her quarry when Nicolette quickly added, "I can do it myself, if you'll kindly lend me the knife and bowl."

The old woman scowled at the girl, but the child's eyes reflected the fire and she could not read them. Her husband loved that hair the most and she felt confident the child was stupid, not guileful. Nicolette forced herself to smile, her cheeks flushing with shame as she spread her legs and reached for the knife.

Taking it with trembling fingers, Nicolette peered at the blade. "What's that?" she asked, her voice cracking. She pointed to the tip of the weapon, but when the witch leaned in for a look the girl pressed the knife to her throat.

"Don't you move," Nicolette hissed. "Don't you speak, and don't you sing or I'll cut you dead."

The witch glared balefully but she did not move, and she did not speak, and she did not sing.

"You tell me what to do," Nicolette whispered, the handle clutched in both hands. "Tell me how to get away or I'll kill you."

The witch grinned but said nothing. The loose beams overhead creaked and Nicolette jumped, the honed blade nicking the witch's turkey-wattle neck. A little blood oozed out and the crone looked worriedly at the girl. Nicolette picked up on her distress and smiled triumphantly.

"If I die it will be after I bleed you out like a rooster," she spit at the hag. "Now tell me quick before I get rid of your foulness and deal with it myself."

"He's already impatient," the witch shot back, raising her voice. "He's et all your hair, and so he'll smell you a mile off. He runs faster through the trees than a stag on the ground, and before the sun next touches this place he'll be eating you alive. Your only hope is to hand over that knife, so I can protect you."

"I don't believe you," the young woman whispered, her eyes welling up anew.

"Then I'll make it fast for you," the stink of spoiled milk hot in Nicolette's face, "better than what he'll surely do."

Nicolette stiffened, breathed deeply, and tried unsuccessfully to stop shaking.

"What do you do?" the girl croaked, cheeks shimmering. "Why? Why do you—"

"Pleasure," the witch snapped. "For me, and of course the taste. For him it's that as well, but also comfort. All that pretty hair he's et will twist in his belly and grow out of it, keeping his pelt thick and warm. Now that you're fit to be cleaned and divvied, he'll burst through that door and take such delight from your misery as suits his appetite."

Nicolette shuddered for only an instant before pressing the blade into the old woman's throat. The hag's arm slapped her head but the girl lunged forward, driving the witch to the ground. The blood spurting into Nicolette's face blinded her, burning her eyes and nose, running into her mouth and down her throat. She choked but pressed harder, the crone bucking and scratching, a wheezing, gurgling fart of a noise escaping her shriveled lips.

Eyes locked shut, Nicolette leaned on the handle until the point burst through the other side. The thrashing gave way to shivering, the crone's legs rattling on the floor. The young woman remained hunched over the witch, the hot liquid warming her hands and face more than any fire could. The roof creaked and the girl leaped to her feet in a twinkling, trying to wipe the blood from her face.

The beams groaned again and Nicolette pawed frantically around the shack until she found the small bucket. Dunking her face in the frigid water she gasped, taking her first breath since attacking the witch. She only brought herself to look at her felled nemesis by imagining the hag regaining her feet behind her. Snapping back to the fire, she took in what she had wrought.

The crone's blood coated the floor from one wall to the other, her head almost severed. Nicolette shook with such passion the knife slipped out of her fingers, and then the fire popped, causing her heart to freeze and her feet to hop, eyes shooting to the ceiling. The silence of the night settled on her, and for the first time she noticed no birds or insects disturbed the stillness in this part of the wood. She swallowed, tasting the bitter old witch in her mouth, and spit on her corpse.

Her heart raced so quickly only her mind could outpace it. The crime that was no crime had spurred her thoughts into action, and she rushed to institute her plan. She held her breath and grabbed the witch by the ears, planting her foot on a gory shoulder and tugging. The head did not budge but an ear came partially free. She yelped, dropping the ear and covering her mouth in a belated effort to quiet herself.

The roof shifted ominously, the girl leaping over the wide pool that shimmered black in the firelight. Snatching the rusty ax, she returned to the witch and, pretending the mess at her feet was an especially stubborn log, raised the ax overhead like a seasoned woodsman. The spattering on her legs bothered her far less than the creaking roof. Snatching the head, she tossed it into the fire, where it sizzled and hissed, the flames dying low.

In the dimness she set down the ax and retrieved the knife, kneeling and frantically cutting the hag's bloody clothes from her body. The witch stank, and her skin had patches of mold and what were surely extra nipples poking from oily creases of skin. She gagged but kept at it, piling the rags beside the sputtering fire.

The husband must be pacing, dust swirling down heavily as she righted the chair before the fire, the decapitated corpse between her and the hearth. Inspired anew, she smeared the cooling blood over her arms and legs and face but could not bring herself to wipe it on her stomach or chest. Donning the filthy, odorous cloth, she forced herself over to the door and with gritted teeth slid the slat from its catch, letting it swing inward.

Leaves swirled around the doorway and all was silent on the roof and in the wood. She backed away, and fighting a sudden dizziness, buried the knife in the crone and slumped down in the chair, the ax again in her sticky hands. Filling her chest with the chill wind blowing against her back, she screamed, but stopped short just as her voice reached its peak. Biting her lip, she waited one, two, three seconds before hoarsely trying to imitate the crone's song. Doubt consumed her but she knew any hesitation would undo her careful ruse, so on she sang, strange syllables sticking in her craw.

Then she heard the tick-ticking of an animal's claws on the stone floor behind her. Rather than charging in and past her to descend upon the corpse as she had prayed, her unseen end slunk slowly toward the hearth. Nicolette sang louder, wishing she could pray to the Virgin instead. The beast sniffed the air, fetid breath stirring the rags on her shoulders. It let out a throaty growl, and it was fortunate she had no water left to expel, although her bottom twitched on the chair and her song cut off as she gasped.

The thing rubbed itself against her side, and she realized the low growl was it purring like the cats her father would not let her keep but drowned in the pond to spite the Devil. She silently pleaded with her eyes to remain fixed on the fire but they gazed down at the brute as it moved to the corpse. It resembled a huge felid, larger than the hungry dogs turned loose into the village streets after curfew. Its mottled pelt dully shone red, black, blond, and brown, with other patches of pink, warty skin where no fur grew. A lanky tail whipped the air lazily, and from distended paw to upturned ass it looked scrawny and ill. She succeeded in keeping her eyes from its head lest she scream.

Directly above the wretched corpse, it sniffed again, its whole body wracked with slight spasms. Nicolette rose with the ax, the chair creaking loudly. It spun around just as she swung, the head of the ax catching it squarely between the shoulders. Its claws tore into her thigh, sending her sprawling across the floor.

She latched her eyelids tight and prayed to her father and the Holy Mother, the creature bawling out a whining scream that deafened her. Her leg must be torn free, so ferociously did it hurt, and she cupped her hands over her ears to shut out the horrible noise. Then the noise stopped. Nicolette remained still for a very long time, and then opened one eye. The shadowy wall before her provided no clue to the state of the beast. With aching slowness she turned her head, the exertion sending pain blasting up from her leg into the rest of her body.

With puffy, bloodshot eyes she took in the sprawled monstrosity heaped atop the witch, the ax handle jutting out of its back. It raised its front shoulders but its hindquarters would not move, foul-smelling ordure leaking from under its tail. Nicolette scrambled to her feet and immediately toppled over, her leg giving out. It tried again, now getting its back legs to jerk. Nicolette stripped off the stinking cloth that stuck to her bloody skin and rose more carefully, taking care not to look at the felled demon.

Not daring to breathe, she moved behind the creature so its eyes could not stare malevolently at her. She found the largest log in the wood pile, and tiptoeing toward it, hurled the missile at its head. The blow slumped the creature again, but through her delirium she saw the fresh gash on its scalp close as soon as it opened, and the blood matting its coat flowed back around the ax blade. The ax handle rocked as flesh knit itself together, and the thing stirred in its forced slumber.

Temples pounding and knees buckling, she leaned against the wall to stay erect. It seemed dreadfully unfair that after all her wiles the beast still lived, and recovered so unnaturally fast that it would soon be upon her again. Suddenly furious, she snatched the ax free and brought it back down where the fur gave way to pale skin below the ears. The body thrashed for only an instant, and she saw with delight that the gaping cut healed much more slowly than the vanished wound in its back, only a raised scar denoting where she had previously injured it.

She hacked again and again until the ropes fixing head to neck gave out in a mess of red, black, and yellow fluids, bones jutting up amidst the pulp. The head rolled into a corner and settled facing her, blood leaking from mouth, ears, and nose, and it blinked its pale eyes. Nicolette began to scream and did not stop until she passed out.

She awoke with a start, the fire dead and the haze of morning filtering into the room. The two monsters lay stacked like cordwood, and to her delight both remained motionless and mangled. The ax she still clutched to her chest, its cold, damp head stuck to her cheek. She cast it away and clambered to her feet. Whimpering, she stumbled out the door into the wood. She walked slowly, wary of her bleeding leg, and eventually came across a stream.

Despite the chill morning air she braced herself against the mossy stones and plunged herself face-first into the shallow water. Gasping and shivering, she righted herself and set to washing off the caked blood, heedless of how viciously the water burned her skin and wounds. She rolled in the leaves beside the bank, steam pouring off her as she laughed, then sobbed, then laughed again. Eventually she calmed enough to recognize how dead and hard her skin felt, and she inspected her leg.

As she lightly prodded the swollen pinkness bordering the four gashes a branch snapped behind her. She knew without turning that it was the creature she had taken for dead, that animal with an old man's face. When she had seen the gnarled but distinctly human head staring at her from the corner after chopping it free of its beastly body only fainting had kept her sane. She knew if she ever saw it again the sight would kill her with fear, and now she knew it could not be killed.

She tried to pray but only a soft groan came out. So instead she began screaming wordlessly to her father and the Virgin and the witch and the trees and the stream. Too weak to run or even move, her courage and spirit spent, she wailed until again the effort knocked her into slumber, her mind shutting in from the strain.

Rolling closer to the fire in her sleep, she wrapped the blanket tight around her. She slowly crept back toward consciousness, fighting nobly to remain asleep. The popping logs brought a smile to her dozing face, and through half-lidded eyes she resolved to rouse herself and tell her father of the ordeal she had dreamed. Surely in the next few weeks they would make the trek into town so she could pray at the church.

Even before she fully awoke the stinging in her leg alerted her that all was for naught. Tears slipped down her cheeks as she opened her eyes, the dark trees towering at the edge of the fire-light. The charcoal burner who had stumbled across her by the stream sat watching, his curiosity mounting. He had of course heard tales of wild people in the woods who ran on all fours and behaved as beasts, but a woodsman hears countless such stories, stories that are thankfully never proven true.

Unquestionably, her oddest feature was her lack of hair, save for the small bit that made him blush when he glimpsed it between her legs. Somewhere between a girl and a woman, he thought her beautiful regardless of her baldness yet feared her to be possessed, or worse still, a witch or spirit. He watched her as she slept with a mixture of awe and fear, wondering if he should have left her where he found her.

Magnus, for that was the charcoal burner's name, rarely saw other people in the wood, and women never. Those he only saw when he dragged his load into town every few weeks, and he had not met the lass who would give a charcoal burner so much as a kind word. Having inherited the trade from his father, at only twenty years of age he had the same blackened nostrils and fingers as those who had been in his business their whole lives.

As he watched the girl cry before she even awoke, his stomach knotted. To properly manufacture charcoal he had to mind the fire constantly for two days and nights, so the few hours of sleep he had snatched the night before meant little. He had the coal-fog on his eyes and limbs, and even with the necessity of warming the strange, naked foundling he had been loath to kindle another blaze. She had slept through the day and most of the night, only now opening her eyes to weep.

She cowered when he approached, but when he offered her

a bit of hard bread she threw herself against him, moaning. He awkwardly lay down beside the fire, her now-warm body vibrating against his. He stroked her bald scalp and prayed for her, noticing the fresh scabs blemishing her pale skin. Soon he nodded off, holding her tightly with his dusty black hands.

Nobody in the village knew her, and while many were kind and offered her niceties, still Nicolette would not speak. Whenever it was asked where she came from her eyes filled with tears and she would point vaguely toward the wood. Despite her silence during the day and the night-horrors that roused Magnus as she whined, kicked, and sweated in her sleep, she seemed fond of him, growing distraught if he left her side even for a moment. None protested when after a week he returned to his business in the wood accompanied by the mute.

She hated the forest but bore it to remain with Magnus, and helped gather and burn and carry and cook and everything else. After a time her hair grew back and her leg healed so one hardly noticed her limp and she could no longer be mistaken for a girl instead of a pretty young woman. Still her voice refused to answer her bidding, but Magnus took to calling her Yew as a woodsman's jest, and the local priest was happy to wed them since she bent her head appropriately during Mass. Although she was generally melancholy, Magnus often succeeded in coaxing a smile or even a small laugh from her. She would kiss him sweetly all over but if he touched her naked body with more than a fatherly hand she would recoil and burst into tears.

Yet Magnus loved her fiercely, and so when he exited the smith's shed after making the last payment on their horse and saw the old man shaking his wife he rushed to her aid. Nicolette's father, at seeing the daughter he had given up for dead so long ago, embraced her passionately, shocked to find her in this town so far from home. He had made the arduous journey to find cheaper hogs rumored to be sold, and at seeing her he wept and shouted with joy.

Grief had aged him far too quickly and at first Nicolette did not recognize her own father and tried to pull away. Then he said her name and she crumpled in his arms. He begged her to explain where she had gone and why, but the words still refused to come, Nicolette shaking her head and pointing to her mouth. Suddenly Magnus snatched her away, dropping his ax and berating the poor old widower. Nicolette's father stared dumbly at the charcoal burner, at his stained face and hands, hands that gripped his child, and realized his worst fears had come true. This soot-fingered brigand had abducted his little girl and cut out her tongue, taking her far enough away that she could not find her way home.

Miraculously, Nicolette's long-useless tongue finally began to obey her again, and she tearfully explained to the angry Magnus that the old man accosting her was actually her father. Her husband understood in an instant, and overwhelmed with happiness at both hearing her lovely voice and her reunion, turned to embrace the old man. Her father had retrieved Magnus's ax from the road and, oblivious to his daughter's words, drove it into the charcoal burner's beaming face.

Everyone in the street screamed but none louder than Nicolette, her husband dropping dead, blood splashing her tear-ruddied cheeks. Men seized her father and beat him mercilessly until a gibbet was raised in that very spot, and before Magnus's corpse grew cold the old man swung for the crows. While Nicolette could finally speak again, it was a very long time before she did anything but weep.

While it might appear this is a grim ending for poor Nicolette, rest assured the truth is even worse. If only such a tragedy had occurred! Rather than splitting his skull and painlessly putting an end to Magnus, Nicolette's befuddled father instead buried the ax in his stomach and hefted it for another swing. Magnus collapsed gasping, only his fingers keeping his insides where they belonged instead of on the street. Her father stared, not comprehending the hardness in his daughter's eyes as she shielded her husband from further harm. The ax flew from his hands as men descended upon him, driving him into the dust under heels and fists.

The gibbet went up and the crowd grew but Nicolette did not watch. The charcoal burner slowly bled to death, his guts trying to twist out around his fingers as Nicolette helped him onto their horse. Despite the forceful bids to help the witnesses offered, all stood back as she got behind her husband, her severe demeanor deterring even the most stubborn. The sensible blacksmith hurried to fetch the priest while Nicolette steered the horse slowly out of town, a crowd slightly smaller than that watching the noose-tree builders following after.

Clearly the man would not live out the day but Nicolette refused to take him to the church for his last rites. The priest caught up to her on the edge of town, the kind old man's face twisted from sorrow and exertion. When she ignored his call, his patience fled and he snatched at the reins.

"Please, dear," he panted, "the only succor you can give him is deliverance into Heaven. Come with me to the church at once, before the life is rattled out of him."

Nicolette did not answer, instead spitting in his face. The priest slipped and fell, shaken to his core. He silently watched them go as a dozen hands lifted him to his feet. Wiping the phlegm from his cheek, he scowled, and called after them:

"Only the Devil is pleased with the road you take! You're damning yourself as well as him! He needs his rites or he will suffer for all time, and you along with him!"

Nicolette did not answer the priest, instead whispering sweetly to her dying love. She urged the horse into the forest, and despite her fresh resolve and purpose her heart quickened as her husband's slowed. She led them deep into the part of the wood where they never ventured, that ancient sylvan realm where Magnus had found her so long ago. The trees no longer struck her as so huge and forbidding, although when they reached the stream the branches entwined too thickly for them to ride and they dismounted.

The front of Magnus's shirt glistened in the departing sunlight and he could no longer open his eyes. He mumbled to her, asking her true name, and, tears again clouding her vision, she whispered it in his ear. He smiled and opened one eye to look at her, then drifted into the slumber proceeding death.

She left him by the bank and rushed into the gloom, becoming more and more desperate as the night thickened. She thought she spied a light, but when she broke through the underbrush the dilapidated shack was as dark as the wood around it. The door had fallen off and the roof partially caved in, but her eyes had long ago become adjusted, and she saw her prize lying where she had left it.

The room stank even after all the intervening years, and she dashed to the heap of rot near the hearth. The headless corpses had grown together, putrescence blurring the boundaries between husband and wife, but resting atop them as if just set down to warm their bones lay his pelt. Even in the dark it shone brown and black and red, and she peeled it off with the ease of removing a sweaty blanket from a tired horse.

As she hurried back, those same roots and trunks that had befuddled her as a child now opened up a path, leading her at once to the stream where horse and husband waited. He did not stir when she knelt beside him and raised his head, but he still managed the occasional ragged breath, his whole body wracked with shivers. Trembling, she took knife from belt and raised him up to slice open his shirt. Armed only with intuition and her nightmares, she removed the cloth, pressed the stinking pelt against his back, and held her breath.

The result could be seen immediately. Magnus's scream sent night-birds into flight and a nearby hare's heart burst in terror. He heaved away from her, thrashing and convulsing, his guts bursting out onto the leaves without his hand to hold them in. Nicolette watched aghast, raising the knife numbly to her own throat lest she had killed her husband. Then, as the horse stomped and pulled at the rope leashing it to a nearby yew, the bloody coils of his insides reversed, sucking back into the wound. Nicolette smiled, then began to laugh and cry simultaneously.

She could not bear to see him suffer anymore, so while he threw himself against the dirt and barked and gibbered, she returned to the hovel to make it ready. The moon rose as she dragged the decomposing remains outside, then took their heads and cast them into the bushes. Being a charcoal burner's wife, she soon caught the dry leaves ablaze and a fire roared in the hearth. She righted the fallen chair and removed the piles of rags, then stripped her clothes and added them to the pile of leaves she had gathered to fashion a nest beside the fire.

Waiting for her husband, she noticed fresh blood dripping down her thighs but knew at once it was only her monthly voiding. Fearing in the dark his eyes might not be as good as his nose, she smeared it over herself, using her fingers to daub her breasts and lips and cheeks. She remembered how she had waited long before, dressed in similar attire, and giggled like a little girl. She did not wait long.

After they made love for the first time in their lives, he dozed beside the fire while she stroked his coat. Although his eyes had glistened with pain and confusion his face held a new luster, only a scar on his belly hinting at what had befallen him that morning. It was her turn to speak all night while he silently listened, telling him how they would leave the wood and journey high into the mountains together. The forest would not remain unexplored forever, and she had many hopes for the two of them. In time he would learn to use his tongue again, but until then she did enough talking for the both of them.

VIII
Enough Distractions

The snow had stopped and the sun had risen. Time passed in silence, Hegel gawking at Nicolette. During her tale she had eaten bowl after bowl of a muddy substance from a bucket beside her chair, but things other than her apparent taste for clay bothered the Grossbart. He shakily stood and cast his bottle into the fire, where it exploded. Drawing his sword, he yelled for his brother.

"On your feet, Manfried!" Hegel kept the blade between himself and the witch.

She clucked softly, not stirring from her chair. Manfried blearily pushed his back against the rear wall and rose halfway to his feet. Perplexed, he looked from Hegel to the seated geriatric. Christ, was she old.

"Calm, calm," she murmured.

"Calm? You goddamned witch, I'll have your head!" Hegel's vision blurred, from fatigue or rage or drink, he could not be sure.

"Witch?" Manfried tried to stand but slid back down the wall. "Is it a witch, brother?"

"You knew what I was when you let me touch up you and your brother," she said patiently.

"That true?" Manfried shot his brother a withering stare.

"Stay the Hell back!" Hegel moved between Nicolette and

Manfried. He intended to hack off her head with a single swipe but was hesitant to approach her. Clearly she possessed dangerous powers.

"Keep your word, Grossbart," she said, eyes flashing even without a blazing fire to reflect in them.

"She summon up that manticore on us?" Manfried's head swam, and his weapons were nowhere to be found.

"Damn it all!" Hegel could not stop shouting. "Wasn't no damn manticore, it's a damn garou, just like I told you!"

"That's French for wolf," Nicolette offered. "Don't think it really applies to Magnus, save metaphorical-like."

"Shut it!" Hegel's temples pounded. "Just be quiet!"

All three were silent. Manfried managed to edge up the wall to his feet, knees wobbling. Nicolette remained seated, staring at Hegel, who stumbled back, gripping his brother's shoulder.

"What's happened?" Manfried hissed in their tongue of two.

"Witch," Hegel hissed back in kind.

"I managed that, what the Hell we doin in its house?"

"You was ill, I dragged you here. She healed you up."

"Don't mean to second-guess, but that sounds awful honest." Manfried peered around Hegel for a better look.

"I paid." Hegel shuddered. "Nuthin honest bout it."

Nicolette had watched them intently during their discourse, head tilted like a curious pet. Now she smiled and leaned back in her chair. It had taken her a moment, but she had it.

"So she's a witch, what you waitin for? Get'er quick fore we's hexed!" Manfried shook his head in an effort to rattle out the sleep-mist.

"What *are* you waiting for, Hegel?" she asked in the same unique cant.

Both stared in shock, their code never before cracked.

"Maybe, Manfried, your brother is a man of his word?" Her smile widened.

"Dunno what word my brother gave, but any words we give's ours to take back when we want, and don't apply to heretics and witches no-way," Manfried fired back, dropping any pretenses at secrecy. "Stab her, Hegel!"

Hegel took a step forward despite the ringing in his ears and the chills lancing through every other part of his body that cautioned against such an act.

"You break your word, Hegel, and I break mine." She leaned forward in her chair.

Hegel paused, like a child working up the nerve to plunge into frigid water. Manfried held his breath, not understanding his brother's hesitation. Perhaps he had already fallen under some charm.

"Why'd you heal us, if that thing out there's your husband?" Hegel asked.

"Husband!?" Manfried slid back to the floor.

"Everything that happens to me or him is Her Will," she said softly.

"Very enlightened," Manfried croaked from the floor. "Least she respects the Virgin proper."

Nicolette's laughter hurt their ears. "Hekate's Will, Grossbarts. The only lady of true quality."

"Heresy," Manfried groaned, the stress taxing his consciousness. "Quick, brother, quick!"

"Hekate?" The name struck Hegel as familiar.

"I'd heard Her Name whispered in my youth, in my dreams. I learned Her Ways mostly myself, but twenty years ago a traveler came to our house, a traveler even Magnus feared. He taught me what I didn't intuit, which I assure you can and does fill volumes." She had the same pleasant tone as when she told her earlier tale, nostalgia bringing a joyous glaze to her eyes.

"The Devil," Manfried managed, lights bursting in his vision. "She met with the Devil!" He passed out again.

Hegel could not move, and while he would later attribute it to some spell, in truth he was too frightened to do anything but gawp at her.

"Not the Devil," she sighed. "Or even *a* devil. A man of letters, a scholar of sorts. He spent a winter with us. I knew how to farm a bit, and Magnus hunted, naturally, but times are always lean when one's appetite is so pronounced. In addition to the unusual seeds from the East, he showed me how to make my own food, as well as auger and curse and all the other goodness the Church warns against."

"We." Hegel swallowed. "We should be—"

"You leave when I say. I lied. I healed you not for Her Will but my own. You will die eventually, Grossbarts, and it will be hideous."

Manfried caught that much, breaking back into consciousness and conversation as though his participation in both had been unfailing. "Yeah, everyone dies, witch, and then we's gonna ascend. Might take us a while, but there'll be no escapin your fate. You's gonna be burnin for all time, long after we's paid any penance we owe."

"Neither here nor there, I certainly don't intend to debate theology with two such learned and pious Marionites as yourselves. If I was to slay you now, no matter how painful or drawn out, you fools would cling to your faith, and cheat me of my reward."

"Damn right we would," Manfried snorted, trying to keep the lights at bay.

"Take that sack down, Hegel," she said wearily, motioning to a high shelf.

He obeyed, telling himself his action was born only of curiosity. It felt heavy and lumpy, full of gravel. He held it out to her, the sword quaking in his other hand.

Shaking her head, she squinted at him. "Look inside."

Unknotting the top, Hegel peered in. His brow knitted, and

he looked closer. Manfried laboriously got back up and also had a gander.

"What's this?" Hegel whispered, paler than milk.

"Teeth?" Manfried pulled out a handful.

"My children's." She sighed.

Manfried hurled the teeth away, wiping his hand on his shirt. "Cut'er!" he yelled but fell on his brother, who dropped the bag and supported him.

"Lean times." Her eyes might have been misty, the room too dim for the Brothers to be sure. "Early spring sowing, to make sure they arrived before the snow. Then I'd have milk to last us through the winter, and some meat as well."

Hegel's sword swayed in his fingertips, its tip brushing the teeth on the floor. Manfried dug his thumb into his brother's shoulder, using all his strength to stay upright. Nicolette cracked her knuckles and yawned.

"First few litters kept us well, but hard times more oft get worse before they're better. After the first couple broods I stopped producing regular, and it's a wonder we survived those years until he arrived. He taught me, yes, bake the bread far faster with a bit of effort, and they grow and plumpen far faster as well. The taste is one to be savored, surely, and I'd not begrudge Magnus anything, and yet…pure instinct, I suppose. Mothers want babes, all there is to it. To raise, I mean, not *that*. So if Magnus had caught you proper we'd have et real well this winter, but now I can have what he denied me through no fault of his own."

"Eh." Hegel's tongue flopped stupidly around his mouth. Manfried's however, worked just fine. It was the rest of his body that failed him. With a string of vile curses directed at the baby-eating, devil-worshipping whore of a witch, he slipped down his brother's side, continuing his volley from the floor.

Hegel stared at Nicolette's enormous gut, which had not been a fraction of that size when she had begun her story the night before. The beast must have put it in there, he thought, magic or no, it must have been the beast. Mary have mercy.

"Growing fast, growing strong." She winked at Hegel, making his knees soften. He leaned against the wall, his brother out of breath from his diatribe. "Vengeance will be wrought not with my hands but by what grows. You'll lose everything, Grossbarts, and you'll know I played a hand in every misery that befalls you. Every dog that bites and every assassin that stalks, every man and woman who turns against you, I will see it in the hoarfrost and the flight of birds and my dreams. My eyes will watch your souls blacken and your bodies fail, and any aid I may offer your enemies will be freely given. I could have slaughtered you when you first came but I held back, and I'm glad I did, for your undoing will become legend."

The Brothers Grossbart knew a curse when they heard one. Hegel, never breaking her gaze, helped his brother to his feet. Manfried no longer pressed his brother, instead snatching a log from beside the dead fire. Righteous indignation gave him strength, and, nudging Hegel, he raised his weapon.

"Given us little choice," Manfried barked. "I kilt plenty, but you's gonna be the best." He took a step toward her but Hegel held him back.

"No, brother, she's dangerous," said Hegel.

"What's a witch do but curse someone? She already done that, and I think I reckon I know a way to break that curse." As he shook his brother off, Nicolette leaned back in her chair and muttered something.

Manfried swung his log but the bag of teeth jumped from the floor, smacking him in the jaw. Knocked off balance, he sprawled on the ground beside the chair. As he looked up what he at first took to be the lights presaging unconsciousness revealed themselves to be hundreds of loose teeth spinning in the air. A single tiny tooth separated from the tempest and slammed into the ground beside his face, embedding in the earthen floor. He covered his eyes with his arms and prayed loudly until he heard them clatter back down where they belonged. Hegel had become dizzy, frozen in place, and no sooner had the teeth returned to the floor than he vomited on the dead coals of the hearth.

"Now get out of my house before I turn your skin inside out." She settled back into her chair.

"Mary preserve us," Hegel whispered, sheathing his sword. Manfried peeked over his elbow, still convinced the end had come. Hegel helped him up, and they groped about the floor, trying to gather their equipment without looking away from Nicolette.

Manfried shook scattered teeth off his bag and slipped it over his shoulder. Everything hurt, ax and mace far heavier than usual. Unsure what had transpired since he had gone to sleep several days before, he had no choice but to trust his brother knew what was going on.

Hegel did not, but he suspected staying in Nicolette's company any longer would drive him mad. Helping his swaying brother to the door, he gave her a final glare. The ways of witches were clearly inscrutable. Hunger overrode his fear, and he turned in the doorway.

"About our meat—" Hegel began.

"Out," she said wearily.

"Or some a that hooch—"

"Out!" She stood, her bloated stomach jutting accusatorily at them.

"We's doin just that," Hegel groused, unlatching the door.

"Fore we do, though . . ." Manfried turned and spit.

"Damn it all." Hegel began shoving his brother out but Manfried stood tall.

"You listen sharp, witch," Manfried spluttered, wrestling his brother in the doorway. "You might a cursed us but we curse you, too. We killed your warlock-beast husband, and you's dyin in this shithole. And we's gonna die, as every man a faith does, but not fore you's pulled down into the pit, the souls a your babes bawlin in your ears, and one way or another the last thing you's gonna see will be us laughin. Too late to turn, you's bound to burn, and when we's done with the Arabs we's comin back to piss on your bones, you nasty—"

Hegel shoved him outside, slamming the door just in time to intercept the dozens of teeth launched at them.

"Let's burn it!" Manfried made back for the hut but his brother knocked him down, wide-eyed and panting.

"You damn fool, you's gonna bring the Devil down on us!" Hegel exploded.

"You reckon your soul's pure enough to suffer a witch to live?" Manfried got to his feet, staring his brother down.

"We's gonna be back for vengeance, I swear it! For now, we gotta move fore she grows some wits and tries to fix us good at present."

Looking around, Manfried nodded. He had almost passed out again, and the witch definitely had her wiles. Floating teeth might be the least of their worries.

They stood in a roughly tilled field on the edge of the forest, and to either side mountains shot up, the hut leaning against a cliff that stretched between the two slopes at the end of the valley. Hegel made for one of the rises, picking his way among the sparse trees.

"Shouldn't we go back to Horse, get some meat?" Manfried queried, following Hegel away from the wood and the shack.

"Nah, even if it ain't been picked clean we'd have a time findin it again. Forest's too big."

"What we gonna eat, then?"

"Put some meat in our bags before. Lost most of it though, that horseskin came loose when I was haulin you through the wood and the rest's in that hut. Full waterskins, though." Hegel began scrambling up the rise.

Manfried followed slowly, his unstrung crossbow bouncing on his back. Hegel periodically waited for Manfried to catch up. An hour later they reached the top, the ridge boxing in the forest behind them and stretching up to a peak ahead. They both looked down on the valley and spit.

Silently plodding down the other side, they took in the unbroken range. More trees speckled the scenery but nothing as thick as the wood of the witch. Manfried slipped several times, lying on the rocks and staring at the gray sky until Hegel helped him up. He felt faint, and even with numerous breaks in their hike he collapsed hours before dark, incapable of continuing.

They were climbing a ridge spotted with boulders and what small patches of snow the sharp wind permitted. Hegel helped his brother to a hollow between two of the monstrous stones and they made camp. Manfried wheezed and coughed, Hegel draping him with their blanket and foraging enough wood to last the night from the nearby trees. Hegel then used rocks to shore up the gap between the boulders in what proved to be an ineffectual attempt at keeping the wind out.

Cooking meat and collecting snow, Hegel crafted a decent stew as the sun set. Manfried slept most of the night, necessity forcing Hegel under the blanket with him. Many times that night Hegel longed for the warmth and windlessness of their past night's shelter, but always came the image of the witch squatting atop him, and he fought back tears.

The morning brought a thick frost to their beards, and within an hour of setting out snow fluttered on them. Both ruminated on their encounter with the witch, Manfried staring at his brother's back and wondering what had transpired during his fever. Hegel focused on the terrain around them in an attempt to free himself from the memory of her foulness.

"Knew she was a witch and still let her touch me?" Manfried demanded while they ate looking down at the morning's ascent.

"Little choice," Hegel replied.

"Could a had faith I'd get better, put your trust in Mary and not some heretic."

"Yeah? You was turnin colors and wouldn't a lasted the night."

"So you risked my soul to save my flesh, that it?"

"Only one riskin their soul was me, so how's bout a bit a gratitude, you thankless cunt?" Hegel bit into his half-raw horse meat.

"Look, brother," Manfried said, adopting a paternal tone. "I ain't mad at you, I's just sayin you need to exercise a touch more discretion, particularly in who you's associatin with. I know your intentions was right, and this time we lucked out as we's both still drawin breath, but next time—"

"Next time I'll leave you to the crow's mercy!" Hegel barked. "You got no concept a what I done for you, and you act like I shit in your beard. Some brother!"

"You got us cursed, Hegel!"

"So? Scared we can't break it? Won't be the first time someone wished us death."

"Yeah, but it's different comin from a witch. Why'd she heal us in the first place? You know that get-us-later meck don't wash."

Hegel grew pale and put his lunch away. "Time we got movin."

"What was the price?" Manfried lowered his voice. "Wasn't your soul, was it?"

"Dunno," Hegel whispered, his voice cracking. "Hope not. Just remember you'd be dead if I didn't do what I done." He marched off, Manfried quickly stowing his things and rushing after.

Catching up, Manfried clapped his brother's shoulder. "I

won't forget. Just gotta be careful now that we got a hex on us. We'll be cleansed a any taint by our own righteousness."

"Yeah. Careful." Hegel had his doubts if anyone shy of the Virgin could clean his sin. He remembered her warmth, and how in his passion he had called her Mary and given his devotion. The knot in his gut tightened every time he thought of it, the only act in his wretched life he actually regretted.

The wind dried their sweat but the chill remained, their teeth chattering whenever they paused to survey the terrain. Hours later they found themselves on a mountainside identical to the last several they had crossed, but Manfried had faith his brother was not leading them in circles. Hegel did not share this certainty, nervously chewing his beard until they crested a pass and he gained proof they were not backtracking—the ridge they traversed fell away sharply into a ravine. On the next mount, directly level with where they stood, snaked a worn road. Hegel shook with happiness, and Manfried showed his improved health by cutting a jig on the scree.

The road stretched on forever but, unlike the first leg of their journey south, the following week on a marked path filled them with expectations of continued good fortune. The road, though poorly maintained, exceeded the one on which they had started their journey in both size and smoothness. They lamented their loss of Horse and cart but tactfully avoided the topic of their dwindling provisions. Even Manfried had to admit that their encounter with the witch and her husband had been a turning point.

"Proves we's doin right in Her Eyes," Manfried said on the eighth day. "We keep up with the righteousness, we'll be sackin them Arab crypt-castles come Easter."

"You think?" asked Hegel. "How far's it to Gyptland anyway?"

"Dunno, and don't care neither. If we's doin what She wills, we's gonna get there by the by, and probably be rich fore we even arrive."

"Suppose so," Hegel concurred.

"We'd burned that witch like I said, we'd probably found some prime ponies loaded with truffles long the way."

"Still might." The idea of succulent mushrooms reminded Hegel they would soon be out of horse meat. Another few days, at best.

"Husband? So you say she told it was a man fore a monster?" Manfried still could not comprehend that their enemy in the wood was anything but a manticore.

"Yeah. Queer tale she told. Mind I drowsed a bit at the slowness, but soon enough got proper strange."

"Kind a wish I'd heard it."

"Nah, you don't. Sad stuff. She used to be a right pretty girl, and honest too, and loved Mary with all'er heart. Kind a woman make a decent wife."

"Now how you know that?"

"She told me."

Manfried snorted. "Yeah, go ahead and believe everythin a witch tells you."

"Didn't say I believed it all."

"But you think she was fit? Ever? Imagine it young and it'd still be all tainted with heresy. No such thing as a pretty witch."

During the intervening days Hegel had often tried to separate one portion of a certain memory from the other aspects. He silently ruminated. He almost had it, but every time his brother would say something like—

"No sir. That witch done fucked that animal-man-thing, fucked'em often, too. And et the babes what come out. Imagine that crusty crone spread—"

Hegel leaned over and vomited so hard his sphincter twitched.

Manfried jumped back from the spray, laughing heartily. Hegel shot him an evil glare through spew-teared eyes.

"That horse not agreein with you?"

"It's that vile tongue a yours. Who'd wanna think a thing like that?" Hegel spit but could not dispel the taste-memory of her.

"Just sayin."

"Well, don't."

"What's that?"

"Eh?" Hegel wiped his mouth and looked where his brother did. The road stretched off around the bend, appearing intermittently down the long ridge, but behind them on the last mountain they had traversed the highway came back into view, and here a large black shape moved. It went quickly, and Hegel could make out both the wagon and the team of horses making good time.

Manfried squinted. "I can't—"

"It's a damn ride, is what it is!" Hegel slapped his brother with his wide-brimmed hat.

"Yeah?"

"Yeah!"

"What they doin comin through the mountains in dead winter?"

"What we doin here? Same as them. Now get to task." Hegel rushed ahead to where a boulder jutted out of the roadside.

"Good lookin out," Manfried said, jumping into action.

They each worked a side of the slab, Manfried with his ax, Hegel with his pick. Every few minutes they would pause and set to, but it still would not budge. Desperation took over, but the more they dug the deeper into the mountainside the boulder went.

"Look," Hegel panted. "We oughta haul that dead tree back a ways over here and wedge it in, try to pry this out."

"What's that?"

"That dead tree was on the upper slope, a little ways back. We hurry, we can get it back here fore——" Hegel paused, seeing the look in Manfried's eyes, and altered his intent: "Or we could just lay that log across the trail stead a this boulder." Manfried nodded slowly, scowling at his brother.

No sooner had they backtracked to the log, scrambled up the roadside, and rolled it back down than they heard the horses approach. They stretched it across the road and waited, and when Hegel caught sight of the wagon rounding the bend they leaned down, acting as though dried, crumbling wood possessed enormous weight. The wagon slowed to a stop and two men jumped from the rear, exchanging words with the driver before advancing on the Grossbarts with crossbows in hand. Seeing this, the Brothers retrieved their own notched crossbows from behind the log.

"Hold, now!" Hegel called when the men came into range.

"Why this?" the bigger of the two demanded.

"Seen yous comin, decided to lend a hand, get this out the road for you," Manfried yelled.

"Why the bows?" the man said.

"Why've you got yours?" Hegel returned.

"What?" The man cocked his ear.

"Come on over," Manfried said, "can't hear you neither."

The men advanced warily on the grinning Grossbarts. When they were close enough to make out their bearded countenances the men stopped. The driver called something from behind but none of the four paid him heed.

"What you doing out here?" the first man asked. He possessed a stringy black mustache that matched both the hair on his head and that of his fellow's.

"Same's you," Hegel shot back.

"Seeing this," Mustache said, "so you move that wood and stand clear and we be on ours, and you be on yours."

"Well, now," Manfried said, "that don't seem fair."

"Why this?" Mustache asked.

"We go through the trouble a movin it and you don't even offer two weary travelers a ride?" said Hegel.

The second man said something to Mustache in a language the Brothers could not understand. Mustache responded in the same, and the second man raised his bow at Hegel. The Grossbarts cradled their crossbows lazily, but each had his weapon trained on one of the men.

"Move back," Mustache said, "and we move it ourselves, and you have no reasons to gripe."

"Fair's fair," Hegel said, immediately regretting the use of Nicolette's phrase.

The Brothers stepped back and the two men advanced. They paused, glancing down at the log. Rotten though it was, they could not move it without setting down their weapons. The Grossbarts beamed at them. The men exchanged more indecipherable words, glaring at the Brothers.

"You win," Mustache said, smiling himself now, "you move, and we give passage."

"What's stoppin you from shootin us when we set down our bows?" Manfried inquired.

"Same as stopping you from shooting we if we do the same," Mustache snapped.

"Righteous Christian morals?" Hegel asked, but made no move to lower his weapon.

"Yes," said Mustache.

"Ain't cut it," Manfried said. "We's pious pilgrims, as shown by our Virgins." He shook his head, the necklace bouncing on his tunic. "Where's your proof?"

"Seeing this," Mustache said, "it is not my wagon or we gladly grant you a ride. So sad, it is not. We are paid exactly so no one gets on wagon. We are paid to move logs. Seeing this, the log must go and you with it."

"Move it, then," Hegel said.

Mustache's smile faded, and he exchanged more words with his compatriot. They began walking backward, away from the Brothers.

"We discuss with the driver," Mustache called.

"You do that!" Hegel yelled, sitting down on the log.

"Should a shot those infidels where they lied," Manfried said.

"How you know they're infidels?"

"You see that one's mustache? And the other's definitely foreign. Finally, when asked for proof a faith they failed to produce."

"None a that means nuthin. You's thinkin too hard, as usual," Hegel sighed.

"Why else they don't give us a ride?"

"Probably cause we didn't offer'em anythin."

"Holy men don't need to pay. Least not to any fellow Christian."

"So you's a holy man now?" Hegel snorted.

"Both a us is. Killed us a devil."

"Wasn't a devil, was a damn man what turned into one."

"Same thing," said Manfried.

"Hell it is."

"Watch that blasphemy."

Hegel perked up. "They's comin back."

Better still, the wagon followed. The second man sat on the bench beside the driver. Mustache walked ahead, smiling broadly but still training his bow on Hegel.

"You win," Mustache said. "Move the log and give some coin and we all be on ours, but you off at the next town. Seeing this?"

Hegel began to answer but Manfried elbowed him, taking charge. "Right equitable. We'll give you all the money we got soon's we arrive."

"Coin now." Mustache sounded immovable.

"No security you's honest, we pay upon delivery," said Hegel.

"No proof you either. Coin now," Mustache said.

"Hey you," Manfried called to the driver. "We'll give you all when we get to a town and not fore, deal?"

"See—" Mustache began, but the driver interrupted with a harsh string of those foreign words, then he looked to the Grossbarts. He appeared their age, with oily black hair and a thinner mustache, and finer clothes than anyone else present.

"No highwaying on this highway, yes?" the driver asked in a clipped accent.

"That's right." Hegel smiled.

"So you have my Christian word on a safe passage. If you will swear the same, we may progress." The driver forced a smile.

"Given," the Brothers said in unison.

"Then move that, and any other obstructions we chance upon, and no further payment will be necessary." The driver smoothed the scalloped edge of his chaperon hat.

The two guards walked to the rear of the wagon, casting foul glances at the Brothers. Manfried kept his arbalest in hand while Hegel lifted one end of the dead log and rolled it to the side, then he picked up his weapon and they both set their feet on it, pushing it over the edge. Watching it pick up speed and finally blast apart on a boulder down the mountainside, they both ruminated on how they might approach a traveling wagon in the future in light of the difficulty in securing passage on this one.

They moved to enter the wagon but all three yipped at them to get on the bench and stay clear of the interior. Jamming their odorous bags under the hanging tarp behind their seat, they were off. A Grossbart sat on either end with the driver and the other foreign guard between them, Mustache presumably inside or on a rear seat.

The rocking wagon provided them with unobstructed views of

the cliffs falling away from the road, and as the day lengthened so did the precipices. The highway wound up into the mountains, the snow and wind and hazy sky chilling the Brothers' bones. Whenever a rockslide or other debris blocked the road they would climb down and move it, but these breaks were infrequent. They moved slowly but still managed a great distance more than the Grossbarts would have on foot before sundown. They stopped in a lightly wooded meadow presiding above the day's road.

The Grossbarts made their own fire farther up the road lest their new friends attempt to flee in the dark. They took shifts, and when Hegel felt his ears itch he ensured that he made a lot of noise loading his crossbow. He heard footsteps retreat back to the foreigners' fire and he returned to his horse-marrow stew.

The next day passed in similar fashion, as did the one after that—except the Grossbarts' rations shrank with each meal. During their nocturnal vigils nothing braved the firelight, so their stomachs remained the only things growling. The third morning never fully came, the flurries replaced by heavy snow blotting out everything but the road in front of the horses. The Brothers debated, in their sibling language, the benefits of abandoning the wagon, reckoning they would make the same time and not have to worry about tumbling over the edge if the horses stepped wrong in the drifts.

They moved through a white fog of snow, steam pouring off the horses, snot freezing in the Brothers' beards. Only the cliffs jutting up on one side and falling away on the other told them they kept the road. Any banter the men had provided over the previous days had frozen on their lips. They traveled slowly, and Hegel sensed something foreboding in the snow, something sinister waiting up the road. He told his brother, who nodded and readied his crossbow. The attack Hegel knew would come never did, and several hours later the foreigners shouted in triumph.

Mustache jumped from the rear and ran beside the slowing wagon, the other guard hopping down as the horses stopped. Hegel felt sick, sweat-ice on his brow and lips. They had to get away but their only option was the void stretching out on all sides, the cliffs having faded away without their noticing. Instead Hegel prayed, begging Mary to take away his frantic disquiet.

"Open up!" Mustache yelled, and his ally yelled presumably the same in his alien tongue.

The Brothers made out a high shadow through the wind-blown snow, and from the rattling sound a barn or other door lay ahead. They kept shouting for several minutes but got no response, and after a quick word with the shivering driver, they both vanished into the snow. The Brothers shifted closer to the driver, crossbows ready.

"Where'd they go?" Manfried asked.

"To open the gate," the driver chattered, his tan skin implying such weather did not suit him.

"Where we at?" said Manfried.

"Rouseberg," the driver replied. "Passed through a few weeks ago, so they should be expecting us."

"Ill name for a town," Manfried decided.

Hegel paid no mind to their conversation. His eyes darted everywhere, futilely trying to spot the source of the danger he knew lurked just beyond his vision. He could not be sure if it was the witch, her husband returned, or something worse.

A groaning came from ahead, and Mustache reappeared, calling out: "Lend us a hand!"

Manfried hurried forward while Hegel refused to budge, trying to warn his brother but unable to speak. Manfried saw a large wooden gate the two men heaved against, snowdrifts keeping it from opening more than a crack. The three kicked and shoved and got soaking wet before it opened wide enough to fit the wagon through.

The driver urged the horses in, Hegel squinting to catch a glimpse of the town. Only a few sagging roofs and shadows of buildings came through the snow, no sounds emanating from the blanketed hamlet. Manfried climbed back onto the bench while the guards closed the gate and secured the supports, locking them into the village.

IX
Odd Men at Odds

Only snow and dilapidated houses greeted the Grossbarts and the wagon-men. Several roofs had caved in from the weight of the snowdrifts and the horses struggled to move the wagon at all. They plodded through the cavernous street until they came to a large building, dark and uninviting as the rest, and here they brought the wagon around the side to a barn. Mustache and the other guard wrestled the door open and the Grossbarts jumped off rather than ride into the black interior.

The two guards waited outside the barn rubbing their hands but the Grossbarts recognized an alehouse when they saw one, no matter how vacant it appeared. They found the door latched and suspected knocking would do little good, but Hegel's dented sword fit through the gap and, putting their backs into it, they dislodged the plank holding the door shut. It swung open and they tumbled in with a mound of accumulated snow.

The grave-wise eyes of the Brothers Grossbart spotted several tables and benches in the darkness of the room, and as their eyes adjusted further they noticed a large fireplace against the back wall. They picked their way through the gloom and upon seeing a shelf of bottles against the back wall they set to business. Each seized a bottle and sampled, Hegel with favorable results, Manfried spitting out a mouthful of greasy oil. They each stowed a bottle of oil and as many bottles of apple schnapps as their bulging packs would allow before turning back to the empty tavern.

"Where's everyone?" Manfried gave voice to his brother's thoughts.

Hegel took another stiff pull of schnapps, trying to drown his paranoia. It only grew worse. They moved along the rear wall until they found an unlocked door and pushed it open. Finding what lay beyond too dark for immediate exploration Manfried went to start a fire and Hegel nosed around the rest of the room.

A ladder extended down beside the fireplace, and Hegel climbed it with his dagger in one hand. It led to a large loft whose ceiling bowed under the weight of snow, particularly under the tarp covering the smoke-hole. Slicing it open and watching the avalanche of snow vomit down, even the amusement of Manfried suddenly floundering under the deluge of frozen powder did not lessen his worry.

Hegel climbed down and rooted about for a rushlight, and once he got it sputtering on the fresh fire he slowly ascended again. Sadly, the loft yielded naught but moldy blankets, rotting straw, and a stinking pisspot. The stench hinted at something more than urine, sweat, and decay, but he could not place it.

Manfried kept busy, first making a snowball with a stone at its core to lob at his unsuspecting brother, and after he heard a most satisfying yelp as the missile reached its mark he scooped up snow with their cooking pot, dumped in the rest of their meat, and hung it from a rung over the fire. He dragged two benches over and got comfortable, scowling at the draft when the other three men entered. His brother definitely had put the shivers on him, but Manfried refused to give in to speculation. After all, free drink and shelter should never be examined too closely.

The driver and his assistants crowded around the hearth, lakes emerging from their boots on the worn floor. Hegel came down from the loft and sat beside his brother. None spoke, all staring into the fire while sensation returned to their extremities.

"Something is very wrong," said the driver, standing and pulling a thin dagger from under his cloak.

"You think so, huh?" Manfried leaned back, his boots heating up nicely.

"You don't?" The driver looked around, and retrieved an unlit rushlight from the shelf.

"He's right," Hegel said, although the warmth had chased off some of his jitteriness.

"So when yous was th. aough a ways back there was people here, eh?" Manfried would not be unsettled. He had battled demons and witches, after all.

"Plenty of them," the driver said, eyes flitting about. "Big town for so deep in the mountains. Many children playing in the snow."

Mustache said something in the southern tongue, and both the driver and the other man nodded. The driver responded in the same language, and glanced back at the door. This skulduggery did not sit well with the Brothers, particularly the suspicious Hegel.

"Speak proper, now!" Hegel shouted, jumping from his stool. "None a that beast-speech, hear? We all speak the same, and if someone don't catch it, well, that's his business."

"Seeing this," Mustache replied, getting up from his bench, "the people may have go to the … the …"

"Monastery," helped the driver. "To what purpose all would go, however, is unclear. The houses look several days vacant at least."

"Yeah," Manfried agreed. "Seen some all boarded up, same as this."

"And there's no one else here?" the driver asked. "Not in the back or front?"

"Well," Hegel said. "If this is the front, no one's here, but we didn't check out the back. No light."

Clicking his teeth, the driver lit his fat-coated reed. "Come along, then."

"You wanna look, go ahead." Manfried tested his stew. "If you catch any more meat or turnips, bring'em on back."

"I'll go." Hegel withdrew his pick, eager to bury its point in the source of his anxiety.

The two other men made no move, finding the puddles at their feet most interesting. The driver spit a string of harsh words of the foreign variety, but this time Hegel smiled at their usage. Admonishments of cowardice he recognized regardless of the language.

"I am Ennio," the driver told Hegel.

Manfried laughed. "He's a *what*?"

"That a name where you come from?" asked Hegel.

"Yes," Ennio said sharply.

"Well damn," said Hegel.

"And by what do I address you?" Ennio asked.

"I's Hegel, my brother there's Manfried, and we's both Grossbarts."

"Seeing this truly." Mustache smiled.

"What's that supposed to mean, dirt-stache?" Manfried glared at the man, who stared back blankly.

"That is Alphonse," Ennio said, "and his cousin is Giacomo."

The cousins stared at the Brothers, the ice thicker than ever.

"Al Ponce?" Manfried grinned at Hegel. "He struck me as a ponce from the moment I laid eyes on him. Ask Hegel, told'em myself."

"Honesty," Hegel said, but his mind lay elsewhere.

The Grossbart and the driver advanced on the back door, Ennio pushing it open and thrusting the rushlight into the darkness. Hegel followed, sweating from more than the welcome heat.

They went down a tight hallway and discovered several sacks of grain and barrels of turnips at the end. Another latched door opened into the snowy void, and they quickly closed it again. Along the hall three doorways draped with cloth revealed sparse chambers with straw mats and nothing else.

Alphonse and Giacomo noticed the shelf where only a few bottles remained, and each took one back to the fire. Manfried considered murder, then chided himself for not hiding whatever would not fit in his bag. Of the two, Manfried hated Alphonse slightly more, what with his bushy black hair and mustache and dimpled cheeks stupidly contrasting his large frame. Not that Giacomo's chiseled face and arms and dark complexion failed to grate on him as well. Like most men who are ugly on both sides of their skin, Manfried detested handsome people on general principle.

"Found us a good place to bed down," Hegel said, stepping back into the room.

"Out here, Grossbarts," Ennio said firmly.

"What's that?" Hegel stopped and turned on the man, pick still brandished.

"We five sleep out here, she will sleep in the other rooms," said Ennio, turning back to the hallway. He added something in his native tongue for Alphonse and Giacomo, and disappeared with his crackling rushlight into the back.

"She?" the Grossbarts echoed.

Giacomo blanched and took a long swig and Alphonse muttered to himself.

"Talk, Ponce," said Manfried.

"None of yours." The guard scooted closer to the fire.

Manfried's boot upended Alphonse's stool, knocking him to the ground. The man scrambled up but Manfried had casually raised his loaded crossbow, its end pressing against Alphonse's codpiece. The startled Giacomo's hand fell to his sword but paused when he realized Hegel's pick had found its way under his chin, the iron point chill against his Adam's apple.

"Talk, Ponce." Manfried smiled.

Alphonse looked at Giacomo, who began shouting at him to do whatever the crazy bandits said. The Grossbarts did not approve of their conversing in an unknown language, so Hegel pressed his tool enough to prick Giacomo's throat. This quieted him instantly, his eyes burning into his cousin's. There would be opportunities to dispose of these two foreign bastards later, Alphonse thought, and did as Manfried commanded.

"The woman is the, the woman of Alexius Barousse," Alphonse said, hoping that would be sufficient. It was not.

"Who's he?" Manfried prodded verbally and physically, the bolt's point rising to jab at Alphonse's doublet.

"A capo, er, sea captain." Alphonse stammered. "In Venezia. She is his, we retrieve her for him, take her home."

"What's she doin up these parts, eh?" Manfried asked.

"She was in…" Alphonse bit his lip, then almost got it correct. "Abbess. She stay in abbess some years in your empire, now we fetch her. Anything happen to us or her, he will hunt you for rest of your lives, and punish—"

"Yeah, I got you." Manfried lowered his weapon. "Now shut your hole. Both a you'd do to remember you owe us your lives."

Hegel followed his brother's lead, wiping the spot of blood off on Giacomo's shoulder and relooping his pick onto his belt. Giacomo relaxed, touching his neck and launching a barrage at Alphonse, who in turn explained the Brothers were moontouched and would be dealt with accordingly. If not now, later.

"Gotta nun?" Hegel asked his brother.

"More likely a sweet piece he wanted off-limits til his wife died or some such. Didn't say daughter or sister or nuthin, but who knows. Poncey's a little rough on the ears." Manfried gingerly touched his cropped lobe.

Ennio returned from the rear hallway, pale and shivering. Alphonse and Giacomo both spoke at once, but Manfried cuffed Alphonse in the ear, encouraging him to talk right or not at all. Ennio narrowed his eyes at the Brothers but seemed distracted. He hurried to the door and ensured the slat locked it firmly, and dragged another bench to the fire. All eight eyes waited for his next move. Sighing, he relieved Alphonse of his bottle.

"Go fetch the grain bag and make some porridge," Ennio said wearily.

Alphonse complained to himself but went into the back.

"Grossbarts," Ennio said. "Any queries should be given to me instead of my associates, as they will provide you with nothing of substance."

"Dunno if that's all true," Manfried said. "What's the girl to this captain—kin or kinmaker?"

"None of your concern, be assured," Ennio said with a frown at the returning Alphonse.

"Maybe yeah, maybe nah," Manfried said, removing the stew from the fire and setting it on a bench. Hegel wasted no time in setting to, dipping his bowl whenever his brother was not slurping directly from the pot. The three foreigners cooked and ate their porridge in jealous silence.

With their stew gone, the Grossbarts gazed at the porridge. Permission was stated by Hegel rather than requested, and they ate the rest of that, too. Pleasantly bloated, the Brothers sipped their schnapps and reclined by the fire. Even Alphonse and Giacomo appeared to have forgotten the altercation, whispering to each other and smiling drunkenly. In view of the porridge, the Brothers let it slide. Ennio disappeared through the rear hall and soon returned with a fresh bit of frost on his hat. He resumed his seat with a sigh.

"The snow has stopped," Ennio finally said, "and the moon is near full, you can actually see about."

"Well, that's somethin, I guess, or you would a stayed quiet," Manfried said.

"No lights." Ennio rolled a bottle from hand to hand. "Not so queer if everyone is here, but they are not."

"What about that monastery?" Manfried said.

"Black. But it can be seen in the moonlight. Usually some lights at those, especially if they have a feast or festival or other reason why town has gone there." Ennio sipped on his bottle, Alphonse's pattern of listening and whispering implying he translated for Giacomo.

Alcohol had blunted Hegel's anxiety about the town but it still twisted in his brain and heart and he brooded in silence. He knew what came next, and did not want to hear it. Something about the unseen woman in the rear also itched at his nerves. He wanted to lay eyes on her to see if that helped, although he suspected it would not.

"So we go out and look around, bang on some doors to ensure, and hike up to the monastery. Even in snow it is close." Ennio set his bottle on the floor and stood, looking at the four doubtful men.

Hegel broke the silence with a laugh, surprised his brother did not join in. Regaining himself, he wiped his eyes. "Have fun! Me and Manfried'll make sure nuthin goes amiss round here."

"Grossbarts," Ennio patiently explained. "We must discover where everyone has gone. Their absence is unnatural. Whole towns do not disappear without reason."

"So? Ain't gonna make no difference where they at. Can't drive them ponies by moonlight on these roads, so we's here til cockcrow at the soonest." Hegel sipped his drink, unable to remember a time when he would less fancy a moonlit stroll.

"Hegel—" Ennio began, but Manfried cut him off.

"Any princes or lords round here?" Manfried said.

"No," Ennio said, not seeing the relevance.

"How'd that monastery get built?" Manfried pressed.

"Looks more of a keep or fortress than a church, so mayhap a duke or count lived there. But that would be long ago, I suppose, or else the monks would not be there now. You think someone ordered the absence of the village?" Ennio perked up, unsure what Manfried implied.

"Nah," Manfried said, "but seein's how you's been so kind's to let us ride, the least me and my humble family can do is spot around the town with you."

"The Devil, Manfried, we ain't..." Seeing the gleam in his brother's eye, Hegel trailed off. The familiar look on Manfried's face clued Hegel in, drunken excitement besting his worry. Cursing his own obtuseness, Hegel said, "Yeah, you's right. I was bein selfish. Right uncharitable a me."

"That's right, brother," Manfried chided. "We's here to do the work a Mary. And She clear as Hell wants us to lend a hand to our friends." Then shifting to their brotherly cant, he added, "And sides, monks' more liable to be decent folk than your average priest. Most a them's shit, sure, but always err on the side a helpin'em out, case they's in good with the Virgin."

Ennio shrugged and made ready to leave, wise enough to recognize that while the Grossbarts were certainly working an angle, there was nothing he could do about it. Besides, if they had murder on their minds then Alphonse and Giacomo would have already been dead and they would have gone after him without pretext. The cousins were tickled to be left behind, wanting nothing to do with the Grossbarts in a desolate town under a fat moon.

No wind or snow disturbed their march but the chill worked into their beards. They brought rushlights but these stayed cold in their belts, the moon reflecting eerily off the snow. Every time Ennio called out into the stillness or rapped on a door the Grossbarts had to suppress the urge to club the idiot. The town consisted of less than a dozen buildings on each side of the road but the knee-deep drifts slowed their progress. The high stone wall circling the houses ended in another wooden gate, and rather than forcing it they climbed a convenient stile and hopped over the side.

Here the road switchbacked up the face of a stern mountain and they could see the silhouette of the monastery several bends away. They did not speak, slowly tramping through the snow until they rounded the final curve and broke off onto the path leading to the black structure. The road fell away on the side overlooking the town, the moon so bright they made out the alehouse, the town walls, and the mountains they had journeyed through.

To their left the monastery wall terminated in a cliff face that rose up into its own shadow, nullifying the need for additional fortifications on that end, and to their right the barrier skirted the drop-off on the other side of the natural shelf and blotted out the view of Rouseberg below. The keep abutted the sheer mountainside, and a wide gap between the edifice's right flank and the encircling wall indicated the monastery grounds continued behind the looming central structure. Ignoring the small wooden buildings annexed along the wall, Ennio stepped forward and cupped his hands around his mouth to hail the monks when Hegel boxed his ear.

"Keep that hole shut," shushed Hegel.

"Where's the churchyard?" Manfried whispered.

"Eh?" Ennio glanced from one to the other.

"The cemetery," said Hegel. "Boneyard? Graveyard? Burial ground? Like a potter's field, only with markers."

"A necropolis?" Ennio's chestnut eyes narrowed to almonds. "What business have you there?"

"Our own," Manfried shot back.

"But what could we find in such a place?" said Ennio with a shudder.

"All questions are answered in the grave," Hegel sagely stated.

"I do not know where it is," Ennio said. "If it was once a castle they might have a crypt in the cellar."

"That's a risk we gotta chance," Manfried said, seeing the concern on Hegel's face. The witch-chills had returned to Hegel, stronger than what he had felt in the town.

"Maybe we oughta just call it done," Hegel said, peering around nervously.

"First we must check the door and try to gain the inside," said Ennio, relieved Hegel had sided with him. Sane men do not poke around graves in the best of times, let alone under a full moon in a suspiciously vacated town deep in the winter-gripped mountains.

"Rot," Manfried snarled. "We check the back, see if it's there. If it ain't, then we pry a window and find the cellar. Don't forget yourself on me, Hegel Grossbart."

Hegel's resolve strengthened at hearing his full name. The spoils were waiting and he had suggested leaving them for the dirt. He shoved past Ennio, reckoning the man's cowardice had rubbed off on him.

Ennio sullenly followed the Grossbarts, cutting between a wooden building and the side of the monastery proper. They were in shadow again, the outer wall and the side of the abbey conspiring to blot out the moon, the crunching snow the only sound. Emerging back into the moonlight, they were in another large courtyard with a single outbuilding set against the rear of the wall where the fortification curved back into the cliff. The trio made for a small doorway in the wall beside the building.

A warm breeze chilled their nerve at the door, a fetid wind blowing from behind. Turning as one, they saw nothing but the rear of the monastery and their own footprints trailing off into darkness. The pungent stench burned their eyes, and all three instantly knew it to be the odor of rotting meat. The draft faded but the stink remained. Ennio had taken a step toward the abbey when Manfried whistled softly.

Beyond the small wooden door a churchyard stretched along the stone shelf, cliffs rising up on one side and dropping from the other until the tapering plateau faded into the face of the mountain. Crosses and other markers jutted out of the snow like wreckage in a flood, and several pale hummocks towered beside the largest mound. To anyone else it would have appeared another vague lump in the powder but the Grossbarts instantly recognized it for a crypt. They hurried through the cemetery, banging their boots and knees on submerged tombstones, Ennio stumbling after.

The stone door had clearly stood undisturbed for ages, and Ennio leaned against it. He covetously watched Hegel withdraw a bottle from his bag and take a pull, then pass it to his brother. Manfried swigged it and planted it in the snow at his feet. While the Brothers inspected the door and counseled in their private dialect Ennio retrieved their schnapps in what he hoped appeared to be a casual manner and crouched in the snow rather than sit on a tomb.

Taking a long pull of the drink, Ennio thought of a certain lady in Venezia who would make him forget all about mysterious towns, strange passengers, and frigid necropoli. He thought of her olive skin and green eyes, of the sweet way she would tease him when he pretended to have left his purse at home. Then he saw Hegel remove a prybar from his bag and jam it into the door of the crypt, and Ennio choked on his drink.

"What you do this?" Ennio coughed.

"Pipe down," said Manfried.

"Ain't doin," Hegel muttered, red-faced and white-knuckled.

"You mean to enter it?" Ennio gasped.

"Course we do," Manfried said, digging the snow out from the bottom of the door.

"Got it?" Hegel asked, setting down the prybar.

"Yeah," Manfried sighed, "but they got us good, too. What you make a this?"

Hegel hunkered beside his brother. Thick stones and masonry sealed the bottom of the door. The Grossbarts had encountered worse. They dug in their bags while Ennio paced, staring aghast at them.

"What could the inside tell us of the town? Or that stink by the gate?" Ennio demanded.

"Nuthin," Hegel said, pulling out Manfried's hammer and chisel.

"Less than," said Manfried. "Inside a graves only tell the future, not the past."

"Common misconception," Hegel agreed, setting the chisel in place.

"What?" Ennio's head swam. "What nonsense are you speaking?"

"Well," Manfried said, raising his hammer. "The content a this here stone-house'll tell us what's to come. If it's full a riches, then we's rich, and if it ain't, we ain't."

"Course there's a deeper meanin," Hegel said, pulling his own chisel out and using the flat end of his pick in lieu of a hammer. "And even if it's empty we's needin all the practice we can get fore hittin up them what the Infidel's got. Heard they's specially tricksome to get into."

Both struck at the same time, the metal ringing out in the stillness. They shared a smile, the familiar sound a balm to ward off the chill of weather and witch alike. A faint echo returned, and at this they struck again, stone splintering off the crypt.

Ennio let fly a string of foreign curses, then remembered himself. "You intend theft from the dead? You're defilers of graves!"

"Ennis—" Manfried began.

"Ennio," Hegel corrected, smashing more masonry.

"Ennio," Manfried continued, "even a half-wit knows it ain't stealin if they's dead."

"Like rape won't take away virginity," Hegel said excitedly, sure his violation at the hands of Nicolette qualified.

"Exactly." Manfried's hammer fell again.

"You damn yourselves!" Ennio spluttered. "This sin cannot be undone!"

"We tithe," Hegel explained.

"Doin Mary's Will." Manfried blasted off more stone.

Ennio turned. "We part paths here and now. Sleep in there, for we will not permit you to enter our shelter."

"You's drawin lines," Manfried said, not looking away from his task.

"Never smart," Hegel grunted, struggling with an obstinate piece of stone.

"Cause then we gotta cross'em," Manfried finished. Many years had passed since the mortar was laid, evidenced by the ease with which it splintered. Further proof of Her Grace.

Ennio cursed them as he tramped toward the monastery gates. The tolling of their iron made him wince. Fifty paces from the door to the abbey grounds, Ennio saw the wooden gate swing inward. No wind followed yet the stink again permeated the calm air and he paused, peering into the black hole in the wall.

A man floated out of the doorway, his naked skin glowing in the moonlight. From the waist down a bestial form propelled him, snorting menacingly, and Ennio stumbled back through the graveyard, begging his unwilling voice to cry out for the Brothers Grossbart.

X
Fresh Paths and Good Intentions

Heinrich stumbled through the snow, his frostbitten feet gone from cold to numb to searing. Of course they had not stumbled across any free-roaming horses, and of course Egon had turned back upon delivering Heinrich to the frost-blasted boulders where the road entered the mountains proper. Heinrich's memory of his friend's hopeless face had faded as if their parting had been years instead of days before. Egon had begged him to turn back, winter coming on far too quickly to risk the mountain passes, but Heinrich would not relent.

Stalactites of frozen sweat, tears, and snot swayed from the yeoman's mustache but he willed himself forward, even as he realized the setting sun likely heralded his demise. He had to catch them before he froze. He had to.

The storm grew rather than abated, and the hazy orb lighting his way grew less distinct as it slipped lower between the peaks on his right. He had enough of the turnips he so despised to feed himself for another week but without wood for his tinder he held out little hope, even with his blankets. Yet Providence had brought him this far, and his continuous prayers that the villains would appear on the road ahead did not fail, even if they were growing less particular in their destination.

Then, through the shroud of snow and twilight, he made out

a shadow sitting on a boulder. Rubbing his bloodshot eyes, he staggered toward it and drew his long dagger. Considering they had left him to suffer in solitude perhaps it was intended he only murder one of them, placing the other in Heinrich's own miserable and solitary state. Heinrich tried to charge but his legs refused to do more than shuffle over the icy stones.

Then he stopped, vision blurring with grief, and he fell to his knees. The figure had turned and he could no longer delude himself, for the swaddled old woman certainly bore no resemblance to either Grossbart. His exhausted wits did not consider why she would be sitting on a rock so far from anything save a frigid death; all he cared about was his own failure. The sun dipped behind the mountains, and Heinrich somehow found the strength to stand and march onward.

"Ho," the crone said as he brushed past her, "there's nothing for leagues save the dens of wolves, and even those will be occupied on such a night. Why not abandon the road and help an old lady to her hovel?"

Heinrich swayed drunkenly but his grief-addled mind refused to allow the intrusion of logic. If he pressed on through the growing dark he would spy their campfire and take them unawares. Only a little farther, surely.

"No?" The woman sighed. "Then that's another old wife dead due to Grossbartery, and with the little ones in my belly, why, two innocent souls beside."

Heinrich stopped, the snow settling on his pack. "What?"

"You heard," she cackled, her laughter like ice splintering underfoot on a frozen river. "You heard, Heinrich Yeoman, digger of turnips, just as you heard your little ones roasting alive in the house you built them."

Heinrich brandished his knife and stumbled back toward the woman, feverish with hatred and confusion.

"Help an old lady home," she repeated. "If you wish to see

those Grossbarts suffer and beg, there's no other way. They are too far ahead to catch on foot, and every moment they spread a wider trail between you and they. But there are ways to find them, Heinrich, ways I know well."

Heinrich stood before her, sweat freezing the dagger to his palm. His teeth rattled, her eyes black specks on a leathery face, and he knew at once she was either witch or spirit. Dejected beyond reason, he attempted to recall the parish priest's insistences that God alone could punish the Grossbarts, and nodded to her. A lifetime of holy terror had convinced him that without a final confession, Hell might be the only place he could again lay eyes on Gertie, his girls, and poor Brennen.

She rose with the help of a cane and together they began trudging up the road. Heinrich lasted less than a mile before his legs went and he collapsed in the thickening snow. He heard her cooing in the darkness, and something so cold it burned pressed against his lips. He had been Brennen's age the last time he had drunk directly from a cow's udder but his gums remembered the method to coax out milk, and with the first drop he felt heat returning to his limbs. His hand went to her flabby breast and squeezed, frigid as what it was, his slurping mixing with her rising moans; a nearby bear retreated up the slope in search of less sinister prey.

"Enough," she said, stroking his snow-dusted hair, "that's not for you."

Heinrich whimpered when she tore her withered teat away, and he regained his legs in pursuit. Her scowl made him reconsider, and together they began walking once more. Unnaturally invigorated, he followed her off the road and down the mountainside, her hunched shoulders all he could make out in the swirling blizzard. That night they threaded through crevasses treacherous in sunlit summer and scaled sheer sheets of rock without incident, arriving in her wooded vale just before dawn.

XI
A Humourous Adventure

The Brothers heaved into each other and the prybar did its job. The slab of a door scraped and groaned, the hinges resisting. Another thrust and they had it, dust indistinguishable from the swirling snow. Manfried tried to light the pig-fat candle stolen from Heinrich's house while Hegel opened the door fully. Then Ennio appeared from behind a mound, gasping and gibbering.

"What're you—" Manfried stopped in mid-sentence.

Hegel's testicles retracted into his body and he swooned, the fear he had smothered returning with terrible vigor. He slowly turned to see the source of his foreboding. Ennio pawed at his legs and skittered past him into the tomb. A naked man astride an enormous hog rode slowly toward them through the church-yard, his teeth sparkling.

The stink rode with him, stirring the stomachs of all present. Manfried scowled at the intruder and loosed his mace from its ring on his belt. Hegel wobbled his head and his prybar, ready to follow his brother. Man and pig stopped between the frosty heaps, four black eyes gleaming in the night. They stared at the Grossbarts and the Grossbarts stared back. Ennio whimpered from the crypt's interior.

"Greetings!" called the man.

"Yeah," Manfried said. "What you want?"

"I want," the man said slowly, "to know just who you are and what you intend by sneaking in here in the middle of the night and opening that crypt."

"We's Grossbarts," said Manfried. "What you think we want? And what you doin on that pig?"

"Why ain't he wearin nuthin?" Hegel asked Manfried.

"You want to steal from the dead, I presume," said the man. "I'm riding this beast as it suits me, and it always behooves a prudent fellow to hold something in the lurch. Finally, I am nude as it is a tranquil night and the cool air helps my skin."

"Full moon," Hegel hissed, and Manfried nodded.

"Yeah, well, seein's how you know the situation, you oughta know we'd prefer some privacy right now. And you's gonna catch a cool death you keep out here without no shirt." Manfried knew how to deal with moonfruits.

"No hurries, no worries." The pig sat down and the man stumbled off its back. He swayed in the snow, a constant cloud of steam rising from him as though he smoldered.

"You are from the monastery?" Ennio asked, having come back to his senses. He stood in the doorway, keeping the Grossbarts between him and the man. Hegel slowly bent and retrieved his loaded crossbow from the step behind his brother.

"Recently, yes." The man tottered but kept his feet, slowly approaching them.

"And you know where the villagers are?" Ennio pressed.

"Certainly. They're inside." The pig rider suddenly succumbed to a coughing fit.

"And?" Ennio had a hand on Hegel's shoulder but Hegel threw an elbow, reminding him not to come too close.

"And?" The man regained himself.

"Look you barmy bastard, he's askin where everyone went and why, so either tell'em and piss off or just piss off." Manfried was known for many things but not for patience.

"I came out of the mountains," the man said, as if that settled it.

"Amazin," said Manfried. "That a fact? Wonder a wonders."

"He was already with me, or I was with him, no matter. We came together, then." The three men peered at the animal while the lunatic continued. "We arrived, and they did welcome us, despite it all, and we were admitted. And when they had all joined us, converting if you will, then we summoned the rest. A certain pattern of bell-tollings brought them running, with their babes and dogs and wives and that was the end." As he talked he staggered slowly toward them.

"That's close as you're gettin, less you wanna see what's under the snow round here." Manfried had traded mace for crossbow.

For the first time the man's smile faltered. "Please, simply a blanket will save me. Will you let a weary traveler freeze? A scrap of cloth, I beg."

"Hey now," said Hegel, "we's bein charitable enough, lettin you get back on that beast and ride out the way you rode in. Monastery's close, warm your bones there."

"What you mean," Ennio called, voice raising, "*that was end*? Something is wrong, Grossbarts! Where are monks and villagers? What they convert to? What was ended?"

"I mean," the man said, all good humour gone, "that was their end. They rest inside, where you will too."

"He's a witch!" Ennio screamed.

The man made to lunge but the Grossbarts hefted their bows demonstratively and he paused, poised to pounce.

"You a monk?" Hegel asked.

"No," the man replied.

"Settles that, then." Manfried shrugged, and they both shot.

One bolt struck the man's swollen stomach and the other his neck. He silently pitched backward, blood geysering toward their feet. He convulsed in the snow, the pig trotting over and snuffling at his wounds.

The Brothers and Ennio cautiously approached the twitching body, each holding a weapon. Hegel felt worse than before, his bowels pinched. The man mumbled deliriously, pawing the pig's snout. Ennio knelt beside him, but not too close.

"What's he sayin?" Manfried asked, recognizing the ranting as the same tongue Ennio addressed the guards with.

"He begs not to abandon him," Ennio said. "They've traveled far, and he has been obedient to his mas—" Ennio rolled away with a squeal. "The pig, the pig!"

"What're you on bout?" Manfried demanded.

"Porco is his master, the pig is Devil!" Ennio kicked away in the snow, desperate to avoid the hog.

"Hmmm." Manfried had heard the Devil would take the form of a cat, but never a swine. Then again, he must come from the same place as Ennio, so maybe the Devil worked different down in the Romish kingdoms. Worst case they would have bacon, Manfried reasoned, and attacked the beast. It saw him coming and bolted.

Ennio got to his feet and joined the chase, Manfried and he pursuing the pig through the snow-draped cemetery. Hegel, however, could not lift his eyes from the dying man. With the man so close, he could clearly make out his features. He stank horribly, his face covered in sores and stains. A dark suspicion took hold of Hegel, and he squatted to get a better look.

The Grossbarts' uncle had taught them to look first under the arms and behind the groinpurse. Of course king and slave alike should be burned, but in practice many who should have met the flame instead sneaked into their ancestral grounds through well-meaning descendants. These tombs should be avoided lest one doom themself before even inspecting other nearby graves for less dangerous bounties.

The bright moon revealed a purplish tint to the swollen lumps under the dead man's arms, great swollen lumps far bigger than

Hegel thought possible. He recoiled, the stink of the man turned sinister. He saw his brother and Ennio chasing the pig back his way.

"Manfried!" Hegel bellowed, backing away from the corpse, "it's the pest!"

"Eh?" Manfried stumbled, the pig avoiding his mace again.

"Leave it!" Hegel's voice boomed out over the valley. "Plague! It's got the plague!"

Manfried stopped dead, then went rolling when Ennio crashed into his back. Getting up and delivering several kicks to Ennio, Manfried wiped the snow off and returned to his brother by the door of the crypt. The pig lay down in the snow beside the dead man, watching Manfried warily.

"Plague?" Manfried wiped sweat from his face, eyes darting to the body.

Hegel nodded solemnly. "Buboes big as my fists."

"Explains him talkin nonsense."

"Does it?"

"Yeah, makes you all touched in the head."

"Where'd you hear—"

"He moves!" Ennio yelped, propped against a stone cross.

"Eh?" The Grossbarts looked, and indeed, the man arched his back and thrashed. His left shoulder swelled and turned black, and he foamed at the mouth. Gore leaked around the quarrels embedded in him, then began spurting out further than should be possible.

"That look right to you?" Hegel demanded but Manfried just gaped.

The curious pig snuffled closer, then screeched and ran off through the churchyard. The man's armpit ballooned outward and he sprayed vomit all over himself. The stench of putrescence grew stronger, the man voiding himself from every orifice. Then he rolled on his side with his left arm twisted behind his head and the pulsing bubo burst, an oozing discharge hissing in the snow.

"Nah, ain't look right to me," Manfried admitted.

The flow of fluids from the armpit quickened and thickened, and then the pus, blood, and biles poured upward into the frosty air, swirling into a hovering humoural maelstrom above the corpse. The growing mass of liquid let off a meaty, musky, hot-rot stench that curled the nose hairs of all present, and before any could move something coalesced within the impossible float-ing whirlpool. The veil of humours parted even as clouds took the moon but the night illuminated what it should have hidden, as though darkness had become black sunshine. The three men stared, each one slipping down into a bottomless pit of his own mind.

A body the size and shape of a barrel jutted up into the air behind the thing's skull-sized head, plates of shell bristling with long hairs. Six willowy, multi-segmented limbs protruded from its thorax, the two pairs in the rear arcing back and up before angling down to make heart-shaped imprints on the corpse with its oddly dainty cloven hooves. The front appendages functioned more as arms than as legs despite their similar four-part build and length, the pair stroking the clump of dagger-length anten-nae jutting out in place of a nose. They saw its hard, shiny face possessed the bulging eyes of a man, the horns and floppy ears of a goat, and small spines running in combs along its cheeks to join the protruding cluster of feelers. It hopped clumsily into the snow beside the corpse of its former host, its cylindrical, bulbous abdomen held aloft behind it to reveal a decidedly human erec-tion of prodigious size, the organ straining up between the plates like a knight's lance or a scorpion's stinger.

Manfried prayed under his breath, Hegel turned to run, and Ennio retched. Wreathed in a thin yellow mist, it dribbled a vis-cous film as it turned its head to each of them in turn. Its antennae trembled and, proving that events can always worsen, it addressed them:

"Grossbarts, eh?"

Hegel slapped Manfried dead in the mouth, bringing him back to something resembling mental coherence. Manfried slung his arm around Hegel's, the woozy Brothers supporting one another. Ennio wiped his mouth and fled with a shriek, and this seemed to decide the matter for the monster. It pounced after Ennio, its spindly legs somehow propelling its bloated form high into the air after the screaming wagon driver. The Grossbarts ran as one but immediately stopped when they saw Ennio and his pursuer were headed for the exit.

"What in fuck?" Manfried panted.

"Uhhh." Hegel felt vomit creep up his throat but forced it down.

"This way," said Manfried, dashing in the opposite direction from Ennio.

The churchyard that had struck them as massive now appeared small indeed. The church grounds sat on a shelf, the door in the wall that Ennio ran toward the only exit. The cliffs rising on one side and dropping on the other met at the end of the triangular plot, affording few hiding places. They could find no purchase to climb up to a higher road or possibly scramble over the abbey walls without disclosing their presence, and, of all the ill luck, the clouds thickened overhead, darkening the cemetery. Ennio's screams drew closer, and they desperately went to the ledge. They saw a snowdrift shining below but could not gauge the drop.

"Rope," Manfried instructed.

"In the bags," Hegel groaned.

"So?" Then Manfried realized they had both left their bags on the steps of the tomb. "Go on back and get'em."

"Nope." Hegel vigorously shook his head. "Let's try cuttin round while it's after Ennio."

"Sound."

They were near the end of the churchyard where the cliffs on either side merged into one sheer curtain of stone. Staying close to the mounds they fled back toward the monastery wall. As they neared the back of the crypt, the hog—having burrowed into a snowdrift—appeared underfoot. It squealed and Manfried shouted.

The light-headed Ennio heard someone nearby but dared not look, the blinding cloud of stink alerting him that his hunter drew closer as well. He angled toward where he hoped the Grossbarts hid. Few men have experienced the terror that drove Ennio forward, few men save the Grossbarts.

Hegel saw Ennio and turned around, running to the ledge. Manfried, still stunned from stepping on the pig, dallied a moment more and so caught a glimpse of the fell thing leaping from atop a tombstone. Its legs shuddered and its heavy abdomen swayed as it landed beside Ennio, the man narrowly avoiding its groping arms.

Hegel lowered himself over the edge, the rock cutting into his chest, his fingers clawing the slick stone for purchase. His boot-tips found a crack, and then another cloud darkened the night, and he blindly scrambled down the cliff. The cloud passed moments before Manfried would have run off the edge.

Throwing himself backward, Manfried slid legs-first over the side. Fortunately Hegel had cleared a few handholds of snow, and Manfried grabbed these as he went over, banging himself against the cliff. Unfortunately for Hegel, his brother's flailing legs kicked his fingers, but Hegel managed to snatch the straps of Manfried's hose before falling. The added weight almost pulled them both down, only Manfried's red fingers keeping them suspended on the cliff face.

No sooner had Hegel rediscovered his handholds and released his brother than Manfried caught sight of the exhausted Ennio lurching toward him. Arms shaking uncontrollably, Manfried scrambled down, pausing only whenever his feet found Hegel instead of the next foothold.

Ennio saw Manfried disappear over the ledge and used his last strength to charge ahead, the thing clumsily bounding behind him. Screaming a final prayer Ennio hurled himself off the cliff, spinning in midair to see if it pursued. It did not, craning over the edge and staring after him. Then his vision blurred as he plummeted, and everything shone white and black.

The Grossbarts heard Ennio tumble past them, babbling as he dropped. He suddenly went silent, and the Brothers did not breathe. The shadow of the cliff obscured the bottom, but judging by the moans that began rising up it could not be too far down. They would have kept climbing but Manfried glanced up and saw the thing just above him, and from his vantage point he clearly made out the circular, winking, hemmorhoidal anus of a mouth behind its central ring of antennae. He had the sense to kick away from the rock face as he let go but still crashed onto Hegel, and both plunged through the moonlight.

At the tavern, Alphonse and Giacomo quickly became blind drunk. They laughed at the Brothers' foolishness and stewed over their threats and arrogant demeanors. It stood to reason such a miserable empire would produce such miserable bastards as the Grossbarts. They had it coming to them, of that the Italians were convinced.

After another bottle they tired of discussing enemies past and present and the talk turned to women. Neither had laid eyes on the veiled maiden they had retrieved but both were convinced she must be gorgeous indeed or else the captain would never have sent for her from such a grand distance. Then they talked of the captain, and how peculiarly he was rumored to behave.

They were both very drunk when the song started, floating out of the back of the tavern. Neither could rightly say what was sung but both found it far prettier than anything they had ever heard. Giacomo got to his wobbly feet and made for the door to the back rooms, but jealous as Alphonse was, he had drunk too much to move. Instead he cried dejectedly until he fell asleep, her music the first truly good thing in his hard life.

Ennio broke Hegel's fall, Hegel broke Manfried's, and together the Brothers broke both of Ennio's ankles. Hegel faceplanted in the snow between Ennio's legs and blacked out. Manfried's tailbone landed on his brother's and he rolled in the snow cursing. Ennio howled and clutched his legs, and would not be silent until Manfried began slapping him vigorously.

Quieted by the drubbing, Ennio followed Manfried's gaze up the cliff. Despite the reemerging moon they barely made out where the plateau holding the cemetery dipped in. Nothing stirred on the ledge. Then horrible shrieks echoed out over the mountains and back again, an inhuman wailing that rattled their nerves.

Hegel came to and wiped the snow from his eyes and nose. Patting himself down, he found everything in order, luck having spared him from impalement on his own sword. Manfried likewise felt bruised but fit, but of course Ennio could do nothing but blubber, his mind as cracked as his legs.

"Leave'em," said Manfried, "we gots to go."

"Need'em for the wagon," said Hegel.

"We can figure it out," Manfried insisted.

"Drivin's fine, but what bout hitchin? Wagon's different from a cart, and we's gonna need to make a sharp exit." Hegel felt a touch ashamed to side with Ennio.

They hoisted Ennio up and carried him between them, elbowing the fool whenever his crippled feet brushed the ground and he cried out. The town wall lay close at hand, and after toiling up and down several small hills they reached the gate. Hegel clambered over and let them in, suspiciously watching the dark monastery looming over the town. Narrowing his eyes, he picked up a shadow flitting over the road past the last bend. Something white moving over the white snow in the white moonlight. Whatever it might be—and he had a fairly good idea on that account—it brought the trembling back to his legs and his brain.

"Run." Hegel snatched Ennio's right arm.

Manfried grabbed the left and they rushed through the wagon tracks to the tavern, dragging Ennio. The poor driver went unconscious from the pain of his lower half bouncing on the icy road. As with the time he had spent with Nicolette, Hegel's anxiety since first arriving had fluctuated mildly but never fully diminished, and now swelled again to mammoth proportions.

The spectral town glistened until clouds again enveloped it with the rightful darkness of night. The Grossbarts did not pause, and when they finally deposited Ennio on the ground outside the tavern fresh snow further shadowed them. When neither guard opened the door they forced it as they had before and dragged the comatose Ennio beside the fire. Alphonse's snoring stopped when Manfried kicked him off his chair and began shouting in his face.

"Where's your man?" said Manfried.

"Shit-sipping bastard," Alphonse slurred.

"Right!" Manfried began pummeling him until Hegel dragged him off.

"Need all the swords we got if that thing comes back," Hegel advised.

"What you did to Ennio?" Alphonse crawled to the driver and shook his shoulders. Ennio immediately awoke screaming and clawing at Alphonse's face. The injured man's bloodshot eyes registered Manfried advancing and he immediately went still.

"Demon," Manfried said, and Hegel did not argue.

"What?" said Alphonse, squinting at the Brothers.

"A demon from the pit!" Hegel exploded. "Somethin from Hell, that sink through your stony pate? A goddamn fiend!"

"What?" Alphonse repeated.

"Pestilence," Manfried proclaimed, pacing the room and pulling his beard. "Had the rot in'em. Came out. Demons and plague, Mary preserve us!"

"Plague?" Alphonse blanched and Ennio moaned.

"Shut your holes, damn you!" Hegel yelled, hurling a chair against the wall.

"Brother," Manfried hissed in Grossbartese. "Need to keep our calm if we's gonna get shy a here and over to the sandy lands. Calm."

"Calm?" Hegel forsook their private lingo. "Calm! Got us a demon after us! Not some manti-what or beastly-man, but a real demon! You seen it!"

"Yeah, I seen." Manfried shuddered. "Maybe it stayed up on the hill."

"Rot! I seen it! It's comin! The witch's curse, Manfried, the witch's curse!" Hegel raged, the foreigners cowering on the floor.

"Faith!" Manfried shouted.

"Balls!" responded Hegel, smashing a table with his sword.

"She's watchin over us!"

"Damn right! Got us a hex gonna last til we die!"

"No, you twat, Mary!" said Manfried. "We live and die by the will a the Virgin! We die when She wills it, not fore! Faith, damn your beard, faith!"

"Faith?" Hegel panted.

"Faith," Manfried sighed, having almost convinced himself. "You know what we gotta do."

"Kill us a demon. For real."

"Mary bless us, we will. Better to just get shy a this place without settin eyes on it again. Now where's that ignorant cunt you was with?" Manfried demanded of Alphonse.

They found Giacomo facedown in the hallway, near the rear

door. He had drowned in a shallow puddle of snowmelt, the water barely covering his nose and mouth. The three mobile men convened in the hall, and after Alphonse told his fractured tale all three glanced at the cloth obscuring the woman's room.

Manfried ripped the partisan down. "What you gotta say?"

The most beautiful woman the repulsive graverobber had ever spied looked up, her supple body partially draped in dirty blankets. Hegel and Alphonse tried to peer around Manfried but his square shoulders filled the narrow doorway. Her pale thigh shone like the moon, and going on the glorious contours of the cloth he doubted she wore anything beneath her covers. She smiled mischievously, black hair glistening down her side, and Manfried suddenly felt compelled to apologize; for what, he knew not. Before he could speak she raised a finger to her dark lips, and they all heard a rapping on the front door.

Hegel and Alphonse rushed back to the main room, and Manfried sorrowfully followed, promising his eyes they would soon take her in again. She smelled different from any woman he had met, and despite the urgency with which Hegel and Alphonse ran to the door he could not tear his mind from her. The night's events were near-forgotten, and his sharp ears were dull to the shouting all around him.

"Manfried!" Hegel barked in his face.

"Eh?" Manfried tried to clear his thoughts.

"It's here!" Hegel's eyes bulged, alarmed at his brother's nonchalance.

"Faith." Manfried smiled dreamily, then shook off her phantom. "Shut it, all a yous!"

The room fell gravely still save for Ennio, who moaned beside the hearth with a bottle clutched in both hands. The knocking did not come again, but something snuffled at the bottom of the door, blowing snow in through the crack. The Grossbarts advanced, the drunken Alphonse following them with rushlight and sword. They stood there for a moment, then Manfried spurred himself into action.

"What you want?" shouted Manfried.

"Let me in," a voice pleaded.

"Why?" asked Manfried.

"Warmth. Christian succor. I'll not harm you, I swear."

"Yeah, and who is you and where you come from?" asked Manfried.

"I'm Volker, I live on the edge of town. I've been hiding, please let me in."

"Oh, rot, you's that same meckin demon!" Hegel shouted.

"Demon? Demon!" The man beat on the door. "Then let me in, for the love of the Christ babe! My soul's in danger, and if it takes mine then yours is damned for not saving me!"

"Maybe open the door and look?" Alphonse turned from Grossbart to Grossbart.

"I ain't gonna dignify that with a response cept to say by my ma's foul mound, how thick're you?" said Manfried, and then raised his voice. "Give us a private discussion, Volker!"

"Hurry!"

Manfried retreated to the center of the room, Hegel and Alphonse in tow. "Listen," he told his brother in their familial language, "it's tryin to trick its way in, might imply it's too weak to bust the door. We wait it out til cockcrow, it'll turn to dust in the sun."

"You sure a that?" asked Hegel.

"What you say?" Alphonse's distress grew with each development, and a council he could not decipher sat poorly with him. The twin glares emasculated his tongue, though, and he went to Ennio's corner to try and calm him. Alphonse's booze-soaked brain could not comprehend much, and he took another pull from Ennio's bottle.

"Demons can't bide daylight, any child'll tell you," Manfried insisted.

"What about that demon in the woods? He seemed to prefer it," said Hegel.

"Now you was the one insistin that weren't no demon."

"Witch told me it used to be a man. You wanna hinge your soul on a witch's word or a child's tale?" Hegel glanced at the door. "Should a drawn a circle in the snow round the tavern, that would a done it."

"How's that different from my so-called superstition?" Manfried demanded.

"Cause it's fact, as our uncle told us."

"So you's gonna believe *that* road-apple? Sides, if that's the case we can draw circles round us on the floor in here."

"Stop him!" Ennio wailed, and the Grossbarts saw Alphonse crouched by the front door, his ear pressed to the wood.

Manfried and Hegel both went for him but before they took three steps the crazed man tossed back the board latching the door. The door blew inward, snow swirling around the manically laughing Alphonse. A silhouette loomed behind him in the doorway, stopping the Grossbarts' feet and Ennio's scream.

"Seeing this, Grossbarts?" Alphonse cackled. "Think you kill my cousin and live? Think you kill me? I have its word!"

Alphonse's left eye sprang from its socket in a spray of blood. His jaw hung loose and the mess of his brains spilled from it, the entire back of his head caved in. He dropped dead on the floor in front of his assailant.

The hog from the cemetery stepped into the room on its hind legs, chunks of Alphonse's skull and hair stuck to its left front hoof. Its black eyes shone and it casually kicked the door shut behind it. The Grossbarts were no longer strangers to sanity-stealing horrors, yet the comparatively simple sight of an animal walking like a man stunned them immobile. Not Ennio, who crawled toward the hallway, refusing to look at whatever had entered the tavern.

"Grossbarts," the pig said, licking its teeth.

Before they had set out into the mountains such a fright would have sent the Brothers reeling into a panic, but having recently experienced equally traumatizing events they shakily held their ground. Hegel began hyperventilating, tunnel vision setting in as he jerkily raised his sword. Manfried held the rushlight steadier than his mace, which shook along with the rest of him. The hog took another step, its hoof clicking on the wood, and the Brothers reacted.

Manfried hurled his rushlight at the pig and ran, and Hegel rushed the beast. A stinking cloud of saffron vapor spewed from its snout, enveloping Hegel as he hacked at it. Reaching the hall, Manfried realized his brother did not follow and turned back to the room, kicking the hallway door shut to prevent Ennio from running out on them. Hooves struck at the blinded Hegel but his sword connected and sent the beast rolling across the floor. He staggered, choking and coughing on the reeking miasma.

"Brother!" Manfried called but Hegel paid no heed, doubled over in agony.

The pig stood on its hind legs again, but the hoof it had killed Alphonse with stayed on the floor where Hegel's blade had banished it. The hog charged its dry-heaving adversary but Manfried intercepted it with a thrown bottle that smashed against its fetlock, knocking it over beside Hegel. It latched onto Hegel's boot with its teeth but he blindly kicked it off, falling down himself.

Manfried rushed the pig with his mace but it squatted and pounced, its misshapen frame belying a diabolical dexterity. It knocked Manfried over a table and pinned him down with its hoof on one arm and its blood-pumping stump on the other. Manfried spit in the porcine face as it leaned in, and he saw dozens of welts and boils coating its snout, one eye crusted shut with pus. Its dripping tongue snaked out toward Manfried, and with dread he saw buboes the size of apples blossoming in the crotch of its arm.

Rubbing his eyes, Hegel saw the beast pressing down on Manfried and he stumbled forward. Hegel's sword slid between its ribs and he toppled it into the shelving, bottles raining on them and smashing at their feet. It bounced off the wall and brought its girth down on him, driving them both to the floor. Blood bubbled everywhere as he tried to dislodge his sword and focused on not being crushed by the braying beast grinding him into the broken pottery, schnapps, and oil.

Ennio rolled away from the reeling combatants and lay pressed against the hearth, the puddle of oil creeping toward his feet. He stuck his hand into the blaze and snatched out a brand, charring his fist and melting the skin off his palm. Manfried caught this from the corner of his eye and kicked the pig's face, then seized Hegel and jerked him out from under its mass. Be it from concern for Hegel's safety or difficulty in forcing his cooked nerves to obey his will, Ennio paused just long enough for Hegel to scramble out of the small pool before he slammed the flaming brand into the oil.

All three were blinded by the jet of flame that rushed over the floor and up the wall. The hog screamed and thrashed, a shadow capering inside a pillar of fire. It tried to stand but collapsed, its bristly coat crackling and letting off thick waves of smoke. The Grossbarts leaned against each other, Ennio shouting triumphantly in his native tongue. Then part of the silhouette split from the twitching bulk and shot through the flames onto Ennio. The man's cheers turned to screams, the wall of the tavern blazing.

The Grossbarts ran to his aid out of instinct, and saw the greatly diminished demon had crawled halfway down his throat. Twiggy, flanged legs and its engorged abdomen protruded from Ennio's dislocated jaw, the golden film coating the thing lubricating its passage into his gullet. Each Grossbart snatched a leg segment and tugged but the brittle limbs broke off, smearing their hands with rank pus. Without legs to hinder its progress it wriggled out of sight, Ennio's neck bulging as it went.

Manfried seized Ennio's tilted chin and snapped his neck, then Hegel kicked his corpse into the hearth.

The loft above had caught, the room filling with black smoke. Ennio's body writhed on the coals and before the demon could escape again Manfried snatched a table and jammed it on top of the possessed corpse. The Brothers heaped stools against that, and then the smoke became impenetrable. Arm in arm they stumbled toward the door when a stray flame ignited the oily Hegel. Manfried shoved his burning brother ahead, crashing through the door and into the snow.

Hegel lay facedown in a snowdrift, steam and smoke rising from him. Manfried remembered the beauty in the back room an instant before a section of the roof collapsed, sealing the tavern-turned-oven. He fell to his knees but before the regret could leave his mouth or eyes she stepped around the corner, clad in a fine black dress with a veil pushed back to showcase her countenance. Manfried forgot his brother and ran to her side but before he could embrace her she pointed to the attached barn, the roof of which had caught fire.

The chaotic night became wilder still as Manfried braved the burning barn, side-stepping the frantic horses. The lax Ennio had not fully removed their harnesses, perhaps sensing the need for a hasty exit, and Manfried tightened their straps enough to pull the wagon out. He found more leather straps and cords and metal things heaped on the floor of the barn, and he carried these out before the smoke forbade him entrance. Now more exhausted than crazed, he returned to his smoldering brother.

Further proof of Mary's Providence could be seen in Hegel's unblemished beard. His pate, however, had felt the burn all the way to the root. His clothes were likewise scorched and ruined and he could do little more than cough. Coughing implied breathing and this pleased Manfried. Dragging Hegel into the wagon, Manfried found its interior to be a plush affair strewn with cushions. Here Manfried promptly joined his brother in a slumber resembling that of the dead, the Brothers Grossbart wrapped around each other in the absence of blankets.

XII
A Telling on the Mountain

The tavern burned all night, taking the barn and several neighboring buildings with it. The snow-laden roofs did not catch easily, though, so the rest of the hamlet remained intact when the Grossbarts staggered out of the wagon. Their normally resilient guts squirmed at the ungodly stench infusing their clothing and hair but the cool morning and bright sunshine quelled their rebellious interiors.

No hair remained on Hegel's scalp, even his eyebrows replaced with black smears and rising blisters. He felt immense relief that his beard had survived, to say nothing of his face. Only his crown and back were scorched, but given that his garments had not survived as well as his body he entered the nearest house to search for new clothes.

Manfried's shoulder throbbed from the demon-swine's hoof, but upon inspection he found himself mostly unscathed. The hand that had seized the demon bloomed with fever-blisters, however, particularly his palm. He spit on it and rubbed it in the snow. Then he began hunting for the absent woman, too embarrassed to call out for her.

Hegel returned to the wagon with several worn but clean shirts and trousers, in addition to the ones he had changed into in the house where he had found them. His right hand also bore the swollen rash, and sniffing it, he found it stank worse than the rest of him. He beckoned his brother, who broke in door after door but gave the interiors only a perfunctory inspection before moving on to the next.

"Brother," called Hegel. "Got us some new attire."

Manfried dragged his boots over to Hegel and donned the clothes, peeling his old hose, breeches, and shirt off in stinking strips. A pair of leather trousers, while superior to hose, hung a little loose for his preference, but he had grown used to such inconveniences. Not once had the Grossbarts worn so much as a sock knit to their specifications.

The horses dozed where they stood, blankets draped over them. The Brothers poked through the black bones of the tavern, hoping to find an unbroken bottle or anything else of worth. They found only the charred remains of Alphonse, and neither wanted to reach into the partially collapsed fireplace to retrieve their cooking pot.

Together they entered the buildings Manfried had opened, and between them found a few sacks of grain, a new pot and more blankets. They went to shove these into the wagon but to Manfried's relief and Hegel's shock the woman reclined inside. Her hair shone, and Manfried reached out to push it away from her face when Hegel snatched his hand and gave him a hard look. Manfried dropped the blankets on the floor of the wagon and angrily closed the tarp.

"Gotta stay pure," Hegel said.

"Who says I ain't?"

"Her much as you. You recollect where that lass was headin?"

"Some fat lord down south," said Manfried.

"Some fat sea captain down south."

"Eh?"

"Yeah, you heard. As in, boats. As in, Gyptland." Hegel grinned, pleased he had worked out the angles himself.

"Hey now," said Manfried, genuinely impressed. "You recollect this captain's name?"

"Er." Hegel's blistered brows creased painfully. "I do believe it was *Bar Goose*. Yeah, I'd stake my take on it."

"What kind a ignorant name is that?"

"They all got'em dumb like *Al Ponce* or *Ennio*."

"Suppose so," Manfried allowed, "but where's this Goose roost?"

"Venetia, I's sure a that."

"What you mean?"

"Eh?"

"*I's sure a that*," Manfried said. "Ain't you sure a the rest? Like his bein named Goose and bein a seaman?"

"Nah, I's sure. Why wouldn't I be?"

"Better be, brother."

"Oh yeah?"

"Yeah."

They glared at each other, then broke up laughing. Manfried spent a time straightening out the horses and piling the pieces he could not determine a use for in the back of the wagon. He led them by the bit to ensure everything stayed in place, then hopped onto the seat beside Hegel, who had half a pot of warm porridge waiting.

"*Need Ellis*, you said." Manfried snorted.

"Aye, coward *Ennio* may a been, but he got pure fore he died."

"Suppose so." Manfried nodded. "Sight better than Ponce lettin that demon in, damn straight. Ennio's sittin with Mary as we converse."

"And what you think a that other one? Drowned in melted snow!"

"Who cares? They's all's weak as these ones, we's gonna be princes a Italia and never need go to Arabtown!"

The day heated up, snow turning to sludge and impeding

their progress until they left the gate and began winding up the road. Here the trail resembled stream more than highway but they persevered and a short time later stopped inside the gate of the monastery. With the demon safely destroyed, they could both retrieve their gear and finally get a peek inside that crypt.

"Be back in a bit," Manfried called to the woman but got no response. He dallied but Hegel egged him on, and they hurried around the side, through the door and into the cemetery. They splashed through the mud and fell upon the sacks they had left behind. Their crossbows were wet but appeared serviceable, and the bottles they had pinched from the tavern were intact.

"Not demon, Devil, witch, or weather will keep us from our richly pleasure!" Manfried toasted.

"Bless Mary, and bless us too!" Hegel intoned solemnly, then they drank and clapped each other on the back.

Stowing the booze, they eagerly pushed open the crypt door and stepped inside. Hegel got their last rushlight aflame and swung it around the cramped interior, revealing three stone tombs. The bronze ornamentation they ignored, setting their prybars under the lids and putting them to their named use. Each contained an older skeleton than the last, but in the layers of dust and decay on the floors of the sarcophagi metal still glimmered. They fished out seven rings and a gold crucifix.

"Can melt him down." Manfried grinned, stowing it in a pouch.

"Beauty better than any woman," Hegel sighed, trying on a silver ring inlaid with green stones.

"Speakin a such," said Manfried, "I oughta check on'er."

"What for?"

"See if, uh, she wants some food. Ain't et in our presence, gotta be famished."

"That's right civil a you, brother," Hegel said. "Just be sure you don't go pissin in our feedbag."

"How's that?" Manfried turned in the doorway.

"She noble or close enough. I'd reckon they's smart enough to figure out we done somethin if somethin we do. So do all you can with your eyes, cause them hands a yours best stick to your own mecky self."

"You got a wicked, unchristian mind." Manfried stormed off, Hegel chuckling and polishing his rings on the step of the crypt.

Leaving the graveyard, Manfried noticed that the drapery covering the back of the wagon hung open. The only things inside were blankets and several boxes. Looking around, he saw a door on the rear of the monastery likewise ajar. Remembering that the demon had hinted at something regarding the abbey, he grabbed his crossbow before advancing. Poking his head in, he found it far too dark to attempt without both light and Hegel. He shouted for his brother, and when Hegel arrived they spent the heftier part of a little while getting the rushlight relit.

"Gonna claim this ax," Hegel informed his brother. "Sword got buried back at the tavern and I might need a sharp edge stead a my pick."

"Yours til somethin better turns up, then it's mine again."

"Proper. My bow looks a mite warped, so lets hope we ain't gotta use'em."

"Whatever you do, don't shoot less you's sure you gotta. No sense puttin a hole in our feedbag." Manfried held up the sputtering reed.

"How's that? Oh."

Manfried led the way, Hegel instantly put off by both the darkness and the eye-watering stench they now equated with the pestilence. At the end of the hall stood a large door, and, exchanging a nervous glance, they shoved it open.

Unmistakably the kitchen, this room housed piles of wooden plates and cooking implements, as well as rotting food of all varieties. The high windows were boarded up for winter, but Hegel noticed a sconce in the wall and removed the torch, lighting it from his brother's rushlight. Manfried went directly across to the opposite hallway but Hegel tarried, inspecting several oaken casks.

"What you got there?" Manfried asked from the hallway.

"Beer." Hegel jammed the bung back in place. "Quality, too."

"Later. We need our feedbag fore we can drink."

"You liked that, did you?"

Halfway down the hall they could go no farther, the stink gagging them. Following Hegel's prudent suggestion, they dipped their sleeves in the beer barrel and held them to their nostrils. They could then advance, although both were becoming heady from the odors.

Passing into the huge chapel, they discovered the cause of the smell. Over fifty bodies were heaped atop the pews, the outlines indistinct from the copious mold growing on them. Children and mothers had rotted together into hideous shapes, the faces of the dead weeping gray slime from every orifice. Monks were piled on women in suggestive positions, the entire putrefying mass an obvious labor of devotion. Even with their ale-soaked sleeves vomit assaulted the Grossbarts' esophagi, and they staggered back down the hall, passing under a large cross smeared with excrement and pus. Shutting the doors on either end of the hallway helped but they could not get the smell out of their noses.

Again Manfried felt delighted and Hegel disturbed by the woman's sudden reappearance. She sat on a table in the kitchen nibbling dried fish from a small crate beside her. Manfried went to her side and reached for a fish but she knocked the lid shut. Manfried felt a mix of anger and reproach, his watchful brother scowling in contempt. Hegel wanted fish, too, but if Manfried would not snatch it away neither would he. Hegel filled his porridge-crusted pot with beer and munched on the least moldy piece of bread he could find.

Manfried stared up at the angelic woman, at a loss as to what he could do or say. She did not seem to mind his attention, which any respectable person would have found disturbing at the least. Hegel kept poking around, and in addition to the beer barrel he found a smaller cask of schnapps. He rolled this out the hall to the wagon, and was dismayed to see the sun already sinking.

"Light'll be gone soon," Hegel informed his brother.

"So we's campin out here."

"Inside? Fuck that. Catch us the pest. Better camp out in that barrow."

"What?" Manfried broke his vigil.

"Sleep with the nobility. Might be a touch dead for your predilection, but one must adapt."

"I swear, brother, you shame the Virgin with your insinuations." Manfried glanced up at the smiling woman, and thanked Mary his beard concealed his coloring cheeks. He did not want Hegel getting the right impression. Not only was she the prettiest thing he had ever seen—save gold—but she tolerated his presence instead of recoiling with revulsion.

"Gotta burn them corpses." Hegel had brought his satchel and deposited his oil bottle on a counter.

"Not gonna waste it on them dead ones?" This brought Manfried away from his infatuation.

"Ain't gonna drag'em to a hole, and damn sure ain't diggin one under'em. Leaves us with the torch."

"Yeah?"

"Yeah."

"Fail to reckon how it's our responsibility."

"Cause it'll ire the Devil."

"Right enough for me." Manfried retrieved his oil as well, then they went to the church.

Each restrained his vomit, oiling the mound of rancid bodies. They heaped pews on the revolting mass and set it ablaze, tripping over each other to avoid the flames. The corpses popped and hissed and smoke engulfed the monastery, the Brothers hoofing it to the rear courtyard. The woman had returned to the wagon, and after cursing each other's foolishness, they risked the burning building to roll out the beer barrel.

That night they stowed the horses in the small stable beside the gate and the Brothers camped in the crypt, thinking it bad luck to sleep in one of the outbuildings after they had burned a church. The woman refused to leave the wagon, and since they had secured the front gate Hegel reasoned she would be safe. Manfried grumbled a bit but soon forgot everything but the joy of drinking with his brother in a ransacked graveyard.

Enough snow remained to offer the churchyard some semblance of solemnity when the sun disappeared and the moon rose. They boasted to each other of their prowess in slaying demons and monsters, to say nothing of cracking open tombs. Then came a period of serious theological discussion regarding the nature of cowardice, evil, and the Virgin. When Hegel shifted the conversation toward women and their natural inclination toward witchery and deception Manfried yawned, replaced the bung in the beer cask, and went to sleep.

Hegel stayed awake long enough to chisel their mark into the front of the crypt's door. His uncle had taught him it was good form to let any Grossbarts who came after know which tombs were already cleaned. Illiterate though every Grossbart was, the symbol was known by all who carried that accursed name.

Late in the night when the fire in the doorway had died, Manfried awoke to music drifting in. Hegel snored beside him, arms wrapped around the keg. Manfried went to the door and looked out, and to his surprise the snow had melted and in the moonlight the cemetery had become a placid lagoon with only the tips of the highest tombstones jutting above the surface. A ripple cut through the water before him and by the glistening pale skin he knew it was her. She clambered onto an exposed barrow, the music even louder now that she had surfaced.

She smiled at him, only the intervening crosses shielding her exposed body. The song touched Manfried in a place he had never acknowledged, and he walked down the crypt's stairs into the water. When it reached his waist he paused, realizing how frigid the pond was. The strength in his legs disappeared, and with a smile on his lips he pitched forward, sinking instantly in the icy liquid.

Hegel sat up in the dark, his heart pounding from a dream he could not remember. He blinked and lay back down, but then he detected a faint splashing in the stillness, and the unease of his unremembered dream haunted him. As he stumbled to the door, the moonbeams reflecting off the snow blinded him for a moment. Then he saw Manfried at the foot of the crypt, face-down in a puddle. Hegel jumped down, rolled him over, and punched him in the gut. Through dark lips Manfried began vomiting water and coughing, and the astonished Hegel hurried back inside and brought him a bowl of the monks' beer.

"What in the name a fuck, brother!" Hegel yelled. "You gotten moontouched or somethin?"

"Dreamin." Manfried shuddered, sipping the alcohol.

"Bout what?"

"Can't really say."

"Get on in," Hegel sighed, helping Manfried up.

Hegel started a new fire inside the crypt and shut the door most of the way. Manfried curled around the blaze, his beard and chest soaking. He nodded off immediately but Hegel stayed awake for several hours, watching his brother. Something worried him, and he went outside to make sure. Right enough, the pool in which he had discovered Manfried drowning was covered in a thick layer of ice except where his brother's face had entered it. A chunk of broken masonry lay beside the hole, and

Hegel had a sick feeling in his bowels. The wind picked up, stirring the snow around him as he stared at the still-smoking monastery. He spit twice, praised the Virgin, and went to bed.

They set off at daybreak. Accusations went back and forth at the wisdom in setting fire to the corpses before thoroughly checking all the rooms for hidden treasure. Monks might not have much in the way of coin, but surely a substantial amount might be found in the abbot's quarters. The initial hope that the stone building would keep everything but the chapel safe had proved false, for the blaze had gutted all the interior rooms save the monks' cells and the kitchen.

They did not trust the meat but besides grain they brought a bushel of turnips and a sack of mildly moldering rye bread. Hegel sniffed out three wheels of cheese, so the breakfast they ate on the bench surpassed any in memory. The road proved treacherous, the previous day's heat combined with a windy night having resulted in more ice than snow. They wound up the mountainside all morning, and when they reached the pass they both spit back the way they had come. Manfried refused to discuss his dream, instead turning the talk to their good fortune. Hegel had to agree, things could not be better and they would doubtless find themselves lords of Gyptland in the very near future.

The sky went gray in the afternoon and snow fell, summoning more curses and a slower road. Despite the deepening twilight Manfried insisted on continuing rather than stopping on the narrow track. When they almost went over the edge of a cliff bordering the road Hegel snatched the reins and they agreed breaking for the night would be a sharp plan. From Hegel's perspective, the only thing dumber than a horse was four horses.

Several miserable days and worse nights later, they plodded along an identically icy stretch of thin road when, shortly before dusk, Hegel began feeling his preternatural worry building up inside like a bad case of gas. He grew increasingly anxious, finally stringing his crossbow and insisting he walk ahead of the wagon to guarantee their safety. Rounding a wide bend with a sheer drop-off on the right and a steep rise pimpled with snowy boulders on the left, Hegel noticed a sharp bump in the road. Pushing ahead, he found it to be loose rocks piled across the trail, lightly dusted with snow. It would take only a few minutes to scatter them enough for the wagon to pass but their presence bothered him immensely. Manfried had brought the vehicle up behind him when Hegel jumped and yelled to his brother.

"Stay clear!"

"Eh?"

"Don't move!" But instead of Hegel, a massive boulder fifty paces up the slope shouted this. Squinting, they made out a dark shape behind it.

"Wasn't plannin on it!" Hegel responded, slowly pulling his crossbow off his back.

"What if we do?!" Manfried shouted angrily at the unseen man, urging the horses on another few steps.

The boulder rocked violently, snow dropping from its summit. "Hell to pay, rest assured! I just want to speak for a moment!"

"Then come down here, so we can do that stead a yellin!" Hegel called. In a lower voice, and in Grossbartese to boot, he addressed his brother. "No highwayman's pinchin our loot."

"Yeah, but if they was thick in numbers they wouldn't risk smashin the wagon," Manfried replied, his own crossbow loaded on the bench.

The man yelled something in yet another language they did not understand.

"Speak proper, you sneak-thievin fucker!" Manfried barked.

"You don't recognize your name?" the man shouted, and the boulder rocked again.

"Easy on, you godless cunt, we gotta woman in here!" Hegel shot back.

"Blaspheme at your own peril, serpent!" The boulder shifted violently but settled instead of rolling.

"What sort a footpad accuses Christian soldiers a blasphemy?" Manfried shouted, sensing a common ground.

"Did not the Son warn of your ravening kind upon a similar location?" he called back.

"See now!" Hegel responded, "We ain't met no sons but we slain a damn demon, so your thievin ass had best recognize the quality at hand!"

The man did not say anything but jumped out from behind the boulder, squinting down at the Grossbarts, which is when Hegel's quarrel struck him. Hegel tore up the slope toward the downed ruffian, pick in hand. Manfried stood on the bench, scanning the snowy scree with his crossbow leveled.

The man had almost crawled back to the log he had jammed under the boulder as a lever when Hegel reached him. The pick rose as the man rolled onto his back, jabbering at Hegel, the bolt skewering his forearm. Hegel almost spiked the man's face but stopped in time, and uttering an oath to Mary, threw down his weapon and knelt beside him.

Seeing his brother duck out of sight Manfried shouted, "Careful, brother! Slit his treacherous throat and get back here!"

"We fucked up!" Hegel responded, his voice cracking. "He's a monk!"

"A what?!"

"A monk, damn you!"

"Oh Hell." Manfried sat down heavily on the seat.

"You's gonna be rightened soon," Hegel told his victim. "Sorry bout that."

The man groaned, allowing his would-be prey to cut off the arrowhead protruding from his arm. Blood splattered on them both when Hegel pulled the shaft out, and continued welling forth even when they bound the wounds in strips of the man's tattered habit. Clapping him on the back, Hegel helped him up and together they slowly went down to the road.

Manfried greeted them with a bowl of beer. "Now then, Friar, have a sip a this and then see how heretical we strike you."

The shaken man balked, but Hegel sealed the offer. "It's made by your folk, so I reckon there's no sin in it."

Gulping the beer and making a face he swooned and fell. Confusion, exhaustion, pain, and exposure had sapped his energy, and he did not awake until the moon had risen and the Grossbarts had made camp down the road. After much haranguing Manfried had consented to the liberation of more blankets from the wagon's occupant, and with fresh snow powdering them they sat bundled up, watching the man stir.

The stanched wound made him whimper even before coming to, and when he did open his eyes he started, unsure of where he lay and the company he kept. Then the man remembered, and he covered his baggy eyes with his hands. His tonsure had grown ragged, tufts of gray hair blooming on his pate above the lanky ring circling his head. His shaking hands eventually steadied, and then Manfried felt comfortable addressing him.

"Apologies to you," Manfried said. "Had we known what you was we wouldn't a shot."

"Never," Hegel agreed.

"But you put us in a spot where we had no reason to suspect, you understand," Manfried continued.

"None at all," Hegel seconded.

"So I hope you's seen fit to grace us with your pardon," Manfried finished.

"Please," said Hegel. "Honest mistake from honest men."

"Could I trouble you fellows for a taste of that stew?" the man asked.

"More than a taste, if you want. We's et already." Hegel offered the near-empty bowl and some bluish bread.

The starved man made quick work of the food and looked up eagerly. Monk or no, the extra loaf Hegel offered came from a heavy hand. The woman never ate the food they offered, though, so an extra mouth would not starve them. Yet.

"Bless you," the man said through a mouthful of mold.

Joyful at this, Manfried quickly offered a bottle. This man sipped, alternating with handfuls of nearby snow. Only when he finished the bread did he speak again, his bloodshot eyes darting between the Brothers and the wagon.

"Forgive my ruse, I meant no harm to such good men," he said.

"No harm wrought, Friar," said Manfried.

"Actually, I am a priest," the priest corrected.

"Glad to hear you wasn't really gonna smash us with that rock," said Hegel.

"Oh, I would have smashed you, make no mistake." The priest's eyes glittered.

"Yeah?" Hegel leaned forward.

"Lord yes, if you were someone other than who you are. You are…" The priest leaned in as well.

"Oh. Grossbarts," said Manfried, realizing it was a question. "Manfried."

"And Hegel."

"Bless you, Grossbarts. I am Father Martyn, and I must beg your forgiveness both for my first impression and for the new imposition I must put upon you."

"Beggin your forgiveness," Manfried interjected, "if you's worried bout somethin you ain't done yet, could circumvent the problem by not doin whatever it is."

Hegel kicked his brother. "Never mind him. We's servants a the Virgin, and intend to do what you beg."

"Thank you kindly. Now please take off your shirts and cloaks," Father Martyn said in a rush, eager to have it said and behind him.

"Now hold on a tic," Manfried growled.

"Please," the priest implored. "I must see. I must."

The Brothers quickly stripped, Manfried more slowly since he had heard tell of certain priests who abused their position to do just this.

"Now raise your arms." Seeing them balk, he added another *please.* The wind chilled their armpits, but the Grossbarts realized his aim when he peered close, almost singeing his stained habit in the process. Satisfied, he took another pull from the bottle and settled back while they quickly put their shirts back on.

"And if you would be so generous—" Martyn began but Manfried cut him off.

"Checked down there ourselves just last night, and mean to check again come morrow to make sure, but no way I's droppin trou for man or God this night."

"Why'd you think to check for that?" Hegel asked suspiciously. "Ain't been an outbreak in what, fifteen years?"

"Mayhap not where you come from," the priest said. "Other regions have not been so blessed. Might I ask why, as you say, you checked yourselves last night if there has not been a pestilence in, as you say, fifteen years?"

"Not where we're from," Hegel said.

"And?" The priest leaned closer still.

"You seem wiser than you's lettin on," Manfried observed.

"You." Martyn pointed a spindly finger at Hegel. "Before you assaulted me you claimed to have destroyed a demon."

"It weren't no assault, was a damn accident, as was made clear, and I didn't *claim* nuthin. I's honest, so's I don't claim, I speak the truth a Mary, simple, unadulterated," Hegel huffed. "I'll tell the tale and praise Her Name, and you'd best listen."

"Hold on that, brother," Manfried said, "til we hear what our holy vested friend has to say on how he came to be waitin for us behind that boulder with murder on his mind."

"What?" Hegel blinked.

"See, I never heard a no priest nor monk intendin a deed like that, and what with his nonchalance bout gettin quarreled by your bolt, accident or no, and the familiar way he's sippin that rot, well, I figure twixt tyin up his wound, fillin his belly, and showin off our pits on the coldest cunt night yet, he owes us a tale fore he hears ours. That seem fair or foul?"

"Manfried." Hegel blanched. "That's no way a talkin to a priest we shot up."

"No, no, your brother is correct," Martyn sighed. "I do owe you gentlemen an explanation. I confess, as much as yours intrigues me, my own has burdened me greatly, and I would be indebted to share the load with such worthy fellows."

"What?" Hegel squinted at him.

"He'll tell us what he been doin led to him bein behind that rock," Manfried explained.

And so the priest did.

XIII
The Start of a Tale
Already Concluded

When I first read the chronicles of the Crusades that my order kept I finally appreciated the necessity of my learning Latin. Doctrine, even the writings of Saint Augustine, had failed to convince me the long years I spent were not in vain, for what boy wishes to spend his best youthful years squinting over a desk, memorizing a language a millennium fallen out of vernacularism? But those accounts of adventure and tragedy in the Holy Land left an indelible mark upon me, as my ability to flawlessly recite them all these years later demonstrates.

I realized my mundane existence held the potential, however scant, of becoming remarkably interesting, of being the stuff my brethren would study centuries after I went to my reward. I confess it was a vainglorious dream, to travel and adventure instead of showing my devotion in the traditional manner, but I was young and naïve and did not yet appreciate that a lifetime of quiet contemplation is as close to physical peace and perfection as we may achieve here. I have made myself obedient, however, and no longer lament my lot, for I indeed achieved my proud ambitions, and I have suffered for them. Our prayers must always be pure, lest they be directly answered!

To understand my condition when I came to the abbey at…at, by Her Mercy, even now I cannot vocalize its name, so does it haunt me. You must understand that I am disposed to the appreciation of certain libations, but I was never discovered or even suspected, for rather than floundering in a drunken stupor drink gave me passion at that point in my life. Due to my, shall we say, exceedingly vocal qualities regarding the nature of man's duty to his Father, I was sent out in the world to proselytize my way into the Holy Roman Empire and to establish myself at a certain abbey.

Again I stress my unwavering faith for even when I drank too much to stand and lay praying in my own sick I knew I remained in His Service, though to an outsider I suppose it appeared that perhaps I lost my way somewhat, for several times I was denied sanctuary at local parishes and had to stay at taverns or farms, where those my age reveled despite the calamitous nature of those times. I would watch the girls dance and only then did my piety tremble like their smooth, plump thighs swaying under their dresses, dresses damp with sweat and youth and—

Ahem.

At one such village a particular lass seemed to shine on me, and so intent was I on talking with her that I scarce remembered to drink and spent the entire night with a blasting headache but a gay heart. We wandered over streams and across fields, and when I brought her to her door she kissed me on the cheek. Such bliss! Her father softened and set down his ax when he threw open the door to discover a young monk chatting with his daughter, and to my shame and inner torment I discovered that my destined abbey sat atop the hill of that very village, and from my cell window I could pick out the light of Elise's farm, for that was the girl's name.

I managed to clean myself up enough to be accepted at the abbey, and in very little time had gotten myself comfortably arranged with the cook. Rare was the day when water passed my lips instead of beer, wine, brandy, or mead, rare as a good Christian in the Holy Land these days. Or anywhere else, for that matter. I know as well as you that all men drink regardless of their link in the chain, but know you must that I drank more than is befitting of any save a drunkard. The faces of my brothers and superiors were as interchangeable as those at my last monastery, although I still shook in my dreams when I remembered the pretty farm girl Elise cavorting that previous spring when I hiked through vale and mountain. Whenever possible I volunteered to take our herbs to the village for market, where Elise would often notice and come running to warm me with her adorable smile, her chest heaving from the exertion. Temptation, lads, shun it, shun it! I prayed and drank and tended the garden and studied and prayed and debated and drank and helped illuminate manuscripts and prayed and translated and drank and prayed. There I would have grown old and shriveled like the fruit of the Lord which I was but instead, instead...

That's better. Good stuff, this. They must be Benedictines, yes? Fine drink, fine, fine, fine. But as I said, was saying, am saying, er, where was I?

Oh, oh oh oh. Yes. Two years passed, was it two? Three? No matter, a little time passed, and then the pest came to our fair empire without warning, and then all flesh and souls were threatened by the Archfiend's plan, for surely, surely he was to blame. At the time, naturally, I did not know this, and shared the base belief that it must be God's Wrath, a cleansing of the Gomorrah we had become. To believe such evil was wrought by His Pure Hands!

What? God's, who else's?

No, no, I did not mean it like that, I meant only that the pest was not His Holy Work but the machinations of the old Serpent again among us. At the time, however, how else could we see it but as another test? The serfs and yeomen who had built their town around the abbey, however, had their own ideas...

That noxious swamp vapors are responsible for the pestilence is documented, and by your nodding heads I see that you are educated men. What is not so well accounted is that in certain rural, dismal places men are so desperate for succor from its ravages that they bow down before the miasma itself, offering devotion in exchange for their lives and those of their families. This diabolical heresy was perpetuated by the cult's ringleader, a man calling himself the Bird Doctor.

He arrived shortly before the pest, and succeeded in gaining the confidence of the foolish members of the village. The abbot brought me personally along to condemn the man as he cavorted in the square, dressed in a suit of raven feathers and wearing a sinister wooden vulture mask. The abbot launched into a diatribe against the heretic and swore if he was not departed in three days' time sterner measures would be taken. The man laughed under his mask and told the assembled mob that only he could ward off the miasma, and continued his strange, lascivious dance.

Contrary to his nonchalance, he left the following morning, wandering down the eastern road, and, they said, dancing and singing as he went. That evening the miller's wife began coughing and by cockcrow had buboes swelling from groin and pits. A family of Jews were passing through, and they could not escape before the town had rallied and caught them. From my cell I heard their screams as they went onto the pyre, accused of sprinkling viper skin into the brook and conjuring forth the miasma.

This time the blasphemous peasants chased the abbot back to the abbey when he tried to intervene, and the miller rode out in pursuit of the Bird Doctor. They returned late that night, and as I drank in my cell I saw their shadows on the moonlit road. After his return, events, as you may suspect, did not improve.

The village was decimated within a week but the abbot refused to allow any of the peasants entrance, swearing they had brought the pest upon themselves by turning their backs on God. I was not then and am still not now convinced he made the right decision, but I was young then and old now, and young men often do very foolish things. When the first of our order developed those damn lumps and the distinct cough we all prayed, and I am sure I was not the only one to eschew water for stouter stuff. Each day several more caught it, and yet Providence spared me, and I drank and drank and drank but could not forget her face.

I packed my belongs, in a drunken fit of hubris convincing myself I could do His Work just as well outside the church as within. I packed my things, mostly bottles, and escaped down to the pest-riddled village in search of Elise. Why do we punish ourselves so?

I saw her pleasant face bloated and gray, staring out from the pile of rotting corpses as I hurried down the rocky path. I found her burnt bones beside the creek, where the heretical peasants had tried to purify her dead flesh. I even saw her embracing the Bird Doctor, licking his hideous mask and cooing to him as I ran through the square. But the worst, which I knew would be the truth as I raced along the outskirts to her house, was that she had contracted the pest but had not yet expired, and I would find her in horrible pain, powerless to help. I was a sobbing man-child as I banged on her door, praying she had eloped with a farm boy before the Bird Doctor arrived.

As I feared, none answered my summons, and in my despair I kicked in the door. The stench tormented me but I fought it with more mead and braved the interior. The wretched, foul bodies were too far decayed to tell man from woman, father from daughter, and I embraced the moldiest of them, wailing her name between fits of vomiting.

I heard my name spoken from the door, and my gagging

throat and breaking heart both hesitated in their course. Oh, her voice, her charming, innocent voice!

. She trembled like a foal taking its first steps, like a novice reciting his first letter, she lived, she lived! Oh, what further proof of His Love, what further proof!? She had meant to flee that very night, having hid in the hay bales for several days, incapacitated with grief and terror. She had seen my approach and raced away, fearing I was the Bird Doctor who had menaced her every day until her parents' passing and her concealment behind the house. Later she told me something inside had made her turn back to be sure, and we agreed it must be the merciful whispering of Mary.

We traveled to a hunter's cabin high in the hills behind the abbey, taking only what food she had in her satchel and I had in mine. Base as I had become, I had also stolen several rushlights, and lighting one of these, I nested us down in that dilapidated shack at the foot of an enormous peak. The heavy pines more than the thin roof kept out the rain, and with tears still glazing our cheeks we acknowledged that we must inspect one another for marks of the pest.

She removed her dress and I my cowl and habit, and our joy at finding each other unblemished soon increased. Do not cast such disapproving looks my way! I shall explain to you as I did to Elise that Martyn the monk is different from Martyn the man, and Martyn the monk's last act as such was to wed Martyn, the man, to Elise. The woman.

Of course it works that way! Who's the priest here? Thank you, Hegel. But you know, after that first kiss we shared this has never tasted as sweet as it once did, and never has filled me with that old joy; only, when I have enough, a blissful absentmindedness.

Yes. We spent days if not weeks there, laboring with all our skill to cope with our grief and our strange new situation. But before I could join us in marriage she had me be her confessor, convinced without immediate absolution she would be forever damned.

That wicked Bird Doctor had taken a strong interest in poor, poor Elise, confirming my suspicions that beneath his avian mantle lurked a decidedly human pair of eyes. But he was more than human both in body and spirit, for before traveling to transmit his ruin he had studied the evil arts. A diabolist of self-professed prowess, he had described in gruesome detail to her how he had used the blood of babes and the fur of rats to summon up an entity from the pit, a demon straight from the old times of darkness and devilry. He welcomed this fiend into his own body and became a demoniac, and it possessed first his bilious humours, growing and nursing and encouraging him in his evil ways. And now he spread plague and ruin and reveled in it, masquerading as the cure for the very malignancy he carried. These and worse secrets he called to her through her bolted door, telling her as soon as the rest rotted alive he would take her as his own and let a similar demon into her virgin body.

My miserable Elise cried and cried, but sometime before dawn her tears dried and we completed a far more pleasant ceremony, with only the flimsy walls and the Virgin witnessing our marriage. Then such heavenly pleasure, and I do not use the word heavenly lightly, I mean—I'm sorry, Hegel, I did not realize such matters would offend. Oh, I see it on your face, no need to protest, I was being most crass, my apologies to both of you and the Lord and both Her and her.

I knew the Lord approved of our union, for I felt Him with me as strong as ever, but I worried about my brethren down below. So when our food ran out, but not our drink, for in that blessed time I drank no more than an old farmwife, I insisted we visit the monastery before traveling south to live our lives together in earnest. Elise pleaded with me not to go but I insisted, guilt at deserting my brotherhood when they most needed me overpowering my desire to carry my bride to safety. I cursed myself for not going to warn the abbot of the Bird Doctor's true identity that first morning as a spouse, regardless of what he might think of me for casting off of my habit.

In many places the pest claimed only a few or at least spared a handful, but in that blasted valley none still lived. The abbey reared up in the twilight, an accusatory finger beckoning me back into the fold. Hand in hand we went inside through the same back door I had sneaked out through, and saw no lights lit for Vespers, the bell tower dark and silent as if it were a league beneath the ocean.

I built a bonfire in the garden to warm my bride and summon any who lived. They were all dead. Elise stayed by the fire but I ran through every hall, opened every door, only to find them piled in the chapel, the stench unbearable, unbelievable. I will not repeat the horrors I witnessed, the blasphemies marking every surface, written in odious— Yes? Sure enough, Manfried, that is further proof that we fought the same evil! No let me fin— Sorry, I get, I get, oh Hell...

Yes please. As I say, it doesn't help like it used to. But it helps. Better, better.

Elise is screaming in the garden, and I run to her, and I see, I see, that filthy, oh Christ, his mask is off and he's got his decaying face pressed to hers, the mask is at his feet and his skin is falling off. I beat him with my walking stick, I hit, I hit, and he fell apart like a rotten roast, chunks of meat and bone and he just fell apart but it was too late. I saw it enter her, oh Hell, I see, I see...

How long have I— Never mind, I'd rather not— Yes, very much so. Better, better. Benedictines, definitely. More? Ugh. First a touch more of this, if it's all the same.

It had her. That demon had her, and only her eyes were her own, and it told me with her unforgettable voice what it would have her do, and I could not move, I was paralyzed with grief.

And it laughed with her laugh, and told me all was my fault for abandoning my brothers and then leading her back to it. It thanked me with her angelic voice! Then it told me if I would give my soul and my flesh it would leave her with no harm done to her spirit or body, if only I would let it inside me. It said a monk would be good sport!

In blackest suffering only His Light penetrates, and it found me then, moments before the demon surely would have had me, and by my own volition. I adored her that much, Grossbarts, that had I, I would, I, I—

I did not. Instead, He inspired me. A demon that demands I offer my soul before taking my body is a demon which *cannot* take my soul unless it is given, *regardless* of what vengeance it wreaks upon my corporeal self! And if a fallen monk is still thus protected, what of an unblemished, edelweiss-pure soul such as Elise's? I began to laugh and it strode closer in her flesh, eager to hear my answer, sure that madness had convinced me. Instead I swung my cane and knocked them into the fire and it pulled me in after, and if I wore a hairshirt then as I do now then we both would be lost.

I managed to douse myself in the snow, although my chest and belly are forever scarred from the blaze. She and it screamed in concert, but in her boiling eyes I still saw nothing but love through the pain. They ran toward the same drift as I but I mercilessly beat them back with my cane, and when she went silent and its blackening shadow tried to slip out I burst its skin with my smoldering cane, and heard it shriek my name as it seemingly expired.

Thank you, very kind. Actually, this one is about empty, do you— Excellent, thank you, thank you.

No. No, oh, but were it thus! What I took to be a death rattle was instead a cry of triumph, for behind me a traveler on horseback had ridden into the courtyard. Even as he retched atop his steed from the noxious mist billowing off her melting corpse the faintest, deflating visage of the thing shot toward me but balked at my flaming stick and instead fell upon this new arrival.

Was he an emissary from a nearby town or brother monastery or a soldier returning from a campaign or a merchant bringing alms? I know not, and I never even saw his face, but that awful night I heard him gag and scream as it slipped inside him, his horse galloping away of its own accord with the unfortunate rider astride it. I knew it had escaped me, but I also knew His Purifying Flame could be its undoing if only there were not other vulnerable victims to be had. Why did it not simply enter my body? Was it my cane which had caught fire and barred its way, or my deep faith that it could not harm me? Had I some immunity of a physical nature to its loathsome pox? I know little more now than I did then, except that my life has revolved around ferreting out that demon and its vile kin wherever they spread their pest.

What's that? Of course, of course. I re-donned my habit then and there and took the vows which I had so eagerly shirked before, again He my only witness, and the only witness that matters. Unlike in my youth, these vows were meant with every fiber of my soul, I wept and wept, my tears sizzling on her smoking remains, and swore I would earn my place by her side as well as Hers in the eternal. I knew He wanted me to do more than even my order would allow, which is why I have become a priest instead of a simple brother. I have spent every moment from that until this searching, searching, for any clue at all! These last few years have actually been more fruitful if more perilous, for instances of the pest are far less common, guiding me ever closer to the victory which it seems you have taken from me. Better, though, for if I had been there only He knows what jeopardy I might have put my soul into, so deeply did I seek vengeance. And there were others between it and me, lesser powers, furry worms hiding inside the demoniacs, and these I ruthlessly suppressed and drove back, but always that one, that powerful malignancy, who prefers to receive rather than steal his steeds, meaning the man harboring it who I pursued through this range was either necromancer or diabolist, warlock or murderer. At the least a heretic, at the very least.

I will not bore you with the struggles I went through in that fair city of Avignon, where lush trees and ornate towers rub each other in grim parody of the state our beloved Church has fallen into. The Holy Office, that very institution meant to hunt it out, admits that heresies exist but questions the legitimacy of witches and warlocks, some even doubting the corporeality of demons! What folly is this? They tell me only women are susceptible, and the victim must always sin to let them enter. They exchange winks and tell me demons reside in the bowels, not the humours, and application of the cross will banish them and save the demoniac. Falsehoods implanted by the very evil we must uproot! We above all others are impressed with this deplorable duty, and yet they do not listen to me, one of theirs who has faced one of Lucifer's! But always, always, I remember her face and the words she spoke before leaving my side forever: we *must* have faith. God *will* deliver us.

XIV
The Monotonous Road

Father Martyn looked from Grossbart to Grossbart, then sighed, pulled his blankets around him, and prayed himself to sleep. Hegel shook his head to dispel the story and left the beard-gnawing Manfried to first watch. Manfried worried the night away, never thinking to wake Hegel until the light slowly returned, accompanied by fresh snow.

Shaking his brother before rousing the priest, Manfried noticed Hegel's right hand appeared as swollen and leaky as his own left hand—the places where their skin had touched the demon. The wounds seemed on the mend but Manfried mentioned the nasty nature of the injuries to Hegel once he had ceased hacking up phlegm and shaking out the cold. Discussing this brought to light a matter both had considered at length but were loath to address. They shifted their gaze from the sleeping priest to the wagon.

"It's gotta be done," Manfried insisted.

"Thought you'd think so," said Hegel.

"She's got it, you want'er in there? Might a dodged it once, but dodgin it all the way to Venetia could prove more luck than even Mary'll dish our way," Manfried argued.

"And if she got'em you's ready to do the deed?"

"Do what I have to."

"Thought you'd say that."

"Dammit, Hegel, I's wearyin a your implications. We's pure, yeah? I reckon the cause a your distress is your own perverted thoughts."

Mistaking his brother's silent recollection and the shuddering that accompanied it for acquiescence, Manfried settled back down. "So we check'er."

"Later, when we got a proper sun stead a that weak," Hegel said, shrugging off the memory of Nicolette like the unwelcome embrace of a drunken relative.

"Sooner the better."

"Can't see nuthin."

"Wager I could feel'em, though." Manfried wiggled his grimy fingers Hegel's way. Hegel almost exploded but caught the mischievous glint in Manfried's eye.

"Now who's harborin shit-stinkin thoughts?" Hegel laughed, and they returned to their Arabian musings. The priest eventually awoke, forgetting his wound and yelping as he reached for a bowl of snowmelt. The Brothers and Martyn wasted little time after that, and made to leave at once.

"Fore we set out," Hegel told Martyn, "got us a passenger needs inspectin."

"In the wagon?" Martyn rubbed his eyes.

"If you's up to it." Manfried spit, perturbed to be denied the task.

"You mean you've not checked him?" Martyn came fully awake.

"Seein's she don't speak, least not our way, we was waitin for an opportune opportunity," Hegel sheepishly explained.

"She? Oh." The curtains over Martyn's eyes lifted. "I'll do the examination, then. If she is poxed, are we up to the task?"

"Damn right." Hegel looked at his brother.

"Yeah, we's ready," Manfried said with less conviction.

"Bless the both of you," Martyn said, entering the wagon.

She scowled at Manfried when the priest closed the tarp behind him, and there followed a brief period of Martyn murmuring to the woman inside the wagon. Then the priest burst out, pale and shaking. Hegel put his hand on his pick while Manfried demanded answers.

"Yeah?"

"Clean enough." Martyn licked his lips.

"What's that?"

"Smooth. Er, her underarms are fine, and the other—"

"The other?"

"The other I did not see. But it felt—"

"Felt!"

"Yes. It felt fine as well. Of course I would have to *see* to be sure, but I don't suppose—"

"No, you'd better not!"

"Manfried!" Hegel reprimanded. "Mind who you's talkin with. All clear, Priest?"

"Clear as well water." Martyn composed himself. "Smooth as down. Saint Roch has blessed her as much as us."

"Then that's us gone!" Hegel and Manfried helped Martyn up onto the bench.

"Kill a thousand saints for some meat," Manfried said, rooting in his bag for the cheese.

"Brother!" Hegel gave him the stink-eye.

"There is no need to amend your typical discourse on my account." Martyn smiled. "I know the difference twixt a turn of phrase and a considered sin."

"See?" Manfried tore into the wheel, Martyn hungrily eyeing the food. "Care for a taste?"

"Very much, please."

"There you are, and some bread beside." Manfried returned the stink-eye to Hegel. The priest gobbled his food, and when they stopped a short time later to clear the road Manfried sloppily transferred some beer into a bottle and all three had a drink. They surveyed the road ahead, the same sparse mountains and stunted trees buried by winter.

"My dear horse gave out not far from here, and I took of his body what I could carry," said Martyn. "Perhaps the wolves have left us some of what I could not."

"Don't wager on a dog leavin nuthin for a man," Hegel said with the air of imparted wisdom.

"Well, Brothers." Martyn looked back and forth, scrunched between the two. "Last night I shared my burdens, perhaps now you might share yours?"

"Ain't really got any," said Manfried.

"Surely, we all have burdens, and in my experience the spiritual weigh heavier than those imposed on our physical backs. How came you to find me on the road, and where are you going, and where have you been?"

"That's Mary's business more than ours, and certainly yours." Manfried took another swig.

"Suit yourselves," said Martyn. "But in the name of your salvation, you *will* tell me what transpired with the abomination you say you killed."

"Not much to tell." Hegel relieved his brother of the bottle. "Seen a demon, killed a demon."

"Easy as that?"

"Easier." Manfried snatched back the beer.

"Tell me. Please."

"Right," said Hegel, and gave a somewhat accurate account of their adventure in Rouseberg. Manfried chimed in only when he deemed it necessary to censor his brother where sensitive matters involving graveyards were concerned.

"Incredible. But you say you laid hands upon the demon?"

"Yeah, when it was crawlin in Ennio's craw. Slipped through, though." Hegel had hoped this failure would not be scrutinized. "Mecky fucker was tryin to get its touch on the whole time."

"Legs busted off, leaked all on us. But we done our all for the poor foreign bastard." Manfried frowned at the empty bottle.

"Let me see." Martyn swallowed anxiously. "Let me see your skin, where you touched it."

Shrugging in tandem, they each showed the palm scalded by the demon's ichors. At first reluctant to touch them, Martyn began prodding and squeezing, then leaned in and sniffed. He recoiled and waved their hands away.

"Despite the stench, they seem uninfected," Martyn said nasally. "Avoid eating or drinking out of them until they return to normal."

"Why's that?" asked Hegel, scratching his blistered scalp.

"Cause they been polluted by a demon, fathead."

"Er, yes. It is amazing, though. As I told you, all who have touched the malignancy have become host to it, yet you two were spared. Did you pray to Saint Roch?" At seeing their blank stare, Martyn explained, "Saint Roch is not yet, er, *officially* canonized, so your unfamiliarity is forgivable. I happen to possess one of his finger bones, to use as a weapon against Devil and devils alike. You may not know him but he certainly watches over you! I have never met any who survived the pest without invoking his name!"

"Til now!" Hegel tried to pass on his swagger through the reins to the brainless horses.

"Ain't the first time, mightn't be the last." Manfried pushed the tarp aside and crawled into the wagon for more beer and a surreptitious glimpse. Neither brother felt the need for saints, having been in Mary's good graces from childhood.

"Eh? You mean you've seen such evil before?" Martyn twisted around to watch Manfried.

"He's referrin to us catchin the pest when we was young, and givin better than we got," Hegel explained.

"You mean you survived the Great Mortality?"

"With aplomb." Manfried almost kicked the priest in regaining his seat.

"Amazing," said Martyn.

"Miraculous is more like it."

"Mind the company, Manfried."

"No, Hegel," Martyn said before Manfried could return fire, "it *is* miraculous. Not one man in a thousand survives the Great Mortality once it has taken hold. I have never personally witnessed such a recovery but have heard tales. The Virgin has truly been merciful to you."

"Couldn't say it better, Friar." Manfried chugged victoriously.

"Between weathering the pest and besting an agent of the Archfiend, you are truly soldiers of the Lord!"

"Soldiers a Mary, you mean," Manfried corrected, and Hegel did not argue.

"Well, I suppose it could be seen as such."

"Drink up, Martyn." Manfried passed him the refilled bottle. "Now you's heard our tale, nuthin left but to shrivel the time's best we fuckin can."

"What is this *fuck*?" Martyn asked.

"What?" Hegel said.

"Who?" Manfried said.

"Fuck," Martyn repeated, "fucking, fuck, fucker—the word you like so much. A slur?"

"Oh, the *word* fuck!" Manfried laughed. "Yeah, a slur, right enough. Village not too far from our birth-home's called Fuckin."

"Why did they name it after a slur?" asked Martyn.

"Oft have I mused the same question," said Hegel.

"You have?" Manfried grinned at his brother's folly. "Hardly surprisin. Nah, Martyn, it's like this. Fuckin's a town filled with men what are assholes, but assholes so mecky it don't serve to just call'em assholes or mecky assholes or even Maryless mecky assholes, gotta get somethin stronger by way a differentiatin, to say nuthin a brevity. Hence, we call someone so mecky they might's well been from Fuckin a fucker or a fuckwit or anythin else related to bein from Fuckin. Yeah?"

"I suppose." Martyn shrugged. "Why are these, these Fuckers, so maligned? Are they pagans?"

"We was in Fuckin tryin to—" Hegel began but caught his brother's eye and piped down.

"Yes?" Martyn pressed.

"We was in Fuckin and the fuckers what lived there done fucked us, which is to say, tried to do us like we was the sort a no-account fuckers what might live in their mecky town. So we fucked them back and fucked off." Manfried was growing exasperated.

"But why—" Martyn started.

"Fuckin Hell, Martyn!" Manfried lost his temper. "It's a fuckin turn a phrase, same's shit, piss, ass, you name it, only worse, cause even if there was a village named Shit it'd be a sight better than Fuckin and the shitters what'd live there would be a right more decent set a souls! Means you ain't fuckin round, means you got somethin serious to convey or you wouldn't bring up the fuckin place! Use it to talk bout nasties and nastiness, as in that fuckin demon tried fuckin us over but got himself fucked in the bargain!"

There was a long silence on the bench before Hegel cleared his throat. "Or the act a fornication. Bein a mecky deed, the term may be applied there as well."

"Fuckin right." Manfried nodded.

Martyn was indeed convinced this Fucking must be a profane place, even if the invocation of its name varied incomprehensibly depending on circumstance. After another lull the priest remembered they had more pressing matters than creative profanities to discuss, and asked, "But what happened after you conquered our adversary? Where were all the townsfolk and monks?"

"In the monastery, in the condition you'd expect from your own experiences." Hegel shivered at the memory.

"We burnt them, too," Manfried hiccupped. "Don't worry on that account."

Martyn sighed. "Then my quest has ended without my presence. But do not think me proud, for I acknowledge you and I are but His Instruments, and His Will has been done. I am solaced that I had tracked it true, and had you not arrived I would have soon after."

"*Her* Will. And that's assumin you didn't freeze, or get et by wolves, or fall into any number a other gruesome ways. Speculatin gets you nuthin but sore, mark me," Manfried philosophized.

"And she," Martyn nodded behind them, "has been with you even before this?"

"She—" Hegel began.

"Has and is," Manfried interjected, "our ward. We's takin her south to Venetia for a sea captain."

"Which captain?"

"Bar Goose. Queer name, I'll allow," said Hegel, saving his brother the embarrassment of having forgotten their future patron's name.

"For what purpose is your anonymous ward traveling through the mountains in the cruel of winter? I did not think any wagons braved such high roads this late."

"To get to that captain, like I just told you," said Manfried.

"No, no, I mean, what was she doing out here to begin with? A foreign bride? A relative?"

"There you go, speculatin. You question why the sun come up and down like it's wont?" Manfried went on. "Why cow taste better than horse, and pig better than either? How bout why you's priest stead a Pope?"

"Manfried!" Hegel's horror mingled with his usual glee at hearing his brother make others look foolish.

"I ain't finished. Got us a holy man obsessed with unravelin the design stead a servin it like everythin from eel to emperor does. Why's we born if we's gonna die? Why's there a Hell if Mary loves us all? If we's slaves to divine plannin, why in fuck's free will an issue? What sort a test got a pre-seen outcome, then a feigned surprise when some cunts fuck up?"

Martyn's entire body matched the crimson rims of his eyes, which jutted out of their puffy settings. He stared while Manfried took another swig, a faint whining coming from the priest's pursed lips. Just when Martyn seemed about to damn them both—Hegel unsure if the noise he kept bottled up was apology or laughter—Manfried finished his speech.

"That's the kind a rot priests been talkin where we come from. Only talk to themselves, mind you, but word always trickles down, specially when you's proud as princes and twice's stupid. You'd think livin as they do, chosen people and all, they'd have more sense than to question a good thing. Heresy is what it is, and worse yet, cowardice. Cryin and carryin on, why, why, why?! I'll tell you, Martyn, I'll tell you honest: kind a maggot askin them questions' too scared to have faith, and that's how he's worse than a simple heretic. Ain't enough his family died, he gotta know why. Why me, why them, why, why, why? Cause you's a cunt, that's why. Cause Her Will is inscrutable, and what's more, none a our fuckin trade. We truck in the flesh, and doin as She commands, showin mercy and acceptin fate for just that stead a raisin them questions what would get you burnt quick you wasn't wearin robes. Gotta believe in a world without answers, a fate without explanation or apology, or you's the cuntiest a the cunts and you's gonna get your precious answer in the fires below!"

The wheels squeaked and the wagon bounced. Hegel sweated,

wondering if their load would soon lighten. His brother usually restrained himself around clergy as there were so many hidden heretics infiltrating the Church but this man had shown remarkable charity, what with not being sore about getting shot. Manfried spoke the gospel, though, and if this priest took offense it was proof of his cowardice.

"Amen," Martyn breathed. "You speak well, Manfried, although I might advise rearranging the order of your points in the future, as most company will not listen so attentively and discern your meaning for what it is. And forgive me if I, through my awkwardness of speech, have implied I do anything but agree wholeheartedly with you. My simple, and admittedly rude, curiosity bested me, but only for a moment."

"Amen, indeed," chortled Hegel, sliding his hand off the pommel of the dagger under his cloak.

"Well, it ain't nuthin," Manfried muttered, delighted his diatribe had pleased the priest. "Just the truth, unfettered by that fancy and meaningless talk so pleases the countryfolk."

"As I told you," Martyn said after sipping the bottle, "although perhaps not clearly enough, it is precisely that sort of doublespeak that has divided Christian from Christian to such grave extent that the Pope no longer sits in his proper place but must dwell in the recently tamed wilds of Avignon, and why I was scorned by some of my brethren for embarking on my journey. They would rather accuse each other of heresy than battle real evil made flesh."

"Cowardice is oft hid under the moniker a common sense," said Hegel, and the others nodded in agreement.

"And you are correct," Martyn continued, "shamed though I am to admit it, that there are many in the Church for whom the Will of God no longer suffices, and they damage not only their own salvation but also the sanctity of the entire institution by focusing more on the questions than the answers."

"What with all them different orders traipsin bout, can't tell one from another," Hegel put in, Manfried winded and content to drink and listen.

"That is not so much of a problem as when the divisions become intolerable." Martyn belched. "The fiend I hunted is indicative of this. I found little support in pursuing a demon that I had *seen*. Sad times when thwarting corporeal evil sent from the Devil to work his mischief is less imperative than investigating rumors of heresy, when the righteous are not even in their city. I found an ally in Jean de la Roquetaillade, a Franciscan gifted with prophecy, but he was imprisoned for preaching the truth—that the End Times have arrived. I met with him in his cell every time I journeyed to Avignon, further proof, further proof! Concern for the souls of man has been supplanted by a desire for power. I prayed that my quest might bring the Church back together, but before leaving Avignon the last time I found myself a pariah and a laughingstock to those who disgrace His Name through act and word, some whispering I was a secret Waldensian! They denied me an audience with Lord Clement, then again with Lord Innocent, and when I recently returned to implore Lord Urban the same curt dismissal awaited me."

"Tragic," said Hegel.

"Tell me, brothers, have you heard of the trial of Formosus?"

Manfried yawned. Hegel blinked.

"Pope Formosus's desecration is most topical, so I will advise you on what befell him and let you two pious wanderers decide for yourself. Several centuries past, Formosus served man and God as all *true* popes do, but even then political machinations were at work, and shortly after his death they exhumed him."

The Grossbarts perked up, such business being their specialty. Hegel forced himself to mind the road while Manfried pried the beer away from Martyn. The priest managed another swig before relinquishing it.

"They accused him of heresy." Martyn's eyes bubbled over but his voice did not quake. "Led by Stephen the Sixth, er, the Seventh, those heretics had him disinterred from his holy resting place and held a trial. With his corpse! His soul long seated in Heaven had the humiliation of watching over while they poked his bones and charged him with blasphemy, devil worship, and every other vile falsehood their wicked minds could imagine. Obviously he was unable to defend his remains, and those criminals hacked off the hand which bore the papal ring and stripped him of his vestments. Then they dragged him through the streets, hurled him into the river, fished him out, and scattered his disgraced bones with those of the Jews."

"Shameful," said Hegel.

"A travesty never to be forgot," said Manfried.

"I often fancied if I were to become Pope, I would petition for the name Formosus," Martyn mused.

"Hey now." Manfried lightly elbowed him. "Ain't someone forgettin their place at the table?"

"What? Never! I simply, er, as Augustine said—"

"Easy on, Martyn." Manfried laughed. "Just meckin up your words. Cowardice is questionin your fate, courage and honor is strugglin to change it."

"But fate is immovable," said Martyn.

"Usually, yeah, but Her Will is for us to struggle and persevere, and part a that is to know the difference twixt what you's tricked into thinkin fate is and what it actually be."

Martyn squinted at Manfried. "Tricked?"

"I reckon it's somethin like this," Hegel piped in. "You think your fate's to struggle gainst heresy back in Roma or Avignon or wherever, but your real fate's to chase a demon up into these hills. So you follow your fate, even though all the rest tries to tell you fate says to stay put."

"Is that what I meant?" Neither brother was sure if Manfried was genuinely asking or being contrary.

"Perceived fate and actual fate. Free will. Heresy. Coward-ice." Martyn slumped forward and vomited all over their feet. Manfried kept him from falling under the wheels and winked at his brother. This priest did not seem a bad sort.

"What kind a priest you reckon he is?" Hegel asked his more worldly kin in their private dialect.

"The superior kind." Manfried shrugged. "From his tale I speculate he's one a them Dominicans. Probable, given his prat-tlin on matters heretical."

"Oh." Hegel quieted, not wanting to sound foolish by asking more.

"Not exact on how he come to be priest in the eyes a men other than the Holy Fucker above," Manfried ruminated. "Can't picture no cardinal nor bishop nor whoever thinkin he'd be fit."

"But you said yourself he seems a the finer stuff," Hegel pointed out.

"Yeah, but definitions vary."

Even buried beneath snow the road remained obvious by the indentation, but they could no longer make it out more than thirty feet in front of the lead horses. Martyn shifted in and out of consciousness between the Grossbarts, ranting on mat-ters Manfried assured his brother would amount to blasphemy in lesser company. This amused them, and they goaded him on as he never disparaged the Virgin, only bishops and priests and monks and orders of monks and nobles and serfs and yeomen and even horses.

They never found his fallen steed but they did not encoun-ter any wolves, either. That night Manfried slept through the darkness, with Martyn filling in for him to make penance for his earlier embarrassment. Knowing the oats would keep longer than the furry bread, they abstained from porridge and cut the moldy taste of the loaves with moldier cheese. The spoiled rye had the odd effect of bringing them vivid dreams, dreams that often arrived before they even drifted off.

Unaware of the source of their visions, all three continued to munch the stuff through the next day, which brought on wilder talks and images. Many times Hegel could not see the horses let alone the road but he kept that to himself, and the beasts trod on without event. The snowy peaks undulated around them, and Manfried and Martyn fiercely debated what this presaged. The snow appeared to rise from the ground instead of fall to it, and each man at times fell into giggling. They did not realize they had stopped until all wore an extra hat of powder, and then started moving again only to spite the lazy horses.

None was sure if they truly entered a wood until they sat around the biggest fire they had kindled since leaving the tavern, and the pine-bough canopy, after dumping its pale payload on their first blaze, kept further snow from drifting onto them. Wolves howled and they howled back, Martyn loudest of all. Of a sudden mind to impress upon Martyn the seriousness of their crusade, Manfried told the priest of their ancestral duty to deny the Infidel anything a Grossbart might covet.

"Prester John," Martyn said incredulously, "is your *grand-father*?"

"Ain't got no kin name a John," said Manfried.

"But you say he is Christian king dwelling beyond the lands of the Arab?"

"Truth be told," said Hegel, "we dunno if he's king or just kingly rich, nor where he lays his beard. We's yet to make his acquaintance."

"We's gonna find out soon enough, mind you, and show him up besides," said Manfried. "Get us enough loot to make our granddad look like a dirt-handed turnip digger."

Martyn laughed. "But stories of Prester John's kingdom date back decades, centuries!"

"Grossbarts been goin south since Moses was a pup." Manfried glared at the priest. "I told you he weren't no John nor Preston nor what, so shut your fuckin mouth fore I hang you up like a scarecrow for them hill-dogs!"

After a desperate pause—wherein both brothers subtly fingered the handles of their weapons, even Hegel unwilling to allow anyone but himself and his brother to disparage their kinfolk—Martyn spoke:

"Well, pardon my fucking mouth!" and then all three were again hooting with unnatural laughter.

Late in the night the sweetest music either brother had ever heard swam out of the wagon, and then Martyn awoke raving and attacked the nearby trees with his fists. Neither brother intervened but instead broke out bottles and heartily enjoyed the spectacle. Only Manfried noticed when the music abated, and he covertly peeled the ice from his cheeks. In the morning he shamefully realized he had not checked if she still sat in the wagon since the day before.

Martyn had excused himself to clean his habit and Hegel snored beside the coals, allowing Manfried to stride guilelessly to the rear of the wagon. He rapped twice on the frame, then clambered inside, closing the flap behind him. Inside he could see only shadows of shadows but heard her breathing and smelled her musky-sweet sweat, an aroma that made him hungry.

"Uh." He swallowed. "That's a fine way a singin you got."

Her clothes rustled and he thought he made out her teeth glittering in the dark. His own sweat stinging his eyes, he suddenly felt uncomfortably hot. Bracing himself, he leaned in until he felt her breath on his cheek, a cool draft in the sweltering wagon.

"Could you...if you...uh, sing it again?" Manfried felt a fool. "Please?"

Her breath came faster and cooler, a vaguely familiar scent tickling his nose hairs. Then Hegel bellowed beside the wagon and she drew back deeper into the darkness. Anger consumed Manfried and he burst out of the wagon, startling Hegel and the returned Martyn. Under their curious look his rage dissipated and he mumbled about getting an early move on. Hitching up the horses, he did not notice Martyn pressing Hegel aside.

"Does he often slip into the interior when you sleep?" Martyn asked.

"Mind your mind," Hegel retorted. "Priest shouldn't think such impureness."

"A man must tame himself before endeavoring to tame another. For the sake of his soul, we should be vigilant."

"For the sake a your teeth, I'd be a touch more vigilant a lip. That's all I'll say, save my brother's purer than you or I." Hegel sullenly climbed onto the bench.

Martyn made the sign of the cross before the wagon and followed after. They broke bread and the bread broke them, that day and those that followed blurring into a harrowing passage not only through the mountains but also deeper, less explored regions. The Fire of Saint Anthony branded their brains, and only fortune spared their extremities from the toxic rye—except for a toe of Martyn's, which fell out of his boot when he removed it to examine the uncomfortable tingling. For two days solid Hegel confused Martyn with the Virgin Herself, usually frightening the priest but occasionally convincing him that he was indeed the Bride of God.

If not for the sensible horses they would have become lost, but to Hegel's chagrin they refused to advance over the precipices or up the streambeds he led them to. Cursing them, he screamed until lights flared up around them but their tusks and legions of legs frightened him dreadfully, dampening his enthusiasm to engage the equines in combat. Mary told him many secrets as they traveled, things that made him froth with anger and cry in despair. Her uncanny resemblance to Nicolette the witch ceased to upset him after the first day, although it kept his thoughts chaste throughout the ordeal.

Manfried once mistook the falling snow for gold and would have tumbled to his death in pursuit had Martyn not convinced him it was a diabolical trap, adder-spit dyed yellow to fool the honest. Manfried crawled under a blanket for several hours to keep the poison from his flesh. When Hegel addressed the priest as the Virgin, Manfried briefly shared his brother's delusion before realizing her to be an imposter, the genuine Mary resting inside the wagon. The things She whispered to him were perhaps the only possible words to make a Grossbart blush. At night, when none truly slept but rolled and raved beside a fire which might have existed only in their minds, Manfried crept under the wagon and prayed until he went hoarse.

Being of the clergy Martyn had a monstrous appetite but it could not contest with that of the Grossbarts, the result being he consumed less bread and could function somewhat like a normal man. While he did not match their hunger, however, his imagination had fed on many tracts over the years and so his visions compensated in wildness what they occasionally lacked in vibrancy. For the demon-hunting holy man their travel led over mountains of ash and through clouds of sulfur, steam and venom raining upon them, the wails of the damned giving them no respite. His beloved Elise remained absent but Saint Roch harried their wagon, his moldering corpse demanding the return of his stolen finger. Martyn hurled the relic into the snow, shrieking his remorse for his own graveyard indiscretion. His speech drifted among the dialects and tongues he had learned, along with a few hybrids of his own devising. A test, he moaned to the lost souls riding beside him, a final test before the glory. Although it meant his damnation, he did not correct the fallen seraphim beside him when the radiant creature addressed him as Mary, Mother of God. He knew himself to be Mary Magdalene, and was ashamed.

Unlike natural dreams, these horrors did not vanish instantly upon their waking but tormented them day and night, subtly fading in intensity until their absence maddened the trio more than their presence had. Stopping the horses late in the third afternoon of their psychosis, Hegel stumbled down to simultaneously vomit and shit while his brother unhitched the horses for the first time in days. The miserable creatures were famished and blistered, the expression of their huge eyes launching the Brothers into another giggling fit. Martyn stayed on the bench, praying and weeping until the Grossbarts started a fire.

The next morn they realized they had left the peaks behind in favor of gentler slopes and would probably not die in the mountains after all. After again reprimanding himself and again checking on the lady who again smiled sweetly at him and batted her eyes, Manfried again readied the horses. Unlike the previous day's gloom and silence, the Brothers and Martyn enjoyed the rough road and biting wind and gruel-turned stomachs.

Nothing could dampen their souls at the first sight of something other than the boundless succession of snowy rocks that had enclosed the Brothers for weeks. They dipped through forested valleys and over grassy meadows, and had they been the frivolous sort songs would surely have been sung; instead they talked of honor, faith, and the gift of prophecy. Had Martyn not shared the bread, he would have thought them heretics of the worst sort.

"Further proof? What further proof you need?" asked Hegel, amazed his sanctimonious brother doubted the truth.

"Could be somethin else, devilry or spells," grumbled Manfried. The idea that his licentious hallucinations might come to pass bothered him in all sorts of ways.

"That *is* possible," admitted Martyn. "The Deceiver might well have given us such visions for the express purpose of fooling us into thinking we were touched by the divine."

"But could even he impersonate Mary so well?" demanded Hegel. "I seen Her Face and heard Her Council. Why would the Devil take Her Guise only to tell me I was servin Her proper? Wouldn't he rather I changed my ways?"

"Witchery can make you see all kinds a niceness ain't really present," said Manfried, unconsciously grinding salt into his brother's spiritual wounds.

"But Hegel's point is valid," Martyn insisted. "Why would the Devil urge us to be truer of faith?"

"That's just what I was sayin," Manfried countered, "bout askin too many questions."

"Exactly! Take it on faith's what you's always sayin, brother."

"Yeah, and I'll take them horrors on faith as proof a evil spite and nuthin more."

"Manfried, if the Lord wanted us to know without questioning there would *be* no faith," said Martyn.

"Priest—"

"Father Martyn, please."

"Martyn—"

"*Father* Martyn."

"*Priest* Martyn," the annoyed Manfried continued, "questionin is fine and good so long as one keeps it all in perspective. Got nuthin to gain, spiritual or other, by assumin we was blessed with sights from Heaven."

"True enough," Martyn confessed.

"But Manfried." Hegel tugged his beard nervously. "There's some other, er, proof."

"You best not be talkin bout what I suspect."

"Yeah, you's probably right." Hegel felt relieved not to address it after all.

"What's this? Come now, Hegel, I am a priest, there is no fear to speak your mind."

"I—" started Hegel.

"Don't." Manfried scowled.

"Oh, shove it." Hegel scowled right back. "He ain't gonna put me on a pyre for tellin the truth bout somethin ain't my fault to begin with."

"Never know." Manfried glowered at Martyn.

"Oh, come now," said Martyn. "Think of me as a confessor if you must."

"Nah." Hegel soured. "I ain't confessin nuthin cause I ain't done nuthin wrong."

"Surely you've not been corrupted by the Beghards?" Martyn grew distressed.

"Ain't let no beggars touch us!" Manfried again considered putting Martyn off the wagon.

"No, no," said Martyn. "A group of heretics calling themselves Beg*hards* have been spreading heresy to the effect that all men exist in a state of grace, without the need for clergy and sacraments. I thought—"

"We's dumb enough to get taken in by heresy?" Manfried demanded, although so far these Beghards did not sound very reproachable.

"Never!" Martyn said. "And besides, they advocate poverty, so surely—"

"Surely?" Manfried breathed in Martyn's face.

"Surely." Martyn licked his chapped lips. "Surely we could forget my folly and concentrate on this fine beverage instead?"

"Surely." Manfried turned back to the horses.

A league of empty road passed before Hegel cracked: "Does it *have* to be a sin to be confessed?"

"If you hesitate to tell a priest you balk at admitting something to God, and He knows already, so the only sin is in obscuring the truth from me, His servant, who can do nothing but help you," Martyn explained.

"Got you good." Hegel sniggered at the dour Manfried.

"So what was it, Hegel?" Martyn asked.

"Yeah, what was it?" Manfried said.

"I, uh, that is," Hegel's nerve slackened as he glanced from eager priest to cross brother, "sometimes, I get, well, spooked bout things."

Manfried chortled. "That how you's gonna put it?"

"How'd you put it?" snapped Hegel.

"Got the Witches' Sight," Manfried explained. "Touched in the head."

"Ain't like that!" Hegel protested.

"Witches' Sight, Hegel?" Martyn asked, again dreadfully uncomfortable to be seated between the two.

"More like, I dunno, a feelin I get. When somethin don't wash." Hegel fumbled with the words like an unrepentant heretic trying to recite the Lord's Prayer.

"A feeling, Hegel?" said Martyn.

"Like my soul knows somethin's gonna happen fore it does, and when it does happen, my soul's always right."

"You mean you have an uncanny intuition?" Martyn asked. "Have you *done* anything to be granted this ability?"

"Prays like the rest a us." Manfried would be damned before allowing anyone, man or priest, to imply anything unsavory about his brother. "He gets his hunches same as us, only his is always right on mark, always just in time, and often enough to be called somethin other than hunches. A boon from Mary."

"Well," Martyn said. "Well."

"Wells make me think a shadowy holes," Manfried said, giving the hard-eye to Martyn.

"Ain't the beneficial nature proof enough the portents, mine and ours, is granted from on high?" Hegel insisted, looking to Martyn for encouragement.

"It certainly adds something to the discussion," Martyn stalled.

"Yeah, but what?" Manfried demanded.

"Er." Martyn brightened. "Yes. That is, I think you should see this as a gift from God. The ways of the Almighty are inscrutable, and as Manfried has pointed out, over-scrutinizing the cause when the result is beneficial does none of us any good. Likewise with our visions. Time will learn us if they were prophecy or simple nightmares, and then we will know and all our debate will have been for naught."

"Whatever they was, they weren't no nightmares," Manfried said with a shiver. "Those only get you in your sleep."

"We were awful weary them last few days," Hegel pointed out. "Besides, ain't nuthin come from arguin, like you always say."

They let the matter rest, each and all feeling more anxious about the matter than before. The road began switchbacking even more sharply as they descended to the foothills, and between sun and beer they felt warmer than they had in weeks. The following day they left the wood and began crossing the vast hills of the southern city-states.

The road stayed fairly level but at midday forked, leading them to stop the horses and curse long after Martyn begged them to desist. Then the heavy cloth hanging behind the bench parted and the woman leaned out between Martyn and Manfried. She wore a purple veil over her face and her dress seemed pristine for having been on her person as long as their sweaty attire had been on theirs. She sniffed twice, fluttering her veil, and pointed to the left-hand fork. Even Manfried found this disquieting, but they set off again, traveling late into the dusk before breaking in a grassy field beside the road.

The weather struck them as balmy even when the wind rushed over them, and the vast hills coated in underbrush were but ant-mounds to the Brothers. They drank and ate and set off at dawn, and followed that pattern for several more days. Twice they crossed other roads that might have led them astray but she always appeared and counseled them on their course. Small towns appeared, then larger villages, and at one of these they spent a night, arguing and bartering with various functionaries until a consensus was reached.

Of those living in the town the barber alone spoke their language worth a damn, and he traded them a modest heap of ancient, disfigured coins for their smallest grave-found ring. Even after they gave a few coins back to that same barber in exchange for being treated their purse still had a little jingle to it, so they purchased clean clothes, had their weapons banged straight by the smith, left their horses with the farrier, secured lodging, and, when the priest disappeared for a time, secured a small pouch of unseasonably early belladonna berries to crush and smear on blades or drop in food, depending on what the situation dictated. Manfried used reason and vague threats but could not coax the woman to leave the wagon, but otherwise they each achieved everything they intended that night and felt rejuvenated the next morning.

XV
Prophets of the Schism

Men gathered around the Grossbarts at breakfast to hear where they had been and what they had seen, but even the priest was reluctant to discuss their adventures. They were indeed on the correct road to Venezia, and against the farrier's insistence to let the horses rest another day they set out before noon. The good food cheered them immensely, and the wheel of cheese Hegel had demanded of the innkeeper would go nicely with the cured pork Manfried had secured from a farmer.

Martyn's crossbow wound had not festered but the barber bound it in a sling, giving him an excuse to indulge in more of the Brothers' beer. They passed several farms before the road arced down into the plains, their wagon bouncing now from the speed instead of the rough trail. After splashing through several creeks they came upon a small wooden bridge spanning a river, and slowed to maneuver across the dodgy structure.

Across the river Clement and Innocent squatted in the tall grass on one side of the road with Urban on the other, arrows notched in their bows. Having drawn the short straw, Benedict hid under the bridge on the opposite bank. He had argued for hacking through the supports but the rest advised that such an action would result in their spoils following the horses and bridge into the drink. Word had come from the farrier's apprentice Vittorio just in time, for as they decided on their plan and settled into hiding the wagon appeared up the road.

The horses slowed to a stop a short distance from the bridge, and the three men on the bench appeared to be holding council. Clement murmured that they were close enough to fire but Innocent urged him to be patient. After a pause two of the men squirmed around and entered the wagon's interior. Crawling forward, Urban saw one of them reappear and hoist a barrel onto the seat beside the remaining man. This fellow again vanished behind the tarp covering the mouth of the wagon, but when the vehicle began moving forward Urban signaled his anxious comrades across the road that everything still looked favorable.

Following Hegel's assertion that something stank ahead and the Grossbarts' subsequent abandoning of the reins to Martyn, the priest broke into a fierce sweat. The Brothers generously set the beer barrel beside him to allay his worry but it hardly helped. The shallow yet quick river shimmered under the sun but Martyn felt only the wind stirring the grass and his habit, and he nervously tried to spy movement in the grass ahead. Without any options, he prayed and let the horses take charge, lazily clipping forward.

Hearing hoofbeats, Benedict moved to the side of the bridge, ready to burst out from underneath and scramble up behind the wagon. The horses reached the river but a sharp twang came from up the bank and something splashed in the water behind him. Spinning around, he scanned the riverside but saw only the leaning reeds and the clouds overhead. The wagon tramped above him, rocking the entire bridge as it slowly crossed the river. Rushing out from under the side, he failed to notice the crossbow bolt that had narrowly missed his neck bobbing rapidly away down the current.

When the horses were almost across the small bridge Innocent shouted, "Stop where you are!"

"I'm a priest!" Martyn shrieked with decidedly more fear in his voice than he intended.

"That means you'll do as we say, yes?" said Innocent, and the three brigands left their hiding places in the grass.

Their appearance—and their physical appearance in particular—impeded Martyn's heart of its usual pace. While wild-stained, their white robes were unmistakably modeled after those of the Pontiff, and above their plain cloth masks perched hats that amounted to blasphemy. Indignation stirred within the weary priest, and he shakily stood on the bench.

"Sacrilege!" Martyn trembled with fury. "You dare?"

"Easy on, old man," Clement called, aiming his bow at Martyn while Urban and Innocent flanked the wagon.

"Mockery of he who rules on earth?!" Phlegm rained down on the bored horses.

"Can't very well all have the same name!" said Urban. "So let's say those who have ruled, what?"

"We're the Road Popes," Innocent said from the other side of the wagon, "and as a priest, you'd best defer to our wisdom."

"Or face excommunication!" Clement hooted, his arms shaking from the strain of holding his bow notched.

"Death," raged Martyn, "death *has* come for you, blasphemers!"

"We'll just have the coin you're carrying and not worry about any of that, if you aren't opposed," Innocent responded.

"The other two are inside," Urban called over the wagon to his allies, and then to the wagon itself, "Come on out now, hop quick or we'll set you on fire!"

Innocent stayed with Clement near the front while Urban moved to the rear, training his bow on the tarp-covered entrance and waiting for Benedict, who had just gained the bridge. The last pope ran toward them, but something about his hunched-over gait prompted Urban to glance back. He did so just in time to see Benedict stop, his robe falling open and a crossbow stabbing out. Only then did Urban notice the copper beard jutting from under the mask.

Disguised in the costume of the man he had just murdered, Hegel shot the pope staring at him directly in the gut. Urban slipped backward and toppled off the bridge, dropping his weapon and howling as he fell the short distance to the river. Innocent turned to fire at Hegel but the bolt Manfried issued from the shallows beneath the bridge struck the bandit under his armpit, tearing through muscle and spearing his heart. Innocent's arrow took wing as his corpse fell, Providence guiding it to strike the half-empty barrel beside Martyn on the bench. The already teetering stash of booze toppled onto the bridge and rolled toward the edge.

With Clement left alone on the road, the Grossbarts' plan became complicated when their passenger's song emerged from the wagon. Martyn screamed at Clement, who responded to the chaos by shooting the priest. Hegel charged around the side of the wagon, clumsily withdrawing his pick from the baggy robes. Manfried saw the beer barrel splash into the water beside him and dove after even though he could not swim.

Slumped on the wooden seat, Martyn moaned and bled, the arrow riveting his previously good arm to the back of the bench. Through watery, squinted eyes he saw Pope Stephen the Sixth— or was it the Seventh?—drop his bow and draw a sword, then Formosus leaped from under the horses and they did battle. Stephen went defensive but Formosus's charge was too quick, and the papal imposter fell to the road under the force of the attack.

His sword arm under Hegel's boot, Clement screamed for mercy. Hegel gave it to him in the form of his pick, skewering the bandit's elbow thrice in quick succession. The third time Hegel left the pick embedded in the mangled arm and snatched Clement's wrist, tugging until the pope's forearm came free and blood misted their faces. Clement went mad with pain and Hegel simply went mad.

"You goddamn heretic!" Hegel shouted, stomping the dying man's jaw. "What you get! What you get, you mecky asshole! Think we's gonna let some fuckin popes keep us out a Gyptland?! Speak that blasphemy now!"

His mask bright red and dripping, Clement lunged up as if to bite Hegel's boot, which impressed the Grossbart enough that he hefted his pick and drove it into the pope's chest, putting a wet, thrashing end to his agony. Tearing off his own ridiculous mask and hat, Hegel turned to his brother, but to his surprise saw only Martyn limp on the bench. An instant later he noticed the music flowing out of the wagon and a horrible, cold sensation soaked his soul.

Manfried had floundered a bit before his feet found mud and he righted himself, wading after the barrel. Before he moved out from under the bridge the barrel reached the center of the current and was whisked away downstream, vanishing around a bend. Manfried splashed toward the bank with the goal of freeing a horse and riding along the bank until he caught it. He had battled a demon for that barrel, and would fight another to keep it. Before he gained the shore, though, he saw the first pope to plunge off the bridge crawling out of the water down the bank.

Manfried knew that the barrel had not jumped off the coach of its own volition. Grinning, he advanced on the half-drowned, perforated Road Pope. Urban's mask and hat were gone, displaying a mildly ugly countenance twisted in agony. Manfried had faith Mary would catch the cask on a sandbar or inlet, granting him the time to twist the bastard's face a little more. Dragging him back into the river, Manfried held him under and wiggled the bolt protruding from his stomach until his mouth stopped bubbling. Only then did Manfried calm enough to hear the music, and his cruel smile became innocent.

Hegel watched Manfried pause over the drowned man, then drop to his knees, the water rushing over his shoulders. Then Manfried slumped forward, his long-haired pate resembling a mossy gray stone in the river. When he did not surface Hegel scrambled down the bank and ploughed into the current, fell, righted himself, fell again, then seized hold of his brother.

Seeing the man's face shimmer and vanish, replaced by her playful countenance, Manfried misplaced his usual wisdom. Her lips felt warm in the cool water, and he felt no shame or reluctance in his actions, even when he jabbed his tongue into hers. He felt a pressure rising in his chest, no doubt his heart swelling with joy, and he pressed harder against her. How she kept singing with her mouth thus occupied did not weigh on his mind.

Snatching a handful of silver, Hegel jerked his brother's head above water. Manfried struggled against him for a moment before blinking stupidly at his savior and vomiting water all over the both of them. His stomach jostled and sour, Hegel returned his brother's volley with his own rush of hot sick. Together they extricated themselves from the river and lay panting on the bank, neither noticing the song had ended.

"The Hell?" Hegel demanded, watching Manfried's victim bob away.

"Eh?"

"What was you doin?"

"What you think? Killin that bitchswine."

"Yeah? Needed to get a closer look?"

"Gotta make sure." Manfried blinked. "Others done the same?"

"Yeah. That priest got stuck though."

"Badly?"

"How should I know? I was fishin you out."

"I's fit, let's see bout the priest."

The arrow had embedded in Martyn's forearm, blood pooling on the bench, and the priest moaned vengeance in his ill-gotten sleep. Hegel's search of the two bodies not given to the river yielded nothing, but Manfried fared better down the road where four horses were tethered in a copse of trees. In a saddle-bag he discovered a small wheel of cheese wrapped in the same yellow cloth as the wheel he had gotten from the inn that very morning. He led the horses back to the wagon to strategize with Hegel.

"Think we got ratted?" Hegel asked.

"Possible."

"That dingy cricket under the bridge *did* bear resemblance to most a them townies."

"I say we hoof on back, sniff round and see if we been cow-arded out," said Manfried.

"Yeah, can't suffer no traitorous churls to keep on bein trai-torous. And sides that, priest needs that barber or he'll bleed out by the look a his wound."

"True words."

They reached the town gate before shut-in and immediately went to the barber's, the newly acquired horses tethered to the back of the wagon. The man's son answered their knocking, and the scrawny teenager's attempts to keep them at the door were thwarted. The Grossbarts carried the groaning priest inside and laid him on the table where the startled barber sat eating his din-ner. The memory of their ring shone in his memory, though, so he went straight to work.

Hegel took the Road Popes' horses to the farrier while Man-fried went to the inn. The farmers turned and silenced at his arrival, Manfried striding in with a papal hat in one hand and his mace in the other. The innkeeper hurriedly offered him a tankard, which Manfried exchanged the hat for. Draining the ale and turning to the curious men, he slammed down the cup.

"There's holy blood on your hands," Manfried told them, but

they did not respond until the innkeeper translated. This drew murmurs but no outright protests or admittances. After giving them another few moments to own up, "Priest might die cause a someone in this town. You give'em to us, we call it square. If not, the wrath a Mary'll descend on all a yous."

The innkeeper turned scarlet but shouted Manfried's meaning in Italian. This got them going. Several men made for Manfried but were restrained by others. The innkeeper slunk off somewhere, and, unbeknownst to all, Vittorio, the farrier's apprentice who had tipped off his cousins to the Grossbarts' worth, waited far out of town for his share of the profit. The innkeeper reappeared with a snarling mastiff on a rope, and shouted at Manfried.

"Get to Hell, you crazy sonuvabitch!" The innkeeper advanced. "You're not out quick, I put the dog on you!"

"That's just fine," said Manfried, backing out into the street. "I see how it is."

"How it is, you stupid turnip-eater, is you crazy! No one here hurt no priest, now go back to screwing that ugly brother of yours!"

Slamming the door, Manfried heard the innkeeper say something to the assembled and then the inn exploded in laughter and cheers. Before returning to the barber he circled the perimeter of the town's wall, his grimace gradually tilting upward. Satisfied, he made his way through the dusty street to the barber, and caught sight of his brother returning from his task.

"Farrier's full a what his beasts leave," Hegel announced. "Got some coinage out'em for them popes' ponies. Still wouldn't spill, though, actin like he didn't understand me."

"Surprised?"

"Course not. Anyone spend that much time around beasts' bound to be shifty. Saw in his eye he recognized them horses."

"That squint-faced lad round? We could beat somethin out a him."

"Prentice? Nah, I didn't see'em."

"More's the pity. No matter, cause I got all the answers we need from the inn."

"Yeah?"

"Yeah."

"Well?"

"They's all culpable," pronounced Manfried.

"Admitted?"

"Same as. Laughed at us, threatened us, and accused us a havin relations."

"Well, we's—"

"Sexual relations."

"Oh. Oh! Come on then." Hegel made for the inn.

"Hold your wrath a touch." Manfried diverted him toward the barber. "Judgment implies forethought in order to judge, and they's definitely gettin some judgment on'em tonight. Startin with that mecky barber."

"Reckon he's in on it?"

"Can't be sure. And when you can't, errin on the side a caution ain't errin at all."

"Reckon them berries he sold us is deadly poison like he claimed?"

"He's a liar he'll burn in the kilns below, and if he ain't his reward'll come sooner than he's expectin," said Manfried.

Martyn slept on the floor beside the fire, his arms slung against his chest instilling him with a pious air his snoring might have otherwise deprived him of. Cipriano, the tall, dark-haired and doe-eyed barber, sat back to his cold meal, his equally gaunt boy Paolo wiping the blood from the floor. The priest would live, praise God, but Cipriano's fingers were sore and shaky and Paolo was quite upset. The young man became infinitely more so when the door banged open and the Grossbarts advanced on the two of them.

"Good news for the father," Cipriano said, setting down his knife. Manfried punched him in the chest, knocking him off his stool while Hegel snatched Paolo by the neck and hoisted the lad onto the table. Crouching over the terrified surgeon, Manfried held up his dagger so the firelight glanced off it into Cipriano's eyes.

"You got more a them berries you sold us?" Manfried demanded.

"What this about?" Cipriano managed.

"You got'em or not?"

"Paolo," the barber said, followed by a string of foreign-talk. Then in proper-speak, "Let him fetch them."

Hegel released the frightened boy, who rooted about in a corner full of boxes and bags. From the bottom of a chest he withdrew a clay jar with a wooden stopper. Paolo brought it to his prone father but trembled so badly it slipped and shattered on the floor, dark purple berries rolling everywhere. Hegel cuffed him and gathered a handful, then guided Paolo back to a chair. He stood behind the boy, awaiting his brother's word.

"You have them, now leave us be!" pleaded Cipriano.

"Thing is," said Manfried, "this burg done sold us out. Set us up. Handed us over to bandits."

"Ain't Christian," Hegel added.

"Wasn't me!" Cipriano gasped.

"Neither here nor there," said Manfried. "See, you also sold us this so-called poison, chance lookin for a little a your own profit fore them popes got the rest?"

"What? So-called? Popes? The belladonna didn't work?"

"Dunno, ain't tried it yet. Hegel!"

"Ready, brother."

"What do you mean to do?" Cipriano almost sat up but remembered the blade hovering over his face.

"A little test," said Manfried. "We feed your boy there some berries, and if he croaks we's square, and if he don't you's munchin iron."

"What?! Please, no, I beg, I beg!" Cipriano degenerated into his native tongue, forgetting the blade and clinging to Manfried's knife arm. His confused son also began crying at whatever he said, prompting Hegel to cuff the boy again.

"Shit damn," Hegel spit into Paolo's hair. "I don't think he's bluffin."

"Me neither," Manfried sighed. "And neither him nor the kid come at us with a blade like old Heinrich's murder-minded wifey all them days back, so mercy it is. Quit womanin and get up, barber."

"Thank you," the man blubbered. "My boy, my life, oh thank you."

"Hell, we ain't bad men," Hegel said, dumping out a sack of the doctor's herbs and filling it with the spilled berries.

"Now where's that ring we exchanged you for them marks we spent?" Manfried asked, dagger still in hand.

The doctor stumbled over beside the fire, lifted a loose stone, and withdrew the jewelry. Meanwhile Manfried retrieved the barber's small pouch of coins from a nearby shelf, from which Cipriano had paid them for the ring in the first place. Manfried tucked it into his own bag. Then the Grossbarts tied father and son together on the floor, the younger shuddering and gaping, the elder issuing gratitude on top of gratitude.

"Startin now," Hegel announced, "you's straight with the Grossbarts. How much we owe you for the priest?"

"Eh?" Cipriano blinked up at them and named a small figure.

"Done. And them berries?"

He named another, slightly higher, figure.

"Done twice. Pay'em, Manfried."

Manfried withdrew the same purse he had pocketed, counted out the coins on the table, and held up one extra. "This is for bein honest with us. And this," he jingled the pouch before dumping the rest of its contents on the table, "is for bein honest with those what come after lookin to run down the Grossbart name. We ain't thieves and we ain't killers, we's just good men been done wrong."

"You gave us a price yesterday for this." Hegel held the ring up to the light. "Was it fair, or was it a little light?"

"Fair," Cipriano gasped, his mind unable to process what was unfolding.

"Good." Hegel put the ring back under the stone while Manfried counted the appropriate number of coins back into the pouch.

"You'd do best by mindin your business tonight," Manfried informed them. "Gather some buckets for your own roof stead a tendin others."

"He's talkin for real, like," Hegel explained, hoisting Martyn over his shoulder. "And if we find out after you's runnin lies or them berries ain't proper, wager on seein us again fore the devils do."

"Mind your father," Manfried said, gently kicking Paolo's chin. "Honest man's rarer than what's under that hearthstone."

The portly militiaman wasted no time in opening the gate for them, being engaged in discourse with one of the farmers from the inn when they rode out. They stopped the wagon a ways up the road and led it off into the grass behind a hill, where they tethered the horses to a stump and crept back in the thickening dusk. Moving around the wall, they came to the spot behind the inn's stable that Manfried had marked by sliding a stick between the slats, and here Hegel helped raise his brother.

The mud of the pigpen broke Manfried's fall and he quickly threw the rope over to his brother. Hegel had reached the top of the wall when someone approached through the gloom with a rush-light. The lad caught a glimpse of silver beard before the owner's mace bashed him between the eyes. Saving the spitting light from the mud, Manfried gave the stableboy a kick for good measure before creeping behind the inn with the little oil they had left.

Hegel darted across the thoroughfare, the nape of his neck telling him he had not been seen. The farrier's building had no lights lit, which suited the grave-eyed Grossbart fine. Splashing oil liberally on the wooden door, he applied even more to the stable. He would have preferred to do the farrier himself but it could not be helped. He chipped away at his flint for several minutes, sweating as the straw refused to catch. When it did the fire leaped up the walls of the building so quickly he barely had time to dash across the street before the cry went up.

The rushlight made Manfried's task far easier, and when he saw Hegel's smiling in the dark he touched off the inn. It went up even faster, and before the Grossbarts scrambled up the pig-fence and over the wall the whole town had come alive with screams. They ran fire-blinded to the road, tripping and stumbling the entire way back to the wagon. Martyn had awoken and gave a shout when they appeared before they pelted him with reprimands.

Regaining the road took time in the dark but when they rounded the hill the glow of the burning village showed them the way. Martyn shook his head to clear it, and looked curiously at the Brothers. They said nothing but their smiles told a dark tale indeed. Too muddled of mind to comprehend anything other than that his right arm now hurt far worse than his left, he asked for spirits instead of answers. Manfried held a bottle of schnapps to the priest's lips until he gagged and spit booze on the three of them. The Brothers joined him, the wagon sporadically drifting off the road. Midnight found them crossing the papal bridge, toasting the memory of Formosus.

XVI
The Gaze of the Abyss

Blubbering and mewling to itself, the pestilential spirit the Brothers had burned out of Ennio paced in the rat hole, the rodent it wore like an exceptionally filthy hairshirt wringing its paws in frustration. Providence had guided its drifting form to the rat it now possessed but the agony of the flames had diminished its power too much for it to make another immediate attempt to enter one of the Grossbarts. Worse yet, the dispicable Brothers somehow seemed immune to its pestilence, and now they were gone, fled, beyond reach. What men would linger in such a place, after all? With the rat already fading and winter driving any other potential hosts to ground save for the few fleas likewise riding the rodent the demon knew it would soon be alone again, and then—it dared not think it, squeaking with fear and fury.

That first night in the rat it had spent digging even deeper into the hole lest the wicked orb penetrate its sanctuary, but now it looked up into the darkness, proceeding with caution up the tunnel. It smelled the ethereal smoke of starfire and tasted the shine of moonlight, and then it ran, ran as fast as it could, out of the hole and out of the house and into the winter-smothered town. It made for the blackened, desiccated remains of the alehouse but of course they were gone, fled, beyond reach, and the tiniest sigh left its snout. It had known they would run, clearly they were not that stupid, they . . .

They had not run. They were that stupid. The demon saw the faint glow of a campfire behind the monastery, in the very churchyard where they had first seen one another. It could not believe its luck and rolled in the snow, cheeping with delight. The short road from town to cemetery would seem many leagues under its current legs, however, and so it quickly hopped up and set to trotting back the way it had come the night before when it had possessed the hog, jumping from hoofprint to hoofprint wherever it could.

The horses whinnied but it paid them no mind, intent on its purpose, and then it saw him, a Grossbart sitting before a fire. It charged, its teeth bared in an approximation of a grin, and then Nicolette snatched it up. The demon felt fingers close around its rat, and before it could escape the rodent the ground vanished and the stars swirled as it hurtled through the cold air, dragged by an invisible arm high above the clouds. Biting and scratching at nothing, it could not fathom what had happened and squeaked its frustration into the blackness. The moon sank and the night waned and it knew dawn would soon arrive, and the demon was afraid.

Then trees appeared below it, and a small field, and a hut. The rat crashed into a snowdrift and felt the spectral fingers release it. Nicolette shuddered as she slipped back into her skin, every bone and muscle sore from a night locked in reverie beside the sleeping farmer as her secret self flew uninhibited by flesh and bone. Shaking out her limbs, she hurried to the door to welcome the guest she had spirited away over the mountains.

The witch stepped outside, where the first streaks of light began catching in the snow. Planting herself before the door, she smiled and fished in her rags for the bottle. The rat scurried toward her but before it pounced she raised her arms with an oath and the creature scurried back as if struck, pacing on its hind legs and staring at the door behind her.

"No soul's lost if it isn't given," she hissed. "I won't have you wearing him like a simple glove. I've read of you and yours, and know no skin but that what carries a soul will keep you when the darkness goes. Deep as the wood be, dare you risk a stray beam touching your tail? Or I might go in after, and drag you into the light from whatever hole you've crept into. No birds sing and no beasts scamper, only the snow and you and I and he inside, who hates them as much as the both of us."

The rat squealed with rage but trailed off as light brushed the laden branches of the wood behind them.

"Quick as sin, make yourself into this." Nicolette held the bottle toward the creature, who hesitated no longer. The rat rolled on its back, a hazy miasma escaping its ass and mouth as it spasmed. The yellow mist coalesced on its belly, a final frosty breath leaving its snout. Then the smoke appeared to suck into the fur, leaving not a trace on the wind. The tiny flea hurtled toward the witch but Nicolette expected this and caught it in the bottle, jamming a wax stopper into place.

Heinrich awoke at sunset, his guts and legs and skin and even his lanky hair sore and weak. She sat humming beside him, and in the firelight he saw how swollen she was of belly and breast. She tossed another handful of herbs into the blaze, making the room fill with noxious smoke.

"They'll be out of the mountains within a week, and they've met another enemy of yours," Nicolette murmured, tapping the bottle balanced atop her belly.

Heinrich rubbed his eyes. "I have no other enemies."

"What will you offer?" She turned her wrinkled countenance to him. "What have you that could be turned against those hated Brothers?"

Vengeance knows neither remorse nor faith, and Heinrich

answered without hesitation, "My flesh is devoted to their misery, and my soul."

"All that is needed." She smirked. "You would share your body with a demon?"

"Eh?" Heinrich tried to remember the words of the priest and failed, instead recalling Brennen's ashen face in the mud. His mind jerked back to the present and he eyed the crone. "You're a witch, then?"

"And one that despises those Brothers. The demon does as well, I assure you of that. Would you become host for it?"

Even a few days ago the thought would have proved anathema to Heinrich but between the priest refusing to help or even condone him and now this so-called witch offering succor, he worried his lip. Demons and witches alike could be tricked, he knew, but he doubted he possessed the wits for such deception. It occurred to him that he would have died without her help the night before, and she might still take his life if he displeased her. In such an event the Grossbarts would never be his, and his failure would be eternal.

"You would need to make room inside that cramped skin, a space as large as your immortal spirit." Nicolette saw his indecision and patted his hand. "I too am prepared to give all that I may, for I loved my husband more than I love my life, and they took him from me just as they took your bride and children."

"My soul, then," Heinrich decided, remembering Gertie thrashing in the mire, dying in agony. God and all His saints had stayed hidden that day, as they did on this. If He wants my soul He will step in now, thought the miserable farmer, but nothing happened. "Summon what demons you may, and inform them my soul is theirs if it means I am the Grossbarts' downfall."

"Unlike others of my faith I lack the knowledge to conjure demons," Nicolette said with a smile. "Fortune's favored us, though, for in spying on the Grossbarts I have discovered one not yet banished to its formless realm, one whose goal is shared by you and me." The flea hurled itself against its prison but Nicolette did not open the bottle, instead continuing to barter with the too-willing yeoman. "That is its price, but we've not fixed mine."

"More than my flesh and spirit?" Heinrich snorted. "I have nothing else."

"Nothing save a father's love for his murdered children."

Heinrich eyes filled and he reached for his knife to cut out her horrible tongue.

"I would have you be a father again, Heinrich," she whispered, stroking her stomach. It pulsated at her touch. "My babes will require a guardian as they grow, a guide to bring them to the Grossbarts."

"Carry wee ones over winter roads? I'll never watch another child suffer, witch, not even to see those Brothers die."

Heinrich had witnessed horrors great enough that he felt himself righteous in accepting his own damnation without regret, but still his bowels twisted in fear at Nicolette's throaty laugh. "You will not need to carry them," she chuckled. "But when you flag they will carry you. Yes, and hunt for you and do all that obedient children should."

"I doubt that. New babes do naught but cry."

"Doubt? Doubt! We'll assuage those, dear master of turnips." Nicolette groaned, her stomach rippling. "I'll free you both, just give your word!"

"You have it." Heinrich stared into the fire. "Give me my revenge and you may take anything I've got that those Brothers haven't yet stolen."

The bottle slipped onto the floor and broke, the flea leaping onto Heinrich. Its body, bloated with even the most diminished form of the evil it carried, popped when it reached his shoulder, a foul golden smoke drifting into his nostrils. Heinrich began to cough and gag, feeling as if a white-hot wire pushed through his sinuses and down his throat. His nose dripped black phlegm and when his boiling guts finally calmed he saw Nicolette had fallen out of her chair, her massive belly heaving.

"Into the wood," she gasped, "find what they buried. Don't return without it, but dare not touch it or such mischief as even I know not will occur. Tongs!" she wailed, slapping the iron tool beside the hearth and arching her back, viscous fluid gushing from between her legs.

Snatching up the tongs and hurrying out of the shack, Heinrich stood panting in the snow. Setting off into the wood, he did not notice that the feverish sweat coursing off him hissed instead of freezing when it dropped onto the ground, nor did he realize his vision was better in the dark wood than it ever had been in the sunny fields of his home. The pain in his sides came in waves but he followed the stream with purpose, almost smelling their stink, almost seeing their snow-shrouded footprints.

Eventually he left the stream, the spoiled-milk stink of witchcraft growing stronger until he picked his way through the underbrush into a small clearing. In the center of it lay a patch of disturbed earth where the snow did not fall, although it lay heaped up to Heinrich's knees everywhere else. Digging in the frozen dirt with the tongs, he saw something shining in what early light penetrated the icy bower. Holding the pelt at the end of the tongs, he marched back through the woods, for the first time reflecting on his superior senses and the impossible nature of the last day's events.

The sun crept farther up as he found his way back to her shack, only a finger of smoke rising from his destination. Stepping over the dead rat by the door he went inside, calling out to the witch. She weakly raised her hand from the floor, two shadowy bulges nursing at her chest.

Approaching the prone woman, even in his madness he could

not control his nausea. After he had expelled what few turnips his belly held, he again stared at the abominations. They were brown and slick, easily twice the size of normal babies, and they chewed rather than suckled on her flabby breasts, milk mingling with blood on the wet floor.

Heinrich snatched a log from beside the fire but before he could act she bellowed at him, "Leave them be! I've done the same to their siblings, leave them be!"

Curious despite his revulsion, Heinrich tossed the wood onto the hearth. Through her agony she continued to instruct him: "Give them the sack hanging above you, it'll take them off me long enough. Long enough!"

Heinrich shakily took down the satchel, and she shrieked, "Tear it open! Spread them on the floor!"

Following her instructions, he opened the bag and dumped out its contents. Hundreds, if not thousands, of tiny teeth scattered on the slimy stones, and the two newborns turned from their meal. Crawling off her, they began rolling in the loose teeth, and while Heinrich watched the small white pegs sank into the surface of their skin, forming new snapping mouths on chests and legs, arms and backs.

"Follow the road through the mountains," she gasped, her gory chest spewing blood, milk, and loose skin. "But do not follow them to the city, for men will burn you alive. Shun even the smallest hamlet, stay to the wilds and journey southeast past the dwellings of men, into the desert. Farther than those ruins that men call holy, where fools battle for stones and dirt until the world ends, always south! That is where you will catch them, in the desert of dead kings."

"Are they—" Heinrich swallowed, seeing the babes' faces were umber skulls, impenetrable pits where eyes should rest. "What are they?"

"Homunculi to inspire envy in all others, my own addition to an ancient recipe." She motioned to a bound pile of parchment, which the illiterate yeoman did not recognize as a text. "A gift from a traveler, long gone. One is Magnus, the other Brennen! But hurry, they return to me!"

True enough, the baby-shaped monstrosities crawled to her feet, their numerous maws snatching out chunks of meat and skin, blood dampening Heinrich's knees where he knelt beside her head. She wailed and he shivered, averting his eyes. Her hands pawed at his face, her voice ragged as she urgently went on.

"They will serve you well, if you do as I say, but hurry." Her eyes were rolling wildly, her grimacing mouth struggling to form words. "Oh my love, my charcoal-man, my Magnus! It was yours first and always, purest and first, and all this for you, I'll bear it! They'll pay for your murder, over and over!"

Heinrich raised the tongs to offer the pelt, hoping to slow their feast, but again she wailed, "No! Not yet! They need it or they'll melt away in rain, but not yet! First my ears, then my eyes, then my nose, and that split in twain! My heart! Half a heart, last!"

"What?!" Heinrich squeezed her hand with his. "What do you mean?"

"One each," she gurgled, her young moving up her thighs, "one ear each, to hear your commands, and so in Hell I can hear the Grossbarts scream. One eye each, to hunt their quarry, and so I can see the Grossbarts die. Half a nose, to smell them out and inhale the last breath breathed by Grossbart lungs. Half a heart to live, to live despite all wounds! My tongue—" But her instructions turned to a scream as they devoured the region whence they had so freshly birthed.

"Your tongue?" Heinrich said to himself but she ended her scream and resumed her frantic orders.

"My tongue," blood bubbled out around it, "my tongue. Tongue."

"Cut in half, so each might speak! Yes?"

She either tried to laugh or to moan, the gurgling making it impossible to say which. "No. My tongue. You eat. Or. They'll eat. You. Alive."

They were spread across her chest and stomach, their mouths chewing in tandem. With unsteady hands Heinrich set the tongs and pelt on a chair and drew his dagger. He sliced off her ears, bloodying his hands. When he held them out a skeletal face snapped near his fingers, but inspiration took hold and, maneuvering around the side, he pressed the gruesome flap of flesh against the side of its head. The muddy surface sank in and the ear stuck fast, Heinrich hastening to give its brother the other ear.

They had almost reached her previously skinned sternum, and Heinrich plunged in his dagger to steal her heart before they could. Entrails wound into their prodigious orifices while he dug past her collarbone, the mix of fever and confusion cheating his act of its deserved horror. Sinking his finger into the muscle, he cut it free just as teeth dug into his wrist. Slapping the creature off him, he left a handprint on its exposed but malleable skull.

Dropping the heart, he carved off her small nose and plucked out her eyes, taking their stringy moorings with them. They were almost to her throat, the crunching of bones drawing his eyes to her lower body. Nothing remained, not even a speck of marrow, and he saw their hands now seemed firmer, more defined. He nearly popped the first eye sliding it into place, and the clay socket tightened around his fingers. The yellow eye dilated and focused on him as he gave one to its twin, and it stretched out a palm split by a snarling maw.

The nose proved difficult but after nicking his fingers and shaving flecks of skin away he managed to split it through the septum, a nostril on each side. These he attached quickly as they moved away, each going down one of her arms. Tearing through her heart, he approached the first, unsure where to place it in the nest of feeding mouths. Moving behind it, he saw an unoccupied space between two enormous sets of teeth, her devoured bones forming jaws even as he watched, allowing it to chew harder and faster. When he pressed his hand toward its back the clay split to reveal a small cave, into which he thrust the hunk of meat. The back closed around his fist but he yanked it out, seeing the heart began to beat and bleed in its new home.

The second had no such vacant area, its entire back snapping and snarling, tongues of mud staining the shiny teeth. Desperately he moved to its front, the last of her fingers disappearing into the mouth on its face. He placed the heart in its stomach, gibbering maws in place of breasts thwarting any effort to place it higher. This scrap also began beating, and the two smaller mouths faded back into the surface, the teeth migrating to form a mouth protecting the heart in its belly. Heinrich fell back, relieved to be done.

They had finished the arms and both scuttled toward the head when Heinrich realized he had forgotten something. Kicking it away, he scooped it up and went for her mouth. They were making for his legs, hundreds of teeth chattering intently as they neared further meat. He cut her tongue free and dropped the bloody lump just as the mouths found his feet.

The chorus of grunts the babes made as they fought over the head made him light-headed, and dropping the dagger he snatched the tongs. He backed toward the door as her skull cracked open, and bit into her tongue. It squirmed in his mouth and he gagged and coughed, the appendage wriggling through his fingers. Crouching to retrieve it, he saw the abominations stand and walk toward him, dozens of smiling mouths turned in his direction. He jumped away and tripped over the stoop, falling outside into the slush.

Standing and backing away, he chewed the writhing tongue,

the flesh attempting to squirm up his throat even as he swallowed. The children followed him out into the morning light, each now grown as tall as his waist. One spotted the rat carcass and scooped it up but the other advanced on Heinrich. He shoved the rest of the tongue into his mouth and choked on it, trying to force it down. The child-thing leaped at him and with a swallow he fell backward, holding up his hands and screaming.

"Stop!"

To his amazement, they did. The monstrosity had landed on his chest but rather than chewing the mouths remained shut, its solitary eye blinking innocently at him. The other ran on all fours to its brother, nuzzling its soft skull against Heinrich's chin.

He scrambled to his feet, knocking the one on his chest to the ground. Its mouths opened and began bawling in union, its eye filling with tears. He saw the indentation of his hand on its cheek and pity consumed him; he knew at once this must be Brennen and the other Magnus. Retrieving the tongs, he picked the shimmering pelt out of the mud and offered it to them. They fell upon it instantly, growling and snarling as each tried to wrestle it from his brother.

The hide tore in half and Heinrich witnessed their final transformation. Steam rose from them as the pelt came alive and adhered to their bodies, the boys rolling in the snow and wailing from every mouth. Heinrich noticed Magnus's face had acquired two more round little eyes from the dead rat, although they had grown significantly larger in the boy's face. One was set in the appropriate socket, the other bulging out in place of a second nostril. The strange skin spread over their clay flesh, and their myriad tongues turned pink and wet as they frothed and spit. Their limbs lengthened and twisted, pudgy hands now furry claws, knees snapping backward and feet lengthening.

The boys wailed even when they had ceased smoking and twisting, and Heinrich knelt between them, stroking their coats.

Unlike those who had worn the pelt in earlier ages neither had fully abandoned his human shape, but neither did they retain a singularly human appearance.

Magnus's black fur covered every bit except the mouths peppering his small body, and while his legs were distinctly rodent-like he managed to stand and walk like a man. His third eye glistened with snot dribbling from his disfigured shard of a nose. In place of his left hand he wielded the giant snout of a rat, its nose snuffling, its growl emanating from every maw save the proper one.

Brennen's coat shone brown and red and white and every other color his twin lacked. Under his bristly hair the handprint on his face remained, finger-sized grooves sunk in over his empty eye socket and where the other nostril would be on a natural creature. His legs were less bowed than Magnus's but his arms and hands bulged with muscle, his long fingers sprouting hooked brown talons.

Heinrich took his boys into his arms until they stopped mewling, whispering his devotion to them. They horrified him, but not as much as he horrified himself, and with the marked difference that they were innocent. Their growling brought a smile to his lips and tears to his puffy eyes.

In fairness to his memory, the Heinrich who left the valley the next morning bore little resemblance, save the physical, to the yeoman who had shared his hearth with his plow horse on rainy nights before building the barn. Despair had yielded to optimistic loathing, an abiding conviction that they would locate the Grossbarts and enact their vengeance. Even when the wind cut and the snow swirled they were warm in the burrows Brennen dug, the twins tightly wedged in the blankets with their arms and legs wrapped around Heinrich, tickling him with countless kisses from uncounted mouths.

XVII
The Difficult Homecoming

Several days after besting the Road Popes, the Grossbarts and company found themselves arriving in Venezia long after dark.

"Real choice swap you rigged for us there," said Manfried, staring down the black canal where the skiff had vanished before the seasick Brothers could raise a fist to stop the boatmen. "A tidy wagon and four strong horses for a one-way trip to an island. Choice, my brother, choice."

"Mary's Sweetness, those cheats done cheated us," said Hegel when he regained his composure. "Pardon me for puttin my faith in my fellow fuckin man! When that mecky mung-gargler said slaves and a boat we all know he meant for the long term and not the short!"

"No matter," said Manfried.

"No matter?!"

"Nope, no matter at all." Manfried flashed his teeth. "I'll allow it might a been nice to keep the boat, but I had a witch-touch a my own on the ride over, meanin we's vindicated true at present, lack a wagon and boat notwithstandin."

"How's that?" Hegel screwed up his face more than nature already had.

"Figured it all went too smooth, yeah? So in such an event

as just transpired, I took me a precaution and left that bottle a apple-water in the boat."

"Why'd you do a thing like that?" asked Hegel, "so if and when they did rob us we'd be down a bottle besides?!"

"That hooch's most powerful fruity, yeah?" Manfried cracked his knuckles. "So I doubt when they find the bottle and set in they'll be tastin all a them barber's berries I mushed down in there. Didn't wanna waste'em all on an eventuality I wasn't lookin forward to or forcin, but I reckon there's enough in there to give'em just what's comin their way."

"Berries? You mean that poison?" Hegel smiled as he realized what his brother was about. "Clever as a crow, you are!"

Martyn swooned as he too understood what had unfolded, and his own part in it brought a massive weight pressing down on his chest. Being the only one of the three who spoke Italian he had quickly grasped that the men of Mertes—the river town across the lagoon from Venezia—intended to swindle the Grossbarts and he had done nothing to stop them, thinking it a fine come-uppance for the twins' arson of the neighboring village. Martyn realized he should have known the Grossbarts would turn the mischief into something worse, and had he but warned either party those four dishonest but likely not murderous boatmen would not be rowing away with a venomous jug of schnapps. His greed to reach a proper city and be done with the whole affair had blinded him, and the realization brought stinging remorse to the priest's eyes.

"Can't all be— Where's she goin?!" Manfried broke off mid-gloat as he noticed the woman disappear at the top of the stone steps leading away from the small dock.

"After the feedbag!" Hegel tore up the stairs with Manfried hot after him.

Cresting the stair, Hegel reeled backward and would have fallen had Manfried not been right behind him. The woman waited for them on a narrow road that sat like a ledge between the tall buildings and the canal. She tapped her foot in the most universal gesture imaginable but the Grossbarts, deciding she had no intention of flight, first went and retrieved their food, schnapps, and priest from the dock. Manfried helped Hegel lash the schnapps cask to his back and then hoisted the provisions.

Their pace and zeal greatly impeded, the trio gained the stairs where the woman waited. Despite the glow seen from the lagoon very few lights burned in this part of the city, and to frustrate them further clouds had blotted out the sky—clouds that appeared meaner than a riled Grossbart. True to its visage, the sky let them advance only a short distance before a deluge crashed down on them.

Canal and road meandered in their course, and then they saw a faint light spilling from a side road. While the woman waited in the road with her veiled face turned toward Heaven, the Grossbarts and Martyn stepped under the overhang of the covered alley. A campfire burned forty-odd paces down the tunnel, a small crowd squatting around it. Hegel and Martyn kept their eyes trained on this lot while Manfried stared at the woman, wondering how long he could bear the music of the rain alone.

"What say—" Hegel noticed his brother's distraction, and resolving to make good after his previous blunder regarding their passage, advanced on the fire alone. "All a yous, listen up! We's lookin for the Bar Goose."

Gray eyes under a filthy cowl flickered up from the fire, intrigued to be addressed in the barbaric tongue of the north.

"I'll say it once more," said Hegel, in no mood to be ignored. "Any a yous tell us where a man name a Bar Goose has his home you might find yourself better for the honesty."

The crutches were snatched and the gambit made.

Hegel turned back to Martyn and his brother to suggest they hurl the lot of rude beggars into the canal and commandeer their campfire. Then he noticed a loping figure had left the circle and was approaching him. Several others were lazily taking their feet, and Hegel put his hand on his pick.

"Barousse!" the beggar called, hurrying toward them. "Barousse!" again, followed by a string of foreign gibbering.

"He say Bar Goose?" Manfried asked his brother, turning back to the alley.

"And that he works for him," said Martyn, his eyebrows creasing.

"That what he said?" asked Hegel, a report of thunder deafening him.

"Barousse!" the man shouted again, and drawing closer, he spoke in their native language. "I am a humble servant of Barousse, how may I assist you gentlemen?"

The other beggars began moving as a pack down the alley, and they all took up the call of Barousse. These shouted that they too worked for Barousse, and they should be the ones to assist. Hegel drew his pick and Manfried his mace, which stopped the gang in their rag-swaddled tracks. An especially grimy old dodger braved their wrath and shoved the man who had originally addressed them.

"Don't trust that Arab cunny! *I* work for Barousse!" The new beggar shouted in passable German as his rival toppled into a puddle.

"Arab?" Hegel squinted through the rain and saw the first man's cowl had fallen away, revealing a dark complexion and a wispy red mustache. "You an Arab?"

"Through no fault of my own!" the Arab responded, standing wearily with the help of his crutches and then lashing out at his attacker with disarming speed. The Arab feigned a punch only to kick the man in the back of the knee, and the surprised Grossbarts saw at once that instead of the usual flesh-and-bone variety the Arab possessed a wooden leg. The usurper fell to the gutter with a shout, and the one-legged Arab broke one of his crutches over the man's back while balancing on the other.

"Come on, Arab!" Hegel laughed, marveling at their good fortune.

"Rest a yous gone." Manfried hefted his mace at the small mob. "Get shy right quick fore we get feisty on you."

The scrawny Arab pursed his lips in dismay at the loss of a crutch but his prone adversary's groans were a bit of recompense. Hegel and Manfried moved in on their guide to get their first gander at a real Arab. The fellow reeked like a sick sow's discharge, and Manfried took a healthy swig of schnapps to clear his mind and nose. The black-toothed Arab grinned at him, shuffling closer and reaching for the bottle. He knew enough to not request such boons from his betters but doubted these bristly bastards were that.

"Keep your stink to yourself," said Manfried, "lest you wanna lose a hand in the bargain."

"You think I…no, no, no, honest mistake, I would not presume, never, not once in all my life would I deign, in front of God and all, no, no, no." The Arab held up his stained palms defensively, the crutch protruding from his armpit.

"Where's the Goose roost?" Hegel asked.

"At his estate, I would imagine. Or is this a riddle? I do love—"

"Damn it, where's his house? Estate or whatnot." Hegel already regretted being taken in by the beggar, and vowed to Mary if he led them anywhere but to the Goose's nest he would throttle him slow.

"Perhaps we will wait out the storm?" The Arab peered around at the torrent obscuring the alley's mouth just behind them. "With your persuasion it is beyond the doubts of such as I that those miscreants could be enjoined to quit their fire to better allow our usage of it."

Martyn brightened and took a step forward but Hegel stepped in front of the priest, eager to be done with the whole affair. Shaking his head, which annoyed Manfried even more than it did Martyn, Hegel motioned the rank beggar closer still. Lowering his voice, he said curtly, "We's set to get there now-ish if it's all the same to you, friend."

"Hold a tic," Manfried muttered in their code, "warmin fore the fire mightn't—"

"No sense gettin warm just to get wet and cold again," Hegel cut him off. "Let's get to step."

"If we are away in the wet," the Arab sighed, "then let us away, for no boats will be found at this late and damp date, and by foot it is some distance. Back the way you have come, I fear."

Their guide led them back into the street, pausing beside their thoroughly drenched female companion. Under Manfried's careful scrutiny he tarried no further and set off in his strange gait. Passing the dock where they had landed, the Arab led them only a short distance down the street before turning inland—or so they thought. After winding through several narrow, dripping alleys they appeared before another canal. This waterway resembled the former enough for the Grossbarts to mutter back and forth about what they might do if this scoundrel was as honest as he had thus far appeared.

They crossed a bridge, and then more serpentine passages brought them to another canal, and eventually another bridge. They trudged on, only Manfried noticing that the woman would have outpaced them all if Hegel's blocky form had not impeded her. No more smiles or songs were granted him, and he wondered what her fate would be once they delivered her.

The Arab talked incessantly of the necessity of staying quiet due to the temperament and crossbow prowess of the local populace but not even Martyn could be coaxed into conversing. The priest's arms felt number than usual, his feet throbbed, his head might be bleeding from a fall he had suffered on the dock, he had sinned to such an extent that several boatmen might find themselves at Judgment instead of their beds come morning, and he was now being chatted up by the Infidel. Father Martyn was in a bad way.

At long last they arrived at the narrowest, darkest passage yet, a tunnel disappearing into the city. After their previous encounters with those of foreign extraction the Grossbarts were ready for treachery. It struck them as conceivable if not outright likely that the Arab had led them in circles while his associates prepared an ambush.

"You tryin to get slit?" said Manfried, snatching the Arab's hair and pressing a dagger to his throat.

The Arab let out another volley of assurances and pledges of loyalty, but he did not seem as frightened as Manfried would have liked. They continued down the alley, Manfried holding tight to the Arab's shoulder, and rounding a bend they saw a house as big as a monastery looming behind a thick wall. The Arab wished another lightning flash would make their arrival even more impressive but the storm had gone. Manfried released him and whistled, Martyn clucked at the uncharitable display of wealth, and Hegel farted, trying to conceal his awe.

A large metal gate separated the massive house and its property from the alley, and through the bars they saw two figures beside a small fire. They must have heard something, quickly pointing crossbows into the darkness where the Grossbarts stood. Before Manfried could further chastise himself for trusting a known Arab one of the guards shouted, bringing five more stout individuals running from somewhere inside the walls. These men also carried crossbows, all of which soon pointed into the alley.

Several of the guards were barking in Italian and Martyn quickly stepped into the light as he responded in their language. The woman moved forward beside him but Manfried did not notice, busy as he was gripping one of the Arab's arms while his brother held the other. In their free hands each held his favored tool, and Manfried put the question to the Arab:

"You in on this?"

"Never. No no no." The Arab shook his head vigorously.

"Time to test his honesty," Manfried told his brother and brazenly dragged him into the light. Not about to doubt his brother now, Hegel stepped in tandem with him, and they emerged from the darkness. The guards became even more agitated at the sight of two burly men with weapons detaining a very excited beggar and a veiled woman clad in a soaking dress.

"Fine welcome," Hegel said, more to the men than to his brother.

"Suppose we could take our company to more accommodatin climes," said Manfried, spitting a clod of phlegm at the guards.

The banter dried in Manfried's mouth at the realization that, in the event this indeed proved home to the Goose, he might never see the maiden again. If it got him closer to Gyptland it could not be helped, but to be fleeced of her after all the trouble they had gone through would not be tolerated. His grip tightened on both his captive and his weapon. The Arab and Martyn went conspicuously silent but Hegel's voice rose in direct proportion to those of the men gibbering at him in their tongue.

"I hear one a yous say *Ennio*? Yeah, I knew the cunt. He's dead. Dead, you jabberin fucker!" Hegel stood proud while Martyn squatted down until his forehead and bandaged arms brushed his thighs in mock prayer—out of the line of crossbow fire, he hoped. The Arab squirmed enough that the Brothers released him of their own accord, and he lamented his folly for not demanding payment in advance.

"You say my brother's dead?" A new man stepped forward and opened the gate, his clothes clean and colorful. In one hand he held a thin sword and in the other a bottle.

"Yeah, sad to say, but he died better than he lived," responded Hegel, put off by the man's fancy dress but heartened by his mastery of the proper tongue. They held eye contact for a long time before the man looked away.

"Difficult to believe." The man took a pull from his bottle, said something unintelligible, and waved his sword in front of the guards' crossbows. They lowered their weapons and the man lowered his head, rubbing his brow. "Too much to hope Alphonse and Giacomo stopped to drink before coming here?"

"Dunno why you'd hope such worthless trash as they'd survive a ordeal what kilt a better man," said Manfried.

"Worthless?" The man raised his head, glaring at Manfried.

"Can't speak with equal authority on the other, but old Poncey good as gutted your brother. Al Ponce paid his price, though, and as the other's kin a his, no water oughta be leaked on his account, neither." Manfried crossed his arms.

"He killed Ennio?"

"Had he three blades he would a tried to plant'em in each a our backs," Hegel explained. "Too weak to do it himself, tried to make a deal so's we'd get ours but he wouldn't get his."

"Lies," the man spit.

"Callin us liars?" Manfried stepped forward. "Us? Watch that mouth a yours, grapesipper, or I'll put it where you can better mind it."

With a swish of a sword the crossbows were raised and the Arab stepped behind the distracted Hegel. Ennio's brother yelled in his language at them, his face bright red. Finishing, he panted and stared, the only noise the fire guttering in the wind. Hegel sensed things might worsen if perspective was not reestablished, and, too involved to notice what the Arab was about behind him, he shouted back at the man:

"Listen! We done what we could for your brother and if it weren't enough that's the Virgin's business! But we did come all the damn way to deliver this Goose's property, and that's what we done, so any pigshit you wanna stir in the mix can wait til we's compensated. My hair's gone, priest's been shot full a more shafts than a fair-haired whore come harvest, and we's in no mood to explain our own righteous fuckin actions at arrowpoint, so calm your dogs! Mecky fuckin gratitude for us what killed a demon in the name a savin your brother!"

"Then get called fuckin liars for stickin the blame on the mecky sap what let the demon in!" Manfried added, nodding at his brother.

"Property...you mean..." The man spoke slowly, his burgundy cheeks fading to a pearly yellow as he finally took stock of the woman standing patiently beside them. "This is her?"

"Course she's the one, you thick clot," said Hegel. "Don't think we wasted weeks comin down here just to get on your teats!"

The man said something in what the Brothers finally realized must be Italian and swayed slightly before shaking himself and straightening his shoulders. After a pause he again flicked his sword and the crossbows sagged, the men grumbling to one another. He turned and walked under the gate before sitting heavily on the ground. While he sat there cradling his head in his hands, the Grossbarts carried on in their private tongue.

"What you make a this?" Hegel asked.

"Bunch a shit."

"Yeah, but what kind?"

"The worst sort. This one's more a ponce than his brother," said Manfried.

"But not so much's Al Ponce."

"Never should a come here."

"Yeah, I bet you'd have other plans for that feedbag."

"Sure turned out to be a feedbag, alright. Thanks for remindin me whose idea it was to come here!" Manfried elbowed Hegel.

"Keen on, the dandy returns."

"Tonight you stay here," the man said. "Clean yourselves and sleep, and tomorrow we determine exactly what you are due. Come inside with what is yours, I will see the lady to her place. I am Rodrigo, and I will have your names before you enter." Rodrigo's eyes drifting back to the woman, he spit an order at one of the least grungy guards, who in turn hurried around inside the gate.

"Manfried," said Manfried.

"Hegel," said Hegel.

"Grossbart," they said together.

"Father Martyn," said the priest, finally reentering the conversation now that it had calmed.

"Al-Gassur Abu-Yateem Thanni ibn Farees," said the Arab, appearing from behind Hegel and the Grossbart-mounted schnapps cask, from which he had filched while the debate raged.

"What are you doing back, you miserable sandrat?" Rodrigo demanded, too put out to revert to the lingua Italia. "When we dismissed you onto the street instead of into a canal it was a boon circumstantial on your not returning."

"I would never offend you or your master, and will leave as soon as payment is received for my efforts," Al-Gassur hiccupped.

"Payment?" Hegel turned to the Arab. "You said you's the Goose's servant."

"I serve him by bringing you here, just as you serve him by coming. If I am correct in comprehending your statements, dear Grossbart, if you request recompense for your toils then is it not only honest that I receive them for mine?"

"A matter to be taken up with the Goose, not us, as we ourselves will do stead a pesterin others in the same predicament," observed Manfried.

"Away, Arab, before your presence brings my wine back to the open air." Rodrigo flicked his fingers at Al-Gassur.

"Course," Manfried said, "comin into *our* employ wouldn't be too difficult, say a bottle a fortnight to be our servant?"

"Agreed, oh charitable masters." Al-Gassur sneered at Rodrigo.

"What game are you at?" said Rodrigo, asking Hegel's question for him.

Manfried shrugged. "Our business is our own." When torn between infuriating a ponce and a beggar he would choose the ponce every time.

"He sleeps with the swine," said Rodrigo. "The rest of you will meet with me on the morrow. Go with him, now." Rodrigo gestured to a gaunt old man who had returned with the guard he had earlier sent off.

"Meanin we's meetin with you *and* the Goose then," Hegel clarified for Rodrigo.

"Captain Barousse's business is his own," Rodrigo replied. "I will discuss the matter with him. But now a good bath for the lot of you, excluding the wretched Arab. He will wash in the garden pool under his guard's supervision."

"I require neither guard nor bath," Al-Gassur protested.

"A guard is necessary to protect your odorous person from my feet, and a bath to protect my nose from yours. Now wait with Marco here." He motioned to a horse-faced fellow of considerable size.

A nod between the Brothers signaled the end of their journey, and they strode proudly through the gate. Martyn nervously followed, having understood along with Al-Gassur the words Rodrigo had said to his men that the Grossbarts had not. While Rodrigo had claimed he would converse with the captain before enacting his plan, both priest and Arab doubted a sea captain of criminal renown would be averse to torturing his guests to discover the truth as his man suggested. Unlike Al-Gassur, Martyn had faith that when Barousse's men came for the Brothers they would find more blood than merely that of the Grossbarts.

The guard who showed them to the door left them with the brawny but aged cook, and she led them through the kitchen and deposited them with a serving maid. The sharp-nosed girl took them through a rug-dappled hallway riddled with doors into a great open foyer, across which they saw an identical hall. To the right the massive front doors towered, and to the left an open stairway rose to midway up the wall, where it split into twin balconies. She led them to the second story, the trio doing what simple arithmetic they could. Manfried counted six guards in total, Hegel three tapestries and the dust squares where half a dozen more had hung, and Martyn two shapely calves on the stair above him.

They followed the balcony to where it ended in a hallway above the one they had passed through below. Three partially filled candelabras lit the way to the first doors on the right and left, which she opened and the Grossbarts claimed. She showed them in and they ran her off.

"Bring food!" Hegel called.

"And drink!" seconded Manfried.

"And fill the bath!" finished Martyn, shrugging at the dual Grossbart glares.

She brought drink first, and when she brought the food she had to go back for more of each. After the second dinner she had time to catch her breath while they bathed, but had instructions to have a third round of both ready on their return. Braised eel, poached eggs, and sautéed carp went into their gullets with the same haste as turnip stew, although both agreed, late in the evening, in private, in their twinspeak, that indeed kings would not eat finer.

At the end of the hall above the kitchen an iron tub larger than many fountains filled the room, a stovepipe from the kitchen helping to heat it and a shallow drainage aqueduct in the floor vanishing into a small hole. Their first warm bath they concurred was far better than a river, and decided that upon their establishing themselves in Gyptland such a luxury would be practiced twice daily. Drowsing in the water, Martyn considered telling the Brothers of what lay ahead, Hegel closed his eyes and imagined the bath full of cowards' blood, and Manfried found himself humming a tune that made the water turn frigid.

They bedded down but not before Martyn cracked and told the Brothers of Rodrigo's intentions. Enigmatically, neither said much but they exchanged a look that bespoke volumes. At least, Martyn hoped for *enigmatically* rather than *drunkenly*, and prayed the volumes would be worth reading once he learned the language.

XVIII
Beards of a Feather

The Grossbarts slept without taking watches in their respective rooms, each starting awake several times from the comfort of his bed. Martyn had stayed in several monasteries that were far more luxurious but he had also spent months sleeping in ditches and barns, and he slept even better than the Brothers, for he had no doubts that whatever befell them he would probably go free. Stumbling to answer the rapping at his door that morning, the priest saw not a serving girl but the Brothers outfitted for battle. Hegel held a cocked crossbow in one arm and his pick in the other, Manfried the same with his mace.

"Rodrigo has sent for us?" Martyn asked.

Hegel grinned. "Nah, we's gonna find him."

"Is that wise?"

"Wiser than sittin in the pot til they set us on the fire." Manfried yawned.

"You wanna hold on to a weapon?" asked Hegel.

"What?! No, of course not."

"Yeah, can't you see his hands are bound up?" Manfried chided Hegel.

Rodrigo cleared his throat behind them in the hall. "Sleep well?"

Wondering why he had not felt the goosechills at Rodrigo's

approach, Hegel overcompensated by thrusting his crossbow in the man's face. Manfried raised his mace and Martyn jumped back into his room and kicked the door shut. Rodrigo blinked at them and extended his open palms.

"What's this, then?" Rodrigo asked.

"Come to torture us, you craven crumb?" Manfried demanded.

"If that's your purpose you should a brought more muscle," said Hegel.

"I wondered if the father spoke properly. Now I have my answer." Rodrigo sighed. "The captain sends for you to dine with him this morning. If you value your pelts I would advise against such hostility, as beating the truth from you was entirely my idea, although the future feasibility of such an option is reliant on how you comport yourselves at his board. Now shall we bring the priest?"

"Nah." Hegel hung his pick and unstrung his bow. "We gotta have a word on private ground."

"Which means no flowery twats in high boots," said Manfried.

"I would like a word in private with you as well, Master Grossbart, but first the captain will have his," Rodrigo growled, turning on his heel and leading them to the stairs.

"Wager you would," Manfried rejoined. "Though you'd be disappointed to find your head fallin to the floor stead a my breeches."

Rodrigo shuddered at the mental image but held his tongue. These bastards were merely tightening nooses around their necks, and Rodrigo knew if they rubbed him off-ways the captain might kill them himself before breakfast. They seemed too proud to deny murdering his brother Ennio, if indeed they had, but already he wanted to see them die simply to watch the sneers fade from their narrow lips.

They went down the stairs and across the foyer to the hallway opposite the wing leading to the kitchen. Two men in chain mail haubergeons slouched against the wall, dipping their heads at Rodrigo. The hallway terminated in an ebon door that Rodrigo gave a series of knocks upon, each Grossbart committing the sequence to memory. Rodrigo then opened the door and motioned them to enter before him. Hegel went in first while Manfried backed into the room behind him to keep an eye on Rodrigo, who followed them in and closed the door.

A massive table laden with plates, platters, and pitchers filled the room, and behind this sat the captain. A light red beard spilled down his shirt and disappeared under the table, instantly warming the Grossbarts to him. His advanced age was shown by his bald pate and ears that sagged with the weight of heavy gold hoops, his muscular frame drooping from lethargy. Blue eyes and a large nose and mouth jutted out from his slightly tanned face, his voluminous hands holding the largest crossbow the Brothers had ever seen. This the captain pointed vaguely between them, and when he spoke he enunciated each syllable so his meaning was not blurred by his thick accent.

"You are the Grossbarts." Not a question.

"Yeah." Hegel lamented unstringing his bow.

"And you's the Captain Bar Goose," said Manfried, his palm on his mace pommel.

"Alexius Barousse." The captain smiled, showing a mouthful of broken teeth.

Rodrigo said something to the captain in Italian that clouded Barousse's face with anger, his nose swelling and his eyes narrowing. Moments before the Grossbarts jumped upon the table to battle the man he bellowed, "I will not have guests worry they are plotted against! In their presence you will speak so they can understand or not at all!"

"Right proper," Hegel agreed, not trying to mask his pleasure.

"Only honest." Manfried beamed. "Chance we could speak without the sneak?"

"Captain—" Rodrigo began.

"You are no longer needed," Barousse snarled, his chest heaving.

"But—"

"I know what you're about." Barousse slumped back in his throne-like chair. "So I'll settle that in your presence. Your names."

"Huh? Oh, Hegel Grossbart."

"Manfried Grossbart."

"Have you come on any other business than returning my property?"

"Nah, but now that we's here there's other business could be discussed," Manfried answered.

"Are you assassins?" The business end of Barousse's crossbow stayed trained on whoever spoke.

"We's never killed none but them what done us wrong," said Hegel.

"Or those what would, given the chance," clarified Manfried.

"Have you brought poison to my table?"

"Yeah, I got some in my bag," said Hegel.

"Only cause we didn't trust our things to be left in our rooms," Manfried added, giving Rodrigo the stink-eye.

"Do you mean to kill me?" Barousse asked in the same manner in which he would offer them wine.

"Not unless you give us cause," said Hegel, and Manfried nodded.

"And you're in nobody's employ but your own?"

"And Mary's," said Hegel.

"Meanin the Virgin," explained Manfried.

"Satisfied?" Barousse looked to Rodrigo.

"How can you trust them?" Rodrigo spluttered.

"How can they trust a man who speaks about them in code

in their very presence? They can't, and I can't trust a man who distrusts me or my company. So out." Barousse set the crossbow down on the table and poured himself a drink, dismissing the dumbstruck Rodrigo with a wave of his fingers. Rodrigo bowed and left without looking at the Grossbarts, slamming the door behind him.

"Lock the door," Barousse commanded, which Hegel did while Manfried approached the table. "Sit and eat. He's lost a brother and you're the ones who were there, so that sits sorely with him."

"Never would a pegged Ennis for the smart one." Manfried fell upon a roast gull.

"Rodrigo's proved himself superior to Ennio in all matters save cart driving, which is why he went and Rodrigo stayed." Barousse drank between words.

"Ennio weren't so bad in the end," said Hegel.

"But it's the beginning that concerns me," Barousse said. "My enemies are legion, hence Rodrigo's protective nature. The green-eared lad fails to recognize that a man who can't defend his own table isn't fit to sit at it. Besides, you have brought back to me what Ennio failed…" Barousse lowered his voice and stared at his plate.

After several mouthfuls of silence, Hegel guzzled some wine and cleared his throat. "We was in the mountains, headin south when we seen your ride comin towards us," he began, and whenever he needed another bite or drink Manfried would take up the reins and continue the tale. They omitted nothing but Manfried's fascination with the woman, even including their debate with Ennio on the ethics of their business in the churchyard. The food grew cold but still they ate and talked, and before they were finished the captain had to retrieve another bottle from the mantel to fill their glasses.

Barousse's hearty laughter when they told of slaying the Road Popes and burning the town endeared him to the Grossbarts, here at long last an honest man. "Many might doubt your tale," he finally said.

"Many oughta get hit," Hegel observed.

"And you say the priest pursued the same demon?"

"Claimed to," said Manfried, "accordin to him the man what had it in'em was a devil worshipper, meanin we kilt us a demon *and* a witch."

"And so you did kill Ennio," Barousse mused.

"Well, yeah," said Manfried.

"Better than gettin a demon in'em," said Hegel.

"Hmm," said the captain, then shook his head. "Demons prowl the wilds. I know this, and I believe you. I will tell Rodrigo what you have told me, and his mood shall change or I will change it for him. Now what kind of reward do you seek for your impressive service?"

"Gyptland," they said together.

"What?!"

"Passage, rather," amended Manfried.

"Once we's landed we can get it ourselves," said Hegel.

"Passage?"

"You's a captain, so that means you got a ship," Manfried said.

"And you want me to take you to the desert?" The captain's face wrinkled.

"Yeah," belched Hegel.

"Ridiculous," said Barousse.

"How's that?" Manfried dropped a duck leg on the floor and stared at the captain.

"I don't sail." The captain stared past them at the door, his fists tightening on the table until they went milky, then managed through clenched teeth: "You may stay in my home until you secure your own passage, that is your reward. We will discuss specifics later."

"What kind a captain don't sail?" Manfried sneered, unprepared for the short shrift this man suggested.

"Leave me. Now." His florid face swelled, and that too began turning white, starting at the tip of his nose and spreading inward.

"We can talk more later," Hegel offered, standing and backing toward the door. The captain had made him go all cold and sober—without letting on in his face, Hegel realized that at some point the captain had picked the loaded crossbow back up.

"Yeah, let the prospect simmer twixt your ears fore givin a final response," Manfried agreed, knocking his chair back and following his brother.

The captain stared wrathfully at them until Hegel unlocked the door and stepped out, Manfried backing out behind him. Pulling the door closed, they exchanged nasty looks and strode back to their rooms. Rodrigo approached them on the way to the stair but thought better of it and diverted his path down the captain's hall. Neither brother spoke until they bolted the door in Hegel's room.

"You like that much's me?" Manfried asked.

"Mecky as it gets," said Hegel.

"Think he can dismiss us like that?"

"Man'll think a lot a things less someone shows'em his error."

"Only sometimes. Oft Mary's guidance's the only thing set one straight."

"Seemed a decent sort til the end there," Hegel ruminated.

"If he holds decent he'll see his crime and make amends," said Manfried, removing his boots.

"And that Arab? We really mean to waste even a bottle on that wretch?"

"First I was thinkin no, just get on Rodrigo's ass a touch, but recent epiphanies got me shifted a different direction."

"How's that?"

"Know how Ponce's cousin and others we seen don't speak proper? And how we can speak like we's always done in the *real* proper way and even that sow what birthed us couldn't comprehend a word?"

"Yeah, so different folk speak different. That's what goes under the term *proper* fuckin knowledge. You just figure that out?" Hegel grinned and dodged a thrown boot. Over the run of their brotherhood they had both developed an almost supernatural knack for dodging expected and surprise attacks alike.

"Don't try actin the abbot with me! Ever think there might be a higher purpose to keepin our swarthy servant about?"

"If you got an example I'll hear it stead a you playin the bishop," Hegel said.

"So we speak our way, others don't, and we also speak the other that men do up north in the Germania or empire or what they call it any given day. But we don't speak what they do down here."

"Agreed."

"But that priest speaks up-there tongue and down-here tongue, just like Ponce and Ellis, and just like that Arab."

"Enni— Oh!" Hegel finally caught on. "But wait, if you's suggestin we use that Arab to tell us what foreigners' sayin, why not use the priest? He ain't the Infidel."

"Fine and good for dealin with the rabble round here, but where's we headed?"

"Gyptland."

"And who lives in Gyptland?"

"The dead?"

"What!?"

"Er . . . gold. And sand."

"Lives, muttonhead, lives!"

Hegel's brow furrowed as he labored to remember their uncle's teachings and other hearsay. "Deadly beasts and monsters?"

"Arabs, you simple slit, Arabs!" Manfried launched another boot, then ducked when it was caught returned.

"Once again, *proper* fuckin knowledge," Hegel complained. "I thought you meant other than them."

"Now how do you suppose Arabs speak?"

"With their— No, put it down, no call for that." Hegel stared hard at the knife his brother brandished. "You mean how's them what live there sound when they speak, like we's doin now, or when we's with others don't understand the way the two a us do?"

"Yeah," Manfried said.

"I dunno, how do they speak?"

"I dunno either."

"Oh."

"But I bet that Arab does."

"Oh! That's brilliant!"

"Yeah, I know it." Manfried imitated his brother: "*With their mouths*. Ignorance ain't a sin but it oughta be."

To Rodrigo, Martyn, and anyone else unfortunate enough to hear them speak the Brothers' voices sounded identical, but to each other subtle differences were noted but ignored except when they mocked each other. They wrestled for the better part of an hour, such commonplace scrapes the source of their prowess in combat with others less Grossbart than themselves. A knocking on the door disturbed their fracas.

"Enter!" shouted Manfried, which set off another row as they occupied Hegel's room.

"Excuse me," Father Martyn said, then louder to break up the melee, "Grossbarts!"

"What?" Blood oozed from Hegel's cavernous nostrils.

"Who?" Manfried's cropped ear had reopened, matting his chin and neck.

"I go to church," Martyn said, unable to keep his head from rocking from side to side at the sight of them. "Perhaps you would care to join me?"

Hegel gave Manfried a concerned look but he need not have worried.

"Nah." Manfried stained Hegel's pillow with his face. "Nuthin for us there."

"But how else will you confess?"

"Confess what?" Hegel asked.

"We ain't sinned," said Manfried, opening a bottle.

"Every man sins, Manfried," replied Martyn.

"Nah, he's right," Hegel agreed.

"Thank you, Hegel." Martyn smiled.

"I mean my brother's right." Hegel sniffled blood into his beard. "We ain't done nuthin might displease Her."

"Nevertheless—" Martyn began but Manfried swelled before him.

"Nevermore, Priest, will you accuse us a sinnin! Think killin demons' a sin? What bout witches? Hackin up heretics require us to lick your ears, that it?"

"Hegel." Martyn looked to the apparently less volatile Grossbart. "I meant no disrespect, to you or your brother, only that we all sin in our weakness."

"Tell him that." Hegel reclined on the broken bed. "Stead a disrespectin us both by talkin to me."

"What was it you said, Priest?" demanded Manfried.

"I," Martyn swallowed pride and spit, "I apologize, Master Grossbart, for implying you had a stained soul."

"I acknowledge your apology." Manfried nodded. "And remind you that any sinnin and weakness on your part don't reflect on us. We ain't no beggars nor beg-hairs nor any other breed a blasphemer. We's Grossbarts, and you'd do well to recollect that."

Disgusted with them and himself, Martyn turned to the door. "I will pray for you, Grossbarts, I hope this is not an imposition?"

"Nah, it ain't nuthin to us." Hegel held a cool glass to his cheek.

"When I give an account of your deeds to my superiors I will do so justly, and I am pleased our paths crossed for even a brief time. Farewell."

"You think bout gettin what's due your way from the captain fore you leave?" Manfried asked. "Cause we ain't savin you a share if you ain't there to claim it."

"Take my share for yourselves." Martyn shut the door on the Grossbarts and strode away, head held high.

Rodrigo intercepted him on the stair and escorted him off the grounds. Certain questions were posed to and honestly answered by the priest, who looked a sight better for his bath. They parted at the gate when Rodrigo caught wind of Al-Gassur skulking in the overgrown garden surrounding the main building. Martyn stepped out into the street and made his way back through the wondrous city toward a reunion with his fold.

Al-Gassur had set traps in the bushes and one yielded a plump pigeon, which he roasted in a dry, ivy-throttled fountain. Hearing Rodrigo approach, he grabbed his bottle and bird but before he could hop away Rodrigo snatched his cloak and spun him around.

"A poacher too, eh?" Rodrigo raised his fist.

"Please speak properly, sir," Al-Gassur pleaded in German.

"What's this shift in tone?" Rodrigo asked, obliging the beggar.

"To please my revered employers, I will only speak so that they too will always comprehend." Al-Gassur batted his gooey eyes at Rodrigo.

"Those ignoble Grossbarts?" Rodrigo scowled, seizing Al-Gassur's earlobe.

"Present," said Hegel.

"And accountable," added Manfried.

"What you doin with our Arab?" Hegel stepped around the shrubbery.

"Merely inquiring as to his presence outside his prescribed chambers." Rodrigo relinquished the ear with a pinch.

"Honorable Hegel. Magnificent Manfried." Al-Gassur awkwardly bowed, concealing the pigeon in his tunic. "I spied you through the boughs approaching, and wondered what purpose such masters as yourselves would find in such a low state as that which I presently inhabit?"

"Eh? Shut it." Manfried looked back to Rodrigo. "Got any more jabber or can we speak to our property in peace?"

"Pardons, pardons." Rodrigo raised his palms and backed away, his immaculate clothes catching in the brambles and spoiling his aristocratic posturing. "I leave you to yourselves. Tonight you will dine in your chambers and I shall trouble you no more until the morrow."

"See that you can keep a promise that simple," Hegel said dismissively. "Now then, Arab."

"Yes?"

"Speak," Manfried commanded.

"Speak what?"

"The words a your people." Manfried gave the sniggering Hegel the hardest eye yet given.

"You mean such words as caliph, ambrosia, and camel?" Al-Gassur could not understand their reasoning.

"Yeah, like them." Manfried's fingers beckoned. "More, and without the proper speech."

"Ah, you wish to hear me speak as I would to a countryman?" Enlightenment brightened Al-Gassur's face.

"Yeah, tell my brother to get stuffed like he was yours stead a mine," quipped Hegel.

"Do it and see what happens," said Manfried. "Say somethin simple, like *the grave's full a gold for those what brave the mold*."

"Immediately, illustrious owner." Al-Gassur bowed, and let out a long string of gibberish—and gibberish proper, as opposed to the language of those who dwell in the sandy lands of the south. Al-Gassur had neither heard nor spoken a word of Arabic since his youth, the bulk of the intervening years spent learning the tongues of those he sought to fleece. The random sounds his mouth produced pleased the Grossbarts, however, who grinned and nodded at his nonsense.

"Told you!" Manfried hooted. "What's that mean, then?"

"The grave holds no gold save for yellow mold." Al-Gassur bowed again, hoping he had remembered the poem properly. He had not, but this did not displease his audience.

"Too oft the truth." Hegel nodded. "He'll do as well as any other."

"Cept there ain't any other," said Manfried.

"Begging more pardons than I am deserving." Al-Gassur's leaden eyes glimmered. "What will I do for?"

"For whatever pleases us," said Manfried.

"Which ain't much presently, so stay unseen and unheard lest you face our judgment," elaborated Hegel.

"The matter of an instant." Al-Gassur bowed even lower, almost losing his pigeon. "I shall be at your disposal day and night, either here or in the porcine quarters."

"How's that?" Manfried looked around.

"The barn." Al-Gassur's retrieved his crutch and slunk away, mulling over his recent employment.

The Grossbarts ambled down the overgrown paths of the garden, clever horticulture making the grounds seem far more spacious than they actually were. Neither would admit how awed he was by their current situation, Barousse's stinginess notwithstanding. When dusk came they invaded the kitchen and made obnoxious demands of the cook and her scrawny husband. They ate two meals there before retiring to bathe, with instructions for the next meal to be delivered directly to the tub.

The Grossbarts basked in the opulent house and slept deeply, awaking the following morning to Rodrigo banging on their doors. He waited with them until food and wine arrived, and when they did not offer him any of theirs he sent for his own. Well fed and tipsy, the Grossbarts finally acknowledged his presence.

"What's the order a the day, then?" asked Manfried.

"You will accompany me to be outfitted for your journey." Rodrigo handed his plate to the hovering servant girl, flashing her an awkward smile. "Thank you, Marguerite. Shall we be off?"

"Wanna talk with the captain," Hegel belched.

"You may request an audience later this evening, but until then, there is the matter of equipping you."

"With a boat?" Manfried elbowed his brother, nodding enthusiastically.

"What? No. With new clothes, and armor and weapons if you require them, as well as any other items you may find essential to your voyage."

"He told you where we's headed, then?" Hegel scowled, displeased the captain would reveal their destination.

"Yes, not that it is any matter to me." Rodrigo stiffened. "There are much more pressing matters facing the captain, and your presence only serves as a distraction to the upcoming trials awaiting our attention."

"*Ours* as in you and us?" Manfried pinned on his cloak.

"As in myself and the captain." Rodrigo led them out.

The Grossbarts insisted they retrieve cheese and bread from the kitchen before embarking into the city. The thronged roads passed around and often through buildings far grander than Barousse's, even the narrowest of the bridges they crossed gilded with ornate carvings. Rodrigo suggested they hire one of the small boats bobbing beside them in the canals to carry them on their rounds but the Grossbarts refused, and their displeasure became compounded when their guide informed them the chief cemetery lay on an island inaccessible by foot.

Winding through the narrow streets they spent the better part of the day purchasing chain mail shirts, shields, new boots, clothes, satchels, and anything else they could think of when it became apparent Rodrigo paid for everything they wanted. Their guide drew the line at a supposed Arab device wraught of iron and glass that not even the peddler could guess the purpose of yet still demanded a small fortune to part with. Several stops at alehouses were made, and by mid-afternoon all three were drunk. Rodrigo stumbled onto a quay, and here the Brothers were afforded their first glimpse of the sea.

"Thought it'd be bigger," Hegel lied, having envisioned a body of water no larger than the lake outside Bad Endorf.

"Course you can't see it all from here," Manfried explained, mistaking cloudbanks on the horizon for the opposite shore. "Said that pond off the Danube weren't big as you'd thought and it still took us forever and a day to get round."

"My brother hated the ocean," Rodrigo murmured, "said it could not be trusted. Seems the road cannot be trusted, either."

"Fall off a wagon, get up and walk." Hegel swayed, staring down the quay. "Off a boat, you can't do nuthin but die."

"Know how to swim?" asked Rodrigo.

"You callin us witches?" Manfried shoved his beard in Rodrigo's face.

"Any man who gets on a boat had best know what to do if he goes over its side." Rodrigo recoiled from Manfried's foul breath.

"Swimmin's for fish same as flyin's for birds," said Hegel.

"Yes, but—"

"But nuthin. Tryin to trick us into drownin?" Manfried squinted in the twilight to see the lie in Rodrigo's eyes.

"I meant to advise you, as any good Christian advises another, and nothing more." Rodrigo haughtily drew away. "By Marco's mighty morals, I meant no trickery!"

"Marco's that ox what minded our Arab when we showed up, yeah?" asked Hegel.

"What?" said Rodrigo. "No! Ah, yes, he is named such as well, I forget, but I meant a different Marco. The saint who guards our city."

"You heard a him?" Hegel asked his brother.

"Course I have," Manfried lied.

"He rests in the basilica I pointed out earlier." Rodrigo clumsily motioned back they way they had come.

"What's he buried with?" Manfried followed Rodrigo's gaze.

"Nothing," Rodrigo said quickly, appalled at what he correctly assumed was the line of thought Manfried had embarked upon. "Back to the manse, then."

They arrived after dark, the tolling of church bells reminding the Grossbarts of Father Martyn. He had appeared an exceptionally unheretical priest to the Brothers, and his donating any share of the loot they might extort from Barousse raised him in their esteem even further. They stumbled through the kitchen, scalding their fingers when they snatched food from the pans. The cook shooed them out, which almost provoked Manfried to strike the woman.

Gaining the opposite hallway, they let Rodrigo take the lead and unlock the captain's door. Barousse stood before the fire, his back to them while they took places across the table. Servants followed them in, cluttering the massive board with steaming platters and bowls. Only when their lessers had retreated and Rodrigo latched the door did Barousse turn to face them.

Alexius Barousse's eyes were rough, purple craters staring out of his craggy face but in their depths lurked no sorrow, only a greedy glimmer to match that of the Grossbarts. He bade them eat and drink, which they did with gusto until heads reeled and guts bulged. Rodrigo nodded in his chair but sobered up when the captain finally addressed them.

"I have sent word for my maiden to be repaired and taken out of dry dock, and as Rodrigo has prepared you, all we need do is wait until she is ready and then we sail south." The captain raised his glass. "We will retake what was lost, and gain what never was!"

In better circumstances Rodrigo would have responded with something more solid than spraying wine from his nose.

"Glad you came around." Manfried hoisted his glass, drunkenness nullifying any surprise he might otherwise have harbored.

"Sensible," Hegel slurred, raising a bottle.

"What?" Rodrigo coughed.

"Too long have I sat mired by a tide that fills my boots but stirs not my soul." Barousse stood and stalked along the table, wagging a finger at the assembled. "Cowardice has haunted me alongside my family."

"What's that mean?" Hegel kicked his brother, who shrugged and repeated the question to the captain.

"Gone!" Barousse thundered. "Taken by Triton or God or whatever dark thing sought a price for my transgression! Gone! Swallowed up, like it swallows up everything from boat to man to mountain! Gone!"

"Leave him alone," Rodrigo hissed, then had wine splashed in his face by the raging captain.

"They will speak! And I will answer! Secrets are for thieves and the dead, and we are neither!"

"True words." Manfried handed a fresh bottle to the captain.

"Over a decade I have cowered and been coward, thousands

of nights tossing in my horrors, thousands of days begging forgiveness, all in vain, in vain! I knew when I sent her away, I knew that first night my woes would not end through such a route! When one spends their life on her back they cannot expect to ride off it. Not without price!"

The Grossbarts loved shouting, and Hegel fired back in turn, "How and why?!"

"My sons! Taken on a skiff not a league out, a day's fishing turned black with their mother's grief and red with their blood! A wave out of nowhere, a maelstrom from the calm!"

"My father with them," Rodrigo muttered, but no one cared.

"And your wife?!" Manfried bellowed.

"Slipped from a gondola into the lagoon, where sea-vines snatched and pulled! So they say, so they say! Not one body given back for their last rites, not one spared an eternity crashing into each other and a million more of the damned, that coldest Hell below the surface!"

"Except you!" exclaimed Hegel.

"Through and to my shame! Watching my fortunes dwindle, my name muddied, my ship eaten by dryrot, my nerve softened, all for a song! Would that I could undo my error, would that I could send her back! But I will! Now, Grossbarts, I will!"

"Who?" Manfried asked, his suspicions cheating him of a forceful yell.

"The Nix! The Siren! She whom I caught! She whom I sent away, but not before she cursed us all! She whom you have brought back! She who took Luchese and Umberto, and dearest Mathilde, who loved me even when I brought a succubus into our home! She who took Italo, and a decade later his son, your brother, my godchild! Ennio, poor, honest Ennio!"

"Come on then!" Hegel toppled his chair gaining his feet. "Let's put'er to the blade!"

"Never!" The captain's cutlass appeared in his hand and sliced the air in front of Hegel. "I would sooner put it to your throat or mine! I have failed enough! No masonry will blot out the sound, not stone nor wood nor crashing coast will silence her! Over the peaks it haunted my dreams, and before I banished her I cut out her tongue with these ten finger bones of mine, all for naught! No scars, no blemishes, just a fat red tongue! Even time fears her and touches her not! If only—" Barousse fell back in his chair, sword clattering on the floor and face in his hands.

"We's experienced in the ways a witches," Manfried murmured after a brief lull.

"Got your paramour, er palomar, uh, best interest in mind," agreed Hegel.

"Erp," Rodrigo managed, every rumor he had heard growing up in the house of Barousse confirmed in a storm of shouting. In his years of service to the captain he had become accustomed to the wild mood swings and tantrums but never had he seen any, himself included, taken into Barousse's confidence so fully. Perhaps the old man had finally cracked, he thought, the strain of the woman's reappearance too much for his injured soul.

"Leave me," Barousse muttered through meshed fingers, and this time the Grossbarts departed without snatching the last word.

XIX
Like the Beginning, the End of Winter Is Difficult to Gauge in the South

Al-Gassur received his payments on time, but that pittance was appropriately supplemented by the food brought to him from the house and the birds he caught in the garden. Fate's wheel had spun him into the yard of one of Venezia's only estates to boast even a tiny plot of land allowed to run so riot. Better still, on the rare days when the Brothers left the manse to Grossbart upon the town he could creep out and spend an honest day begging without the worry of being absent when sought. Confident his employers would not notice the discrepancy, he periodically unbound one leg and wrapped the other, lest his limb atrophy from lack of use and truly become lost. A veteran of a vague crusade inspired more charity in the populace than a simple Arab come to the city by Providence and his own two legs.

A sneak by nature as well as trade, Al-Gassur eventually overheard enough from the kitchen windows and the guards to ascertain the destination of the Grossbarts. The years of rotten food, alcoholism, and exposure had not dulled his wits but sharpened them, the mendicant well aware such an opportunity came to a man only once in his existence. Knowing his ruse could not last forever, he struggled to tame his forgetful tongue, scouring the streets in vain for another Arab to teach him what everyone assumed he knew.

One sun-broiled Mediterranean morning several months after the arrival of the Grossbarts the twins found themselves again wandering the ill-kept gardens when they noticed Al-Gassur perched in the boughs of a lime tree. The fellow had shimmied out along a high branch that stretched over the top of the garden's wall, and here he sat conversing, presumably, with someone on the other side of the wall. Cat-paw quiet, the Grossbarts crept underneath him to better eavesdrop but upon hearing the incomprehensible tongue of Italia they resolved with a glance how to handle the situation. Hegel dropped to a knee and Manfried sprang from his brother's shoulder, seizing the Arab by his good leg and bringing them both crashing to the ground.

Hearing hurried footsteps fleeing over cobblestones on the other side of the wall confirmed their suspicions as to the duplicitous nature of their servant, and Manfried held the stunned cripple while Hegel drew his knife.

"Time you's clean a spirit," said Hegel, showing Al-Gassur his own terrified expression reflected on the blade.

"Please! What?! No no no, let me explain!"

"Explain away, traitor," said Manfried, tightening his grip around the Arab's pinned arms.

"Traitor? Never!" Al-Gassur did not struggle, the panic leaving his face as he met his own reflection.

"Own up and we'll make it quick for you," said Manfried. "You was tellin your heathenish relations bout our plans, wasn't you?"

"Givin'em time to ready for our arrival," Hegel clucked. "And after all we done for you. Shameful."

"I would sooner cut the tongue from my own mouth and feed it to that Rodrigo before I would slander my benefactors!" Al-Gassur said. "I merely sought to find the reason, for your mutual benefits, as to why the two of you, and by extension myself, have been forbidden to leave the grounds these last weeks."

"Forbidden?" Hegel laughed. "We ain't forbidden from nuthin!"

"Bide, bide," said Manfried, recalling the alcoholic distractions and bathy diversions placed before them whenever they had intended an outing over the previous month.

"Bide what?" asked Hegel in their twinspeak. "He was talkin foreign!"

"True enough," Manfried replied in kind. "But sounded right Italia-talk to me, not that Arab gibberish. Implies he mightn't be fibbin this once, least not completely. Hear'em out, and if I gives you the nod gut'em then."

"Fair's fair," Hegel said, reverting to the common language. "Tell us quick and true who you was talkin to, and spare no details if you want spared."

"And every other applicable item to boot," said Manfried, "bout what you been doin since we showed up and put your mecky Infidel ass honest in this house."

"Yes! Please! At once! Honest and without hesitation!" Al-Gassur may have carried on like this for some time had Hegel not wiggled his knife at the Arab. "From the beginning then, and if I may presume to suppose you might be willing to sully your nobly forested mouths with a bottle that my own corroded lips have blemished, I would be elated to share my unworthy beverage as well as my tale."

"Huh?" said Hegel.

"Ifing Master Manfried sees fit to release me, I would like to share my bottle of wine," Al-Gassur clarified.

"See, our company's makin you more honest by the moment,"

said Manfried, giving the man a final squeeze before letting him go.

Finding the bottle unbroken in his bag, Al-Gassur fished it out and took a swig before offering it to the Brothers.

"While the gutter has served as residence and employer for most of my time in Venezia, I have occasionally stooped to labor in more, as you say, honest ventures. An especially upstanding and chivalrous youth of noble standing spied me in a crowd and perceived I possessed all the graces required to be an ideal servant, and so I served in one of this fair city's most highly houses."

Al-Gassur spoke a variety of truth, for the young man in question indeed found the Arab to possess certain graces—said graces being an appearance and demeanor assured to raise the rancor of the youth's father. While Al-Gassur was never caught in the act of embezzling his master's sugar and pepper, the lad had tragically been slain in a duel with an equally shallow coxcomb and that very afternoon Al-Gassur found himself discharged.

"After I had done all I could for him, my original benefactor, and, dare I say, friend," Al-Gassur continued, "I found cause to advance myself. We are aware, are we not, that any worthwhile city, like any worthwhile pudding, holds a thick layer of fat atop it?"

Hegel nodded at this while Manfried futilely tried to think of a way of applying the analogy to graveyards that was not distasteful to his delicate sensibilities.

"So I found employment with our mutual and dearly departed friend and confidant, Ennio, in this very house," Al-Gassur said, omitting the detail that Ennio had hired him primarily to irritate his brother Rodrigo; a trend that, once established by his first master, served Al-Gassur all the days of his pragmatic life. "The barn is therefore familiar to me upon this, my second tenure in the House of Barousse. The matter of a missing cake from the kitchen's windowsill undid my previous employment, despite the obvious, blatant, and irrefutable proof that the guards set me up. Nestore, God bless and keep him, has found work for me to perform down these days whenever I am not actively serving you."

Nestore, the cook's husband and supplier of groceries, had taken to Al-Gassur at once, their mutual dislike of honest labor surpassed only by their affection for excessive drinking. Ennio and Nestore were the only ones who had stuck up for Al-Gassur when he was found munching the cake intended for Barousse's board. The first night the Arab spent back in the barn Nestore and he had celebrated with the exquisite schnapps Al-Gassur had stolen from Hegel's cask during the Grossbarts' first, stormy discourse with Rodrigo before being admitted to the grounds. The schnapps was supplemented with Nestore's cheese, sausage, and, of course, cake.

"Fascinatin," Manfried yawned. "Much as I'd love nuthin more than to hear your whole fuckin life told from when you crawled out your desert womb down to the present, with every time you copped a hot squat laid out in detail, time's an essence where savin lives is concerned."

"Saving lives?" Al-Gassur blinked.

"Yours," said Hegel. "You get on with who you was talkin to just now or you get cut, you loquacious piece a shit."

"Naturally, of course, without pause! My advantageous placement in society allows me to catch the random rumor, the occasional whisper, and a nightsoilman I keep company with often gathers gossip along with the excrement he dumps in the canals. A consequence of our long-standing friendship is that he, on occasion, will pause underneath our esteemed host's wall when he sees a rock balanced on the ledge, as he did today. I have known, as all with wits who dwell in this city do, that the doge harbors a strong disdain for Captain Barousse, although precisely why is all merely conjecture, and so I thought to enquire of him particular details, details which may explain why Barousse feels the need to keep his beloved Grossbarts safe behind these walls."

"Right," said Manfried. "We's finally fuckin gettin somewhere. You been consortin with shit-takers, which is fittin in light a your shitty nature. Could a said that in one word."

"Now brother," said Hegel, "no call in runnin down nightsoilmen, we wouldn't a gotten out a Bucharest without that sound fellow lettin us hide in his cart."

"Thanks for remindin me bout another one a your blessed schemes," said Manfried. "Buried alive in devil-dirt ain't exactly the fondest memory I got, and might not a been the only way out that situation. Now stow the reminiscences long enough to see if we got to kill us an Arab."

As the Brothers had not switched to their private dialect, Al-Gassur wasted no time in relaying the rest of his information. "According to my friend, the most immediate defamation goes like this: a certain merchant of certain repute harbors certain wanted brigands who reputedly sacked a certain village to the north, the same village a certain mistress of a certain prominent official hails from. That both her parents burned to death in the ensuing fire is no less certain. Worse still, her only brother and several of his friends were found murdered in the river shortly after."

This tale the nightsoilman had told gelled with the doge's emissary paying a visit to Barousse several days before, only to leave red-faced and cursing a short time later. Further confirmation came at once from the Grossbarts, who grinned at each other.

"Called us *certain* brigands, did he?" said Manfried. "Tomorrow you's puttin a stone out for your friend, then me and my brother can endeavor to impress on his *certain* ass the utility a usin proper language stead a slanderous terminology."

"Not his words, I assure you, but the words of the rumor!" said Al-Gassur. "He also says a new wrinkle has been revealed, namely that the, ah, *accused* brigands are in fact the leaders of a certain heretical sect calling themselves the Road Popes, and these blasphemous bandits have stolen much coin and spilled much blood which might have otherwise gone to Venezia, prior to this most recent and heinous and by no means proven crime of arson and murder."

The refutation of this rumor came to Al-Gassur in the form of a sound beating from the Brothers, who were more than happy to blame the messenger.

"Your life's spared for bein honest," said Manfried as he boxed the wailing Arab's ear. "That skin a yours' a different matter, phrasin them lies like we's them fuckin popes!"

"Easy on," said Hegel, jumping back rather than delivering the intended kick to the prostrate servant. "I just got me a touch a the chill."

"Someone's raisin a ruckus out front," said Manfried, his uncropped ear cocked to the side. "You's square enough for masonry now, Arab, make sure you keep yourself that way."

A breathless Father Martyn argued through the gate with the guards until Rodrigo and the Grossbarts arrived simultaneously, admitting him and leading the nervous fellow inside moments before several of the doge's guardsmen arrived. Barousse's guards were equally surly to the pikemen, who left after issuing several oaths and proclamations for the neighbors' benefit. To the observant Al-Gassur—who had slunk back to the barn to watch—trouble hovered over the Barousse household like the nightsoilman's swarm of flies.

"Heretics," Martyn panted as he sat down at Barousse's table.

The captain, perpetually distracted of late, picked idly at a fish bone, but the Grossbarts took interest in Martyn's return, his bruised face, and his vague proclamations regarding blasphemers of a yet-unnamed stripe.

"You ain't talkin bout us again," Manfried informed him.

"Or is you?" demanded Hegel.

"What?" Martyn rubbed his swollen cheeks. "No, no, no. Lord no. I mean the Church."

"That's better." Hegel reclined in his chair.

"Which church?" Only Rodrigo appeared dismayed by this.

"*The* Church." Martyn sipped more wine. "The only Church. The worm of corruption has been unearthed but I cannot exorcise it alone. How long? How long! Back to Formosus, certainly, but farther still I fear. Longer than my order has professed to battle heresy, certainly, certainly. Who remains untouched? Aquinas? Augustine?"

"Those weren't priests chasing you, they were guardsmen. Why?" Rodrigo pumped Martyn with all the subtlety of a burly child priming a spigot.

"Hounds, nothing more!" The priest swigged at their mention. "I bore their scorn before, for the name of God and man, but no more! Roquetaillade was right, rotting in prison for speaking the truth! End Times are upon us!"

"Calm yourself," said Rodrigo.

"Cease thy blathering!" said Martyn. "Nothing can be done for it! The Antichrist strides among us, gentlemen, he breathes and stalks and spreads ruin! Prophecy which they called heresy! They must have known, but feared martyring him lest he too rise. Saint Roquetaillade!"

Seeing his brother's confusion, Manfried clarified. "To get sainted you gotta die someways awful. Catch the wisdom?"

"Evil clever." Hegel nodded. "Didn't reckon the clergy might be so underhanded-like."

"That's just it," said Martyn, unswallowed wine spilling from his mouth. "Always, always! I offered to bring you before them to validate my tale but they would have none of it! Accused *me* of harboring a demon, me! Meanwhile the Great Mortality has not returned over spring nor summer in any part of the continent! Any! We smote it from the Earth, and yet *we* are deemed wicked, *we* are deemed guilty of blasphemy! We who put our lot with the lowly and craven, we who suffer alongside serf and cow, through winters without turnips and summers without wheat!"

Manfried scowled. "Seein how we's not yet royalty, I's a touch curious as to your choice a phrasin it *we we we*."

"They would not let me see him! I thought this Gomorrah's ill relations with our Mother Church would facilitate my immediate departure but alas, they are again close as brothers! I meant to stay only a night before journeying weeks, all to sit patiently for months seeking an audience in Avignon while hordes rally at our gates, that old Serpent never absent, our second fall!" Martyn babbled, then calmed, a rain-drunk creek of words. "I have not left the city since I left you, Grossbarts, seasons have passed and I have abided, imprisoned and tortured like the last Cathar to wither and die! That's what they did to the surviving Albigensians, you know, not a quick death for them! They sent for an inquisitor to bring me to the Holy Office, I heard them! Escaped in time, through His Will! Delivered back to you despite pursuit! His Will!"

"What's he on bout?" Hegel asked his brother.

"Parrently implicatin our good name in some fresh shit." Manfried was on his feet. "What in Hell's wrong with you?!"

"Demonslayers, are you not? What worthier devil than the Archfiend, our nemesis! Of course I brought the title Grossbart into the field! Humble though you now seem, I know of your greatness, and would be remiss not to draw you into my company, lying as you do somewhere between laity and clergy. Even Saint Roquetaillade and Saint Roch quail before your sanctity!

I have dreams, Grossbarts, and in them He has commanded me to do what is just! I thought that meant informing his so-called Holiness of the situation we endured, only to be undone! Not even exiled but imprisoned under his orders; his orders that the inquisitor pry the truth from my lips like some recalcitrant Judas!"

"You's mixin up tales, you drunken sod." Manfried shook his head, abandoning his efforts to decipher the ravings.

"Nah, keep talkin like that," Hegel insisted. "Whatever he's sayin sounds good to me. You's always speakin on how corrupt them priests and abbots and all is, and here's your proof!"

"He was proof enough fore he went incomprehensible." Manfried lowered his voice. "Seen how he looked at her."

"How he looked at *who*?" the captain unexpectedly joined the discourse.

"I have weaknesses!" Martyn shouted, the indignity of being talked about as though he were absent intolerable after months of such treatment. "I have passed every test, though, every one! Oh Elise, poor poor Elise, I tried, I tried so hard but I was weak! But not a woman have I touched sinfully since I accepted my mantle so long ago! In this forgotten time it matters not, for all that should go have gone and all that remain until the End are those now twice-damned and twice-fallen! And still I abstain from temptation, still and forever!" He gulped a final gulp and pitched forward, moaning on the table.

"Shit," Rodrigo said after a brief silence.

"Nuthin so sweet," said Manfried.

"So what'd he say?" asked Hegel.

"You heard, same as us." Manfried poured more wine.

"Yeah, but what's he mean?" Hegel pressed.

"He means we're in more trouble than just harboring the both of you," Rodrigo sighed, "unless we turn him over."

"To who?" asked Hegel.

"The Church, the doge's guard, whoever. He's wanted, same as the two of you."

"What's this bout us beein wanted?" Manfried's interest renewed at the prospect of an honest Arab.

"Murder, arson, and some other crimes less polite. Don't think we've asked you to stay within the grounds this past month for the pleasure of your company." Rodrigo kept glancing at Barousse for support but the captain stared at the wall, his face vacant.

"Wondered bout that." Hegel took the bottle his brother offered. "But no mistake, had we more shoppin or carousin to do we would a been gone like a goose in winter and come back if and when we wanted. But the end's what? We ain't turnin'em over to them heretics."

"So that I'm not misunderstanding, by *heretics* you mean the Church?" Rodrigo spoke slowly.

"Yeah, thems what think wearin fineries and havin precious baubles is intrinsic to their devotion. You know, heretics," said Hegel.

"We would all be burned if your feelings were known," Rodrigo hissed.

"Mind the lip, lad," Manfried belched. "That priest is the best we's seen in our time, and less he proves otherwise anyone callin him out on heresy is workin for Old Scratch themself."

"We're dead!" Rodrigo jumped up, knocking Hegel's feet off the table and spilling wine on the dozing Martyn. "Denying them you is difficult, but his presence will make it impossible! Even now they will be preparing an assault, and if not that, a siege! An inquisitor has been sent, and we hold the object of his summons! Dead and damned!"

"Sit down," Barousse said wearily. "Shouting like that soused church mouse'll do nothing for any of us. You want to cut your ties and float on your own, I won't stop you."

The quivering Rodrigo did not sit, but nor did he leave or interrupt.

"Grossbarts vouch for him, good enough for us," Barousse continued. "Besides, the Church is nothing to fear. True Venetians will never cower before a pope. They threatened excommunication when your dad and I were trading with the Saracens all those years back. Never stopped him cold, nor me neither."

"But you were never caught." Rodrigo crumbled.

"Who's saying we're caught now?" Barousse demanded. "They can suspect all they want, but won't heave that one on us until they're sure. And they won't be sure until they break in the gate. It's late now, so the soonest they'll come for us is tomorrow morn."

"Exactly!" Rodrigo began shaking again. "We can't fight them all, and the ship isn't nearly ready!"

"Your dad should of named you Tommaso!" Barousse stood, shaking even more fiercely than Rodrigo. "Don't trust your captain no more? Doubting me always? Think I've gotten so chair-softened I'd let some pikeman or prelate slit my throat? Think I'd turn over my loyal men rather than fight it out?"

"Captain, I—" Rodrigo stared at the floor.

"Out, Grossbarts, and take the priest!" Barousse shouted, but when they reached the door he added, "Come armed to my room around Vespers, we'll work on our stratagem then. For now, I have a mutiny to quell." He turned back to Rodrigo but to the young man's relief the captain's fury had dissipated, leaving a mischievous grin in its wake.

The Grossbarts could easily have carried Martyn but instead each held an arm and let his legs drag—all the better to upend several small tables. He frothed and groaned the entire way up the stairs and, lacking a third unlocked room to dump him in, they slung him onto Hegel's floor. Shouting until the servant girl Marguerite arrived, they enlisted her help in the transfer of

Hegel's bed into Manfried's room rather than share the room with Martyn. Only by mutilating the frame, tearing the mat, and impressing four of Barousse's hired muscle were they able to perform the task.

Tramping through the dark tunnel beneath the house to carry out the captain's orders, Rodrigo again turned his thoughts to his deceased brother Ennio. With all the madness the Grossbarts had added to his life he had been left little time to reflect on his own affairs instead of Barousse's, but with this newest catastrophic twist he again reflected on what impact the Brothers Grossbart might have had on the passing of his last living kin, and how he might have averted it had he accompanied Ennio instead of remaining behind. He resolved to visit a chapel as soon as this business was past, a single tear escaping his eye. Had he known what chaos approached he would have wept more.

Directly above Rodrigo, Al-Gassur spied on the artisans laboring in the garden. For several weeks the men had arrived at dawn and left at dusk, felling fruit trees, shaving them down, and lashing them together. Gauging by the massive boulder delivered and harnessed to one end of the contraption it neared completion, and now the men patted each other's backs after a successful trial of winching up the stone and letting it drop again. Stranger still, the captain himself made an appearance, the cook brought out food and drink, and her husband Nestore brought oil lamps, with the clear purpose of persuading the men to work through the night. Had Al-Gassur actually seen the combat in which he claimed to have lost his leg he might have recognized the device.

Leaving Martyn to recover, the Grossbarts went to the captain's bedchamber for the first time in the many months they had spent under his roof. It lay across the foyer from their quarters, the entire opposite wing a single chamber. Knocking on the door they received no answer but then he suddenly appeared behind them on the stairs, head high and jagged teeth shining in the light of the setting sun filtering through the windows. Unlocking the brass door, he beckoned them in.

They found themselves encaged, thick iron bars stretching from floor to ceiling in a wide box around the door. Only when Barousse had locked the door behind him did he produce another key and open the door of the cage. His room dwarfed most buildings they had entered, with a huge tub set into the right side of the floor stretching from one end of the room to the other. Stepping over the shallow aqueduct that led from the bath into the opposite wall they noticed the massive bed and table, ornate clothes strewn everywhere but inside the pool. Both recognized the shimmer of stray coins underneath the flotsam of loose clothing, and even the briny odor of the bath added to the majesty of the place.

"Can never be cautious enough," Barousse explained, locking the cage behind them.

"Right opulent," said Hegel.

"Yeah," agreed Manfried, the tub immediately capturing his attention. A shadow flitted under the water without raising a ripple and he held his breath, but she did not appear.

"Fancy it, do you?" Barousse stepped in front of Manfried, obstructing his view.

"What's that?" Manfried blinked.

"My property." The good-natured Barousse of the doorway had vanished, replaced by his moody doppelganger.

"Course," Manfried said, holding Barousse's gaze. "Anyone but a fool'll preciate what you got."

"Appreciate or covet?" Barousse's fiery eyebrows wedged against each other.

"Preciate, verily," Hegel interjected. "We's here by your grace, don't forget."

"Yeah, captain." Manfried shook his head to clear it. "What

warrants our presence at Vespers when we oughta be prayin like decent folk?"

"Pray with me, Grossbarts." Barousse's voice cracked and he fell to his knees before a large shrine set in an alcove, snatching their shoulders and pulling them down with him. His beard bunched up around his neck as he whispered in another unknown language, water leaking from his squinting eyes. The Grossbarts grumbled in their own tongue to the life-sized statue of Mary for patience, strength, and inspiration. And lots of gold.

Then Barousse's tone hardened, his words entered the vernacular they understood, and they began punctuating his rapid prayers with amens:

"And grant us the will of arm and spirit to destroy those in our way, we who are kings amongst yeomen, we who have served the lot of Job, survived the trials of Abraham, all without respite or mercy. We will not let them slander us and the good Lord through us, and we will not surrender to those blasphemous idolaters who control the Church and the city. We will be His Sword and His Vengeance on the betrayers of man and God!"

Barousse's voice rose to a roar, and he bruised their shoulders under his fierce clutch. "We will be the horsemen returned, the Scythe of the Lord! We will hack our way to the deserts despoiled by the Infidel! We will hurl their souls to Judgment, and those of their bastard families with them! We will take what they have stolen! We will kill as He kills until there are none but we left in the Holy Land! Every loss we have suffered will be avenged upon His enemies ten thousandfold!"

Hegel nodded and amened, but Manfried's attention drifted to the pool beside him, and then he saw her for the first time since they arrived. Without making a sound she had emerged from the water and bridged her arms on the rim of the tub, her pointy chin resting atop her hands. She blinked her almond eyes, her face and hair slick and dripping onto her tub-obscured chest. Then she smiled and disappeared silently under the surface before Manfried could get a proper gaze at her. He realized she must be nude, and nervously glanced at Barousse and Hegel, who were both shouting now.

"And blood and fire from Mary!" Hegel hollered.

"And the moon will plummet, raising the tides to swallow the flourishing Sodoms! Avignon and Roma, Paris and Praha! München and London and Jerusalem and Cairo and Constantinople! The heathen East and the heretical West alike! Damn them all!"

"Damn them all!"

"Damn." Manfried swallowed, then, seeing the statue of the Virgin jump toward them, "Damn!"

"Enlightenment is upon you, Grossbarts!" bellowed Barousse, holding them tighter lest they flee or attack the moving statue. He need not have worried, for the draft tickling their beards told the truth. The seasoned Grossbarts snatched hold of Mary and pulled her farther out, allowing the winded Rodrigo to emerge from the passage. He stank of fish and mold but his frigid countenance warmed at the embrace Barousse delivered upon him.

"Success, my son?" Barousse squeezed Rodrigo.

"Success," Rodrigo squeaked, the tears on his cheeks more from the captain's choice of words than his ferocious hug. "Here he is."

Barousse released the young man and turned to the fellow the Grossbarts stared at. The sinewy man blinked and pushed back the wisps of hair in his pale eyes, the Grossbarts recognizing him for a beast of pure muscle and vigor despite his years. The captain and the man sized each other up, a faint smile playing at Barousse's beard.

"Captain," the man clipped, bowing his head, and then Barousse hoisted him up and spun him around, laughing.

"Angelino!" Barousse said when he managed to quell his joy and set his friend down. "Too long, too long!"

"No fault of mine, Captain." Angelino winked.

"Alexi, always Alexi to you!"

"And that'll be *Captain* Angelino to you, from what the boy says." The new arrival grinned.

"Well, well, well." Barousse feigned amazement. "Captain, eh? Fair enough, though I would have had you my mate again on the old haunt if time would permit."

"The trappings may seem lesser, and the title as well, but if we indeed have a day's notice a few of the old bones can be unearthed and dried out enough to join us. According to his nephew here Sergio won't be putting in for another few weeks, which is doubly ill for he kept a bit better watch than I on where the crew's drifted over the lonely—" Angelino peered over Barousse's shoulder and blanched, then slapped his friend in the face.

Only with the barrage of Italian Angelino emitted did the Brothers notice they had spoken in German before. Barousse's entire face turned the color of his reddening cheek and he swelled up to smite the smaller man, who shouted and shook an accusatory finger in Barousse's face. Rodrigo recognized the dire turn and, seizing Angelino, dragged him back. Hegel knew better than to touch the trembling captain, instead stepping in his line of sight and offering him a bottle.

"Nuthin a drink won't fix," Hegel announced. "Why's it you two was talkin proper and switched to Papal, eh?"

Barousse let out the breath he had bottled since being hit and focused on Hegel, snatching the wine from him. Angelino had thrown off Rodrigo and now dressed down the younger fellow, punctuating his rant with gestures at Hegel and the captain. Barousse guzzled the entire bottle, red spilling down his beard onto his boots. Then he dropped the wine, pushed aside Hegel, then Rodrigo, and threw his arms around Angelino, crying like a fresh orphan. Rodrigo hurried over to Hegel and walked him to the narrow window overlooking the garden, which they both

found intensely interesting while Barousse blubbered and snot-
ted all over Angelino's shoulder, the older man's fury gone as
quickly as the captain's.

Hegel peered down at the lamp-lit garden and the reflecting
pool where he and his brother had clandestinely practiced swim-
ming when all in the house slept. Looking back around the room,
he saw Manfried lurking at the edge of the bath. Containing his
own rage, he succeeded in crossing the room without arousing
Barousse's or Angelino's attention, the two now exchanging
whispered oaths.

"What're you doin?" Hegel snarled, noting the silhouette
ghosting about under the water.

"Just lookin." Manfried would not meet his brother's eye,
clumsily stowing something in his bag.

"Keep away from there," Angelino called to them, and all
three hurried back to the altar.

"My word, my word," Barousse mumbled, having sat on a
chest.

"Course, sir." Angelino nodded. "These lads'll come with me
now, then?"

The Grossbarts looked to the captain, who nodded but did
not return their gaze. "I'll need them back fore dawn."

"That the chest, then?" Angelino smiled.

"Yes." Barousse wearily stood and clapped Angelino on the
arm, his good spirits returning. "It is, it is. And remember, sparse
at best. Less mouths to feed."

"On that end I'll fit us with water and supplies and what few
can be trusted for such a jaunt."

"Angelino," Barousse swallowed, "I intend to avenge myself
on the doge, meaning we'll be hunted if ever we return with less
than an army behind us. Still in league?"

"No question," Angelino said. "Now let's see what you got
here."

The chest contained gold bars. Hegel and Manfried saw Mary's Mercy shining up at them and silently gave thanks. Then they began stuffing them into the leather satchels provided by Barousse until not a speck of gold dust glittered in the empty box. Rodrigo and Angelino could not carry as much, which suited the Grossbarts perfectly. Leaving the captain to prepare, they followed Rodrigo into the chute behind the Virgin, clambering down iron bars set into the wall.

The rungs were mossy and the satchels heavy, and twice Rodrigo almost slipped but caught himself. The bath's aqueduct emptied into the shaft, the stink of mold a familiar tonic to the Grossbarts. Angelino's boots rained filth down on Manfried, prompting him to hurry and thus increasing the muck he dislodged upon his brother.

The sound of running water rose up around them, and then Hegel went weak in the knees when his feet found slick stones instead of a rung. Rodrigo flicked his flint, burning their eyes. Not until Manfried and Angelino reached the bottom did the wick catch, illuminating the pit.

Stone and earth bled together along the walls with only the narrow shelf they stood on evidencing the channel's man-made nature. In the dim light the waters were black as the walls and ceiling, the path obvious as the shelf broke off a few feet downstream. Rodrigo led them along the mildew-rank outcropping, their pace sluggish to avoid slipping over the edge. Across from them smaller channels intermittently joined the main flow, fell breezes wafting along the streams.

A narrow canal emerged from the wall in front of them, dirty water pouring over their shelf. Rodrigo knelt and shone the candle up the passage, and with a sigh stepped into the stream. The rushing water came up to his knees, and he plodded up this new channel with the others following. The ceiling sank lower until all four were hunched over like flagellants, the frigid canal deepening to their waists. Those reproachable Grossbarts naturally felt at ease, and wished they had learned of this part of the city earlier.

"I do not know if our captain had these built or if they were already here," Rodrigo explained as they moved away from the roaring main flow. "Have to mind sudden storms; a shower above will fill these in an instant."

"Figured all a them canals might lead to a place like this." Hegel nodded. "But what's it for?"

"It is for nothing," said Rodrigo, "save for us."

"Why's it you and the captain speak proper to one another?" Manfried asked Angelino.

"Custom," Angelino said, ducking under some dangling rot. "Many here and more abroad don't speak it so we got in the habit of that. Less worry of your words being stolen if they're not understood."

"Sound," Manfried agreed.

"Easy on," Hegel growled, his brother having walked into him.

"Quiet," Rodrigo whispered, blowing out his candle.

All eyes picked up on a faint oval of yellow ahead of them in the black. Rodrigo did not advance to the canal's mouth, however, but crept forward only a few feet, brushing the clammy ceiling with his free hand. Tripping after him in the current, Hegel saw him stop and then stand erect, his head and shoulders vanishing into the ceiling. Rodrigo began climbing, and stepping after him Hegel saw a hole open above and, groping for rungs, followed him up.

This shaft widened as they climbed the short distance to the surface, the odor of rotting fish overpowering their senses. Rodrigo stopped so they all stopped, and he awkwardly reached up and fiddled with something. With a metallic squeak he freed his quarry, and several pounds of putrid fish and crustaceans cascaded down on them. Rodrigo crawled up and out of sight, then Hegel went through, and he turned to help his brother and Angelino.

Thick iron bars covered the mouth of the pit, but Rodrigo had freed one and rolled it aside. Their eyes watered from the heap of decomposing sea fruits choking most of the grate, generations of interlocking bones and scales preventing the mass from slipping down to its intended grave. With the others shaking the filth off, Rodrigo gave the dark alley another glance before kneeling and refitting the dislodged bar.

The pack of stray dogs they had frightened off with their unexpected appearance slunk back, growling at the interlopers. Before Hegel could brain the closest beast Rodrigo reminded them of the necessity of secrecy, and that making the pack howl with pain and bark with fury would not be in their interest. They circumvented the animals, who returned to gorging themselves on the freshest and rolling in the oldest of the refuse. The candles remained unlit but after the sunken avenues the waning moon served well enough, Angelino replacing Rodrigo as guide.

As the older man led them through the labyrinthine passages Hegel sometimes felt eyes watching from side avenues and black windows, but they met no one on the streets. Small bridges were delicately trod, the report of boot on wood breaking the stillness that earthen streets afforded them. The sound of the sea grew, feeding the Grossbarts' unease. Having avoided the city's pageantries as strictly as they abstained from fasting during Lent, the Grossbarts' only indications of the Venetian people's character came from the dour men skulking in the streets and rowing through the canals when the Brothers had vainly quested for a landlocked cemetery. The tomb-burglars assumed they might be sold out for half a ducat by any and all witnesses to their nocturnal sojourn.

Angelino stopped once and drew them all into a crack between two moldering buildings, and they heard footfalls approach, then depart, along a nearby alley. Even in this dismal quarter the edifices towered over them, blotting out the sky. Returning to the road, they went only a few more blocks before Angelino ducked under an arch and rapped softly on a small door.

From within came a knocking in response, to which Angelino softly whistled. The door swung open, and Angelino stepped into the dark interior. Rodrigo followed, then Hegel, with Manfried nervously gripping the pommel of his mace in one hand and holding the satchel of gold closer with the other. In the blackness someone closed the door behind him, and just before Manfried could draw his weapon a second door opened ahead of them, scalding their sensitive eyes with light.

The small tavern had tables made of driftwood and a bar consisting of a dozen oars lashed together. Behind this stood a gnarled stump of a man whose curdled-yellow eyes bespoke blindness. A gargantuan man closed the second door behind them, the only other occupant a short, black-haired fellow drinking by the hearth. Angelino led them to his table and the barkeep brought ales, the ox looming over them. Manfried exchanged hateful glares with the muscle while Angelino and the short one carried on a hurried conversation in Italian, which Rodrigo unsuccessfully tried to join.

Just when Manfried had resolved to call his adversary out Angelino turned to the Brothers and addressed them in German:

"And this priest Barousse says you bring, is he to be trusted?"

"More than most, but that ain't sayin a whole lot." Manfried slurped his ale.

"But he traveled with you and that thing you returned to him?" Angelino insisted.

"Thing?" Manfried narrowed his eyes.

"That slant-eyed slattern," the short man said in broken German.

Sensing his brother tense up, Hegel quickly interjected. "Yeah, the priest was with us most a the trip."

"And," Angelino frowned, "did anything unnatural befall you, either before or after he joined with you? Water-related, I mean; drownings, floods, that sort?"

"Yeah, before—" Hegel winced as Manfried kicked him under the table, but he kicked back and continued. "Yeah, fore he come one a Barousse's men drowned in a pool no deeper than a turnshoe-top, and my own brother here almost went the same."

"Told you, I was sleep-wanderin'," Manfried said, cheeks flushing under his beard.

"And after he came with you?" Angelino pressed.

"After, I don't recollect nuthin cept—" Manfried viciously thumped Hegel behind the knee. "—cept my brother here almost drowned again in a river." Hegel scowled at Manfried.

"And where was the priest then?" the short one asked.

"Oh, he'd just been shot for the *second* time." Manfried glared at Hegel.

The two Italians reverted to their tongue, prattling back and forth while the Grossbarts had their own private discussion on the importance of clarity of meaning as related to physical inter-actions. Rodrigo saw his brother in the bottom of his mug, and strengthened his resolve to have a solid pray on Ennio's pass-ing. The men turned back to the Grossbarts, who had likewise reached a consensus, welts and bruises rising on the thighs and calves of both.

"Glad as I am to again serve my friend and captain," Ange-lino addressed them, "that thing he keeps is no good to any man, and I won't suffer to be in its presence any longer than I must. I tell you now as I told him, when the time comes for us and it to part company over the side it goes, no matter what he says. You two are his inspiration to finally be rid of it, and return to Arab lands besides, so we must all be agreed before we set out. I am the captain of my vessel, not he, and as long as you are on my ship and I am taking you to your goal you will obey my orders, not his. Agreed?"

"See here—" Rodrigo started.

"Do not mistake my tone for hostile, boy," Angelino shot at Rodrigo. "I served the captain for more years than you've lived, and toiled beside your departed pa and absent uncle. I was one of the few who was with him on the boat he brought it back to, and I'm the only one of those present still drawing breath stead of brine, so I know of what I speak. One thing's more important than coin, and that's being alive to snatch more."

"We's agreed," said Hegel, nodding at the wisdom.

"And you?" the short one asked Manfried.

"Didn't take your name," Manfried drawled.

"Giuseppe," the diminutive fellow replied.

"Well, Seppe," Manfried began, even Hegel anticipatorily holding his breath, "I's inclined to take my brother's position. You and Angelino's in our service to get us to Gyptland, with the arrangement bein we'll do everythin in our power to keep us on course. Not bein familiar with such matters, we'll defer to your judgment as we would a hired wagon driver."

Giuseppe's already beady eyes tapered further but he held his tongue and turned to his employer. After looking from Grossbart to Grossbart Angelino's face lightened and he raised his mug:

"A sound agreement. Now which one of you is Heigel?"

"That's *Hegel*," Manfried said, pointing to his brother.

"And he's Manfried," said Hegel.

"Good, good. I'm Angelino, as you already know. The one behind you is Merli, and he'll be taking that gold off your shoulders."

"The Hell he will." Manfried stood up.

"Grossbarts." Rodrigo stood as well. "These men would

sooner steal from the Pope than the captain. Give them his property."

"That don't mean nuthin at all," Manfried retorted, "just said, honest-like, bein alive's more important than anythin else, includin friendship."

"If you don't give it to him," Rodrigo growled, "you can't very well carry more when we come back."

"Suppose there's a hint a wisdom in that," Hegel allowed, setting his satchel on the table. "So we leave yous to put this on the boat, then fetch the captain and come back?"

"We sail tomorrow," Angelino said firmly. "Captain might have no future here, and maybe I don't either, but I'd just as soon not attract any more attention by leaving at night. At dawn I'll fix it so my girl's waiting at the dock right out that door." He motioned to the latched front door none had entered through. "I'll have Merli wait here so anytime after dawn you all come here and we push out. Course she's a wee brim compared to Barousse's, so we'll have to hug the coast a little tighter, add a few days or weeks to the passage, but I'm staking my life alongside yours she'll do us good, if a little cramped. So we're straight on who's coming, yeah?"

Rodrigo nodded. "The captain's contingent and you and yours."

"Good, good. We'll load the gold, then, and make ready to depart. Well met, Grossbarts." Angelino added something in Italian to Rodrigo, which he smiled faintly at before turning his satchel over to the men. To the Grossbarts it felt like dumping their war chest into a bottomless chasm but they had little choice. Escorting them to the back door, Angelino again embraced Rodrigo, shook the Grossbarts' hands, and let them out.

XX

Venetian Heartbreak

A chill and salty wind stung their faces, any speed they gained from being unburdened of their gold negated by Rodrigo's paranoia and unfamiliarity with the exact route home. Just as they rounded the last corner before the grate, Hegel experienced the familiar prickling of hairs and tightening of gut. Before he could say a word, over a dozen figures rushed from either side of the alley, swarming the trio.

Rather than hacking into them, the attackers fell upon their waists with sharp rocks and rusty knives, trying to cut off their purses and weapons. None of the figures reached up to Rodrigo's chest, and their stink gave them away for a band of street urchins. The first to reach them hurled a bowl of liquid into Rodrigo's face, blinding him.

Prepared for nothing more than drunken merchants returning from the Whores District, the children began screaming as Grossbart iron was in hand and use before they could be mobbed. In an instant the children were fleeing, but Manfried's mace shattered a dawdler's hip and sent him rolling. Hegel brought his pick down on another's back, pinning him dead before he could blink. Manfried put a stop to the wailing of the injured boy by stomping his neck while Hegel poured water into Rodrigo's eyes.

The pack split down the alleys, the cry of murder echoing off walls and into windows. Manfried snatched up Rodrigo while Hegel clumsily loaded his crossbow but they had all fled into the darkness. With Hegel watching their backs they hurried the short distance to the end of the alley, running off the dogs with sharp kicks. Bells began ringing, and as the half-blind Rodrigo felt through the muck for the loose bar they heard the approach of angry men. Rodrigo went down first and Manfried after but as Hegel knelt to unload his crossbow he heard footsteps. Crouching with his bow trained at the alley's intersection, he saw a child hurry over to the boy Manfried had killed.

Hegel bit his lip, the lad not twenty feet away but focused on his dead friend or brother. Placing one foot on the first rung, Hegel slipped the slightest bit and his pouch clinked against his side. The child's head spun around, and in the moonlight Hegel saw a crying girl not yet ten years old. They stared at one another, the girl slowly standing while Hegel's free hand snuck to his purse. The girl straightened as Hegel held up a gold coin. With an unspoken prayer on his lips, Hegel twisted the coin so it shone in the dimness, and then the girl twisted on her heels to flee.

Hegel's left hand dropped the coin and steadied the arbalest, and before the gold hit the street he fired. The coin still plummeting, Hegel knew he had acted too hastily, his shot off the mark. At the twang of his bow, however, the girl instinctively jumped to the side and caught the bolt in the nape of her neck.

The coin bounced and the girl spun against the wall, hair swirling around her head, and to Hegel's amazement her face was gone, replaced with that of Brennen—the murdered son of Heinrich the turnip farmer. Momentum propelled her into the wall and she slid down it, rolling to face Hegel. Brennen's face had fled back over the mountains to his grave, her features still bulging but again unfamiliar and feminine. The head of the arrow shone at him under her raised chin before she slipped forward. Bubbles rose around her ears as she drowned in the widening pool of her own blood. The bells were almost upon them. Snatching up his dropped coin, Hegel descended the ladder and slid the bar back into place. Holding his breath, he scrambled down into darkness.

The return took even longer, the children having stolen Rodrigo's candle. In perfect darkness they picked their way back, Manfried taking the lead and Hegel assisting Rodrigo. They went back up the chute and into the glow of Barousse's chambers, the man himself seated before the Virgin, eager for news. None were given to idle chatter, and the captain's mood turned as acerbic as their odor. All three went to the bath in their wing that Barousse had prudently ordered for them. Despite going to bed immediately after their bath, each stayed up long into the night thinking of women—Rodrigo intent on the Virgin and how she might intercede on behalf of his dead brother, Manfried mulling on the so-called Nix's song, and Hegel unable to free his mind of the girl he had ruthlessly murdered.

The result of their nocturnal meditations was that none rose with the sun; instead all were roused later in the morning by the clamor of Barousse yelling in the foyer. Eighteen men waited outside the gate for admittance, men Barousse had no intention of letting in. The doge, a cardinal directly from Avignon, a chevalier from north of there, and fifteen of the doge's guards waited impatiently, their words and the words of Barousse's mercenaries rising to shouts. Rodrigo hurried outside after his captain while the Grossbarts made for the kitchen, disgusted their tugging at the bell rope had not summoned breakfast.

The doge, whose name, despite common usage, was certainly not the Italian term for prostitute, smiled at the approaching Barousse, Cardinal Buñuel ineffectively counseling him against rashness. At his holy toady's insistence, the doge had withdrawn the archers he had ordered to snipe from the rooftops, although usually the doge was anything but obedient to the Church. Times change, however, as they are wont to do, and doge and cardinal both hoped Venezia's strained relations with the Papacy might be eased for their mutual benefit.

Sir Jean Gosney sweated under his visor, not for the first time internally bemoaning the dictates of formality that forced him into his iron shell. The cardinal dismounted from his horse and stepped toward the gate, and the doge and the knight silently did the same.

The pikemen bunched up on either side, their three betters standing before the gate with reins in hand to enter as gentlemen. Instead of ordering the gate opened, Barousse stopped before it and belched. The cardinal winced, the doge scowled, and the knight wrinkled his upturned nose.

"What do I owe the pleasure, with my fast hardly broke?" Barousse asked.

"Listen, Alexius," the doge began, "you know why we've come, and any pretensions that you don't will be seen as admission of guilt."

"It is *Captain Barousse*, if you do not mind, Doge Strafa— Doge," Barousse said, flashing a smile at the cardinal. "And who are your guests?"

"I am Cardinal Buñuel," the red-frocked man said sharply.

"And I am Sir Jean Gosney of Meaux." The armored man bowed. "A chevalier in the service of the cardinal."

"Now that we're acquainted, it's time you turned over to us those whom, for the sake of this city's honor as well as your own, we are willing to assume you were incarcerating on our behalf." The doge clicked his boots together.

"The Grossbarts." Barousse's smile widened. "And the priest who sought sanctuary here, yes?"

"He is no longer a priest." Cardinal Buñuel wiped sweat from his brow.

The Grossbarts found Martyn in the kitchen wolfing down cold bacon with his left hand, the right one, which the Road Popes had injured, now lame and dangling. He sloshed a glass of wine in their direction and returned to his meal. Hegel poked his head outside while Manfried shouted into the cellar. Together they checked the servants' quarters off the hall to the foyer. They were vacant of both people and belongings, irking the Brothers further.

"Where'd they go, then?" Manfried demanded.

"Dismissed." Martyn swallowed. "This morning, sent them all off. Those men working in the garden last night as well."

"Stands to reason, I suppose," said Hegel, he and Manfried sitting down beside Martyn to eat.

Captain Barousse's grin never faltered, unnerving Rodrigo even more than the wary doge. "With pleasure will I give them to you, for, as you say, I only meant to keep them until your arrival. Frankly, I began to worry I would have to send for you to relieve me of them, so slothful was your pacing."

"What?" The doge blinked, unprepared for this turn.

"I suspected they might be ruffians, but without your confirmation I could do little but stall their departure. Then this lunatic ally of theirs arrives dressed as a priest and spouting six kinds of heresy, and I have to hold my sword for a full day and night until you deign to visit. Honestly, Strafalaria, any grudge you bear me should not have delayed your dutiful action to deliver me from such blasphemies." Rodrigo covered his gaping mouth with his hand, never having seen Barousse so alert.

"What is the delay we are now experiencing, then?" Cardinal Buñuel asked. The doge was overjoyed Barousse's bluster had not distracted the cleric but was disappointed the use of the hated moniker Strafalaria went unnoticed.

"This and nothing more," Barousse said without pause. "Until this very moment I could not confirm the Grossbarts were indeed wanted by you. I would have my men bring them to you this instant but they are pious Christians like the rest of us, and refuse to lay hands upon the priest and those with his blessing, by whom I mean those bearded bastards, until such time as a higher authority, as it were, confirmed for them the priest was indeed a heretic and not simply, ah, confused."

"He has confirmed it!" The doge haughtily declared.

"Only by assuming the priest lodged within is indeed the priest he seeks." Barousse extended his palms. "So you see my conundrum?"

"Did he give the name Martyn?" asked the cardinal.

"He did not give any name at all," answered Barousse.

"Then let us in and we'll have a look!" said the exasperated doge.

"I am not in the custom of taking orders when I have done nothing to deserve the overthrow of my command," Barousse said, quickly adding, "but to prove I have done nothing wrong, I will gladly welcome you, revered cardinal, to enter as my guest and confirm the identity of the priest, at which time *my* men will take them out and give them to *your* men."

"What are you scheming?" the doge shouted, earning a stern look from the cardinal and a hidden smile from the chevalier.

"And you would prove my innocence by invading my home and seizing those who you would dub my guests? A display born of perhaps pernicious intent?" Barousse fired back, Rodrigo nervously glancing at the assembled guards, who numbered nearly twice those in Barousse's service.

"Deranged or not, he seems far from stupid enough to bring all of Christendom down upon his head by doing me harm," Buñuel whispered in the scarlet ear of the doge. Then, turning back to Barousse, he raised his voice. "And surely, as my host, you would consent to my bringing a guest whom I vouch for, the honorable Sir Jean?"

"Without reservation, and the doge as well if— No?" Barousse masked his displeasure at Strafalaria's shaking head with an even broader smile. "As you choose, then. Now, if I may have the good doge's word his men will not attempt to storm my residence when I open the gate, we may get this over with and I may finish my repast."

"That's fine." The doge grimaced. "You have my word. If they are not returned with the felons in very short order you also have my word they will come in whether you open the gate or not."

Barousse waved his hand dismissively while the gate swung open, the captain's men clearly as relieved as the doge's that things had ended thus. The cardinal and the chevalier left their reins in Strafalaria's hand, making him wish he had brought a page along. The gate clicked shut again, and Barousse winked at the fuming doge before escorting the men into the house. Rodrigo hurried around the side to the kitchen door, dumbstruck that the frenzied plan Barousse had whispered to him on the short walk to the meeting had unfolded so flawlessly but worried the Grossbarts would not be where the captain insisted they would be. Their presence in the kitchen was not surprising but still a relief, prone as the Grossbarts were to thwarting expectations.

"To arms, Grossbarts," Rodrigo panted. "Our enemies are upon us."

"How's that?" One hand went to Manfried's mace but the other stayed on his cheese.

"The doge has come to arrest the three of you, bringing with him a French knight and a cardinal as well as men, but the captain has outwitted them, and now," Rodrigo tilted his head toward the sound of the great door in the foyer opening, "he has lured the doge's guests inside, and we must take them prisoner. Now! And by force!"

Shouting reached them, and still chewing their breakfast the

Grossbarts hurried down the hall after Rodrigo. Martyn followed at a sensible distance, a bottle in his good hand. Entering the spacious chamber they saw four of Barousse's men aiming crossbows at two impressive figures, one bristling in plate and chain armor, the other draped with lily-white, coal-black, and blood-red cloth. Both were shouting at the pleasantly smiling Barousse, but they quieted when he stepped forward and laid the edge of his cutlass against the cardinal's throat.

"Better." Barousse nodded. "Much better. May I present Cardinal Buñuel and His Lordship Sir Jean Gosney of Meaux. Cardinal, Sir Jean, this is Hegel Grossbart and Manfried Grossbart, my two advisors. Rodrigo you have already met, and who is this? Ah, of course, the supposedly defrocked priest, Father Martyn."

"We are already intimately acquainted," Martyn sneered, making directly for Buñuel. "You have erred in the introductions, however, captain, for this man has no authority over a servant of God. This heretic presided over my torture! How dare you wear those robes in my presence? You are hereby excommunicated!" To the delight of Barousse and the Grossbarts and the horror of everyone else, Martyn slapped the cardinal in the face. He then twisted around and stormed back to the kitchen before he committed greater sins.

"Blasphemy," Buñuel gasped. "Seize them, Jean, dash their mouths!"

Like many veterans of his age and country, Sir Jean had been captured and ransomed several times in his life, and found the arrangement far more comfortable than a martyr's death. His command of Italian therefore failed him, and he unfastened his helm to better demonstrate his obedience. Bowing to Buñuel, he remastered the language of his captors and turned to Barousse.

"If you will give me your demands I will shout them to the doge, and I vouchsafe he will prove more honest in his negotiations than most." Sir Jean shrugged at the livid cardinal.

"Tell him to wait until Vespers for your release, at which time I will have received a full pardon from Church and city for my regrettably forceful keeping of both of your company," said Barousse. "Furthermore, all of my men and guests will likewise receive identical pardons, I will be recompensed to the sound of one thousand ducats, and receive the word of both of you as well as the doge that this matter, soon to be forgiven by the Lord, will be forgiven by you personally as well. Tell that weasel to wait at his palace for any further demands, which shall be sent before dark."

"Churl!" Cardinal Buñuel spit. "Think you can imprison us by sword and get whatever you desire? Heaven is not granted to such rogues!"

"Imprison?" Barousse adopted a pained expression and sheathed his sword. "Never! You are free to leave at your will! Of course, if you choose to leave before I grant it my men will murder you where you stand. But imprison? No, no. No irons, no cages, simply hospitality as befits men of your station."

The Grossbarts were staring at the weathered chevalier, who without his sharp-visored hounskull helmet looked decidedly less intimidating. His paunchy jowls were smooth, and what few scars he possessed were shallow and indistinct. Compounding matters, he had lathered himself with perfume, reminding the Brothers of the witch's pungent hut.

"Hop to, then." Barousse had moved to the door when the cardinal, who saw the fear on the faces of his guards, addressed the crossbowmen.

"By directing your weapons at me you have damned yourselves! Only if I live may you be absolved!" Then the cardinal broke for the door.

Hegel caught him in the shin with the haft of his pick, sending Buñuel sprawling in the doorway. The Grossbarts snatched him up and held his arms while he spit and kicked, his normally placid nature undone by the indignity. With a nod from the captain they dragged him to the kitchen while Barousse, Rodrigo, and the guards supervised Sir Jean's recitation of demands to the furious but not entirely surprised doge.

The doge left his pikemen blocking the gate and rode off while Barousse shut the door and clapped Rodrigo on the back. The scheme had succeeded more than even he had hoped, and after apologizing again to Sir Jean, he disarmed the knight and escorted him to the dining chamber along with three of the crossbowmen. With the servants dismissed, Rodrigo hurried to fetch wine and food for the captain.

Loading up several plates with what little cold meat the again-feasting Grossbarts had not already claimed, Rodrigo descended to the cellar for wine. Gasping at the sight awaiting him, he raced back up the stairs and shouted at the Brothers, "What have you done with the priests?!"

"Put'em down there." Manfried tossed his crust at Rodrigo. "As you's just seen, I imagine."

"Fools! That crazed priest's killed the other one!" Rodrigo yelled.

"Goddamn it all!" Manfried jumped up. "I told you to tie him good!"

"I did!" Hegel followed. "If he's so worthless as to be slayed by a trussed-up man he deserves what he gets."

They stumbled down the stairs and saw the naked Buñuel swaying from the rafters, ordure dribbling down his legs. Martyn had traded his worn robes for the scarlet-piped finery of the cardinal and prayed fervently in a corner, oblivious to the ruckus he had caused. The Grossbarts relaxed upon discovering the miscommunication and Manfried chastised Rodrigo.

"Gotta use them eyes, boy." Manfried shook his head. "With the clothes switch I can see the cause, but even a cursory glance would tell you it was the other way round. Bein perceptive'll keep you alive longer than runnin hither and thither squawkin all kinds a meck."

"Your mad friend did it, as I say! Your pet heretic killed the cardinal!" Rodrigo hunched over and vomited.

"That ain't gonna help the stink." Hegel retrieved a bottle of wine from the lattice rack.

"Look," Manfried addressed the gagging Rodrigo, "either my way or yours, only Mary knows which is right, which is mine, a course, but that defeats the purpose. Point is: either I's right, and a man a Mary's Will, committed to righteousness, has hung a heretic, which is his duty and obligation, especially considerin said heretic mocked us all by pretendin to be pious."

"But—" and then Rodrigo dry-heaved.

"But we could have it your way," Manfried continued, "and assume it was the red and very dead cardinal what was the righteous one, meanin Martyn's a heretic, and worse still, one what murdered a man a Mary. And since he's aligned with us, we's all accomplices."

"There has to be another way." Rodrigo wiped his mouth.

"Certainly," Manfried continued, raising his voice. "We turn Martyn over to the doge and explain the mistake, and hope he's the understandin sort. You got no time to snot on your sleeve, so take the sensible reality a things: we's doin Mary's work, and this cardinal asshole did worse than interfere, he blasphemed, and we ain't gonna tolerate that."

"Have a drink," Hegel quietly offered, but when Rodrigo raised his head he saw the Grossbart handing it to Martyn.

His psalm trailing off, Martyn opened his eyes and took in Hegel. The doorway above him ringed Hegel in light, and Buñuel's dangling legs seemed as wings to the demented servant of God. The bottle shone red in Hegel's hand as he repeated the offer.

"I am not worthy of these stolen robes, let alone your mercy," Martyn murmured, fumbling at his sash.

"Hold a tic." Hegel put his hand on Martyn's shoulder and squatted down. Taking a cue from Manfried, he coached the priest. "We's agents a Mary, and from where we stand, you came by them robes and whatever station they imply through your own fuckin piety. We ain't heretics, we's bout the only ones sides yourself knows how corrupt and wicked what they call *the* Church is, with that bastard you hung bein prime example. So wear them vestments with dignity and pride, *Cardinal* Martyn." Hegel wiped imaginary dust from Martyn's shoulders.

"But—" Martyn's eyes shone.

"Sides," Manfried called, sensing Rodrigo's defeat and his brother's imminent victory, "how else is a one-armed priest gonna hang a heretic cept through the power a faith and the Will a Mary? Throttle, maybe, but really..." Manfried chuckled, impressed by Martyn's follow-through.

"From Judas onward," Martyn shouted, springing to his feet, "let the betrayers of our Lord hang as did the first! To Roma, Grossbarts, and then to Avignon!"

"Shut it," Manfried sighed. "Hegel, cut down the dead one and take'em out to the stables. Cover'em in Martyn's clothes, and take his sorry ass too, but mind he keeps his head down lest spies spy our ruse."

Hegel climbed a barrel and cut down Buñuel, spattering shit everywhere. "Why I gotta drag this meck about?"

"Cause I gotta bring wine to the captain and inform him a recent events," an exasperated Manfried explained. "Now get to it so's we can reconvene with some wine a our own."

To dry Hegel's pissiness, Manfried helped haul the corpse to the kitchen and then intercepted Rodrigo coming up the stairs from the basement. Leading the shaken man back down, he pulled a bottle from the rack and opened it. After a guzzle, he gave it to Rodrigo and hoisted several fresh ones. Leaving the basement laden with booze and entering the empty foyer, Manfried caught wind of the Arab hobbling along the second-story railing toward the captain's chambers. "Get down here!" Manfried barked.

"Illustrious Master Manfried!" Al-Gassur turned, his unseen grimace of dismay instantly replaced with a winning smile. "Here you are! I have scoured and scoured, only to see that we have exchanged placements, with I above and you below!"

"You dirty sneak." Manfried waited at the foot of the stairs. "What're you doin in the house?"

"Seeking you, of course! From my stable bed I witnessed this morning's display, and when no word was sent I thought I might advise you of the imminent peril."

"What imminent peril?" said Manfried.

"Why, that facing us all, for with the doge so angered and his men imprisoned, I thought—"

"You thought that your lowly fuckin observations would be superior to mine?"

"No, certainly not, I only wished to—"

"Sneak in unobserved and pilfer what you could before desertin us?"

Al-Gassur faked a laugh rather convincingly, and pretended to slip in order to pat his vest and ensure the purloined silver candelabra did not bulge too much.

"You's underfoot from now til I say otherwise, understood?"

"Yes, Master Grossbart."

"Good. Take this wine." Manfried shoved the two bottles under Al-Gassur's crutch arm and led him to the dining chamber.

Through the open door they saw Barousse and Sir Jean laughing as though they were lifelong friends. The French knight found the captain to be the worst example of nouveau riche mercantilism tempered with deplorable manners and a liberal dose of insanity, while Barousse judged the nephew of the Vicomte de Meaux to be a spoiled fop oblivious to his situation. This did not prevent them from carrying an animated conversation about Sir Jean's period of imprisonment in England after the Battle of Poitiers. The mercenary guards nervously nodded at Manfried and the Arab.

"Manfried!" Barousse called, "you've brought more wine, excellent! Rodrigo seemed peaked so I sent him to have a rest."

"Rigo tell you what's happened?" asked Manfried, and when the captain shook his head Manfried snatched the bottles from Al-Gassur. Setting one before the captain and opening the other himself, Manfried took a pull before saying, "Got new developments, could set us back."

"What sort?" Barousse's voice hardened.

"Cardinal's dead," said Manfried.

"That's too bad." Barousse shrugged. "Can't be helped, I suppose."

"I sent Hegel to put'em in the barn, and had Martyn follow wearin the cardinal's robes, so's the men at the gate'll think he's still breathin."

"Sound," Barousse agreed, then suddenly stood. "I'll attend to the remains better than they, serve a belated lunch to the lady of the house, then fetch you and Hegel to assist me with finalizing certain matters. That is, if you would entertain Sir Jean while I perform my errands?"

"Think I can manage," Manfried sighed, sitting in Barousse's chair. No sooner had the captain excused himself than Manfried snatched the glass away from the petulant knight and handed it to his hovering servant.

"Care for some wine, Arab?" Manfried asked, eyes locked with Sir Jean.

Al-Gassur bowed and poured from Barousse's bottle, sharp enough to see the game and stay respectfully silent. The Arab slurped and smacked, Manfried's lips curling up in direct proportion to Sir Jean's frown.

"I's seen your sort before," Manfried said after swirling some wine in his puckered mouth. "Ridin about, puttin on airs. I seen you."

Sir Jean would not have learned German even if given the chance, believing the Holy Roman Empire and its guttural tongue to be beyond contemptible. Instead he smiled slightly at this peasant's coarseness, which earned him wine splashed in his face. Sir Jean's hand went to his empty scabbard and his cinder-hued cheeks turned ashen, his blue eyes bulging. He told Manfried precisely what he thought of him, starting in French but shifting to Italian for the benefit of the watching guards and the Arab.

Al-Gassur began translating, at which point Sir Jean went paler still and his diatribe dried up. Manfried nodded appreciatively and stood. Sir Jean did not shrink away but leaned forward to accept the blow that never fell.

"Tell'em to take off that armor," Manfried ordered Al-Gassur, who went to task.

"Tell him I will do nothing he commands, but will wait for the captain to return," Sir Jean interrupted.

"Begging your apologies, dear Frenchman," Al-Gassur said, taking liberty with his duty, "but I believe Master Grossbart is seeking a provocation to murder you. I would do what he says, unless you are ready to end as the cardinal did."

"Cardinal Buñuel's been killed?" Sir Jean swallowed. "Are they mad?"

"Quite. Now haste might be a better ally than even myself…"

Manfried checked his urge to strike the Arab, *Buñuel* being recognizable in the stream of nonsense. Sir Jean stood and reluctantly removed his armor, which took quite a while without his squire. Manfried circled him, paying close attention to how the iron carapace fit together.

Hegel scowled at the sun, at the guards curiously watching them, at Buñuel's twisted rictus, and at Martyn. Dropping the real cardinal in the hay, Hegel seized the bottle the new cardinal had stowed in his armpit and set to prowling around the stable. Martyn wiped his excrement-covered hands on the side of a horse, which Hegel glared at, daring the animal to make the first move. It blinked and he resisted the impulse to slay it.

"What is that?" Martyn motioned out the door.

"Eh?" Hegel looked at the apparatus constructed in the back garden. The main supports rose nearly as high as the house, a huge beam balanced between them with one end tethered to something behind the shrubbery. Utterly baffled as to the purpose of such a device, he lied to Martyn.

"That's the instrument a our victory," said Hegel.

"You know of its purpose? Wonderful!" Barousse came from the house.

"Er." Hegel scratched his beard.

"Grab hold of the body and bring it with us, and you shall help me ready our final blow." Barousse veered off toward the contraption, and with much cursing Hegel and Martyn followed, towing Buñuel's corpse.

Closer inspection only perplexed the two more, but Barousse took hold of a wheel and with Hegel's assistance winched down one side of the teetering shaft. Attached to the end sat a spacious wooden basket, which they unceremoniously dumped Buñuel's corpse into. Several guards watched from the terrace, in theory minding the rear wall lest the doge's men storm it.

"I told the builders it was to be filled with an anchor's weight worth of flowers to honor Strafalaria," Barousse grunted, leading Martyn and Hegel onto the terrace and through the back door, "so it should be calibrated proper. I've got an actual anchor to drag out, lest a boulder undo the counterweight and foil the accuracy. That, along with the cardinal and a few hundred ducats ought to ensure the streets are thronged and our flight unnoticed."

"A sound scheme," Hegel acknowledged, possessing all the mechanical intuition of a mule.

"What is its purpose?" Martyn asked, earning him Hegel's silent thanks.

"You'll learn soon enough." Barousse rubbed his palms together. Entering the rear door behind the central staircase, he motioned toward the dining room. "See that your brother hasn't murdered our other hostage, and make sure the twit doesn't learn of our scheme. I'll be back as soon as I attend to my business."

Barousse's face darkened as he hurried toward the kitchen, while Hegel and Martyn went to see what Manfried was about. Retrieving the bucket of live sardines from beside the kitchen table, Barousse saw Rodrigo coming up from another wine-run to the cellar. Sloshing back across the kitchen, Barousse turned to the flushed young man.

"I know I've been difficult, at times. Hell, most of the time." Barousse stared into the bucket. "I'd have lost myself years ago without you and Ennio, and I'm sorry about how it's all played out up until here. I'm sorry about your brother, son. And your father."

"I, uh, thank you, thank you so very—" Rodrigo did not know quite how to respond to the words he had always longed to hear.

"Now get on with it, and focus sharp or I'll put you off the boat." Barousse winked, momentarily forgetting his purpose. A fish splashed his boots, and the calm passed. "Don't stand there gawking, leave the blasted bottles! Get to the Grossbarts and send them to me. Kill the snob if he gets crafty."

Barousse ran back to the foyer and up the stairs, unsure why his vision had gone misty in the kitchen. Unable to dispel his grin, Rodrigo raced across the house, seeing the captain disappear on the second story. The guards almost shot Rodrigo when he burst into the room, and all his pent-up happiness burst forth in hysterical laughter at what he saw.

Sir Jean sat stripped of all but a loincloth and the Grossbarts stood on either side of him, Manfried wearing the upper half of the knight's plate armor and Hegel awkwardly attaching the greaves to his own knobby legs. The inebriated Al-Gassur wore the helm and sat in the captain's chair, clumsily fitting the neck of a bottle under the jutting visor. Martyn sprawled in another chair, his ripe Cardinal's robes hanging off his spindly arms like blood-trimmed bat wings. Fixing the codpiece into place, Hegel rapped it with his knuckle and smiled knowingly at the stewing chevalier.

"The captain requests you in his quarters." Rodrigo giggled. "I'm to watch the Frenchman."

"Watch his mouth most close a all his bits," Manfried advised.

"He don't seem to say much without his iron, though," noted Hegel, and the two departed.

They clanked up the stairs, each thinking his brother had received the better half of the unwieldy armor that barely stayed on their bodies in its fractured state. The captain admitted them, taking notice of the Arab for the first time. Ushering them in but leaving both door and cage ajar, he motioned to several open chests. These were full of coins, with many more scattered all over the rug. The Grossbarts hid their greed and amazement far better than Al-Gassur, who licked his lips and positioned his crutch so it might catch on the floor and send him sprawling. Before he could act Barousse addressed them, bringing a thankful lump to the Arab's throat.

"Carry these outside to the garden," the captain ordered them, "and quickly, for if I know Strafalaria we will be blessed indeed if we have until dusk to prepare."

"Might I fill a sack, as my deformity prevents me from carrying an entire chest?" Al-Gassur asked.

"There's a bucket there." Barousse nodded toward the tub, which Manfried immediately hastened to before the Arab could move.

"Why we takin'em out back stead a through the you-know?" asked Hegel, keeping an eye on his brother.

"A ruse, dear Hegel," Barousse explained, hoisting a chest, "a ploy to distract the populace. In Angelino's tub we'll not leave the harbor without being nabbed if any see us board. No, we must keep eyes elsewhere, upon the ruins of the doge's manse, the fire of my own, the miracle of a golden rain upon the streets! Hurry, you hounds, hurry!"

"Don't be callin me no beast," Hegel grumbled, lifting a chest.

Al-Gassur pretended to tie up the hem of his gown-length tunic when the bucket crashed into it, bashing his fingers. Manfried laughed while the Arab flung himself to the ground, secretly tickled the mangy bastard had eased his deception. He groaned and rolled on the floor and before he had recovered sufficiently to stand his pointed turnshoes and hidden pockets had eaten a dozen loose ducats.

"Quit that bellyachin," Manfried ordered, cuffing Al-Gassur's ear.

"Apologies, apologies," the Arab whimpered, clumsily filling the bucket and his sleeve with coins.

They trotted downstairs and out the back, the baffled guards staring as they dumped the contents of the chests into the contraption's receptacle on top of Cardinal Buñuel's stinking corpse. The sight made all three laugh and Al-Gassur obediently joined in. Panting, Barousse turned to them and wiped his pink brow.

"Back inside," said Barousse, "one more load."

Their excitement at more carrying turned to seething anger when they saw the massive anchor against one wall of the foyer. Much shoving, cursing, straining, and tugging followed, but finally the iron behemoth lay beside Buñuel's corpse in the coin-filled receptacle.

"Crucial," Barousse gasped, "crucial. We. Don't fire. Too soon. Hell."

"At your word." Hegel shrugged at Manfried. "But now lets get some a them sausages and wine."

Barousse licked his lips. "Wise enough."

Manfried circled the contraption and then went around the side to the kitchen door after foiling Al-Gassur's attempt to lag behind. Hegel reminded the men watching the back door of what befell thieves, and Barousse added that shortly all would set sail with far more riches in their coffers. In the dining room, Sir Jean's attempt to bribe Rodrigo had earned him a bloody nose. Despite his manners and fine clothes Rodrigo was not of noble or landed stock, and so naturally he hated those who were.

The guards likewise despised Sir Jean for his fortuitous birth and homeland but, unlike the frazzled Rodrigo and the belligerent Grossbarts, their fear grew with each insult the noble weathered and each blasphemy Martyn spoke. The guards and Sir Jean both believed the day would end with all of their necks in nooses unless a miracle transpired.

XXI
The Conflagration of Desires

An hour before sunset fifty pikemen relieved their compatriots outside the captain's gates. Two of Barousse's men nervously waited until a spokesman for the doge arrived, offering them amnesty if they peacefully admitted the doge's force if and when such an order came down. This was the offer the mercenaries had agreed would buy their surrender after hearing of the cardinal's murder, wanting no part of the inevitable massacre. The leader of the doge's pikemen insisted they were positioned only to prevent escape, but to prove their loyalty Barousse's men hastened to inform him of Buñuel's passing. Not caring a jot for some French brat and doubting the doge did either, the pikemen demanded admittance at once. A guard hurried to unlock the gate when an arrow fired from one of the house's windows struck his traitorous leg and he went down howling. Then everything soured and to this day Venetians whisper that in the time that followed the eyes of God averted from Venezia.

Hearing a scream from the front, Barousse released the lever on the trebuchet, and the Grossbarts cheered as the anchor, coins, and cardinal soared into the setting sun. Rodrigo hurried about the second floor, having already doused every room of the first with oil. The mercenaries who had guarded the chevalier took shots from the room formerly occupied by the Grossbarts, Sir Jean and Martyn watching the catapult from the terrace.

Sir Jean stared in shock, his urge to flee around the house forgotten at the sight of Barousse's nerve. The trio of crossbowmen with them on the terrace let out three shouts and three shots as pikemen flooded around the stable side of the house. Martyn fled inside and Sir Jean followed, terrified he might be caught between crossbow volleys or cut down by his rescuers before they identified him.

From the window one of the guards hurled an oil lamp at those swarming the front door, setting several ablaze and then catching a bolt between his eyes. He pitched foreward on the sill while the other two mercenaries retreated to the hall, the doge ordering an abundance of archers to make up for his earlier error. The two remaining guards saw Rodrigo rushing down the hall, laughing nervously.

The ground quaked under the Grossbarts' feet from the counterweight's impact, the hastily constructed catapult ripping apart and collapsing behind them. With the first step toward the house Al-Gassur realized he would be overtaken by the pikemen, so, snatching out his dagger, he cut the binding on his mock-lame leg, threw the crutch over his shoulder, and dashed after his masters.

On the raised terrace Barousse's crossbowmen fired a second round but similarly armed members of the doge's force responded in kind. Two of the mercenaries collapsed, riddled with shafts, but the third had ducked inside for a lamp to hurl. Coming up the terrace stairs with Hegel in the lead, the Grossbarts were each struck with several bolts. The quarrels bounced off Manfried's shoulders and Hegel's legs, their purloined plating saving their lives, Al-Gassur in pursuit but far enough back to avoid the volley.

Barousse did not share their armor, thus the two bolts striking his shoulder and the third hitting his thigh embedded in flesh. Ignoring the wounds, he knocked his remaining guard over as he burst into the house, causing the poor man to fall onto his lamp. The lamp shattered, engulfing him in liquid fire. The Grossbarts sprang over the flailing man as he burned alive, and Al-Gassur did the same moments before the pikemen reached the terrace. If the Grossbarts noticed their manservant had miraculously regained his missing appendage they did not mention it, instead tearing out from behind the now-flaming staircase and following the wounded captain up to the second story.

With Barousse's guards hurling oil lamps from the second story onto the invaders at the doors below, the walls of the entire house soon crawled with fire, arrows whipping through the smoke-clogged windows. Al-Gassur overtook his masters on the stairs, his crutch bouncing in their sooty faces. The railings beside them cracked and hissed and their boots smoked as they reached the distraught group of Rodrigo, Martyn, Sir Jean, and the two remaining guards waiting at Barousse's locked door. The Frenchman wore the quarrel of one of the doge's men through his bicep from an attempt to flee out the front, and his golden tresses were singed from his subsequent reentry through the burning doorway.

Fumbling with his keys, Barousse shook the smoking walls with his laughter despite his grievous wounds. One of the guards swayed from the heat and pitched backward over the railing before any could stop his plunge. Throwing open the door, they saw several pikemen had braved the inferno and rushed up the stairs behind them. Barousse turned to battle them but the Grossbarts dragged him inside and slammed the door, knowing he had the only key to the cage in which they all now huddled. He unlocked this, and they pushed inside at the same moment that Al-Gassur brushed against the smoldering door, his oil-spattered clothes immediately catching fire. The others dived away from him as he charged Barousse's oversized tub and hurled himself into the water, his mustache crackling along with the rest of him.

Al-Gassur had always equated asexuality with practicality, but when he opened his eyes under the surface the stinging salt water filtered the woman floating before him into an angel of all his repressed longing, an embodiment of femininity that melted his heart as it solidified other regions. Barousse charged after the errant Arab and hoisted him out of the water by his hair, the woman darting away to a dark corner of the pool. Sir Jean attempted to make a spectacle out of his wound but his vocalized pain merely earned him a cuffing from Hegel. The chevalier swooned when the remaining guard carefully removed the bolt from his arm. Hegel grinned and put his pick's tip under Sir Jean's chin, helping him find his feet again.

Manfried had followed the captain, viciously kicking Al-Gassur as he yowled on the floor. Necessity had driven the Arab to do what Manfried had longed to every time he entered the room. Barousse snatched a sheet from the bed and scrambled over the rim; up to his waist in the water, he whispered to the woman.

Timber collapsed outside the door, the pikemen hacking their way in, screaming as the floor gave out and they plummeted into the inferno, the one who had snatched the railing suffering longer than his countrymen before he too let go, the flesh of his fingers welded together. Martyn stomped around the room screaming damnation, his spit hissing on the smoking carpets.

"To the Virgin!" Hegel bellowed, hoisting a satchel from those piled on the table and shoving it under Martyn's left arm.

Barousse shielded Manfried's view but then she stepped past him in the bath, her body swathed in wet, translucent linen. Al-Gassur crawled after the last guard and Rodrigo, who disappeared behind the statue of Mary. Hegel seized his brother's arm and pressed a satchel to his chest.

"This ain't Gyptland, brother," Hegel intoned, his eyes locking with Manfried's.

She took another step toward Manfried, the waters parting for her, but he found the strength to turn away. Sir Jean and the guard had followed Rodrigo down the shaft, with Martyn close after. Al-Gassur reached for a coin on the floor but it burned his fingers, and somewhere in the room bottles began exploding, flames belching and broken glass snowing down on them, each shard radiant in the blaze that consumed the walls. Then Hegel hurled a sack full of ducats at the Arab, who heard the chinking of coin and grabbed it along with his fallen crutch before vanishing into the passage.

The captain shouldered one of the satchels but six remained, and these the Brothers clumsily threw past Mary into the chute. A fearsome tearing sound arose behind them, and they saw the entire massive tub pitching upward for an instant before being swallowed by the house, the floor between them and it collapsing. Hegel dived behind the Virgin and shimmied backward into the shaft, but to his disgust he saw Manfried turn to something out of his periphery. Hegel descended only a rung before he envisioned that treacherous woman undoing both Barousse and Manfried.

A rafter fell from above, driving the woman to the floor. The captain vainly tried to lift it, screaming as the smoldering wood blistered his hands. The stink of burnt skin and other meats permeating his nose, Manfried turned away from brother and Virgin to help the captain. She did not shriek or moan or cry, but smiled up at them as they lifted the burning log from her pinned legs. She scooted out and they dropped it just as the floor caved in beneath the beam.

A chasm now separated them from the Virgin, flames riding the squealing walls around their small island of floor. The captain's face fell, his tears popping before they reached the ground.

Manfried grabbed hold of the woman, steadied his boots, and hurled her over the fiery gulf. Her head struck the Virgin's feet and she lay still, and the captain let out a wail as he jumped after her.

He almost made it.

His legs dangling in Hell, his fingers splayed and gripping the smoking floor, and his eyes fixed on her countenance, Barousse struggled to lift his weighty frame. Manfried went after him, overshooting his mark and pitching into the Virgin. He knocked the statue loose of its base and it toppled sideways, tearing through the burning wall as if it were wet parchment. On impulse he reached to stop Her fall but then he felt a lady's hand on his ankle and he saw another woman smiling up at him despite the blood running down her forehead. The captain forgotten, he knelt to kiss her when Hegel appeared out of the passage, spoiling his objective.

Seeing her turn to Manfried instead of him, Barousse released his hold and closed his eyes. Hegel leaped at him, having moored himself to a rung with a length of rope. He caught one of the captain's hands but flat on his stomach could do no more than hold on, staring into the surprisingly calm face of Barousse.

Manfried lifted her up, the sheet sticking to his armor, but he looked away and pushed her gently into the passage. Hegel grunted and twisted, the captain slipping from his grasp when Manfried joined the struggle and together they hauled Barousse up. Another chunk of the floor gave way beneath Barousse's chest and they almost lost him before all three tumbled backward into the nave. Hegel cut the rope and scampered down the rungs, Barousse shoving Manfried after him. The captain went last, the bars scalding his palms, the last view he had of his home obscured by waves of heat and smoke.

Rodrigo moved down the narrow shelf beside the channel. The tallow he had lit from the walls before descending illuminated Sir Jean and the guard behind him, and Rodrigo handed each of them a candle of his own. Sir Jean lacked the strength to assault them or flee, panting against the wall with his bare feet dangling in the water. Martyn and Al-Gassur came next, several satchels landed behind them, and then nothing.

When all had realized the remaining four must be cooked alive they shouldered what bags they could carry and turned their backs, only Martyn staying behind to pray in the flurry of embers coming down the chute. The stone ceiling shook and they quickened their pace, only to stop when Martyn let out a triumphant shout. In the glow of the shaft they saw the pale woman emerge alone and unblemished.

Then Hegel dropped, shouting, "Slow on, you mecky assholes!"

Manfried fell the last few rungs and almost rolled into the channel but Hegel helped him up. The Brothers narrowly avoided being crushed under Barousse as the captain popped out, having nearly become stuck in the shaft. Grabbing the remaining satchels he pushed them ahead down the shelf to where the rest waited, flaming debris bursting out of the chute behind them and backlighting their progress.

The woman looped her arm through Barousse's, smiling at Manfried as she did. They rushed through the tunnel, their lights extinguishing one by one from dripping water and splashing filth. At the very moment they reached the ladder the last tallow went out, and they stood waist-deep in the sulfurous water.

"How many of my men are with us?" Barousse asked.

"We're all your men, sir," Rodrigo answered.

"No, no, my personal brigands," said Barousse.

"Me and Hegel both," Manfried replied.

"I know that." Barousse's voice rose. "I mean the men I hired to keep my manse, those that would make up our crew onboard Angelino's."

"Mine ownself," the guard put in, "being Raphael."

"Who else?" said Barousse.

"Mine ownself alone," Raphael responded, clearly struggling with his German.

"Shitfire and brimstone." Barousse rubbed his blackened brow with blistered fingers.

"There be also mine, eh, the," Raphael mumbled something in a tongue none present save Sir Jean understood, then brightened, "the hostage! Still I maintain hostage."

"The knight?" Barousse squinted in the blackness, then switched to Italian: "You're still with us, eh Jean?"

"*Sir* Jean," the knight shot back.

"We don't need any witnesses," said Barousse. "Raphael, slit his throat."

"Wait!" Sir Jean yelped.

"Wait," Barousse allowed.

"Hurry," Hegel added in German, starting up the ladder.

"While our plan has heretofore been flawless," Sir Jean stalled, "murdering me might foil it."

"How's that?" Barousse drew his cutlass and made toward the sound of Sir Jean's voice.

"If my body is found down here, or washes out in the canals, what then? They'll know people escaped the fire!" Sir Jean smiled at his own wisdom. "And if you are discovered after we leave here, there's still my priceless value as ransom."

"Shall mine ownself slay him open?" Raphael asked in German from behind the knight.

"Nah," Barousse whimsically decided. "Can always do him later. Don't see how we're going to get anyone to pay a priceless ransom, though. Up, then, all of you."

Hegel had chased off the dogs lurking at the mouth of the pit, taking his usual obscene pleasure in bashing one's snout with his pick. The barking bounced down the alleys but in contrast to the quiet of the previous night the entire city reverberated with noise. Manfried came next, sliding in the fish-mire in front of Rodrigo. The rest followed, with the woman coming last after Barousse. Hegel had advanced to where their alley crossed another but found no trace of the dead street urchins. Leaning against the wall, he saw the setting sun alone did not light their way, a distant glow implying Barousse's house still burned.

The alleys were desolate save for a few drunken beggars, whom Barousse ruthlessly ordered put to the sword. Manfried and Hegel laughed at Sir Jean's offer to assist, instead taking the duty upon themselves with aplomb. Al-Gassur recognized one of the victims as a swindling chum of his named Six-Toed Pietro, and his dislike of the Grossbarts shifted to outright hatred. The Arab attempted to make his escape of their vile company but they set him back on course with a series of kicks, and he cursed himself for rebinding his leg in the subterranean passage. The yelling of the murdered sots drew no attention, and they arrived at the back of the tavern without further incident.

Angelino ushered them into the back room and through it, the blind barkeep the only other man present. The party fractured and rejoined beside the hearth, dragging chairs and wringing their clothes. The blind man could not leave his bar before the Grossbarts descended, liberating him of cup after cup of ale. While the old man's face sagged he did not protest when they rolled a barrel out from behind the bar.

Angelino grinned at Barousse. "What've you wrought?"

"Brought him the Hell he would've had rain down on me." The captain smirked.

"Rain is right! A golden shower for Venezia, eh? If I didn't know where certain things was located I'd surely compete with the throngs to snatch a few ducats for myself."

"And did the anchor make a sound impression?"

"Anchor?"

"An anchor right on Strafalaria's head, if my laborers constructed it proper."

"Something to hope, to be sure, though I can't testify to whether it struck true or not." Angelino noticed the woman and winced. She sat on the floor with her ear to the wall beside the barred front door. "Christ."

"You're a good man," Barousse whispered, squeezing Angelino's shoulder. "We'll be rid of her soon."

"Not soon enough," Angelino said, and, seeing the pain on his friend's face, added, "Not too late, either."

"Where's Seppe at?" Hegel interrupted.

"On the boat," Angelino replied, "soon as the rest of your men pull in we'll pull out."

"What other men?" said Manfried.

"The rest of the crew you said were coming." Angelino cocked his head at Barousse, "What, you said more than six but less than twelve besides this lot?"

Barousse shook his head sadly. "Wasn't wagering on all but one of my guards being stomped like grapes."

Angelino bowed his head. "Oh Hell, Alexi, you mean we're to sail to the ends of the ocean with this lot and nothing more? Not even a skeleton, just a bunch of loose bones!"

"Can't be helped." Barousse shrugged. "So let's get a move on."

Angelino again glanced at the woman. "You're sure there's no other way than on board with us?"

"Angelino," said Barousse, "please—"

"Can't be helped, I heard, I heard," said Angelino. "Giuseppe won't like it, though."

"Giuseppe?" Barousse scowled. "Say he isn't."

"He is." Angelino scowled right back. "As captain, I choose my crew. And if I don't have a say in who you take, you sure as shit don't get a word on my choices."

"Who else is aboard?" Barousse asked.

"Find out soon enough," Hegel advised. "Oughta left by now. Hey you bitchswine, give me a hand with this!"

Ripping his eyes off her, Manfried made sure the bung fit snugly before tilting the barrel over and rolling it toward the door. The others crowded around the door behind Angelino, Raphael being sure to stay behind Sir Jean at all times. Hegel marched back to the bar and fished out Al-Gassur, who had slipped behind it and feigned sleep. Sending the Arab on his way, Hegel reached in his bag and removed a gold bar, turning to the blind barkeep.

"Any man you fence that to tells you it's less than genuine you bite his face, scream for help, and hold on to that til the watch comes," Hegel said.

The barkeep burbled something unintelligible, maybe Italian, maybe not, but the gold disappeared regardless. Turning back to the nervous group, Hegel grinned and drew his pick. The captain extended his hand to the woman, who took it and rose beside him.

"Bid your city farewell and good passing," Barousse announced. "Only the most foolish of you would dream of setting your eyes on it again, for now our crimes can scarce be counted. We must turn our back on it for all time, and with the grace of God we will come to a better end than all who dwell here. Their curses will not find us, and the judgment they would seek to level will go unpronounced."

Rodrigo closed his eyes and whispered goodbye to the only city he had ever known, the place where his family had lived and died for generations. Martyn yawned and Al-Gassur seconded it, while Sir Jean's eyes welled at the realization that he would not actually be rescued. Raphael clung to the captain's melodrama, the mercenary having less idea than anyone else what destination they made for.

"Straight out and up to the end of the dock," Angelino informed them. "They'll hoist a light soon as we open the door so we're all sure of course, but anyone you see to right or left catch and kill, young or old, man or not."

"Get on, then," said Manfried, hefting his loaded crossbow.

"Mary bless us," Martyn intoned, and Angelino threw open the door.

Subtlety had no place in their flight to the boat, the group all but whooping as they charged. Sheer ill luck had brought a tipsy couple toward the alehouse to celebrate the five ducats that had dropped into a gutter before them earlier in the evening, and Al-Gassur and Rodrigo averted their eyes as the Grossbarts did their business. Manfried's bolt caught the surprised young woman in the chest, and before her head cracked open on the stones Hegel had thrust his pick through her beau's neck.

No other witnesses stirred and the Grossbarts quickly rolled the bodies off the quay and returned to their barrel. Rolling it up to the ship they heard a heated argument between Giuseppe and Barousse but before they could contribute Giuseppe had relented due to Angelino's intervention. They took their time getting the barrel safely up the gangplank and a pair of burly young toughs in tarred breeches untied the ship. While the Brothers were curious as to how the vessel moved, Barousse hurried them out of sight below deck, and hopping off the ladder they saw their compatriots lounging in a large, barren room. Only when the sailors lowered their beer barrel did the Grossbarts relax, confident Gyptland lay just across the sea.

"This boat got a handle?" Hegel asked the massive sailor named Merli.

"You'll get your sea legs soon enough," came the reply.

"You take the piss again and I'll bring the red to yours," Hegel said, irritated by his brother's amused snort. "A name, boy, heard tell they name these things."

"*The Gorgon's Kiss*," said Merli.

"Well," said Manfried. "That's a pretty name."

XXII
Sins of the Father

After many days on the road Heinrich and the twins approached a village. Heinrich insisted they wait until after dark to investigate but when no fires were lit and only the wind stirred they investigated the empty hamlet. A flame-gutted building gave Heinrich miserable cramps, armpits pulsating and blood blistering his arteries. The feeling dissipated, only to return when they passed the scorched monastery during their ascent. They stayed to the roads, it being winter in the wilds, and while the boys ran down any game they scented Heinrich saw neither breathing man nor beast until they left the mountains.

Heinrich's intuition and the lads' noses guided them down the left branch when the road split on the high hills past the forest. They took to traveling from dusk until early morning, spending the daytime foraging, hunting, and sleeping in the deep thickets choking the knolls. They skirted the towns and houses that now dotted the landscape, despite the curious youngsters' whines of protest. The twins grew with each meal they caught, each now standing as high as Heinrich's shoulder.

Dozing by a creek late one afternoon, Heinrich awoke to a wail echoing through the ravine. Both boys were absent and, hope blossoming in his breast, Heinrich dashed through the brambles to the road. Sliding into the gulley the trail ran through, he saw several prone figures on the road and a few more running in opposite directions, Magnus pursuing one group and Brennen the other.

Loath as he was to see them feast on innocents, Heinrich knew any witnesses would spread the word of their presence and then men unaware of their situation would be hunting them as they hunted the Grossbarts. The screams deteriorating into squeals just up the road, Heinrich drew his dagger and approached the half dozen prostrate men. Several of them bled from deep bites speckling their bare torsos and torn breeches but Heinrich realized that while a few were unconscious the rest were fervently praying, eyes shut, brows wedded to the dirt. Save for one dressed in white robes their backs were scratched and bleeding, as if they too had run through brambles.

His long knife gripped in one hand, Heinrich bent and retrieved one of their scourges from the dirt. The barbed flail dripped onto the dusty road, and Heinrich smiled as he realized their identity. He had not seen a flagellant in over a decade, most vanishing along with the plague they had sought to avert with their corporeal mortification.

Crouching behind one of the men, Heinrich reached around and slit his throat. The flagellant thrashed forward, a font of blood splashing the feet of the man before him. They knew he was among them without opening their eyes and their prayers grew louder even as their numbers dwindled with each slash of his dagger. Now only two remained, his boys baying like packs of hounds on each side of the road.

Underneath his skin, deep in his veins where blood, phlegm, and black and yellow biles pulsed against each other, Heinrich's companion protested angrily at this murderous turn. Upon first entering the turnip farmer it had felt relief to inhabit a host as eager for the same end as itself, but now the deranged man refused to do as he was bidden. Dead men's ability to spread the blessings of the pit were negligible, and one after another Heinrich was insensibly murdering all of the potential carriers.

Leaving the presumed leader unscathed, Heinrich began lashing the other man mercilessly, blood spattering on the high leaves over their heads. The man's prayers remained strong even when most of the scabbed skin on his back came loose, but when the white of his spine shone in the dappled sunlight he shrieked and writhed, allowing Heinrich to flail his stomach, arms, and face. Only when the wretch went limp, his exposed musculature quivering in the chill wind, did Heinrich turn to the robed leader.

Long-festering frustration partially sated, Heinrich addressed the praying man he mistakenly took to be a priest. "Remove your robes."

The man continued to pray, his voice cracking.

"Remove them!" Heinrich barked.

Still the leader prayed. Heinrich swiped the scourge underhanded so it whipped beneath the man's neck, wrapping around his throat and chin. Yanked backward, the man choked and spluttered as he landed on his rear, his eyes still closed, his lips resuming the prayer as soon as the scourge slackened.

"Pray for them!" Heinrich shouted. "Pray for my family!"

Dragging the lash free in a welter of blood, Heinrich dropped his dagger and brought the weapon back down with both hands. Heinrich's delight grew with each wet smack of the scourge, the pleasurable warmth in his guts recalling the sensation of eating a bowl of Gertie's stew, or watching Brennen pull his first turnip. He remembered how pleasant his wife had smelled after they made love, how Brennen laughed and clapped when his mother made shadows on the wall, how his littlest girls would kiss him on his cheeks simultaneously. Inside Heinrich the demon continued to plead for the man's life, a whisper trickling through his mind like the fluids dribbling down his victim's face, but Hein-

rich would not heed the council. It was not enough that those
who wounded themselves to stop the plague become hosts themselves. They were servants of a God so cruel He would absolve
the Grossbarts, and so they must be punished as only Heinrich
and his lads could.

After a time Heinrich realized the man had expired and he
whipped an exposed skull, embedded strips of scalp, hair, and
gore dulling the scourge's impact. The skeletal face now resembled those of his boys who sat watching him, gnawing on flagellant bones. Glancing at the carnage, Heinrich now saw only
Gertie bleeding to death from an ax wound, Brennen's gurgling
throat, the blackened husks of his daughters, and the four children they had buried before, some still from Gertie's womb,
others living a year or five before being stolen by God. He heard
the screams of his little girls, smelled the stink of gravedirt and
his burning home. His face hard, he spit in the dead leader's gaping mouth.

"Let us be demons, then!" Heinrich screamed. "Let us be the
pestilence upon those that would abide such cruelties as this! Let
us riot and rampage upon the servants of that devil in the sky
who deceives the whole world into His worship! Vengeance is
our name and deed! Vengeance for every murdered child, for
every raped woman, for every soul who toils only to see all they
have loved and wrought wither and sicken, suffer and die! No
absolution! No confession! No last rites! Grossbarts, we come for
you!"

Magnus and Brennen howled from every mouth and wept to
see their master weep. The scourge bit into Heinrich's back with
every oath but his tears were not for his own anguish, they were
shed for every innocent who held false hope for some final apology, some explanation. As he threw down the barbed whip and
fell to his knees, the terrified boys hastened to lick his wounds
and whimper their devotion.

By dusk they had removed the bodies from the road, the twins devouring a mind-boggling amount of flesh before lounging in the shade, their stomachs distended, every tongue lolling. Heinrich had meticulously cleaned the scourge in the stream and donned the leader's soiled robes. His ablutions complete, the moon dangled low over the thickets as they again sought their bearded quarry.

XXIII
Ever Southward

Below deck, the forecastle housed a table, a few chairs, and several water and beer barrels. A narrow hall staggered around the masts to the back of the ship, with two rows of bunks depressed into the walls on either side. At the end of the hall a storeroom contained nets, food, and everything else, and there the captain and his lady established themselves. With two people occupying a sleeping space where fifteen would fit, there were not enough bunks for the crew and the Grossbarts' party; they traded off the beds with the men toiling above. They, of course, being everyone except the Grossbarts, who were quickly avoided by the crew due to the twins' tendency to jab anyone foolish enough to disturb their sleep.

When the Brothers stirred late the following afternoon they saw one of the young sailors from before and the lummox Merli sleeping on the bunks opposite them. Extrication proved especially difficult for Manfried, who had gone to sleep with his shoulders still plated in iron. Even their toes and fingernails were sore from the previous day's exertions but they awoke laughing at the memory of their triumph. They staggered to the open room and guzzled water, paying no mind to the half-naked Sir Jean or his shadow, Raphael.

"Where's the rest?" Hegel asked after dunking his face in the water barrel and leaving a sheen on the surface.

"Aboveward." Raphael nodded to the ladder. "Taking sunny, salty air. Captain with them, want to council at you."

"Speakin ain't your strong suit, is it?" Manfried leered.

"Truly honest, mine ownself prefer the tongue all men speak." Raphael rattled his loaded crossbow at Sir Jean, making him flinch.

"True words," Hegel agreed, and they went above.

Crawling into the blinding square of light, they crouched like beasts freed after too long in a cage. When their eyes adjusted the Grossbarts reeled from more than the rocking of the ship. On all sides lay water, vast hills and valleys of the stuff, glowing in the sun without a hint of land to be found. Both felt extremely queasy and took small pulls from their skins, and when Manfried spilled his drink refitting the stopper, Hegel noted with interest that his brother's apparently held water for a change.

Two masts towered over them and the country-born Brothers knew only that the ship exceeded any barge they had seen, and was therefore enormous. Men seemed to be everywhere but there were actually only three sailors at work besides the sour Giuseppe and good-tempered Angelino, the relatively small size of the vessel forcing the men to circumvent the Brothers numerous times during their slow advance to the stern. Climbing the stairs to the raised section in the rear, they found Barousse talking with Angelino, and both men hailed them.

"Well met and mornin to the both a yous, too," Hegel greeted them.

"Yeah," said Manfried, his eyes casting about for the Arab.

"Feel that?" Barousse inhaled, his stained bandages fluttering like pennants. "The breath of the sea is the breath of God. Small wonder our ancestors worshipped her."

At this Manfried caught sight of the woman through the sails, her back to him astride the figurehead at the front of the ship. "Gotta get below," he muttered.

"Hold, Manfried," Barousse said. "With my men deserted or dead we've only enough hands to keep us on course for half of every day, and the wind blows better at night. I'd hoped to reach our conquest sooner, and with your help, along with the rest, we can double our speed."

"Later, then," Manfried said dismissively. "Fetch me when the moon's up, this glare's no good for my eyes."

"We'll send up the others prompt, though." Hegel hurried after his brother and addressed him in their private tongue. "The captain seems much improved for bein on the water and speaks wise in the whole, but I wonder at his choice a words."

"How's that?" Manfried ducked under a sail.

"Shit, I dunno, it just puts me off. Like sayin we's gonna reach our conquest. All the words he could a used he said *our conquest*."

"So?"

"Well, that could mean what or who we's gonna conquer."

"Course it does, thicky."

"But couldn't it also mean us bein conquered? *Our conquest.* Not the way I would a phrased it, not at all."

"And you would a used some choice bit a French, or maybe Latinish? Keep in mind he might be Roman but he ain't out the Holy like us, so likely he don't know no better words for the point he successfully made. To me, at least, not bein keen on pissin bout every little detail!"

They reached the ladder, the woman just ahead over the prow, her arms entwined in the railing. Manfried clambered onto the raised platform of the bow, telling himself he went up instead of down solely to avoid his brother. Hegel knew exactly what his brother was about and followed him up.

"You gotta put that feedbag out your mind," Hegel said softly, sensing the true reason for his brother's sudden ire. "It won't bring you no good at all. You gotta look at somethin, look to Mary."

"Now I reckon you'd best mind your own choice a words," Manfried growled, facing Hegel. "*It's* a *she*, same's the Virgin."

"*It's* a damn witch," Hegel snarled back. "Your eyes always been sharper than mine, when they get all smeared with cherry paste?"

Manfried thought about punching Hegel's fat nose until it smeared some cherry paste of its own, but before he raised his hand a stronger impulse reared up in his mind like an angered eel. Manfried suddenly wanted to shove Hegel over the railing and into the sea, but the desire passed as soon as it came. Manfried felt light-headed and slowly turned to look.

She sat where she had before, waves jetting up spray across her front, only now she watched him. Her delicate lips were pursed but her eyes shimmered and she smiled softly, her hair lathered around her chest and neck.

"I'll do you fore I touch him!" Manfried shouted at her, scrambling down the stairs and then the ladder, his chest burning.

Hegel remained above, puzzling over his brother's outburst at the woman and glaring at her. She returned his stink-eye, her ruddy mouth twisted into a sneer. He made as if to strike her but she did not give him the satisfaction of even twitching her nose.

"I's onto you," Hegel hissed, "you damn witch."

Quitting the platform and gaining the ladder, Hegel reeled as he suddenly pictured his brother pitching over the side of the boat with the woman in his arms. He imagined them spiraling down through the depths and could see himself distorted through the water, looking on helplessly from the ship. Then they sank past the light, and in the dark the woman began to change into something else, her skin distorting in his brother's arms.

"You alright?" Rodrigo asked from below, and limply clinging to the ladder, Hegel vomited all over him.

Al-Gassur, Sir Jean, and Raphael laughed heartily at Rodrigo's expense, the young man shuddering with revulsion as he waited for Hegel to descend so he could climb above deck. Rodrigo knew better than to waste fresh water, even in such unpleasant circumstances. Hegel dropped the last few feet and staggered to an unoccupied chair while Rodrigo went up.

Manfried returned from his bunk with a loaf of bread, half a cheese wheel, and three sausages. He wordlessly ripped the bread and cheese in two, handing the smaller pieces and one of the sausages to Hegel before sitting in another chair. Here the Grossbarts experienced their first taste of the monotony unique to long sea voyages. They sent the smaller sleeping sailor, the Arab, Sir Jean, and Raphael above to help sail, and two sailors soon replaced them in the room. After these two guzzled some beer and conversed in Italian, they went to the bunks. The sun set and finally the Grossbarts deigned to speak to one another.

"Where's Martyn?" asked Hegel.

"Cardinal's lyin in a bunk, jabberin at the wall as he's wont." Manfried rose and took some beer. "Think he might a gone from unorthodox to unhinged."

After another long pause, Hegel cleared his throat. "What I said earlier—"

"Already forgotten." The twin forces of alcohol and denial had finally convinced Manfried the impulse to murder his brother had been some variety of seasickness. The last thing he wanted was Hegel prattling his old line.

"Remember, then, and fast. I had me a vision."

"A vision a what?" Manfried snorted. "A grain bag with an adder in it? I already seen that vision mine ownself. Ah Hell, that crumb Raphael's got me talkin stupid now."

"Don't you make light a me!" Hegel lowered his voice and leaned in. "Always had somethin different, you know well's me, Hell, you's the one who told me it was Mary's blessin. Well, this weren't no feelin nor sensation nor what have, this was a damn vision. I seen it!"

"Seen what?" Manfried continued while Hegel stared at his own puke-flecked boots. "Seen what, O great oracle? Got somethin worth tellin then tell or don't give me no grief bout visions a Mary."

"Weren't no vision a Mary," Hegel snapped, "was you. You and her. Sinkin to the bottom a the sea. Worse yet, it was by your own will, jumpin overboard with her all up ons like she was a bag a riches."

"Shut your mouth," Manfried whispered, but Hegel would not be denied.

"And when yous went under where the sun don't reach she started turnin into somethin else, somethin strange. What she really is under that pretty skin, I imagine."

"What's that mean, *turnin into what she really is?*"

"Witches do that, brother." Hegel's nausea returned. "They can hide themselves, make'em look different, make'em look like somethin a man would want, somethin a man couldn't refuse."

Manfried's laughter was genuine, which made Hegel's bile roil up even hotter as his brother laid into him. "So cause we kilt us a witchy-man up in them mountains and seen that other you's a damn authority on'em? Maybe stead a headin south we could move up to Praha, get you work at that universalality they's built so's you could teach the world all bout witchery!"

"Listen." Hegel choked his stomach back down his throat where it belonged. "Listen."

"I's listenin, you just keep sayin *listen, listen.*" Manfried smiled.

"No you ain't, you's doin what you always do and makin fun a me, when I's tryin to save your soul and your skin besides." Hegel wanted to strike his brother, to tie Manfried down and make his condescending eyes see the same vision that had burned Hegel's brain.

"All right, brother, calm your damn self, I's listenin," Manfried sighed.

"Close your eyes."

"What?" Manfried laughed again but stopped at the seriousness of Hegel's expression. "Right, right."

"Now imagine you's in Gyptland, in a big old graveyard, and you's in the middle a all them princely barrows, crackin into the biggest tomb a them all."

"Easily done. Where you at?"

"Shut it! Pretend I's dead."

"What?" Manfried opened his eyes, "Don't jest bout that sort a thing."

"Just do it, you mecky bastard!"

"Fine! You's dead, brother, dead as that cardinal! And I's in the biggest cemetery in Gyptland, at the biggest crypt in the place." Manfried closed his eyes, the fantasy setting a familiar one that occupied his thoughts for at least an hour on any given day.

"Now wait fore you blurt out somethin, just wait til I say when to answer this next part. The crucial aspect is you hold that tongue a yours, if you's able."

Manfried remained silent to prove he could, though it irked him. Hegel continued, "So you crack open the door, and quick, think bout it but don't say, would you rather see a big heap a gold or that woman reclinin on the floor, smilin up at you?"

Manfried's grin turned as south as a Grossbart's predilection and his face drained of color but he did not open his eyes. Hegel relaxed, seeing the severity of the situation had finally sunk in. Neither spoke for a long time, and finally Manfried cracked one lid, then the other. Hegel thought he detected a tear shining but it might have been a stray reflection of the glorious sunset they were missing in the dank hold.

"Let's kill us a witch," said Manfried, jumping to his feet.

"Easy on, Master Inquisitor." Hegel rose and filled the cup, passing it to his livid brother. "Gotta ruminate on the proper way to handle this."

"Simple. Bash her face and hack off her limbs. Cut up them pieces into smaller ones and burn'em. Take care not to breathe the smoke."

"When I get that post up in Praha I'll put in a good word for you."

"Burnin's what's done with witches, as you well know from experience and common fuckin knowledge besides."

"Considerin this boat's nuthin but kindlin, that oughta be simple," said Hegel. "Course, we could save ourselves the bother and just jump into the sea right now."

"What you suggest we do? Sit down here and wait for the witchery to get outta hand?"

"Seein's you's accepted she's a witch implies to me the situation what was outta hand's played back into ours." Hegel motioned above. "But I doubt the honorable Barousse'll come round so simple. So we wait til he's below and she's above, then we pitch'er to the fishes."

"That's sound, seein's how fraid a water she is."

"That's why I's always on you, you cunt, cause soon's it's your turn to point out a minor flaw in a plan you get airy as the goddamn moon on me. So we'll hack off her head and cut out her heart, keep'em stowed on the boat till such time as we can burn'em, and toss the rest a her brineways."

"That's better thinkin, but hold that tongue, others approach." Manfried nodded to the legs coming down the ladder.

"Sure, brother, seein's how they can't even speak proper I's sure they'll understand what we say in a tongue that not even thems what can speak proper understand. Sound, sound."

Above deck, Barousse's eyes raised to his intended, still perched on the prow like a petrel. He tried to recall the face of his drowned wife Mathilde but could not, unaware that as he did he whispered her name. Angelino tactfully departed to harangue one of his men for a slack tacking of the sails.

When the sun departed Angelino went below, followed by his old mate Giuseppe, two sailors named Karl and Lucian, Sir Jean, and finally his keeper, Raphael. Of the newcomers Raphael had proved the most useful, being young and strong, whereas Sir Jean and Martyn had only two fit arms between them.

Al-Gassur had stayed up late the previous night whittling a peg to replace the one he had dropped when fleeing Barousse's burning manor, and to his relief none had seemed to notice his shifts from cripple to biped to cripple again. He remained atop the foremast, watching the moon rise from his crossbeam. The woman below did not escape his notice, and as the city of his birth was home to Christians, Turks, and travelers of all sorts, he alone of those who had ever laid eyes upon her recognized her features as distinctly Eastern. He did not stare long, however, for every time he stole a glance she would cock her head and return it, her smile reflecting the moonlight.

Not wishing to leave Barousse alone with only the woman and an Arab, before retiring Angelino called for more hands. Merli and the other sleeping sailors, Leone and Cosimo, were roused and went above, cheese and bread in hand. The Grossbarts followed, not wishing to spend another moment around the whining knight.

Cardinal Martyn regaled Sir Jean, Raphael, and the sailors with the ballad of the Brothers Grossbart as well as he knew it, embellishing nothing. Angelino joined them, eating and drinking in silence. Giuseppe reminded Angelino that never before had he permitted such things spoken of on his vessel, but coming from a member of the church Angelino allowed it. Until, that is, Martyn came to his fifth cup of beer and the slaying of the heretical Buñuel, at which point Karl and Lucian blanched and Angelino stood with a forced laugh.

"Enough tales for one night," Angelino said. "Now let's get some rest so by dawn Leone, Cosimo, and Merli may get theirs, as well as those heroic champions who now toil at our meager sails."

"It's all true." Martyn clambered to his feet. "Do not doubt them or my telling of them, lest you risk His Wrath."

"You risk some wrath of your own, talking such things as demons and witches on this boat." Giuseppe stood as well.

"Come, sir." Raphael pressed another cup into Martyn's shaking hands. "Get us some sleeps, yes? And in the morn you could lead ourselves in prayers, and after hear mine own confession?"

"Certainly, certainly." Martyn bobbed his head, looking even older than his many years.

"Sleeps good." Raphael excused himself, assisting Martyn to a bunk and crawling into one closer to the main room, where he overheard Sir Jean whispering his situation to Angelino. To the guard's relief, Angelino laughed Sir Jean off and trudged past him to a bunk of his own, followed by Karl and Lucian. Even the tart-faced Giuseppe would hear none of it, leaving the knight to nurse his arm and the beer barrel.

Above deck, the Grossbarts devoted themselves to learning the nuances of sailing. They shouted back and forth to the captain at the stern but mostly listened to Cosimo and Leone, their assistance being constantly required on the two masts. Merli mumbled to himself the whole night but not once did he address his colleagues. The Brothers' work would have proved easier had they stowed their weapons below deck, but even leaving their layers of plate and chain below had taxed their nerves.

The waning moon and clear sky allowed the twins to take in the details of the sails and rigging, but their refusal to ask for instructions or admit any errors forced the experienced sailors to work twice as hard. Manfried lost his balance drawing his mace upon discovering the Arab atop his mast, and while the Grossbart recovered Al-Gassur scampered down. Such pleasant distractions were rare, however, and by dawn the Grossbarts agreed that of all the modes of travel, none stank worse than sailing. For their triumphant return from Gyptland they resolved to fill a canoe with loot and simply row their way home.

At dawn they retreated to their bunks after another huge repast. Undoubtedly, of all the ships sailing all the seas that year, theirs was the finest-provisioned. Barousse slept alone in the storeroom when his intended would not come down from the figurehead, and all were asleep before the sun had fully risen.

Day and night rotated several more times, although to the Grossbarts' consternation Sir Jean's wound improved despite his complaining. Martyn and Al-Gassur drank more and more, the cardinal blessing the cups and bottles before each sip to purge the taint of heresy. Al-Gassur's insistence of his Christianity did little to assuage Martyn's doubts. He had never heard of a Christian Arab, and in the absence of a Christian pope, he himself remained the absolute authority on earth.

Sir Jean spoke little, working the sails lest Raphael be permitted to physically coerce him. The knight ineffectually tried to convince himself things were not as bad as they could be—he had escaped his enormous debts, after all. Raphael ingratiated himself to the Grossbarts by constantly ridiculing Sir Jean and telling them of the epic battles of the White Company, in which he had served as a lieutenant for a short while before realizing how miserable an occupation it was. This Hawkwood fellow in charge of the mercenary army seemed like a good sort considering he besieged the Pope until he got what he wanted, although his Britannic lineage seemed highly doubtful in light of his supposed prowess.

The sailors grew warier still of the cardinal, especially when their confessions were met with giggles and an unseemly pressing for details when carnal sins were admitted. While relieved the ship had not sunk and none of his men had drowned, Angelino hated the woman's presence on the prow, and once he saw Barousse slip her a fresh fish that should have gone to him as captain. The suspicious and displeased mate Giuseppe held his tongue regarding the woman but slyly gathered information from the besotted cardinal regarding the Brothers' presence in the house of Barousse.

The Grossbarts did as Grossbarts have always done, drinking and scrapping and eating far more than their fair share. With a half moon in the sky they clambered up the ladder for another night at the rigging. Hegel let his brother lead so he could watch the back of his head and ensure it did not tilt toward the woman. When Manfried turned to have a word with Barousse at the stern, Hegel did exactly what he had instructed his brother not to do.

The waves broke just below her, the spray causing her wet black hair to swirl around her head, shining green and blue by moonlight. Pressed closer by his instinct, Hegel climbed the stairs onto the bow, where he made out her milky arms resting on the dark wood of the figurehead she straddled. The linen sheet clung to her and trailed down into the black water, but through it he saw that her glossy white skin darkened whenever the sea doused her with another wave.

The water sent ripples of blackness up her legs and arms, her flesh erupting in a dark rash that faded as soon as the spray fell and the water dripped from her. He craned his head farther as another wave broke, trying to catch a glimpse of what effect it had on her face. Then his boot slipped on the deck, and he tumbled forward, only to have Manfried seize his beard and yank him back. Instead of pitching over the front of the ship he fell back, bruising his scarred buttock on the platform.

She twisted around to watch them, smiling the smile that has damned men and women and ships and empires. The Grossbarts stared back, even Hegel moved by her unwholesome but absolute beauty. Barousse appeared between them, casting his finger at her.

"I've told you!" the captain raged, "leave them be! I've been true as my word, what more do you want?!"

Her lips parted, and all three leaned in to hear the first words to ever leave her mouth. Her small teeth stretched further and, completing the yawn, she turned back to the sea. Barousse took a step forward and Hegel stood, Manfried's hand going to his mace. After a long silence Barousse wheeled and stomped back to the stern.

Leone and Cosimo watched, but seeing no more would come of it they hailed the Grossbarts to lend a hand. Hurrying away from her, Hegel understood his brother's fascination better, and he cursed himself for almost making a similar error. Manfried restrained his urge to smite her where she sat and went to work, gnawing his lip until it stained his beard.

Everyone slept in his bunk save Martyn and Al-Gassur, the cardinal praying while the Arab pretended to do the same, getting ever more intoxicated. When Martyn's quiet prayer rose to a wailing canticle Al-Gassur could stand no more and went above deck. Turning away from the masts to avoid being impressed, he went up to the bow and sat behind the returned captain.

The brine splashing from below mingled with that flowing from her eyes as the ship at long last entered suitable waters, and she stood on the figurehead. She held no hope of Alexius returning her to her distant home, yet he had brought her this far, and for that she could almost forget the years of bondage, years that were dull but flitted by so quickly she scarce noticed. He knew what came next, for she had shown him, and he was eager to pay the final cost to settle the matter.

Ever since reaching the lagoon outside Venezia she had fought the urge to return, but the sea is deep and dark and not all regions are half as accommodating as the balmy waters where her kind had always flourished. Although she was once hailed as a goddess, over the long centuries men had come to regard her and her sisters as mere devils or monsters. She was entirely indifferent about the shift, for she craved the veneration of humans no more now than she had in ages past. She simply wanted the freedom she had always enjoyed, aside from her various tenures as land-wife to those eager fools who sought her company.

As the first syllable left her mouth the gentle waves cupping the boat glowed, and as her voice rose so too did the sea emit brighter and brighter luminescence, a sea-foam-shaded light shining on her joyous face. For all the ages she had lived and all the leagues she had swum, the thrill of the song remained the rarest and sweetest delight, a feat possible only on a sojourn to the dry world. It being the last opportunity she might have for millennia to enjoy herself in such a fashion, she sang all the louder, summoning all of her world who might listen to the requiem of her voiceless, earth-treading days.

Merli jumped over the side of the boat in his dream and regained his senses when a very real wave swallowed him, the giant sailor instantly aware that for him every seaman's nightmare had been realized. A large black shadow bobbed out of the glowing wave beside him, and he knew it boded ill. Like any drowning man, his body reacted before his mind could halt it and he kicked toward the shape, desperate for anything to cling to, but then Merli saw orange eyes flicker on the shadow and on dozens of similar creatures all around him. His fingers brushed scales and spines and he went under, and whether they spirited him down to behold unimaginable splendors or devoured him on the spot is not recounted here.

Al-Gassur awoke without realizing he had fallen asleep and, rubbing the salt from his eyes, saw Barousse release the anchor. It splashed in front of the ship, the cable uncoiling from its spool. Sitting up, the Arab felt his eyes fill with tears as he heard the sweetest song imaginable drifting from just over the bow. Then a shadow fell from the top of the high mast into the glowing sea, plummeting as silently as the anchor.

Below deck, Angelino, Giuseppe, Lucian, Karl, and Sir Jean drowned in their nightmares, their dreamships dashed on the music dripping down through the planks. Raphael had risen to piss and, seeing Martyn's head submerged in the water barrel, yanked him out, only to have the cardinal shove him off and submerge himself again.

Atop the foremast Leone stared at the end of the crossbeam from which Cosimo had jumped, too startled to move. On the rear mast Hegel attempted to prevent Manfried from doing the same while not slipping himself, one hand wrapped in the rigging, the other clutching Manfried's breeches while his brother tried to scramble to a higher diving point. Then a horrible groaning smothered her song, the entire ship jerked to the side, and even those in the depths of their night visions started awake.

In the dark men tumbled out of their berths into one another, slamming into the forecastle walls as the ship violently tilted. The barrel upended all over Martyn and Raphael, and the young brigand rolled in the water, keeping Martyn's head above the shallow surface and slapping the Christ back into him. The cardinal began hacking up water and his eyes focused on Raphael, who released him and joined the sailors rushing up the ladder.

A second shock rattled the masts, and the suddenly suicidal

Manfried's head knocked against the crossbeam with enough force to loosen his teeth. The rigging Hegel gripped swung him away from the mast and his brother, and before it swung back Hegel saw Manfried open his eyes and shakily stand on the crossbeam. Hegel screamed impotently, but instead of jumping to his doom Manfried turned and snatched at his swinging brother. Her song unbroken, the Brothers locked eyes, blood leaking through the gaps in Manfried's grin.

"Witchery out a hand yet?" Manfried helped Hegel untangle his arm from the ropes.

"Fuck that witch and double fuck Barousse he tries to keep us from righteousness!" Hegel began descending the mast, the light of the sea brighter than the moon.

"Hey!" Manfried noticed Leone standing on the opposite crossbeam, his head tilted down at the water. The sailor did not hear, carefully edging toward the end of the sail. Knowing what he was about, Manfried snatched out a dagger and hurled it at the man. His aim true despite the rocking vessel, the blade stuck in Leone's leg and sent the man spinning off the crossbeam. He disappeared with a crash into the hold, which was better than the sea by Grossbart reckoning.

Al-Gassur followed as she quit the bow and made for the stern, throwing himself at her feet. She raised the Arab up with her voice, her discarded sheet entangled on the figurehead. Her body blinded him, not with lust but with awe. Stroking his chin, she stole his heart as sharply as if she had done it with a knife.

Dropping off the mast, Hegel saw them and moved to crack her head open when the ship again tipped and he lost his footing. Karl led the charge from below and was therefore the first to tumble down the suddenly steep deck and over the railing. His pick embedded in the planks, Hegel shot out his hand and seized the sailor's arm. With Hegel secured in place Karl's legs dangled over the edge, and as the ship teetered further, a wave splashed onto the deck, immersing the sailor for a moment.

As the glowing water retreated, Karl shrieked and Hegel caught sight of a long shadow beside the man that disappeared with a splash. Hegel hoisted Karl back onto the ship, Angelino and Giuseppe arriving to help as the ship rocked back the other way. Karl kept screaming and as he toppled onto the men they saw that from the belly down nothing remained but strings of meat. While they all slid down the deck entrails spilled out from where Karl's legs ought to have been, his would-be saviors coated in his blood, the man's scream finally catching in his throat at the realization that he was dead.

Rodrigo slipped in the spilled water below deck and knocked the wind out of himself when he fell. Lucian and Raphael hung on to the ladder as the ship pitched about, and then emerged to the sight of a radiant ocean and Karl's upper half gliding across the deck. The waves had climbed along with her song, blazing spume crashing over the railings and soaking all. Manfried released his grip on the mast when the ship settled as much as it was likely to, and he saw her shove the Arab toward the edge and flee back to the bow. Manfried gave pursuit, the sprawled trio of Hegel, Giuseppe, and Angelino finding their footing as she danced past them onto the platform.

Between the rising groans of the timber and her song the men's shouts went unheard by each other, but all were clear on their purpose. Angelino's dread became complete when he saw that not only was the anchor dropped and doubtless moored, but Barousse stood before the windlass used to winch it up with his sword drawn. The woman stepped behind him, singing directly into his ear, and then she turned and let her song bound out across the roiling, luminescent ocean. With each note the sea grew fiercer despite the still air, and the taut anchor cable tugged

the nose of the ship down so the figurehead could kiss the sea
before rearing back up.

Al-Gassur held on to the open lid of the hold as the ship
swayed, and he saw the barely alive Leone sprawled in the shallow water atop the layers of hidden gold bars. Had the hold contained seawater and caught fish instead of Barousse's fortune
topped with a little fresh water the man might not have broken
his hips when he fell from the mast. Al-Gassur reached out to
Leone and drew Manfried's dagger from where it jutted out of
the sailor's thigh.

Martyn raved and prayed below deck, wondering if perhaps
all was not as the Grossbarts claimed and he, through no fault
of his own, championed sinners instead of saints. Sir Jean's limited knowledge of sailing and his absolute terror propelled him
through the storeroom door with a satchel in each hand. Rodrigo
tried to stop him and was promptly knocked unconscious by the
crazed knight, who opened the ship's only porthole and shoved
the satchels out into the sea in a desperate gambit to lighten the
load, radiant water rushing in with each sway of the ship.

Manfried barely noticed Barousse in his eagerness to reach
the woman on the bow, and almost had his face split for his over-
sight. Instead he jumped aside, sliding to the edge of the railing.
Hegel circled Barousse, trying to get at the woman he shielded.
Angelino shouted something about the anchor but even those
who spoke Italian could not hear over the song and the crashing
waves. Giuseppe knew without being told, however, and slunk
after Hegel. Raphael and Lucian drew up short behind Angelino, Raphael unsure of whose side to fight on given his bought
loyalty to Barousse and Lucian simply scared of getting near the
enraged man.

Regaining his balance on the platform of the prow, Manfried
went in for another assault and managed to back Barousse into
the anchor winch, the man slipping in the salt spray and falling

flat on his back. Hegel headed for the woman but then the prow bucked again and he slipped, skidding toward a gap in the railing. Manfried caught his brother before he went over, dragging him away from the edge. Hegel tried to stand but his leg buckled, his left shin black and swelling from where it had connected with the railing. Angelino was not so lucky, the poor fellow tumbling over the side of his ship as it dipped violently back down, his last thought before he struck the blindingly bright water that his best friend had sent him to his doom.

Scrambling upright, Barousse noticed with dismay that Raphael was delivering the final strike needed to sever the cable. The ship swerved as it came free, and to Hegel's horror he saw an enormous shape moving under the luminescent water where the hacked end of the hempen cable disappeared. As if sensing his gaze it dived down, sending up a brilliant wave that washed everyone but the woman and the Grossbarts off the bow and onto the deck.

Having seen him creep up on Barousse and the woman, Al-Gassur pounced on the upended Giuseppe but the mate hurled the Arab off. Lucian and Raphael clung to a mast to avoid being swept into the sea, and Alexius Barousse again regained his feet. The woman gripped the same railing as the Grossbarts and her eyes narrowed at them, her song trailing off. Her teeth appeared longer in the sea-light, and they saw her dripping body bulged and pulsed, her skin darkening in wide splotches. As she pivoted and sprang over the railing Manfried grabbed a gaff pole from its mooring in the rail and swung, smacking her side.

Seeing the woman disappear over the edge, Barousse wailed and charged back toward the prow to follow her into the ocean but Lucian kicked his legs out from under him. Giuseppe scrambled to his feet and was hurrying to put an end to Barousse when Al-Gassur tackled the mate, pitching them both on top of Barousse and Lucian. Raphael decided to side with the majority and administered a sound kick to Barousse before the restrained captain freed an arm and pulled his former hired man down onto the pile.

Using every remaining drop of stamina, Manfried held on to the gaff with both arms, Hegel limping as fast as he could to his brother's aid. The woman went berserk on the end of the pole, her left arm skewered by the barbed hook. She dangled in the water up to her waist, her other arm pulling on the gaff to drag Manfried down with her. Then Hegel reached them and grabbed his brother around the waist, tugged him away from the edge. Eyes tightly shut from her surprising weight, Manfried opened them only when he heard her flop over the edge of the railing.

Her bright lips again parted to release her song, her soft eyes meeting his hard ones, but Manfried could not hear her music over his own scream. Having finally pummeled Barousse unconscious, Lucian, Raphael and Giuseppe looked up and joined the Grossbart chorus while the Arab began laughing the desperate, howling laughter of the deranged. Below, Sir Jean dropped the box he held, bursting gems and coins and jewelry onto the floor beside the concussed Rodrigo. Martyn stopped praying and withdrew a bottle, guzzling what he thought might be his last taste on Earth.

The thing writhing on the bow resembled the woman they had brought through the mountains from above the navel, but even here differences were legion. Her small teeth had lengthened, sharpened, and multiplied, several rows of them glittering in the moonlight as she snapped at them. Several gashes had opened on either side of her throat, and water bubbled out of these as they descended upon her with pick and mace. Their weapons tore through the webbing between her fingers, smashing her hands down into her face and chest. Her blood proved red, thankfully, but they kept screaming, mashing her skull and driving her ribs out through her back.

Even with her song forced back down inside her she flopped around, her sinewy body slapping on the planks. The smooth skin of her stomach appeared translucent where it met the scales coating what had been her legs, the new and shimmering eel-like appendages tapering to splayed fins. This abominable region of her body continued twitching even after they used hatchets to remove her arms and head, and Manfried carved out her heart with his knife.

Giuseppe and Lucian retreated below, sallow and shivering, under the pretext of locking up the mutinous Arab in the store-room. Raphael swayed aimlessly on the deck, gibbering to himself in his native tongue. A sound slap from Hegel set him a little straighter, and he assisted in transferring her prodigious remains to the hold lest they reform in the again-dark and calm sea and she return to life revenge-minded. In the hold they found the dazed Leone, who passed out as soon as he saw what they carried. They dragged him out and shoved her in, then bore the sailor under.

Sir Jean had eventually calmed after the ship stopped creaking and swaying, and realizing he had struck Rodrigo unconscious, surreptitiously made his exit. Finding Martyn dozing on the floor, the knight liberated him of his bottle and righted one of the chairs. Giuseppe and Lucian found him there, and after shoving Al-Gassur into the storage room without noticing the still-prone Rodrigo they picked up their own chairs and wordlessly joined him in drinking. Worrying he had perhaps erred, Sir Jean did not mention his exploits in the storage room, and the sailors did not mention their adventure above.

Manfried came down next, and Hegel lowered Leone until the sailors could catch him and set him in a bunk. Raphael remained on deck securing Barousse's arms and legs with rope after he had determined the captain lived. Binding the man's bleeding forearm, Raphael looked up to see Manfried and Hegel emerge with bottles under their arms. The Grossbarts advanced on Raphael and sat on the loose rigging between him and Barousse.

"Didn't make those too tight?" Manfried asked.

"Tight secure." Raphael stared at the tilted bottle at Hegel's mouth.

"But not tight enough to wring new harm out a him?" Manfried insisted.

"Mine ownself is capable adept of tie a man," Raphael snapped.

"Tone, boy," Hegel growled, handing him his bottle.

"Mine thanks." Raphael tipped the bottle.

"Wise a you not usin a blade on'em," said Manfried. "Weren't no fault a his, and what made him that way's dead, so's when he awakes he'll be right in the brainpan again."

Manfried could not know how wrong that statement would prove. They made no pretensions at working the ship, and had they run aground the Grossbarts would not have known it. The three put a powerful drunk upon themselves, Hegel insisting to the others that the worst was yet to come, for his bones told him and they never lied. On this matter, the Grossbart had the gift of prophecy.

XXIV
The Execution of the Grossbarts

Al-Gassur slept in a corner, his mind reeling through subterranean oceans with his new brother and their nameless wife. Barousse and he were now closer than kin, as wedded to one another as they were to their mutual intended. Her song bonded the three of them eternally, and in the darkest depths with worlds of ocean above, and that mounted by worlds of earth to further block out the light of sun and moon, Al-Gassur knew he had finally found a home where he would not be judged for his appearance.

Awoken from his dreams by shouting, Al-Gassur rolled about chortling with sleepy laughter. Having pressed an ear to the door the previous night he knew what they were about above deck, and fully approved of the plot. The ruckus brought Rodrigo back around as well, the young man's head pounding and every fiber of his body sore from the involuntary sleeping posture Sir Jean's fist had granted him.

Blearily gaining his feet, Rodrigo demanded to know what had transpired the previous night but the Arab responded with a fairly convincing imitation of Rodrigo's deceased brother and Al-Gassur's former master, Ennio. Making for the smaller man to wring the truth from him if need be, Rodrigo startled Al-Gassur into action. The shouting above them grew louder,

Rodrigo intent on his purpose, but even with one leg his quarry eluded him.

"They're hanging them!" Al-Gassur finally hooted as the two danced about the tiny room. "Death to the Grossbarts! Death!"

"What?" Rodrigo paused. "What does Barousse think of this?"

"Bound and beaten! Those bastards killed her and now they'll kill him and then me!"

"The Grossbarts?" Having spent the night crumpled on the floor, Rodrigo could perhaps be forgiven for not intuiting the events that had transpired after Sir Jean knocked him out.

"Death to the betrayers! Justice meted out for their crimes! For Six-Toed Pietro, cut down in the street! For my brother Barousse and for our wife! Justice!" Al-Gassur closed his eyes, and Rodrigo resisted the urge to strike the former tenant of the Barousse stable.

"Shut your mouth or you'll wish the Grossbarts had gotten you," Rodrigo spit, but his dramatic exit was foiled by the realization that the door was blocked from outside. Cursing, he drew his sword and hacked at the door.

Hegel's dreams cautioned him of what came next but when he opened his eyes and mouth to warn his brother the treacherous mate Giuseppe had already slipped a noose around Hegel's neck and the crippled Leone lay on the hold, a crossbow pointed in Hegel's face. Sir Jean had gotten a loop over Manfried's head and Lucian's cutlass poked the Grossbart's belly. The Brothers exchanged a glance but did not move, recognizing the nervousness of their captors as potentially lethal. Now that it had occurred, being taken while asleep on the deck of the ship struck them both as being a rather embarrassing and avoidable circumstance.

Raphael lay bound and bleeding beside Barousse, the conspirators' plan to enlist him thwarted by Sir Jean's wrath. The knight insisted the young man would remain loyal to the Grossbarts as an excuse to soundly beat him, and hopefully worse. The nooses stretched over the crossbeams, but all agreed it would be better to humiliate the Brothers first.

"What's this treachery?" Hegel demanded.

"You're mutineers, and as captain, it's my duty before God to see you hang," Giuseppe breathed in Hegel's ear. "I told Angelino not to take on this voyage, and had he listened to his mate he would be alive and you dogs would already be dead."

"A fine thanks for us savin your lives," said Manfried.

Sir Jean called to Giuseppe in Italian, and the man repeated it in German: "He wants to thank you for denting his armor and making it stink like a serf's crack."

Dinged and smelly though it may have been, Sir Jean had donned his armor again before sneaking upon the Grossbarts. He kicked the rigging by Lucian's foot and nodded down at Manfried. All four then had a short and heated debate over whether to risk tying the Grossbarts' hands before hoisting them. Deciding they could always shoot or stab them if they got themselves loose, they decided on their course.

"After we cut off your heads to present to our doge we sail home!" Giuseppe announced. "With Barousse's besides, we shall receive a hero's welcome, saying naught of your idiot captain's gold."

"You ready, brother?" Hegel asked in their secret tongue, but before Manfried could answer or act Giuseppe ran back down the deck, jerking Hegel to his feet. Tethered by his neck and bouncing on a swollen ankle, Hegel's hand went to his belt but all his knives were gone. He caught sight of a scarlet sash poking out from behind the mast, and hatred mingled with his gloom.

"You snivelin twat!" Hegel gurgled. "Supposed to be with us! Supposed to help us fight Her enemies!"

"The Will of Mary will be served." Martyn sheepishly stepped out from behind his cover. "We are but instruments of a greater will."

"Damn you!" Manfried elbowed Sir Jean, his elbow shooting pain up his shoulder as it connected with the knight's armor. "You's goddamn heretics, all a yous!"

"The pity's we can't burn you!" Giuseppe yanked Hegel off the ground, the Grossbart seizing the rope with both hands to avoid a snapped neck. Swinging around, he kicked at Giuseppe but the man hoisted him higher. Hegel's feet futilely tried to find purchase on the sail behind him.

"By my brother's beard, better yous crucify us!" Manfried howled, kicking at Lucien.

"An excellent idea!" agreed Martyn, who cut loose two lengths of cord and began shimming up the mast with his good arm.

"Hey now," Giuseppe called, "we haven't the nails or the time."

"Actually," Martyn panted, pausing in his ascent, "rope will suffice, for it is God that does the slaying."

Sir Jean asked Giuseppe what in the Hell was going on, but rather than supporting his new captain the knight cackled when Giuseppe translated. The suggestion also calmed the condemned, so Giuseppe relented—at least for the first Grossbart. He rasied Hegel higher, and the Grossbart eventually swung in enough that Martyn could grab him. Of course, this meant Hegel could also grab Martyn, which he did even though it meant his life.

The noose tightened around Hegel's throat, throttling him as he throttled Martyn. Then Hegel saw the handle of his dagger jutting out from Martyn's robe and he released his grip, fumbling around until he hooked an arm over the crossbeam. He glared at the sputtering cardinal, who nearly fell from his roost.

Exchanging whispered oaths with Martyn, Hegel relented and had his arms loosely tied around the crossbeam to give the appearance of being bound while his hands and elbows truly supported him. From here he realized the rope around his neck stretched over the opposite crossbeam, meaning he would still be hanged if he came loose or Giuseppe tightened the tether.

On the deck, even Giuseppe had become distracted by Raphael, who had worn through his bindings on a jutting nail and tackled Lucian. Manfried snatched hold of his noose and jumped away, pulling Sir Jean with him. The knight knew better than to release the leashed Grossbart and was dragged forward as Manfried swung away, nearly tripping over Lucian and Raphael. Martyn stopped halfway down the mast, Hegel's dagger set conspicuously on the crossbeam behind the Grossbart's left hand.

Giuseppe realized the situation had changed and yanked on Hegel's rope with all his might, then tied it around the railing behind him. Martyn had bound Hegel just tightly enough to appear convincing, but with the rope tugging him up toward the foremast's crossbeam he could not slip his arms out in time. Hegel felt the cord cut into his neck, able only to choke and pray.

Still suspended by his own rope, Manfried swung back toward the knight. Lucian and Raphael rolled beneath him, each with a hand on the hilt of Lucian's sword. Sir Jean accepted Manfried's legs squarely in his chest and fell backward, but since he held tight to the rope this caused Manfried to ascend higher into the air. Giuseppe hacked at his flailing legs but before he found meat Leone let out a yelp and fired his crossbow.

Rodrigo had appeared by the ladder, and Leone's bolt sailed over his shoulder. The sailor frantically began reloading while Giuseppe charged Rodrigo, who had no idea why events were unfolding thus but drew his sword lest the incensed first mate run him through. Sir Jean scrambled upright, lowering Manfried in the process.

"Hegel!" Manfried yelped, catching sight of Rodrigo.

Rodrigo glanced up at the crucified Grossbart and almost lost his ear for it. Giuseppe's cutlass brushed his face but Rodrigo parried it and backed away. The head conspirator compensated for lack of skill with ferocity, whereas Rodrigo's lengthy training was supplemented by little experience in the school of actual combat. The young man's brilliant feint therefore slipped past his rival's blade and tagged Giuseppe's left hand, but then Rodrigo had his scalp clipped of flesh and hair by the enraged Giuseppe.

Lights began appearing to Hegel, legs kicking and teeth gritted. The sounds below faded and shadows filled the perimeter of his vision, closing in around the growing specks of light. Then they were swallowed by the black tide, leaving Hegel alone and blind.

Martyn shimmied back up the mast out of self-preservation but when he reached the crossbeam he realized what had happened to Hegel. Getting his balance on the crossbeam, he bumped the dagger with his knee and it tumbled into the hold. Unsure what else to do, he began untying Hegel's arms with his only usable hand.

Raphael kneed Lucian in the groin but the sailor headbutted him, breaking the brigand's nose for the third time in his life. Another crotch-shot from Raphael, and Lucian released the sword and consciousness just long enough for Raphael to seize the weapon and scramble to his feet. He booted Lucian in the face, returning the nasal favor. Half-blind from the blood and pain radiating from his nose, he spun around for a target and found Sir Jean within range.

The knight felt his panic returning as things became less like butchering the uppity peasants comprising the Jacquerie in his native province and more like the brutal battle at Poitiers, although there he had laid down his sword and enjoyed a comfortable period of relaxation until his ransom was paid. Naïve though he might have been, he knew better than to expect such honorable treatment from this lot. He released the rope, dropping the suspended Manfried onto Raphael's shoulders. Both men fell to the ground and Sir Jean drew the sword he had found the night before.

Rodrigo stumbled back with blood burning in one eye and dodged the next swipe of Giuseppe's sword. By Providence they had battled across the deck until they were near Hegel's rope, which Giuseppe inadvertently severed when Rodrigo ducked. The rope snapped past Giuseppe's face and on reflex he jumped back, his knee buckling on the lip of the hold. The head conspirator fell backward into the exposed hold and went under the brackish surface for a moment, then came up to see the unmoored Hegel tumbling toward him. Martyn had freed Hegel's left arm and had made enough progress with the right that when the rope went slack Hegel slipped out of the bond and fell.

Leone's crossbow popped again, and this time the bolt found flesh. The horrified sailor thought for a moment Rodrigo had actually caught the arrow out of the air, but then blood poured out from either side of his hand. Rodrigo stared at the arrow skewering his hand and wondered why it did not hurt, and suddenly it did, severely. Leone dropped the crossbow and fumbled for his dagger when the tip of Rodrigo's cutlass passed between his teeth and out the back of his neck, blood misting Rodrigo's face as he twisted his sword to free it.

Spying his mace on the deck, Manfried lunged away from Sir Jean while Raphael swung at the knight. The mercenary's blade bounded off Sir Jean's plated chest and the chevalier cracked Raphael in the skull with the pommel of his sword. Raphael slumped at Sir Jean's feet and he delivered a vicious kick to the man's stomach. Before he lost himself in stomping his former guard, Sir Jean spotted Manfried dashing up the deck and gave chase.

Giuseppe saw Hegel plummeting down directly on top of

him, but before he could move the Grossbart landed. Even with his soul to Mary's Breast, Hegel's body tallied another mortal sin when his dead weight drove Giuseppe's head under water and split his skull on a submerged gold brick. The corpses of Giuseppe and the woman-thing broke Hegel's fall better than the water and gold bars had for Leone the previous night, and when the cold liquid coated the Grossbart's back his lungs drew in on reflex, his prodigious neck muscles loosening the noose. The foul nature of the air he inhaled, stagnant with the murdered monster's fishy musk, caused him to begin coughing and gagging. Hegel Grossbart again drew breath, but only because the physical world so offended his dying senses.

Manfried snatched up his mace in one hand and his brother's nearby pick in the other, and spun toward Sir Jean just as the knight brought his sword down. The cutlass exploded when it met Manfried's swinging mace, metal shards bouncing off Sir Jean's plating and embedding in Manfried's skin. In the same motion Manfried brought the pick up between the knight's legs, its metal tip punching a jagged hole in Sir Jean's codpiece and what it covered.

Drawn so close, Manfried could not dodge Sir Jean's broken sword as it thrust at his bruised throat. Before it reached flesh the knight curiously released the weapon and awkwardly slapped Manfried's face, the discharged blade clipping Manfried's uncropped left ear and tumbling over the rail. Rodrigo's sword had not penetrated the thick iron covering Sir Jean's forearm but had succeeded in both disarming the man and incensing Manfried even more.

The numbness in Sir Jean's genitals turned to searing agony when Manfried yanked the pick out, and before he could recover Rodrigo and Manfried had knocked him to the deck. His armor sagged inward wherever the mace struck, bruising his skin and the organs beneath. The tip of his nose flipped off under Rodrigo's blade, erupting blood and snot, and thus disenfranchised of even an honorable death, he covered his face with his hands and waited for a strike to end both humiliation and life.

"Keep'em where he lies, but kill'em and you's next," Manfried snarled at Rodrigo, whirling to find his brother.

Martyn saw Manfried stalk around the deck calling for Hegel but the cardinal did not answer, instead cowering at the top of the mast and praying. Then Manfried saw his brother lying in the hold—face pale, body motionless. Hegel's panting had slowed to an imperceptible wheeze, but Manfried hauled him up and over his shoulder as if he were merely too drunk to stand. Swaying back to Sir Jean and the suddenly crying Rodrigo, Manfried dumped Hegel onto the prone knight.

Hegel landed face to face with Sir Jean, and the knight removed his hands from his own mangled features to shove Hegel off of him. Ignoring Sir Jean's pawing hands, Manfried hauled his brother higher until his limp body blocked the chevalier's mouth, what remained of Sir Jean's nose too full of blood to draw breath. Manfried pushed down on Hegel's back and smothered the knight until his thrashing softened, and then Manfried stopped to allow Sir Jean a solid gasp before pressing the human pillow of Hegel back into place.

Muttering curse after curse, Manfried continued this rhythmic pumping of Hegel's chest against the knight's head until the action painfully wrenched Hegel away from Her Bosom and into Sir Jean's. Hegel's hands twitched, then flopped up to the painful bulge under his chest. The Virgin returned what man had taken, and opening his eyes, Hegel Grossbart promptly gouged out those of Sir Jean.

"A miracle," Manfried whispered.

"A miracle," Martyn gasped.

"Glub," the asphyxiating Sir Jean gurgled, his eye sockets now bubbling along with his nose.

"Ugh," groaned Hegel.

"A goddamn miracle!" Manfried shouted, "Praise Mary!"

"Praise," Hegel managed. "Us."

"Let's get that off," said Manfried. "I accept you's shaken by Her Power, Rigo, but quit cuntin off at the eyes and help me get this noose off a him."

Rodrigo obeyed, but with the fight won his wounds set to paining him until he could barely stand. They set Hegel against the side of the rear mast and got a bottle to his lips. On the deck lay Raphael, Lucian, and Sir Jean, all too beaten to move, and Martyn hurried down his mast to join the victors. As he approached Manfried stood and snatched his collar, hurling him to the ground between Hegel's legs.

"You want I open'em now, or you'd rather after a rest?" Manfried asked.

"Please!" Martyn yelped.

"You accept Her," Hegel wheezed.

"I do!"

"You accept Her Miracle?" said Hegel.

"I do!"

"I died." Hegel blinked at his brother. "I seen Her."

"You's a martyr." Manfried bowed his head.

"She brought me back," panted Hegel.

"A true miracle!" agreed the desperate cardinal.

"Then you's absolved." Hegel closed his eyes, trying to remember what he had witnessed but the image had faded like a leaf in winter. "Same with the rest, brother."

"What?" Manfried could not believe his cropped ear.

"Any who'll accept the truth be spared," Hegel rasped. "Save that snobby French and that schemin Seppe. They's past mercy."

"Even asleep you slayed Giuseppe!" In his haste to impress Martyn made a severe tactical mistake.

Manfried reminded Martyn of the divine nature of things by cuffing the cardinal.

"In death," said Martyn, "even in death, you smote the Judas."

"That rich one." Hegel motioned toward Sir Jean. "Get'em out that armor and hoist'em up where he put me."

Rodrigo had disappeared, however, leaving Manfried with little choice but to perform that particular task himself. He left his brother to drink with the cardinal and stripped Sir Jean of his battered plate. Sir Jean resisted only slightly, intent as he was on his ruined face.

Next Manfried saw to Raphael and Lucian. Both came around following a dousing from the rain barrel, but with their bloody faces he could not tell them apart until Raphael spoke in his broken German. After quickly outlining the situation to the miserable men, Manfried insisted Raphael translate for Lucian, who eagerly accepted the heavenly course of events and even tried to kiss Manfried's feet.

"Get to Hell," Manfried spit. "See this bastard don't get so much's a knife long as he's on this boat."

"Why not a knife for him?" Raphael asked, gingerly touching his broken nose and wincing.

"Cause he can't be trusted!" Manfried shook his head in frustration.

"Yes, so why not a knife for him?" Raphael gestured toward his throat.

"Cause Hegel's restored his grace and we ain't forsaken murderers!" Manfried rapped Raphael's brow. "Now get a move on helpin me cross that French."

"Thanks to the Virgin!" Al-Gassur announced his presence, having had time to swallow his disappointment. "Bless Her as She blessed you and he and even I! A miracle!"

Under the pretext of helping untangle the excess rigging to

lift Sir Jean, Al-Gassur went to the side of the forgotten Captain Barousse. He had watched the entire event from where he lay trussed between the masts, several times serving as a stone for men to topple over in the battle. His placid eyes and expressionless face transformed at the sight of the Arab, however, tears brimming even as a grin split his swollen face.

After discovering Sir Jean's jettisoning of every crust and crumb—including both of the Brother's private food satchels from their bunks—Manfried rooted through all the bags in the common room, and ransacked the other bunks looking for hidden cheese or sausage. He found enough to last him a day, and again cursed their recent softness. They should have stashed extra provisions somewhere lest this sort of idiocy transpire. Making sure none approached the ladder he took the slightest of sips from his personal waterskin, rolling the water around in his mouth with his eyes closed. Then he filled a bucket from the beer barrel, thanking the Virgin that had not tipped like the water.

XXV
The Monotonous Sea

Hegel quickly recovered enough to direct the others about, but the sunlight playing on the sails and the gentle ocean distracted him. Raphael and Lucian used the two nooses intended for the Grossbarts on Sir Jean's arms while Martyn attempted to administer confession to the pain-maddened knight. Unable to decipher the nauseating sounds and loath to look upon him, Martyn hurried through the last rites. Had Hegel noticed the cardinal's actions he would have tossed him overboard but the Grossbart had adopted a contemplative mood, which he thought befitting for one recently risen from the grave.

When Raphael informed Hegel of Sir Jean's readiness for punishment the Grossbart ordered the corpses of Giuseppe and Leone given to the sea following a thorough search of their persons for valuables. Manfried reappeared, lugging up the bucket of beer for his brother. He noticed Al-Gassur whispering to the bound Barousse and helped his brother stand so they could hold council with the captain.

"Another miracle," Hegel pronounced.

"Glad you's returned to your senses," said Manfried.

The captain said something in Italian to Al-Gassur and both giggled, staring up at the Grossbarts.

"See now." Hegel scowled. "None a that."

"My brother informs me you both look ridiculous," said Al-Gassur.

Manfried informed Al-Gassur of the prudence of silence by slapping his face until his hand stung. At the first blow Barousse set to baying like a hound and straining at his ropes, snapping his chipped teeth at the Grossbarts. Hegel responded by pouring wine into his biting mouth. The captain calmed at the taste, and tilted his neck to better guzzle.

Kicking the Arab toward the ladder, Manfried ordered him below. "Get Rigo to come help reinstate the captain in his quarters."

"Barousse," Hegel said, "you's all right now, Captain?"

Barousse removed his lips from the bottle and spit wine in Hegel's face.

"She's dead," Hegel hissed, "dead as the rest a them what'd undo us. And now we's Gyptland-bound. Look to Mary, Captain, look to Her!"

Barousse pissed himself, his eyes rolling back and red drool coursing between his jagged teeth. Hegel sighed, the sight of the once-great man so reduced oddly reminding him of his formidable hunger. Manfried returned from running off the Arab, and hearing Hegel's stomach complain, opened his sack. They moved downwind of the captain to eat, and Lucian and Raphael went below rather than ask the Grossbarts for a share. They soon returned, even paler than before.

"What will mine ownself eat?" said Raphael.

"Here." Hegel tore a portion off his cheese wheel and tossed it his way. "Drink enough ale you won't feel the pangs so."

Sir Jean lazily dangled between the masts, and Lucian began punching his naked chest and screaming in Italian. The Grossbarts had a laugh at this, although only his cheese prevented Raphael from becoming equally hysterical. Below deck he had tried to get some information from Rodrigo on how they might catch fish but the man had been unwilling or incapable of speech after hearing Raphael's account of the previous night's madness and the change wrought upon their captain. That Lucian and Rodrigo—the only two people on board who knew anything about sailing and the sea—were clearly pessimistic about their lot rattled Raphael's nerves.

The new and terrible emotions killing a fellow human being stirred inside Rodrigo mingled with his concern for his captain, and to escape the howls of the Arab emanating from the store-room he eventually went above deck. His puffy eyes were ill pre-pared for the radiance of the sun, and by the time they adjusted enough for him to squint and make out the deck he saw that the joint efforts of the remaining crew had resulted in Sir Jean's cru-cifixion on the crossbeam of the foremast. Ignoring the sadistic turn events had taken, he slowly walked to where the captain lay.

The bound Barousse ignored Rodrigo, his eyes fixed on the sea. Rodrigo sat beside him on the deck, and without knowing exactly why, laid his head on the captain's shoulder. Closing his eyes, the young man wondered if life would ever be enjoyable again. Then Barousse bit into his ear.

Yanking away, Rodrigo left his right earlobe in Barousse's mouth. Clapping his good hand to the wound, Rodrigo stared at the captain as he chewed. Rodrigo stumbled away, weeping from more than the searing pain.

Witnessing Rodrigo's mishap and unconsciously touching his own cropped ear, Manfried called for Lucian and Raphael, and while Rodrigo watched they unwrapped the captain's ropes and maneuvered him to the ladder. Barousse would not or could not stand, so they dragged him and lowered him down to the com-mon room. From there the three men went down and Rodrigo stumbled up the stern to Cardinal Martyn. The two men did not speak but stared behind them at the point where the emerald sea met the golden sky.

Late in the day the Grossbarts insisted Rodrigo and Lucian ensure their course remained true. Even if either had known much about navigation any maps stowed in the storeroom had gone with their food into the brine. With everyone except Al-Gassur and Barousse working at the sails the two sailors could not be sure they were directed anywhere save generally southeast. Both had insisted they should cut north in search of land where food and a new crew could be taken on, but the Grossbarts would hear none of it, insisting faith would suffice.

That night Rodrigo, doubting he would live long enough to find a more acceptable man of the cloth, attempted to unburden himself by speaking with Martyn. Concerned for the souls of his captain and his brother even more than for his own, the injured fellow was disappointed when the cardinal insisted on confessing to him instead, raving of demons and the death of his lover Elise. Raphael stayed awake even after Lucian, Martyn, and Rodrigo drifted off, trying futilely to pick out comprehensible words from the Grossbarts drinking above deck and the voices from the storeroom.

After much debate, Manfried's logic regarding the purifying nature of flame won out and the Brothers set to building a fire on Sir Jean's shield. By its light they saw his silhouette flat against the sail, a wide stain running down beneath him. Hegel suggested they test it on the Arab in the morning, a wise course by Manfried's estimation. As a final precaution Hegel only cut from the twin tails farthest from where they joined her human skin.

They stayed up most of the night smoking the meat, hoping the delicious aroma did not mask poison or curse. After the lid to the hold and the chairs from the forecastle were ash they agreed they had enough to last until Gyptland, provided they ate sparingly. So they hacked off part of the railing and smoked another pile, now getting dangerously close to where questionable meat became cannibalism. This they hid in their sacks and pitched the coals into the ocean, disappointed that the waves gobbled up the pleasant hissing they longed for.

They slept in shifts while the stars twisted and the ship rocked, both grown accustomed enough to the motion that they no longer became sick. Manfried spent his watch patrolling the deck and squinting at the impenetrable depths. Hegel spent his at the top of the mast, whispering to Sir Jean the theories he feared to tell his brother. He felt safe in doing so for the knight had finally died in the long interval between his crucifixion and Hegel's taking him into his confidence. Neither brother touched the sails or rudder, imagining that such actions might indicate their lack of reliance on the Will of Mary.

Raphael led the exodus from below shortly after dawn, Rodrigo glumly accompanying Lucian and Martyn. The Grossbarts greeted them in their customary fashion, which is to say they ignored them. Raphael cleared his throat, and when the Brothers did not respond, he turned to the other three.

"We've got fish to catch," Raphael said in Italian.

"What I say bout talkin that code?" Manfried demanded, now paying attention.

"The sailor doesn't speak any other way," Rodrigo sighed, motioning to Lucian. "All he said was we should try for some fish, but I don't know how he means to do that with the net's moorings ripped off along with the winch."

"Drink ale," said Hegel, "and pray."

"Yes!" Martyn agreed, "it's the only means!"

"What are they saying?" Lucian whispered to Raphael in Italian.

"That we'll eat you if you keep talking," was the mercenary's response, and that quieted him.

"Fish's been caught," Manfried announced, "but fore anyone eats we feed it to the Arab. Check it ain't rotten or poisonous."

The incredulous group all spoke at once, but Manfried dismissed them with a wave of his loaded crossbow. They noticed the flanks of smoked meat laid out on the deck and their mouths watered, more than one moving to snatch a piece. The crossbow brought them short, and now Hegel stood on the edge of the hold and addressed them.

"We'll eat if the Arab's alive by sundown," Hegel rasped, "and neither me nor my brother nor any a yous'll have a taste til then. Now mind Rigo, as he instructs you on how to steer this raft to Gyptland."

Manfried took a large hunk below, leaving the men to untangle the rigging and fiddle with the sails. They had shoved the beer barrel in front of the door, Rodrigo having smashed the latch the day before. With a few groans Manfried slid it back enough for him to push through. Al-Gassur apparently valued his life enough to have not untied Barousse but the two lay side by side in the center of the room, four eyes shining at Manfried.

"Got somethin for you to eat, Arab," said Manfried.

Al-Gassur had not grown lax as the Grossbarts nor as unfortunate as they, his satchel still bulging with fruit, cheese, sausage, and bread he had nicked prior to Sir Jean's ejection of the provisions. This, compounded with the mutual distrust he shared with the Grossbarts, dissuaded him from accepting any such gifts. The brief period he had spent in their company cautioned against outright refusal, however.

"Many blessings to you, dearest Manfried," Al-Gassur cooed. "Perhaps you've also deigned to feed our captain, and also brought something to wet our tongues?"

"All a them empty bottles beside yous implies drinks been provided from that crate," Manfried observed. "And for the captain, everyone knows fish ain't proper for those ill a mind, which is why I brung'em cheese."

"Fish, for me?" Al-Gassur suspicions increased along with

his supplications. "Please, honest Manfried, deliver me this too-worthy feast!"

Manfried tossed him the fish, waiting until the Arab had bitten off several pieces and swallowed before turning away. The sight of Barousse eyeing them like a simple beast annoyed him to no end, and he wished the captain would either perish or recover. Still, Mary's Will would be served, inscrutable though it may have been to Grossbarts and lesser men alike. Shoving the barrel back into place, he did not see Al-Gassur spit out the meat he had concealed in his cheek.

"They're eating her?" Barousse laughed and cried.

"Our wife," Al-Gassur moaned, pressing the fishy pulp against his cheek.

"My bride."

"How shall we avenge her?"

"With their blood," Barousse wept, "with their bones and souls."

"She is gone," Al-Gassur lamented, "gone, gone, gone."

"But you shall have another." Barousse's sob melted into a cackle. "You'll bring another up, and she'll be yours, while I swim with mine through what estates the kelp grants us. More than their Mary, more than my Mathilde."

"What do you mean?"

"Release me, brother." Barousse became perfectly calm. "Cut my bonds, and I'll show you."

Deranged as he had become, Al-Gassur still balked at the request. Stalling, he said, "The Grossbarts will return, I am sure of it. Better we wait until the sun is gone and they shun this room."

"Avenge us when I go, brother, and you'll be rewarded." Barousse closed his eyes and hummed a tune they both knew well, though his simple human instrument failed to capture its essence.

Above, the men had discovered where the meat had come from when Lucian peered into the hold. After he recovered from fainting he crawled away from Hegel, gibbering every prayer he knew. Raphael was likewise disgusted and swore he would die before putting such vileness in his mouth, Martyn encouraging his denial of witch flesh as a source of sustenance. Rodrigo smiled at their indignation, not at all surprised by this newest sin but unwilling to partake. He climbed a mast while they murmured their disapproval out of range of Grossbart ears.

Of all the men, excluding the risen Hegel, Rodrigo had suffered the worst injuries the day before. The patch of exposed skull on his scalp, his punctured hand, and his masticated ear still bothered him less than the decline of his captain, the only family he had left. Sitting on the crossbeam beside Sir Jean's wilting head he looked to the sea, wondering how he could go on if Barousse died.

The day meandered by, the men's despair countered by the Grossbarts' optimism. Surely the sandy lands of gold lay behind the next cloudbank, and even late into the afternoon they watched the horizon expectantly, positive that any moment a shore would appear. It did not, and while the winds were stronger at night the men were exhausted and again went to bed hungry in their bunks. That Al-Gassur seemed fit as ever did not sway any but the Grossbarts to sample her flesh.

The Grossbarts ate copiously, arguing whether their meal tasted good or not. Manfried found it gamier than most aquatic meat, while Hegel thought it especially fishy. His dislike of four-legged beasts in no way impinged on his enjoyment of their seared flesh and organs.

"Odd," Hegel said after they had eaten, "we's seen us what now, three witches and three monsters?"

"You's calculatin improper," Manfried belched.

"How's that?"

"One monster, that mantiloup or what have you, the witch what served'em—"

"He served her," Hegel interjected.

"Moot. Then we got that witch come with the pig. And he got a demon in'em, so that's one more a each."

"That's where you's off, cause the man's a witch, the demon in'em's a demon, and that pig makes three."

"Three what? No, shut it. That pig was a pig was a pig. A pig what got a demon in it after we kilt the witch." Manfried shook his head at his brother's obtuseness.

"How you know it weren't his servant, or the Devil?"

"I don't, same as you, so in the absence a evidence we's gonna assume it was simple swine got possessed by a demon."

"If it was Old Scratch he wouldn't well let some mecky demon in'em." Hegel reasoned. "Would a come at us himself."

"See, that's bein sensible." Manfried was impressed. "So that's two witches and two monsters, and she what we just et makes three."

"Three what?"

"Hmmm," grumbled Manfried. "Witches? Witches."

"Witches, in my voluminous experience as a tutor in Praha, do not have goddamn fish parts stead a legs." Hegel made a big to-do of straightening his beard and sniffing his knobby nose.

"Hmm."

"Monsters, on the other hand, have all kinds a weird animal parts. What makes'em monsters, after all."

"Witches might have tails," Manfried said after another bite. "Just not ones that big."

"Granted, maybe a little cow tail or cat thing or what, might even have seven tits like a bitch, but this mess—" Hegel squeezed the greasy meat between his fingers. "No sir. But then a monster don't cast charms and such in my knowledge, so I figure she counts for both."

"Eatin a monster's no sin," Manfried philosophized, "but eatin a witch is, cause they's more or less mannish, so long's we stay south a the navel we's safe."

"The truth, unadulterated by rhetoric. Don't taste too bad, neither, if I's to be honest."

"But that broaches another curiosity," said Manfried. "We can agree a demon's different from other monsters, requirin, as the cardinal told us on the mountains, a body, preferably a witch, to ride round in like we's on this boat."

"Cause like us, it might float for a little while fore sinkin below without somethin solid to rest on," Hegel agreed.

"The good Virgin must a given you some extra brains while you was dead. Any rate, demons different from monsters. Look nuthin like anythin I ever seen."

"Yeah?"

"Whereas the monsters we seen, namely our dinner and that mantiloup, they look like people what got beast parts," said Manfried.

"Fish ain't a beast, we's been over that," Hegel pointed out.

"By my fuckin faith, Hegel, you know what I mean! Part eel or snake or fish and part woman and part beast and part man is still closer to the same thing then that demon was to anythin, man or beast. Or fish."

"Yeah?"

"So why's monsters always a mix a man and critter?"

"In our experience, that's indeed been the case," Hegel mused. "Operatin, as we now do, on the assumption that what we's et is monster stead a witch."

"Right enough! I ain't et no damn witch! Only the top part is witch, what we's munchin is pure monster."

"Suppose so. But I harbor doubts as to whether that thing in the mountains had a witch's head and a monster-cat's body. Seemed what might a been a man become a monster."

"So it's possible monsters is just men, be they heretics or witches, get turned into somethin." Manfried bit his lip, staring at the pile of uneaten meat.

"Or monsters might be beasts that change partly into men. Or women."

"That's pushin reason a little hard," Manfried argued. "I don't believe it's possible she was a fish what turned into a woman."

"But she didn't speak. Fish don't speak."

"And they don't sing, neither. Sides, plenty a monsters I heard bout ain't nuthin like men or women, just pure monster."

"Like what?" Hegel demanded.

"Like dragons and unicorns and such."

"But we ain't never seen'em, so they might be nuthin more than tales."

"Not necessarily," said Manfried.

"No, but hearin bout somethin don't make it real. I know Mary's real cause I seen Her, and I know demons' real cause I seen one a them, and I know weird fuckin fish witches is—"

"I follow, I follow," Manfried groused. "But we knew witches was real fore we ever saw one, and sure enough, we was right on their account."

"Yeah," Hegel allowed.

"So monsters, in our experience, is part man and part beast, although the possibility exists they might be parts a other things all mixed together, like a basilisk. Part chicken and part dragon."

"That ain't no basalisk, that's a damn cockatrice."

"A what?!" Manfried laughed at his brother's ignorance.

"A cockatrice. Basilisk's just a lizard, cept it poisons wells and such," said Hegel.

"That's a scorpion! Although you's half right—basilisk'll kill you quick, but by turnin its eyes on you."

"What!?" Hegel shook his head. "Now I know you's makin up

lies cause any man a learnin'll tell you straight a scorpion ain't no reptile, it's a worm."

"What worms you seen what have eyes and arms, huh?"

"Sides from you?"

The debate raged for some time, eventually deteriorating into a physical exchange. Hegel was happy to be alive and kicking his brother, and Manfried felt the same. When they took their shifts each thought of irrefutable points to make in the argument that qualified as such only in the loosest sense, considering they shared roughly the same opinion on this, as in most matters.

When all below fell silent below deck Al-Gassur lit a tallow in the storeroom. By its scant light he cut Barousse's bonds, and in a moment the captain had wrested the knife away and pinned Al-Gassur to the floor. The Arab's misery that his suspicions regarding Barousse's intentions had been proven true became compounded by stark fear as Barousse began acting even stranger.

His face hovering above Al-Gassur's, Barousse used the knife to slice open his own cheeks and brow, carving deep gashes that leaked blood into the Arab's open mouth. Then the captain held the knife to the Arab's throat and began licking Al-Gassur's face, sucking on the ends of his mustache and prying open locked eyelids with a meaty tongue. Al-Gassur gasped when the salty appendage wriggled under and pressed against his eyeball, the jelly coming off on the rough tongue. Only the blade nicking his neck prevented the Arab from screaming; he was well aware that if he so much as coughed he would slit his own throat.

Suddenly as the bizarre and lascivious assault had begun it ended, and Barousse reared to his feet. Al-Gassur cowered, begging his brother to forgive whatever trespasses he had inadvertently committed. Instead Barousse wildly cut through his own clothing with such vigor that in moments he stood nude before Al-Gassur, his old wounds and fresh cuts gleaming black in the candlelight. One hand gripping the knife, he seized Al-Gassur's hand with the other and yanked him upright. He hugged the Arab, who shivered at the wet embrace, his filthy clothes now glistening with fresh blood.

"In my travels I met a traveler," Barousse whispered, releasing Al-Gassur and rushing to the scattered boxes. "I was a traveler, and he was a traveler, and for a short time we traveled together. Traveling. Travel, travel, the only life worth living. I had a wife, and two young boys but still I traveled, if you understand."

"I under—"

"Traveling is best done with other travelers. The sea forces you among men, but not all are travelers at heart. The man, like me, was more than a man who travels because he can, but a traveler who travels because he must."

"I too have traveled. I must confess—"

"He told me." Barousse opened a box of jewelry and threw it against the wall, scattering a fortune along the floor. "I did not ask, just as you did not ask, but he told me, as I tell you."

Al-Gassur remained silent, watching the captain ransack the other boxes until he found the one containing his clothes, the last chest Sir Jean had made to discharge before he slipped, banged his head, and realized the ship had also calmed. Barousse began chortling with laughter, tears and rivulets of blood pooling around his bare knees. Al-Gassur brought the tallow closer while Barousse began tossing fur-trimmed tunics and boots around the room.

"He knew I could not be fully happy, for I traveled despite my hard-fought wealth, my beloved family, my comfortable station. I think that is why, it must be why. Yet I wonder, often, often, especially after they died and I banished her, I wondered. You will fear the sea and her but more than that you will fear returning her, you will regret everything, as I regretted everything. Yet in the end, you will be as happy as I!" Barousse shook with laughter, his naked body matted with dried blood and waste.

"East is their home. You travel to where ships are known to have sunk, spits of stone far out to sea, desolate island cliffs, hidden reefs that rape ships bellies, you go alone. I left my ship and all my men, and rowed close to a desolate island farther east than I had ever gone, past Cyprus, to the very brink of the Holy Land. There must be no moon, not even a shaving, when the sea is lit only by stars and your fear, and there you wait with a sturdy net."

The captain must have located his quarry, for he stopped rooting and leaned back, a thick black coat held in his shaking hand. He delicately ran the knife up and down it, prodding until the Arab heard a faint metallic jingle. Then the knife sank in and Barousse sank down, sliding his hand into the hole with the gentle air of a midwife assisting a small woman's first child into the world. Al-Gassur's candle reflected off something, and he peered over Barousse's shoulder.

"If you search it out you can find cable thin as rope but far stronger. You noose it over the end, and drop it into the sea. Ensure it is a ship's length long, to reach her depths. Then you wait, but not long. When you feel the tugging haul it up, slowly and gently as the first time you made love to your wife. You will hear the splashing beside your boat and then you must cast the net, and carefully, for one chance is all a man is allowed. Haul it on board quick, but do not look or all is lost! Above all, do not look until you have found a beach or rock where you can drag the net, and only then! And that, dear brother, is worth all sacrifices you have made and all tragedies you will suffer, the first sight of her! Only then will you return to your ship and the world of men, bringing what you have earned."

Al-Gassur held out his trembling hands and took the artifact. The sides of the small bottle were twisted and warped, and rather than having a stopper the neck ended in a smooth glass circle. A strange object sat in the bottom, a lump wrapped in sealskin, and the awed Arab saw that it exceeded the neck of the bottle in size. Either the bottle had been blown around it, or it had somehow grown after being sealed inside. Most curious of all, the glass felt warm to the touch, and pressing it to his cheek, Al-Gassur thought it pulsed like the chest of a small animal.

"Always conceal it, from moon and sun and man alike. Here, with roof above and floor below and walls on all sides, here it is dangerous enough." Barousse ripped a piece from the coat and covered the bottle in Al-Gassur's palm. "Never let it see the open sky, even when you put it to use, keep it wrapped in cloth and let the sea strip it of its mantle. Now that you have seen it, never risk it again, never!"

"Brother, I will never have faith in any but you." Al-Gassur bowed.

"I love to see the trembling of the tiny birds," Barousse whispered in a strange accent, and before Al-Gassur could question his meaning warm liquid splashed the Arab's face.

"I'll see you rest with her, brother," Al-Gassur vowed, the room tinted burgundy from the blood in his eyes. Barousse flopped forward, the knife buried to the hilt in his bare chest. A fevered smile contrasted with the horror in his foggy eyes, and his lips continued to move long into the night. And so Captain Alexius Barousse left the world of men and Grossbarts, leaving his legacy in the hands of those who still praised his name.

XXVI
The Children's Crusade

In the days that followed Heinrich's donning of the flagellant's robes, the boys remained obediently silent but would abduct any solitary travelers from the road and bring them before their stepfather, who would lecture the near-catatonic victims before allowing the twins to eat. With each gobbled victim the demon raged and worried at Heinrich to spare the potential converts but still the man overpowered his fiend. Heinrich's fever never slackened, imbuing his limbs with an unwholesome vigor instead of weakening him, and without even noticing he lapsed into cannibalism when Brennen offered him the pinkest parts of the unfortunates they seized. The demoniac could no longer bear the sun, making the twins dig him deep burrows when no caves or thickets could be located. Worry plagued Heinrich, who had never seen a map but whose belly compelled him southward.

The night after they passed a town half-ruined by fire, his boys raced ahead toward a campfire beside a small river. They were in grasslands now, which afforded them few places to hide during the day, and Heinrich would have forbidden their investigation had he not held out hope for discovering the Grossbarts before they eloped by ship. The customary shrieks were quickly silenced, and as he waited by the riverbank Heinrich's excitement waned, suspecting as he did that a Grossbart may curse and shout but will not shriek even if his genitals are gnawed by piglets.

The twins splashed through the current and deposited their charges before Heinrich, his disappointment sweetening at seeing their white vestments. Priests were better than nothing, but before he could launch into his diatribe they had rolled over, revealing their papal masks. Snatching them off, he peered into the unfocused, rolling eyes of the young men.

After he splashed them with water and booted them several times they began to speak, Magnus and Brennen eagerly watching from the shadows. The gibberish they spouted made no sense to Heinrich, who sighed and resigned himself to never knowing how they came to be dressed in such a manner. After all, the yeoman-turned-prophet only recognized a pope's attire from a triptych he had seen long before and for all he knew most residents of the Papal States dressed that way.

Relieved to see an actual priest after being assaulted by devils, Paolo begged for mercy, explaining that only his desire to see his father avenged persuaded him to don the baggy garb of a Road Pope. Vittorio saw the beasts skulking in the weeds and knew at once this cruel-faced man could not be a priest, and so he tried to barter his friend's soul in place of his. Heinrich raised his flail, knowing his words would be lost on these foreign heretics, when Paolo cursed their name, bowing his head and weeping.

"What name did you speak?" Heinrich demanded, unaware that the witch's tongue knew all others, and he now addressed the lads in Italian.

"The Grossbarts!" wailed Paolo, tearing at the mud, his mind broken. "Those goddamn bastard Grossbarts! They burned us, they burned my father! They burned us! Bound and helpless, we could not get loose before!"

Unfortunately, while they understood him, Heinrich had not nibbled Nicolette's ear and so all he comprehended was the name Grossbart and the youth's rage toward them. Seeing this gave the demoniac pause, however, and Vittorio joined in cursing them, his hatred genuine as they had murdered his cousin Giovanni—known to his victims as Clement.

"Quit your barking!" commanded Heinrich, and the young men resumed their terrified prostrations, moaning and scratching at their faces in shock. "I only wish to know if you hate the Grossbarts more than you love the Virgin or your souls or the Great Demon of Heaven."

The two nodded vigorously, begging for mercy. Paolo tried to explain that before being set upon by monsters they had been journeying south in pursuit of the Grossbarts but Heinrich silenced him with a gentle flick of his scourge. He told them to merely shake their heads or nod, for he recognized that they understood his words. They nearly snapped their necks so vigorously did they assent.

"Then you will be spared," Heinrich said, and the twins wailed in disappointment until Heinrich commanded they be silent. "Put your masks back into place and swear to uphold my will in our quest to undo the Brothers Grossbart!"

They swore and nodded, clumsily refitting their masks with hands bruised raw from the teeth of the twins. Turning to his boys, Heinrich insisted they do nothing to harm their disciples, but to ensure they did not flee he assigned Magnus to mind Vittorio and Brennen to Paolo. The brothers jumped back into sight, bringing on another fit of tears and convulsions from the would-be Road Popes.

That night they took the sacrament of human flesh Heinrich offered, never suspecting the two abominations understood every word they whispered even if their master did not. Vittorio's fear that they would have to kiss certain parts of the demons' anatomies proved unfounded, although that was little succor. Escorting the novices back to their fire to retrieve their packs and weapons, Heinrich asked the lads if they knew which direction would take them to the sandy wastes of the Arab.

Being a barber of deserved reputation, Paolo's father had known and passed on everything he understood of the profession and, unlike many of his trade, he had acknowledged that many advances had returned from the Crusades along with relics and other, more physical rewards. Whereas the average bumpkin might have pointed vaguely southward and picked his nose, Paolo motioned east, nodding his head vigorously when Heinrich narrowed his eyes. The fellow again pointed east, then curved his arm south, which seemed to please Heinrich.

They set off at once, the minds of the young popes irrevocably contaminated by the night's horrid events. Without map or road they braved the wilds, Heinrich demanding the twins carry him over even the smallest stream rather than dampening his toes. Inexplicable impulses such as these beleaguered him and in the humid afternoons when sleep escaped him he would hear a soft, slithering voice that did not belong to him or any of those present, a whisper goading him to perform stranger rites still. Compromise was eventually brokered.

Now when they passed villages one of the novices would be forced to attempt a clandestine entry to deposit hunks of Heinrich's rotting flesh in the wells. Where this proved impossible Heinrich would grow irrational, and order his boys to kidnap individuals from outlying farms so he could embrace and kiss them wantonly until they retched. Then they would be released, under a warning that if they spoke of what they had witnessed the demons would appear before them but to remember all was the fault of the Grossbarts. Few ever spoke again, the plague taking their lives before they sufficiently recovered from their horrors to think properly, let alone communicate beyond moans. In this fashion the Great Mortality enjoyed a brief renaissance in those regions, Heinrich's retinue leaving plague and ruin in their footsteps as they marched to war against the Grossbarts.

XXVII
Rhodes to Gyptland

Hegel awoke with a start, the fever finally broken upon his fire-bald pate. Looking around the dark room, he felt for his pick on the bed beside him and grew anxious at its absence. His armor lay draped over a nearby chair but when he attempted to stand his legs shuddered and he fell to the floor. Lying still for several moments, he listened to the drone of voices outside the door. Closing his eyes, he tried to remember what had happened before his illness but all he remembered was the vicious drubbing they had administered to the Arab at finding Barousse dead under his watch.

The door flew open and Hegel's eyes glazed at the brightness flowing in, the unmistakable silhouette of Manfried framed in sunlight. Then the door closed and Manfried helped him onto the bed, placing a bottle in his hands. Hegel drank and coughed, his brother grinning at him until he returned the wine.

"What happened?" asked Hegel.

"Her Will fuckin served." Manfried had a sip. "Not up on the specifics, as I's just risen myself. Seems maybe we shouldn't a et that witch after all, tried to poison us even in death."

"Told you's much. Probably why my recollections ain't comin."

"Told me's much? You certainly *ain't* recollectin proper."

"What you got? I got that Arab beggin when we put Her Will into him and little more."

"A day or two after that him and that mutinous Lucian was on the beams and I fired a bolt at'em."

"Sport or necessity?"

"Suppose it must a been one a the two. Pinned Lucy to the mast with it, clean through the brainpan. Even Rigo laughed at that one, bastard's body flappin and danglin til the bolt snapped and he fell."

"Anythin else?"

"The Arab wouldn't come down so I was gonna fell his roost. Didn't get round to it, apparently."

"Got airs on, thinkin we's gonna stand for him wearin the captain's flag like a cassock." Later things were coming to Hegel now, things involving the Arab. "Didn't he make at you with a knife?"

"Don't think so." Manfried knit his brows. "If he did, must a put'em proper, as I got no such wound."

"But after you kilt that Lucian?"

"Hazy at best. We's sailin, and they's fishin but ain't catch a tadpole. Ended up cuttin the Judas knight off the mast cause his rot was workin on the sail. Then we pitched'em overboard, along with the rest a them dogwhores."

"Captain Bar Goose included?" asked Hegel.

"You takin me for a heathen? Barousse we left below."

"And the witch?"

"Someone put her over when we was asleep. Martyn won't own up, but we'll beat it out a him when you's feelin revived."

"So we in the sandlands yet?" Hegel asked after a period of silent reflection.

"Nah, but gettin closer."

Hegel blinked and rubbed the down mattress with his surprisingly clean palm. Looking back to Manfried, he scowled and said, "So when was you thinkin bout stoppin with the tooth display and tellin me just what in Her Name is happinin? What it is, cause I know you didn't stitch me this softness out a old turnip sacks."

"Come and look, brother." Manfried finished the wine and helped Hegel rise. "Come and take a gander at Her Benevolence."

Arm in arm they went to the door and Manfried led him outside. Light blinded Hegel but his brother moved him forward, the sounds of the ocean nearly suffocated by the clamor of men and the nickering of horses. Even the presence of equines could not diminish Hegel's awe when his eyes finally took in their surroundings.

They stood on the deck of a massive ship, fully three times as large as their original vessel. The dozens of men did not rob him of breath, nor did the cheer that went up from them at his appearance. What shocked even a living saint was the fleet of ships cutting the sea around them, a prodigious, floating forest of masts, many of them flying huge white sails emblazoned with blood-red crosses.

"We was delivered to an island." Manfried's swept his arm in front of them. "An island full a honest men just itchin to head south and get a piece a what the Infidel's holdin."

"Mary bless us!"

"Yes She has! Martyn!" Manfried shouted, and the cardinal appeared across the deck. "Come and hear it from his mouth, brother! That fool's made amends in full to Her Eminence."

"Brother Hegel!" Martyn panted, scurrying up the stairs to the raised deck. "The Virgin's caress has balmed you once more from the grave, delivered into such hands as are scarce fit to stroke you!"

"You didn't leave him alone with me whiles I was under, did you?" Hegel muttered to his brother.

The first thing that set Hegel on edge was Martyn's reluctance to drink with them. Under threat of harm he relented and sipped at his wine, his thirsty eyes drinking more of it than his lips. As he talked he forgot himself and drank more of the wine, but before they could open a second bottle his story had concluded.

Martyn's rendition shared a number of similarities with the actual event, but this could be attributed to coincidence. Their ship had indeed floated unmanned for several days while they all raved and weakened from dehydration, and they had floated into the current surrounding Rhodes. Here their ship was sighted and brought in, and within two days of arriving they had set out again, this time in the company of hundreds of men intent as they on reaching the domain of the Infidel. Martyn's implication that they had left entirely under his command as Mary's chosen representative on Earth is where the tale began to stray from the truth.

After years of unsuccessfully petitioning king and pope, duke and emperor, King Peter of Cyprus had completed by his own hand preparations for a crusade. Admittedly, the Hospitallers of Rhodes had not intended to invest themselves fully before the arrival of Cardinal Martyn and his followers. The news that Pope Urban V had died, and the subsequent mutilation of his corpse at the hands of heretics, caused more distress among the holy men than can be adequately conveyed in simple words. The similarity between this atrocity and that which had befallen Formosus so long past did not escape their notice.

That Cardinal Martyn seemed out of sorts was to be expected, they reasoned, and his overindulgence in beer was attributed to the lack of any other drink upon their wrecked vessel. Ten of the Hospitallers' most zealous Imperial brothers were granted permission to serve as Cardinal Martyn's guard despite the balking of the grand bailiff. The earnest knights persuaded the grand master that because the cardinal was of the rare number from their homeland they had as large an obligation to his safety as to Rhodes' defense. All assumed bed rest and water would restore the cardinal to a more reserved demeanor.

The shifting of targets from Palestine to Alexandria actually had been influenced by the Grossbarts. Among the proposed plans drawn up on Rhodes, landing in Egypt to take the Infidel unawares Peter had previously thought to be the most foolish of all, despite the economic advantages that the destruction of Cyprus's chief competitor would yield. After hearing Cardinal Martyn's tales of the Brothers' near-saintly closeness to the Virgin, the confused heir to the throne of Jerusalem went to the hospital beds of the Grossbarts. The grand marshal of the Hospitallers could not speak German either but as he hefted the military weight of the order he accompanied Peter, praying the Cypriot ruler would defer to the wisdom of a direct assault on his rightful kingdom.

Bidding his host to wait outside the arched door, King Peter entered the private room intended to quarantine those damned with the pest. The sight of those pilgrims basted with fever, rolling on their cots and groaning Her Name, broke his proud heart. Shame scalded the righteous king's cheeks, the misery of these two men moving him in ways unfamiliar. Even when demons rose to thwart them they had persevered, and now the cost of their devotion was made physical upon their flesh. Kneeling between their beds, he closed his eyes and prayed.

"If only you would give me a sign as sure as that which moved these Imperials to find me," Peter whispered.

"Gyptland!" the silver-bearded man moaned.

"Gyptland!" the copper-bearded man repeated.

Leaping up, Peter stared intently at the men, the word precise despite the language. When he later discovered they only spoke German his belief in a higher answer seemed affirmed. If Venezia and other papal kingdoms had come around and were sending men as Martyn implied, the force leaving Rhodes could secure the port city on the bank of the Nile, assuring a safe landing for the others before pressing inward. The murder of the Pope might bespeak an infiltration of the Arab subtler than that of the Turk, and an army could be lurking in ambush for them at Palestine. A man rarely has his prayer answered so quickly and assuredly, even a king. Alexandria, then.

"And you talked'em into sailin right away?" Hegel asked the cardinal.

"We arrived on the very day they were to leave harbor, but they delayed long enough to hear and heed my council." Martyn smiled and reached for his glass.

"*Our* council through *your* lips," Manfried corrected. "Credit yourself by creditin us."

"Ah." Martyn nodded. "My tongue tripped over my pride."

"And the Arab?" Hegel asked.

"No doubt dozing in the desert." Martyn smirked. "Unsuspecting their days of idolatrous sloth are waning."

"No, you twit, the Arab what was on our boat. The mecky little cunt with the mustache," Hegel clarified.

"With the horses." Martyn tapped his foot. "Below, where he belongs."

"Keep him outta trouble." Manfried nodded. "And the captain?"

"Who?" Martyn blinked. "Barousse?"

"Who else?" Hegel opened the other bottle of wine.

"He's, well, he's dead." Martyn glanced nervously from brother to brother.

"We know that," said Manfried. "What they did with his flesh and bones?"

"Buried him in the churchyard of the Knights of the Hospital of Saint John," Martyn answered. "He received final absolution and reward for his devotion to the cause."

"Knights a what?" Hegel asked, remembering Sir Jean's treachery.

"The Hospitallers." Martyn's pupils crested the tops of his eyes. "They who saved us, and now journey with us on their ships?"

Manfried scowled at this but Hegel seemed satisfied. "If they's takin us to Gyptland I reckon they's likely not heretics, brother."

Martyn spluttered on his second glass of wine and set it on the table. "I would not talk so of these men, Grossbarts. The wild hair of youth must be tamed, and you must master that tongue of yours, especially in the company of cardinals and monastic knights, to say naught of the king."

Manfried hooked his foot under Martyn's chair and pulled, sending the man toppling to the floor. "I'd mind that tongue a yours, lest it get slit like a serpent's!"

"See now." Hegel leaned in. "You sayin there's a king round here? He a relation to old Charles back home?"

Martyn picked himself up from the floor, eyes narrowed at Manfried. "You bed in the cabin reserved for he, who, in his benevolence, granted it for your convalescence. As you both seem recovered, I'll send for him, as he has anxiously awaited your council."

"Send up Rigo and that other, we got words for them, too." Hegel reclined in his chair, enjoying his drink.

Rodrigo had been taken onto the ship by force after insisting they not inter his beloved captain in the Hospitallers' cemetery and that he instead travel with them. Only Martyn's insistence on the young Italian's faith spared him the noose when he kicked and fought rather than leave the side of the festering remains.

Despite his wish to put his brigand days behind him Raphael had little choice but to follow after hearing every last gold bar on board their boat had gone with the cardinal. Being better sorted after a day's rest and drink than any other save Martyn, the mercenary conned his way into a suit of armor and new weaponry before joining the grief-addled Rodrigo in the new ship's berth.

Raphael and Rodrigo dutifully came to the cabin and drank with the Grossbarts. Raphael had also noticed a distinct shift in Martyn's character, suspiciously observing the man rarely drank more than a sip or two of wine, and never stonger stuff. Any hopes the mercenary held of thanks from Grossbart lips now that they were in good health dwindled as they badgered the two about slacking at the sails and letting Martyn call the shots. Furthermore, there was the question of where exactly all their gold had gotten to.

"The prie— Er, the cardinal say he takes care of that." Raphael looked around but Martyn had vanished.

"Mecky fuckin hole!" Manfried yelled. "Martyn! Where's that trickster?"

"What was you doin while our gold was gettin cardinal-touched?" Hegel asked Rodrigo.

"Nothing," Rodrigo replied, his once-bold face wearing a wan grimace.

"Gotta been doin somethin." Manfried considered slapping the man to get him to pay attention when the door opened and the King of Cyprus entered.

The Grossbarts blinked at the friendly, immaculately dressed man approaching their table, accompanied by several no less suave advisors. He congratulated them on their recovery and praised the Trinity, offering his condolences for their illness and loss of crew. Then he exuberantly launched into the specifics of their plan, righting Martyn's spilled chair and joining their table. They did not understand a word he said, and Manfried rose to strike the dandy for his ill manners. Rodrigo finally smiled, expectantly watching Manfried, but Raphael intervened as translator.

"This own person be the king," Raphael explained, slipping from his chair and kneeling.

"Oh," said Manfried, and extended his hand. "Manfried Grossbart, servant a Mary."

"Hegel Grossbart, living saint." Hegel held a bottle in one hand and offered the other.

Peter coddled Manfried's hand in both of his and pumped it excitedly as Raphael translated. The murmurs of his advisors that these men had not showed proper supplication was quieted with a word from Peter, and with their flawed but earnest translator resuming his seat the men talked of Gyptland, Jerusalem, and Mary. Rodrigo occasionally interrupted with harsh statements on the nature of devotion and eternal rewards, and if either brother had understood Italian they would have struck him for his foolishness. Luckily they did not, and in light of the man's loss Peter took no offense, so only the advisors and Raphael were concerned by the fellow's vindictive pronouncements.

Had Rodrigo accurately interpreted the dialogue between Peter and the Grossbarts the Brothers' gross blasphemies would surely have caused trouble, but he did not and the tongue-tied and awestruck Raphael could not have conveyed the extent of their heretical ramblings had he even been inclined. Instead, all save Rodrigo and the worried advisors enjoyed the wine and conversation, supplemented by a feast brought to them by servants toiling somewhere below. Although a touch put out that they had not offered him back his cabin, Peter left satisfied they were indeed divinely inspired, and the Grossbarts agreed the king was not such the cunt for being a noble.

Time passed, the Grossbarts spending their days in the ordinary fashion of fighting, eating, and drinking, and their nights in the extraordinary company of a king. The cardinal often joined them but abstained from helping translate as much to save his own skin as to save theirs; instead Martyn glumly watched the imported tiger lilies he had plucked from the gardens of Rhodes lose their ginger luster and become ashen. Rodrigo was excluded from these repasts as his offensiveness was easily understood by Peter; the despondent man would gaze north from the stern, his tears joining those of Mary, which fill the oceans of the world.

As the ruby clouds swirled atop the horizon like steam atop a stew, Manfried strode up beside Rodrigo. The Grossbart had noted the change in the man's demeanor, and such melancholy sat poorly with Manfried. The boy would either straighten out or go over the side, because with Gyptland at hand he would not tolerate such folly.

"Still worryin on the captain's account?" Manfried shook his head in disbelief.

"He was all I had," Rodrigo sniveled. "First my mother, then father, then my brother, and now him. All dead."

The tears returned but before Rodrigo could turn back to the sunset Manfried had snatched him by his hair, tugging on his healing, scabby scalp and turning his head to face him.

"Tell me he ain't better served where he's at," Manfried snapped, and when the lad dumbly stared at him he went on. "Still the doubter, eh? You say he ain't better served with the Virgin than on this lousy boat with a company a blood-handed men?"

"I want him—"

"You want him what? Alive and pained stead a at his reward? Want him to suffer long with us? Selfish, that," said Manfried, still gripping Rodrigo's hair.

Rodrigo's scalp peeled back a little as he went for Manfried's throat, stopping when his perforated hand tried to close around the Grossbart's neck. Then the young man slumped and Manfried released him.

"Think on it. He's gone where we all will, Mary be praised.

You think to imply other than he's better now than fore and I'll prove you wrong. Course, heretics don't never reach where he's at, meanin if you do wanna see him and the rest a your morally skint kinfolk again you'd best straighten your mecky ass out."

"You know nothing!" Rodrigo screamed, his face shining. "Nothing! He was sick of mind when you came, and you made him worse! I knew you'd bring his end!"

"Men bring their ends on themselves," said Manfried.

"He listened to you!" said Rodrigo. "Years I obeyed him as a son obeys a father, and for what? You come into our house and suddenly it's you and not me he trusts!"

"Way the wheel spins," said Manfried, with what he assumed was a sagacious air. "Maybe if you'd been a better son to 'em he'd never a set foot on that boat. Maybe he'd a listened to you." The Grossbart did not look at Rodrigo as he left, his satisfied smile unseen by all but Her.

In the sea-bound stable, Al-Gassur showed the bundled relic he had begun to think of as his brother's heart to the horses, which stomped and whinnied whenever the item left his cloak. He regaled the steeds with the legend of Barousse and whispered in their long ears how he would sell the Grossbarts to the first Bedouin slavers they encountered. Then eastward for him, to find a sea containing a bride of his own, and perhaps to meet his brother again under the waves.

When they sighted the coast Hegel and Manfried slapped each other and King Peter on the back until welts rose. At dawn they coasted into the harbor of Alexandria and the Grossbarts led the charge down the docks, armor and weapons glowing in the autumn sun.

The massacre that ensued is well documented elsewhere, neither women nor children spared from butchery. The unsuspecting citizens fled as best they could but not before the waves splashing the quays were crimson and the gutters filled with blood. Unlike many of the Hospitallers and Cypriots, the Gross-barts and Raphael took no pleasure from the slaughter, going to task as men have always toiled—with bored disdain. Al-Gassur followed the Grossbarts from a safe distance, liberating bottles and coins from the dead and the dying left in their wake. Rodrigo refused to partake or even watch, creeping back onto the ship and drinking himself into a miserable stupor.

Breaking into a multi-domed manse, the Grossbarts found their way to the larder and wiled away the twilight hours drinking syrupy wines and gorging on strange meats and fruits. There they spent the night, Raphael forced to take first watch and Al-Gassur shoved outside until daylight. At dawn they wandered the vacant streets, idly making toward two monoliths rising in the distance. Standing before Cleopatra's Needles, the Brothers yawned.

"What you make a all them shapes etched on there?" Hegel peered at the black obelisks. "Reckon there might be someone under them?"

"Might be." Manfried pressed his cropped ear to the side of the less worn monument and banged with his mace. "First let's see if there's some kind a door up here."

There was not. Disgruntled and sweating, unable to find portal or crease, they sat between the two, chewing their beards. Before they could resume their efforts one of the Hospitallers in Martyn's service spotted them and brought them to the cardinal and the king, who had established themselves in a palace.

The Grossbarts would look back on the time they spent with King Peter as if recalling a fairy tale, with embellishments added only through a failure to recollect the specifics. They characteristically avoided the bridge over the canal leading to the battle lines, where the city's inhabitants successfully held off the crusaders, instead surreptitiouly crossing in quieter quarters to vainly prowl for tomb-cities. They were undeniably sloshed for the bulk of their stay in Alexandria, which ended up being only a few days. After their unsuccessful attempt to pry open the solid stone of the Needles, they shunned the column of Diocletian towering nearby and so never discovered the Catacombs of Kom el Sho-qafa or the Christian and Jewish cemeteries thereabouts.

Their innate gold-hunger led them at last to the alabaster tomb of that mighty city's mighty founder, but his gold casket and bejeweled scepter had been pinched long before. They were impressed by the quality of workmanship but annoyed their pre-decessors had not marked the grave in some way to denote its hollowness, which would have saved them time and toil.

Finally, at long last, the red glimmer of evening revealed to them the grand graveyard of Chatby, and both were struck mute by the sheer volume of stone markers and crypts. A number of other crusaders were already at work, and rather than risk draw-ing Mary's disfavor by associating themselves with amateurs they returned to the palace to coerce the king into putting a stop to the looting so that they might do it properly.

The next morning, however, word arrived that the Mamluks, those slaves-become-masters who ruled all of Gyptland, had a massive army approaching the city by sea, land, and river, and despite Peter's protests the fleet prepared to abandon its con-quest. Standing on the dock that final morning with the hordes of the Infidel entering the rear of the city, the Grossbarts dis-missed Peter's pleas to accompany him back to Cyprus.

"Shit, sure we got plenty a gold, notwithstanding that what the cardinal donated." Manfried shot a glare at Martyn. "But that's missin the point."

"Yeah," Hegel explained, "you gotta have faith there's still more gold locked up in them heathen tombs."

Peter nodded at Raphael's translation that faith was indeed more valuable than physical wealth, and through the interpreter Peter gave his assurance that he would return with a larger

army. This the Grossbarts agreed to be the sensible option, there
being no way they could transport all their loot in a canoe as
Hegel had originally theorized. So king and Grossbarts parted
as allies and almost equals, neither party knowing what Mary
held for them. Before he could rally another crusade King Peter
would be assassinated by papal schemers eager to suppress what
would become known as the Grossbart Heresy, and as for what
befell the Brothers themselves, one must press a little further into
Gyptland.

Rodrigo's attempt to stow away back to his captain's bones
was thwarted by snooping knights, and he was escorted back into
the Grossbarts' company. Al-Gassur beamed at the ships, waving his brother's swaddled prize as they slipped out of harbor.
The ten Imperial Hospitallers resolved to stay with the cardinal
after the Grossbarts convinced Martyn his aim of returning to
Rhodes might be unsound. The winking reminder that perhaps
word had come from Venezia regarding the future of the papacy
convinced Raphael to stay as it did the cardinal.

Having little interest in meeting the Mamluk host, the sixteen
men boosted a small galley and set off down the canal leading
to the Nile and the tombs of legend; the defenders on the bridge
retreated to join their reinforcements and thus allowed the
Grossbarts to slip away. Only as they whisked down the canal
and passed the enormous eastern necropolis did they realize how
ripe with graves was Alexandria. The remorse such an epiphany
brings might cripple a lesser graverobber, but these were Grossbarts, and after the initial cursing the disappointment instead
honed their gluttonous appetites.

To think the Grossbarts were happy now that their lifetime
goal was fulfilled is to misjudge them completely. They found
no wonder in a river flowing north and were intensely put out
to have ten heavily armored men crowding their vessel who
answered to Martyn instead of them, even if the crusaders were

the ones doing the rowing. Only with kicks and punches were they able to convince Rodrigo of the necessity of his helping pilot the boat, fiddle with the oarlocks, and do everything else required to keep them moving. From their vantage they made out only sandy banks and silt-muddied water, small and dank islands rearing up where tributaries joined and broke from their liquid road.

After they had dropped anchor the first night in the boat, the Brothers stared upriver long past moonrise. Raphael, Rodrigo, and Al-Gassur joined them, and for the first time since meeting all five shared a drink in silence, putting aside the crisscrossing paths of mutual aversion to stare at the moon-glowing river and listen to the bizarre conglomeration of sounds. The quiet of the scorching day had worried the seasoned Grossbarts, who knew full well silent places in nature often bespeak demons, but the cacophony of nearby splashes, chirps, and whistles could hardly be viewed as preferable.

They started again when light crept over the bank, and at a fork Rodrigo directed them up the left channel. The Grossbarts grew increasingly frustrated as the day waned and no steepled churches emerged to herald plunderable cemeteries. Only the sun shone gold, turning the river all manner of strange colors that evening, the bank to their left replaced by an endless bog.

No sooner had they dropped anchor than the darkness fully settled. Then they all saw the lights ahead, as if a small city slowly drifted toward them on the current. The Grossbarts hissed orders and gathered their arms, but when the lights grew closer and larger they realized flight could be their only salvation as the massive ships approached.

Raising anchor they awkwardly maneuvered about and rowed downstream, picking up the current and flying over the black water. The ships disappeared around the curve and the nose of their boat slammed into something. The sound of splintering wood is not something to take lightly on a river, and water had flooded the galley up to their ankles by the time they had freed themselves from the submerged log. They managed to reach the nearby bank but the hole punched in the side made further use of the boat impossible until they could fix it—assuming, of course, that they could.

The ships reappeared around the bend and the Grossbarts hopped overboard, Rodrigo and Martyn joining the Brothers on the swampy shore. As they unloaded the boat, Martyn struck the cackling Arab in the mouth, sending Al-Gassur tumbling into the mire. The Hospitallers trudged dutifully after as the group splashed through sludge and waded through pools, collectively collapsing behind a mucky island no bigger than a half-sunk wagon when the ships came within earshot, men rushing about on deck and yelling to the vessels behind them.

A collective groan washed over the party as lights fell on their nearby boat, everyone digging further into the filth. Rather than stopping, however, the first ship glided past and the men began to hope. Two more ships, and then the last, a great whale of a galley, rows of oars raised as the current swept them along. From this final boat several smoldering bundles fell into the Grossbarts' beached ship and the waterlogged vessel unexpectedly exploded in flames. Then the ships were gone around another bend, leaving only the moon to display the smoke rising from where their boat had sat.

While neither would admit it, that night, soaked to the bone and coated in mud, was the most miserable the Grossbarts had yet experienced. The twitterings and slurpings rose to a raucous cheer, mocking their dejection. Not one voice broke the silence to lament their lot, the slime around Al-Gassur vibrating from his repressed laughter. The summit of the gelatinous island proved no more dry or pleasant than its base, and before the sun even rose they tramped back to the ruins of their boat.

Rodrigo and Al-Gassur walked downstream a bit to laugh without fear of reprisal until they both collapsed. Their shared mirth quickly degenerated into a fight when Al-Gassur again imitated the deceased Ennio, lying in the mud and whispering to the livid Rodrigo how the Grossbarts had murdered his brother. The incensed man reopened his punctured palm during the fracas, the sight of which cheered the gloomy Grossbarts.

"Back to Alexandria, then?" Martyn said hopefully, nudging the burnt out shell of their galley. "We've only gone a few days upriver, so surely—"

"Surely that city's thick with Arabs by now," Manfried said.

"Them boats wasn't carryin pilgrims such's us, mark me," Hegel agreed.

"But without a boat, how will we travel?" Martyn asked what he thought to be a rhetorical question, being as they were surrounded by swampland.

"Unlike yourself, we didn't sail out the womb with boats stead a feet." Manfried shouldered his pack. "Given as I am to thinkin fordin yon river might prove a task what with our armor and such, I move we hike upstream as we's been."

"Damietta is east of Alexandria." One of the Hospitallers broke with the clump of men and motioned away from the river, over the bog. "That is the closest other city."

"Seein as you's speakin proper, I find it disconcertin you think so simple," Manfried replied. "If we's trekkin through marsh, might's well do it next to clean water stead a that meck."

"Farewell, then," the man said, filling a waterskin from the river. "Cardinal, I assume you will travel with us?"

Martyn looked to the Grossbarts, who were both smiling at him and shaking their heads, hands on pick and mace. "No," he sighed, "I have faith Mary will guide us."

"Fine." The warrior-monk stood, the previous days in close company with both cardinal and Grossbarts having convinced him of their madness. "When we reach Rhodes I'll inform the king and the new Pope of your decision."

"New Pope?" Martyn had nearly forgotten his own previous delusions that these men had based all of their decisions upon. The Hospitallers convened, and several of them exchanged soft words before three split from the pack and marched to Martyn. These men knelt in the muck and pledged their continued dedication to his safety while their brothers turned their backs on the Grossbarts. Of the three Moritz spoke both Italian and German while Bruno and Werner knew only German, their voices unwavering as they dirtied their lips on the silt of the Nile.

The other seven Hospitallers marched toward the rising sun. Just out of sight of their former company, they were cheered to discover the bog yielded to lush farmland and bountiful orchards. They rested in the shade of an enormous tree and gorged themselves on dates, unaware that a salamander had nested in the roots and infected every fruit with its dread toxins. They all began convulsing and sweating blood, and only after their organs burst from the heat did their suffering end.

"Settled then." Hegel nodded south up the river. "Get Rigo off our Arab and we can move on."

The bloodied Al-Gassur assured the Grossbarts they had made the correct choice, for just up the river lay churchyards grander than Alexandria and Venezia combined. A week passed and no cemeteries appeared, only the swamp they plodded through and the river bordering it. A viper bit Werner in the hand when he filled his waterskin and within an hour the knight expired, bloated and rotting as if he had spent weeks submerged in the Nile.

Even the mighty rations of the Grossbarts dwindled, and one evening when they scrambled up a rare dry prominence a crocodile attacked Bruno. The beast exploded out of the muck bordering the rise, its huge jaws latching onto his leg. The knight, confronted with the ancestral nemesis of his kind, let out a scream as the dragon yanked him into the water. The Brothers Grossbart came to his rescue, but while Hegel's pick skewered its brain, in the chaos Manfried snapped Bruno's neck with his mace. Only after did Hegel realize the rolling monster had slashed open his boot and shin with its claws. They smoked the salty, wet crocodile meat with the dead shrubbery shrouding the top of the mound, even the wounded Hegel happier for the encounter. Moritz and Martyn interred Bruno in the mud, and the Hospitaller cross they marked his grave with found its way into Al-Gassur's bag.

In the days that followed the pain in Hegel's leg worsened, as did his attitude. Manfried's attempts to figure where this new monstrosity fit into their growing catalogue went unanswered by his limping brother. Hegel stole the Arab's crutch but even with a peg leg and no assistance Al-Gassur moved quicker than he. Huts could sometimes be dimly seen on the opposite bank but no men called to them and they knew better than to attempt a crossing. When Hegel felt the old itching at his neck he turned and saw a large ship creeping up the river behind them. They all stopped, agreeing they had no choice but to hail the galley.

"Now remember, Arab," Hegel cautioned, "you's the only one can speak like them, so be sure the meanin's clear. They take us to the tombs and they get some gold but not a coin fore then."

"Of course, my kin in lame." Al-Gassur bowed.

"And recollect right what happened to every cunt what tried doin us wrong or sellin us out," Manfried added.

"What if they attack us?" Martyn worried his lip.

"Then we strike them down with the power of the Lord." Moritz drew his massive sword, raising himself in the Grossbarts' estimation.

"And if they don't stop, but row past us?" Martyn insisted something must go wrong.

"That is reason Her Goodness Mary grant our ownselves crossbows," Raphael said, lying in the mud to notch a bolt.

"Finally in decent company," Hegel told his brother in their twinspeak.

"Close's we's liable to get, any rate." Manfried also cocked his arbalest, switching back to German. "Here they come, so do your stuff, Arab!"

They began jumping in the muck, yelling and waving their hands, even Rodrigo excited by the prospect of escaping the swamp. The boat slowed, the bearded men at the oars staring at them in shock, those striding on the deck excitedly yelling. Al-Gassur invented word after nonsensical word, tears of pleasure at the Grossbarts' imminent undoing cleaning his mustache.

The rowers at the front locked their oars and stood as the boat glided toward the shore. The standing men withdrew bottles, knocked them back themselves, and tossed them to the rejoicing men on the bank. Nothing is less cautious than a fiending alcoholic, only Moritz abstaining from the drink. Yet when Hegel tilted a gifted bottle that old witch-chill rushed up and down his bones, his belly twisting around his spine. He slapped a bottle out of Manfried's hand and drew his pick.

"I don't believe them boys was actually drinkin, brother. Drink's probably got some Arab barber berries in it or such, so lest you's eager to wake up in some new place with all sorts a nasty to deal with I'd abstain."

"I's had enough a that shit to last a lifetime," said Manfried, firing his crossbow into the first Mamluk to hit the bank, and together they joined the fiercest, greatest battle of their lives.

XXVIII
The Rapturous Hunt

The winter ended as Heinrich's new family journeyed, the heat increasing even in the dank belly of the southern forests of Wallachia. Over hills and rocky mounts, through sunny glens and shadowy gulches they crept, never doubting their purpose. Vittorio talked incessantly while Paolo had not spoken since he recognized the grotesque buboes bulging under Heinrich's arms when the man removed his robes to pop blisters and peel skin, depositing them in a river upstream of a mill. Paolo had certainly become mad as a mooncalf but his education stayed with him. Only when Vittorio scratched at his groin and armpits did the barber's son inspect his own, and at seeing the purple swellings he rejoiced to know he would soon die. He did not, nor did Vittorio, nor did Heinrich.

When they skirted the massive city of Al-Gassur's birth Heinrich danced lewdly by moonlight, reciting litanies inspired by the whispers he heard not in his ear but in his heart. Drawing symbols in the dirt with a woodsman's severed finger, Heinrich repeated the words that freed similar beings from their torment, granting Paolo and Vittorio the same privilege he enjoyed.

Crossing the channel proved nigh impossible with the three demoniacs' aversion to running water but they managed to steal a boat and float across without dampening themselves. They were almost apprehended by mounted Turks several times in the barren regions they crossed, but they hid in caves when the numbers were too great and descended on smaller groups, again devouring all but one or two, leaving those to stagger home, infecting their loved ones and ranting the cursed name Gross- bart that all three of the possessed chanted hatefully.

Into the wastes, those born men now appeared barely more human than the twins, both of whom had grown to the height of horses from constant feeding. Their buboes big as the honey-melons so loved in those regions, their pace weakened but their intent did not, Vittorio and Paolo eagerly following their brothers into combat with men who shrieked and fled at their approach. Their guts sagged with black and yellow biles, the humours churning but refusing to burst from their copious sores and wounds so that they were able to drain them only into the pleading mouths of their victims. Any oases they traversed rot- ted to desert at their presence, and for months they ate only men; all other creatures smelled their evil from great distances and could not be caught even by the twins.

The things inside them communed while their hosts slept, delighting in the willingness of their servants and bartering with their still-imprisoned kin for information regarding the Gross- barts. Those without form could do naught but enviously watch, but the two released into the Italians had dutifully scoured with sight not constrained by space before being granted their salva- tion. They were very close indeed; fortunate, for the oppressive heat that cooked them even as the seasons changed threatened to slay their mounts before they captured their game, and in such desolate regions they might not find replacements before being thrust back into the place they had so vigorously fled.

XXIX
Like the End, the Beginning of Winter Is Difficult to Gauge in the South

Outnumbered five to one, and with Cardinal Martyn and Al-Gassur swooning from the soporific-laden wine, the Grossbarts may well have met their end there on the bank of the Nile had chance not favored them. The impressed men working the oars of that particular galley were prisoners and not birth-slaves, and just as their Mamluk masters had once spurned their bondage and usurped their keepers, so too did these slaves revolt upon witnessing the Grossbarts' resistance. Chained in place though they were, these wretches thrust their oars and feet before the charging legs of their masters, slowing the Mamluks attempting to join the fight and winning the day—a boon that none of the victorious Europeans would ever acknowledge.

When the last Mamluk contributed his lifeblood to the ruddy fluids of the Nile, the Grossbarts took stock of how the battle had gone. They now had a boat and slaves, and despite the odds only Moritz—the last remaining Hospitaller—had expired from his wounds, a long handle jutting ominously out from between the felled man's helm and breastplate. Raphael had seen enough carnage in his days with the White Company to know that he too would doubtless join the slain knight before the sun set, for in addition to the pommel that had smashed most of his teeth, his left wrist had caught a blade that nearly severed his hand. Spitting gore and tooth-gravel, he desperately attempted to stanch the wound even as his legs gave out.

While Martyn and Al-Gassur were rolling in the sand and vomiting from their poisoned beverage, the battle seemed to have restored the melancholic Rodrigo to a more chipper mood. He actually laughed periodically as he made the rounds, shoving his sword repeatedly into the prone figures of their attackers. Manfried noticed Raphael's mortal condition at the same time the still-chained-in-place and now-screaming slaves drew Hegel's attention to the fact that the last Mamluk had destroyed the rear of the rapidly filling galley. Knowing they could not possibly remove all of the boat's supplies before it sank, Hegel begrudgingly used a key he had found on the body of the lead Mamluk to free the slaves and enlist their assistance. Not only were the supplies rescued but the slaves were able to haul the prow farther onto the bank, meaning the vessel could be repaired.

"Well, Saint?" said Manfried.

"Well shit," said Hegel. "We's in Gyptland proper, so let's get this done and find grandad's loot."

Manfried took one look at the wrecked boat and began smashing wood free for a decent fire, and Hegel set to helping tie off Raphael's filthy wound. To the horror of all but the Grossbarts, who laid out the first slave who moved to stop them, a bonfire soon raged where the boat had rested. At one point Raphael pitched forward unconscious and by the time the freed prisoners dragged him back the flaming Providence had taken his left hand but seared the wound shut. The result was that the loyal thug lived, although weeks would pass before any could distinguish individual words out of the one-handed man's shatter-mouthed gabble.

The grandly inflated horde of Grossbarts and Grossbart followers progressed up the Nile with a simpleminded tenacity. The wound of the captain's passing still festering in his heart, Rodrigo took masochistic succor from their situation, as did Al-Gassur, who despite it all maintained his ruse of being fluent in Arabic by babbling at the freed slaves—a rude assortment of betrayed generals and too-bold beggars who stayed with their liberators more for the food than for the company. Cardinal Martyn believed he had converted a few of the Moslems, and those he had not spared him a beating out of respect for the Grossbarts.

The grains and dried fruit went quickly with so many mouths but the Grossbarts paid no heed to Martyn's entreaties to ration the remainder—each brother carried a full satchel reserved exclusively for himself and suggested the cardinal do the same. Had they stayed on the river they might have made progress toward reaching at least a small settlement but the Grossbarts insisted that with the swamp bordering the river given over to sandy wastes, forays in pursuit of the tomb-cities were now mandatory. Every few days the water ran low and back they trudged to the Nile to refill their skins, even Hegel and Manfried finally growing weary of the venture. Despair threatening to cripple the spirits of all, Martyn made another entreaty for the Grossbarts to confess their sins.

The party sat in yet another cemetery-free valley amidst the countless dunes, this one thick with enough dead trees to stoke two fires. The thirty-odd freed prisoners sat some distance off at their own blaze, debating amongst themselves the practicality of turning on the Grossbarts as opposed to simply quitting their company that very night. Had one among them understood the words spoken at the other fire—or the reverse—then blows would surely have been the result, but as it stood the majority of the Moslems had at the very least lost their curiosity as to what the bearded Christians intended by hiking into the desert and then back to the Nile several times a week as the food supplies dwindled.

"Told you twice now and I ain't sayin again," Manfried grumbled through his last mouthful of dates. "We's got nuthin to own up."

"Everyone must confess, Manfried." Martyn bowed his head. "I will not judge, only He is allowed that."

"*She*," Hegel corrected, "and it can't hurt, brother."

"So why don't you do it then?" said Manfried.

"She's already seen my sins and absolved me." Hegel looked to the spectral ceiling of the heavens. "Every rotten trespass I committed washed clean."

"But you admit you have sinned!" Martyn said, excited they were making progress. "So why not confess them to me, absolved though you may be, so your brother can understand that which he does not realize are sins still must be confessed!"

"Well shit." Hegel rubbed his hands and bit his lip. "There was that witch."

"Which?" asked Martyn.

"Witch?" asked Manfried.

"That one up in them hills. Alps." Hegel looked his brother in the eyes. "Guess I oughta come clean with you seein as She knows it anyway. I done that witch."

"The witch what lived in the valley with the mantiloup? What you did to'er?" Manfried asked.

"No, confess to me," Martyn insisted.

"Shut it," said Hegel. "Yeah, that's the witch. I, uh, done her. Physically."

"Kilt'er? When you did that?"

"No, meckbrain, carnal-like. She, uh, sexed me."

"What!?" Manfried burst out laughing. "Ain't proper to fool with me, Hegel. *That* old thing?"

"Some a us what possess a proper palate recognize mutton's superior to lamb." Hegel crossed his arms.

"Women ain't the same as meat!" said Manfried.

"Tell that to the lady-fish we et on the boat. But the point with the witch is I should a known better but I didn't, so I lost my purity. But She gave it back to me. Mary I mean, the Virgin, which is what the witch's spell made her seem like." Hegel spread his hands. "See? No shame for those in Her Graces. Confess to me and you's absolved same as I."

Martyn wanted to interrupt but could not retrieve his lower jaw from the sand. Manfried continued to laugh until Hegel punched him. Then he tried to talk several times but kept chortling every time he opened his mouth.

"That old thing?" Manfried repeated. "Christ, brother!"

"Why you think I done it, huh?" Hegel said, furious. "Think I was aimin to knock my Grossballs gainst some witch's stinkhole? If I hadn't you would a died from that sick wound a yours, you selfish cunt! That was the price."

"Should a let me die!" snorted Manfried, but observing the pain in Hegel's face he sobered. "Thanks, brother, that's better than I deserve. Had no inklin you had to suffer like that on my account. Damned pious behavior."

"I'd feel a sight better bout it if you came clean yourself so I wouldn't have to worry bout you burnin in the pit." Hegel gave his brother the eye. "Thought's sinful as deed, Manfried."

"Is it? Yeah, I reckon it is." Manfried squinted into the shadows behind them, as if the secret lay hidden in the dark beyond the firelight. "Guess I done some things I shouldn't, thought some things worse than what I did besides."

"Come on, then," Hegel prodded. "Out with it, and spite the Old Boy."

"Uh, well, that nixie…" Manfried swallowed.

"Yeah?"

Martyn wanted to interrupt but his curiosity overpowered him and he remained silent.

"Well, I, uh, kind a got a fondness for her and that song a hers." Hegel nodded while Manfried continued. "Reckon some a them things I was thinkin was put there by her witchery, but some a them, er, probably come by my own volition. Mecky thoughts, things what'd shame the Virgin."

"And what'd you call her?" asked Hegel knowingly.

"Eh?"

"By what name was she called in your thoughts, brother? I know cause I's guilty's well a callin a witch by Her Name." Hegel bowed his head. "Terrible sin."

"Does it count if you say it stead a me?" Manfried kicked his brother. "So yeah, I reckon lackin a better title the name Mary might a been used. I'd creep into that wagon and watch but I never touched her, well, uh, never *meant* to touch her. Then that time in the river I was kissin that Road Pope, thinkin it was her. If I was right a mind I never would a laid one on her, let lone no bandit."

"There it is." Hegel sighed.

"But that ain't the worst, brother!" Manfried said anxiously. "I done worse yet. Wickedness to blush Scratch's smooth cheek. See, when we was with the captain the first time we met Angelino, he was fightin with Barousse and you and Rigo was off lookin outside and I was, I was…"

"Whatever it was, you's forgiven soon's you tell me," Hegel said gently.

"I was fillin my wineskin from her tub, and since then on anytime I was feelin low I'd take a sip out a that salty bathwater, even after she went monstrous." Manfried's shame brought his chin low. "Still got a little bit left." Manfried kept his head bowed until he heard a strange noise and looked up. "You laughin at me, you hag-touchin degenerate?"

"Hey now." Hegel covered his mouth with one hand. "Just cause you's forgiven don't mean you ain't a mecky whoreson! Her *bathwater*, brother? Disgustin!"

"Well fuck you and your witch-kissin ways!" Manfried shouted.

"Calm yourself!" Hegel swelled up, then relaxed at seeing Manfried's eyes threatening to pop. "Calm, calm. Mockin a man's confession's a worse sin than any either a us done, so you got my confession on that too, fair? Hell, you wanna keep drinkin it, it's alright now cause I bless you and I'll bless it too, make it holy water. It's alright, brother."

"It most definitely is not!" Martyn roared, and Manfried socked him in the gut.

"You got any interest in delayin your reunion with the fuckin infinite, you shut your mouth in the presence a the saint!" Manfried roared back, and Martyn keeled over clutching his stomach. "Go on, brother."

"I was bout done," Hegel said, then looked around at the shining eyes watching him from across the fire. "Anyone else wanna be washed clean?"

Raphael stood and walked to them, plopping down and addressing Hegel directly for the first time since losing his hand and most of his teeth. He told them of all the atrocities he had committed during his service in the White Company. The mercenary army had taken part in all sorts of debauchery involving wine, women, and extreme violence, and Raphael confessed until the tears came and he shook with remorse.

"You's forgiven, boy." Hegel exchanged a shrug with Manfried, neither having understood most of what was said. "We's all sinners in this mecky world."

"I too have something to confess." Al-Gassur giggled, crawling toward them around the fire. "But first, is my miserable, lowly Arab-self allowed the same benefits as you?"

"Long as you don't keep prattlin on and own up already," Manfried said.

"And no revenge will be inflicted upon my flesh for whatever evils I have done?" Al-Gassur pressed, the hoax that had kept him laughing all these months almost told.

"Yeah, yeah, spit it," said Hegel.

"I, I'm, I'm not—" Al-Gassur tried to say it but his whole body trembled with mirth. "I am no Arab!"

"No Arab what?" Hegel's eyes were slits.

"No Arab at all! Not even a Turk!" The laughter overpowered Al-Gassur and he rolled in the sand.

"Heth mwad," Raphael guessed.

"No!" Al-Gassur hooted, "Neither mad nor Arab! I am from Constantinople, probably the same stock as the rest of you! Born a beggar, yes, but an Arab? Not on your souls!"

"What are you, then?" Hegel asked. "Not honest, whatever the breed."

"My father was a Wallachian peddler." The memories of his youth calmed Al-Gassur's delight. "He took my mother to Constantinople to practice his trade. But he was robbed and beaten, and without any coin to even travel home he moved to the only place which would take him, the Jews' quarter. I was born there, and so to the ignorant city folk I was a Jew. My father and mother both died when the rival Christian merchants launched one of their attacks on the ghetto, killing anyone they could catch. But not I!"

"That don't tell us why you act the Arab." Manfried had risen to a crouch.

"Even the exotic Arab with his thirst for Christian blood is less despised than the Jew," Al-Gassur hissed. "And a converted infidel, one who fought for the Pope in a crusade, can coax coin from even the least charitable Christian. As a young man in the ghetto what chance had I as a beggar or anything else, when all who see you know you for a Jew? I adopted a new name and what name I had is long forgotten."

"So you ain't a Jew or an Arab, is that right, Arab?" Manfried insisted.

"No! Yes! The golden horses and other riches my father believed to stand in Constantinople as proof of the city's wealth were long before stolen by Venetians in a crusade as noble as that on which we are now engaged, and that is why I journeyed there. I intended to abandon my Arabian ruse along the way but it stuck fast and earned me as much pity and drink as it did beatings. My true ancestry won my father naught but a broken heart and an empty pouch, and had I adopted a Jewish name be assured the beatings would have surpassed the mercy, especially in those plague-ridden days when every scapegoat was whispered to have horns beneath his pointed hat."

"So how'd you learn to talk like'em?" Hegel asked.

"The few Arabs I saw in my youth taught me a bit, and while I had forgotten it all by the time we met, our recent company has rekindled the spark of language so that I may speak a little instead of simply spouting nonsense that would only fool a Christian." Al-Gassur puffed out his chest, waiting for the blows to fall.

After a long silence, Hegel and Manfried exchanged a glance and began to chuckle. Raphael and Rodrigo soon joined in, and all four laughed until their ribs ached. Al-Gassur and Martyn looked on amazed until Manfried recovered enough to ask another question.

"And you got nuthin else to confess? No other lies need tellin? Last chance!" Manfried's smile was too broad, too honest.

"What, er, no?" Al-Gassur had not expected them to be amused, but then they fulfilled his expectations by leaping upon him,

Hegel holding his arms and Manfried seizing him around the thighs.

"We'll make you honest yet, Arab!" Manfried began tearing Al-Gassur's breeches. "What's under here, then, a stump? I seen you runnin in Venetia, Arab, seen you runnin with both legs!"

Al-Gassur struggled but they held him fast. Blocking the man's view of his own exposed lower half Manfried revealed the bound leg and tore the rags keeping it lashed against thigh and ass. Then Manfried drew his dagger and pressed the dull side against Al-Gassur's knee.

"Gonna cut it off, Arab, so's you ain't a liar no more!" Manfried dragged the metal across his skin, making the beggar scream and wail. Then the Grossbarts let him go, and he scurried away into the dark while they laughed and laughed. They had not had such sport since they first came to Gyptland.

Heartbroken that his confession had not bothered the wicked twins in the slightest, Al-Gassur took succor in that he no longer needed to bind his leg. In the dark between the fires he stealthily extracted his hidden treasure from his smaller bag, as well as the spool of thin, flexible cable he had found in Alexandria. He noosed one end of the line around the swaddled bottle and the other around his thigh, then stuffed the bottle back into his satchel and shoved the bag up the front of his short tunic to serve as a false potbelly. Only a searching eye would notice the cable leading from the top of his breeches to the bottom of his shirt; having robbed him of even the satisfaction of his deception, Al-Gassur had little doubt the Grossbarts would soon turn to his physical possessions, but if they wanted his brother's heart they would have to cut it out of him.

"I have a confession as well," Rodrigo said after the cackling at Al-Gassur had calmed. "When I came above deck on the ship it wasn't to save your lives, it was to watch you hang. I wanted to witness your suffering, for I blamed you then as I do now for Ennio's death."

"What brought illumination to your ignorant fuckin ass?" Manfried said.

"One fool shot a bow at me and then the other tried to stab me. Has a way of making a man come round." Rodrigo, like Al-Gassur, waited for a kick that never came.

"Killin them bitchswine only penance you needed, boy, so I pronounce you clean," judged Hegel.

"Heretics!" Martyn pointed at them. "By Mary's Virginal Belly, you are heretics!"

"Stow that noise," Hegel said, "or I'll demote you to bishop."

"Blasphemer!" Martyn snapped. "Only the Lord may judge me!"

"Heth a thaint!" Raphael wagged his stump from Hegel to Martyn. "Know your own pwace, Pwiest!"

"Just cause you ride with us don't mean we won't execute your ass," Hegel reminded Martyn. "You been slippin of late, but despite all a your recent blasphemin I got faith you hates demons and witches and such, so you's probably goin upways if I put you down like a blood-simple hound. If not that's your own mecky fault. What was it you said bout us bein tools and Her Will bein done?"

All eyes were on Cardinal Martyn, who stood on shaky legs surveying the four men he had shared so many days with. Everything seemed so utterly wrong that he turned away without a word and stalked off, the jeers of the Grossbarts following him into the night. Instead of making for the other fire he wandered out into the open desert, a cool wind rinsing his mind free of the Grossbartian dust that had coated it for so long even as his good hand stripped him of the murder-bought cardinal's vestments. Scaling a dune he followed the ridge until the rosy full moon again slid under the clouds. Completely naked, drunk, and crazed through the clarity of just what he had been up to over the last year of his life, Martyn looked back at the twin campfires and wept.

Closing his eyes, Martyn remembered the past for what it was and not what he had made it. His thoughts turned away from the lies he had almost believed, all the way back to Elise bidding him farewell before entering the convent where she would live out her days without him. The Bird Doctor had come for them in the garden but while Martyn fell to his knees in terror she had seized up his staff and beaten the avian-masked demoniac into the fire. When the unclean spirit abandoned its vessel and came for them she stood strong, her fiery staff between them and possession. Then it had entered the unfortunate rider and fled, and the two of them had wandered south. Even after Elise had disappeared behind the nunnery's gate Martyn could not believe her decision, and a year passed before he picked up his cowl and staff and went in search of vengeance.

The broken man did not hear the sand shifting as the behemoth rushed up the dune behind him, instead the soft, warm cadence of Elise's voice bringing tears to his cracked cheeks. Martyn did not feel the warm breath emanating from Magnus's dozens of mouths behind him, tightening his hand on her shoulder as she told him they must part and seek solace in God instead of each other. The massive rat's head Magnus had in place of a left hand accommodated all of Martyn's lame arm and part of his chest into its mouth before snapping shut. His body was acting curiously and his chest boiled, but in the cloister of his mind Martyn finally forgave her for abandoning him, although even as he died he could not forgive himself. Perhaps God would, he thought, and then thought no more.

"Martyn." The thing inside Heinrich spoke with the farmer's mouth as he rode up astride Brennen. "A monk, one of the only to escape me in years past. How might one doubt the existence of Fate, with such proof as our happy reunion down all these days?"

Heinrich had nothing to offer but a dull push to keep moving, to find the Grossbarts before he fell into the eternal sleep. His tenant merely directed the eyes they shared toward the two campfires blazing at the base of the dune, and tears of happiness dribbled down into Brennen's mouths. The husks of Vittorio and Paolo appeared in the moonlight, and, inevitable as death itself, all five rushed down the hillside and fell upon the Grossbarts.

XXX
Their Just Reward

"Martyn's hereby relieved of his duties," said Hegel with a nod into the darkness where the cardinal had disappeared. "I reckon that makes you high priest or prelate, brother."

"An honor I's happy to receive." Manfried gurgled as he drank heartily.

"Rigo and Raph, you two's bishops, Hell, you's a bishop, too, Arab." Hegel nodded at his own wisdom and the returned Al-Gassur.

"Why not a cardinal, O font of the ages?" asked Al-Gassur.

"That title's been corrupted, as has pope." Hegel hiccupped. "Fact is, ain't been a legitimate pope since Formosits."

"Shame he had to go heretical on us," said Manfried. "Martyn weren't a bad sort fore his office went to his head. Sayin that rot bout you not beein saintly."

"I did die a horrible death," Hegel agreed. "That She saw fit to raise me up only proves Her commitment to spite that celestial rapist and his so-called martyrs. Any real saint ain't gonna stand quiet for no martyrin, believe you me. Urgh!"

Hegel finished his proclamation by spraying vomit into the fire, bringing on a cheer from his brother. Never before had Hegel felt the Witches' Sight come upon him with such speed and violence, and he battled his rebellious body to warn Manfried. Finally swallowing back the puke, he gasped, wild eyes roving over the skies and sand.

"We's in a trap! Arabs!"

The freed slaves rushed an masse to the Grossbarts' fire, experience having taught them to hasten when Hegel craved their audience.

"How's that?" said Manfried, hopping into a squat and eyeing the horde of foreign allies suddenly crowding the edge of the fire.

"What kwan ower ownswelves dew?" Raphael panted.

"Suffer!" a voice crowed from darkness. "That's all I've left you, Grossbarts!"

"Who the fuck—" Hegel began.

"Who else but your nemesis?!" Heinrich shambled into the firelight, flanked by Paolo and Vittorio. The young Italians' tongues were too swollen for them to speak, but they grinned and drooled on their papal robes at seeing their quarry. In one misshapen hand Heinrich lazily dragged the scourge up his bulging stomach and chest, his sullied robe and rotting flesh peeling off like a roast turnip skin.

The stench overpowered them, even the Grossbarts gagging on the suddenly wet air. The slaves wailed at the uncomprehending Saint Hegel to banish the demons, some fleeing and others praying. Raphael and Rodrigo vomited at the stink of pus and carrion, and Al-Gassur burst a blood vessel in his eye staring at the festering men. The only pale areas on their blackened skin were the weeping pustules that glistened like the moon.

"Heinrich?" Hegel could not feel his legs, dizzy from the reek.

Manfried squinted. "Who?"

"Yes!" Heinrich hooted. "It is we!"

"Who?!" Manfried repeated, refusing to believe it. "Nah it ain't!"

"Mecky dirt-fuckin farmer!" Hegel stepped toward him, hefting his pick. "What you done to yourself?!"

"We've joined!" Heinrich cackled. "The one you thwarted in the mountains as you did me!"

"Witchery!" Manfried shouted.

"Yes!" agreed Heinrich. "She is with us as well! You killed her husband as you did my wife, and now her children will end you as you ended mine!"

"Moonfruit let that demon in'em!" Hegel exclaimed, recognizing Heinrich's rotten appearance for what it denoted. "The one what slayed Ennio and them monks and the rest a that town!"

"Eh?" Rodrigo wiped the slick vomit from his lip and drew his sword. "He's the one?"

"That's it, ain't it?!" Hegel demanded. "Confess now fore we smite you twice!"

"Yes!" Heinrich bellowed. "Now see what came from the witch's loins, Grossbarts, see what you have brought out of Hell upon you! Brennen! Magnus!"

"You's *still* a fool!" Manfried said. "Who's that skulkin behind you in them robes, eh? Couple a crumbs from that town we torched outside Venetia, or is there true popery at work?!"

Hegel felt his guts try to flee north and south simultaneously, he alone comprehending the nuances of the situation. How might a harvest spring forth but with a planted seed? Before he could recover, half a dozen slaves on the edge of the firelight disappeared, yanked backward into the darkness without a scream among them—but their fellows who had seen what had taken them supplied shrieks to go around. All assembled felt hot wind stir their hair, a wind that pushed and pulled like a rapid tide, a wind born of dozens of massive mouths breathing in unison.

"Draw circles bout yourselves!" Manfried shouted before seeing the towering abominations.

"Use fire on'em!" Hegel shouted, spinning into a crouch and leaping at the shape blocking out the moon beside him.

Sheer idiotic rage allowed the Grossbarts to act, everyone else catatonic. Heinrich and his disciples chanted from across the campfire, the enormous twins among the company and devouring two slaves apiece with the maws on their legs. Magnus thrust his left arm at Hegel, the snarling rat-hand snapping its jaws over his head.

Hegel's pick went into Magnus's groin with a dull thunk and he jumped back, blood jetting into his face. Then the monstrosity's leg kicked out, the mouth on the sole of its hairy paw just the right size to bite off Hegel's head. Galvanized by the Grossbarts' heroic charge, the remaining men took action: a Syrian pederast jumped under Magnus's extending leg and deflected the foot before it could decapitate the saint. The mouth snapped over Hegel's head and the unbalanced beast stumbled back. Before the child-rapist could move, jaws behind Magnus's knee opened and bit off his face, chewing the man's triumphant smile as he fell dying to the sand.

Brennen swiped a hand at Manfried, the Grossbart parrying three of the sword-sized claws with the haft of his mace. The pinky talon, however, went under Manfried's weapon, through a gap in his plate, and the claw sunk through his mail shirt as though it were knit of yarn instead of iron. The force of the blow sent him rolling ass over head across the sand, his mace flying into the sky. Before the creature pounced a figure flitted in front of its sole eye, scrambling away into the darkness. Bellowing with every mouth, Brennen forgot Manfried and pursued the fleeing coward.

Looking back, Al-Gassur could not even piss himself before a huge hand closed around his left leg, the teeth thereon holding it tight. Brennen lifted his victim to drop the morsel into the central mouth on his cyclopean face but then the satchel housing

Barousse's relic slipped through Al-Gassur's torn breeches and dangled beside him. The mock-Arab noticed this and invoked the name of the captain, slapping the bag into one of the mouths. The lips encircling his leg parted in surprise, and Al-Gassur fell to the sand.

The witch-born beast howled in Al-Gassur's face, dozens of mouths blowing the stink of his own death upon him. The beggar saw the bottle tumble out of the ripping satchel, and the small vessel containing his brother's heart blazed with a pale yellow luminescence as the glass shattered in the gnashing teeth of Brennen's hand. Al-Gassur closed his eyes, unaware that the loop of cable on the bottle's neck slipped down a prodigious tooth and cut into its gums as the monster chewed glass and glowing relic.

Just as there exist dark things that traverse oceanic abysses as if they were dry land, so too do fell beings troll the skies as if they were seas. The releasing of the artifact from its glass prison brought the attention of one of those, which might otherwise have failed to notice the object from such a distance. With the speed of God it descended from the heavens in pursuit of the shimmering prize for which all vile powers lust. Before Brennen could swallow the scorching relic a shadow even the moon feared to illuminate plucked him up with the ease of a falcon snatching a rodent. Blood splashed across Al-Gassur and he opened his eyes to see the beast vanish, but before the first syllable of thanks could leave his lungs the spool of cable he had attached to the bottle, and his thigh, burst from his satchel. Bonded to Brennen by the suddenly taut line, Al-Gassur shot into the sky and out of the knowing of the Grossbarts.

Two more convicts were torn apart by Magnus's voracious legs and right arm, the rat-faced left hand intent only on devouring Hegel. The creature had regained its balance and pressed forward, murine jaws tearing into Hegel's left hand and coming away with the Grossbart's two outer fingers and sword. Hegel responded by burying his pick in its snout but the arm drew back and Hegel released his weapon lest he be pulled any closer to the behemoth.

Drawing his prybar, Hegel jabbed the comparatively normal but massive hand snatching at his face. Then the other arm returned, the bestial face wielded like a club. Hegel sprawled on the ground under the impact but rolled away before the toothy feet could fall. He spied Manfried's mace on the ground beside him and snatched it, but this distraction enabled the three-eyed horror to focus fully on its quarry, all other victims forgotten in its rage.

The pick-skewered rat-hand leaked blood from its clamped jaws, but as it fell they again sprang open to rend Hegel's exposed back. Manfried swung his ax over his prone brother's head, exploding rat teeth and severing the lower jaw. Magnus's mouths shrieked and he threw himself atop them, desiring only to crush and chew their defiant bones. Rodrigo snatched Hegel and Raphael seized Manfried, each jerking a brother in a different direction. The beast crashed to the empty ground, two pairs of men spinning almost out of reach.

The jaws on Magnus's left elbow tore into Rodrigo's leg, taking away a massive dripping chunk. Had Raphael not already lost his left hand it would have disappeared into the snapping mouth that grazed his bandaged wrist. The skeletal outline of Magnus's face twisted toward Manfried and Raphael, the warped nostril billowing, two eyes shining black and the third yellow. The remaining two prisoners, one a hardened killer who had that very night determined just what the Grossbarts were after in his homeland and the other a young Moslem noble who had never struck a foe, swung their swords into the backs of Magnus's ankles. The biting teeth on the creature's feet kicked as Magnus tried to right himself, legs as thick as tree trunks pumping the air as the convicts hacked.

The four men near Magnus's head and arms scrambled back only to leap again into the fray, the downed creature's bellows of fury turning to wails as ax and sword and mace fell on every limb. A foot found the noble's chest but his last blow cut the mighty paw free and the young man fell backward, the jaws gnawing his bare chest despite being severed. Tendons popped in the other leg, the more seasoned prisoner dodging the deadly kicks as he cut ever deeper. The mangled rat-head became mush under Hegel's mace and then came loose from Rodrigo's stabbings, and Magnus's right arm flew off at the elbow from Manfried and Raphael's onslaught.

Swaying in the moonlight, Heinrich called his son's name over and over but his child had departed, taken by something even fouler than he. Staggering toward the Grossbarts and their followers he raised his dull scourge, grief dampening his cheeks for the first time since abandoning his humanity. Poor Magnus bawled as the bastards dismembered him, the child rolling toward one group only to have the other hew into his exposed torso.

With the arm removed, Manfried pressed in to hack the thing's head open when the barbed scourge whipped around his face and pulled him off the beast. Heinrich's stench blinded them as he swung the flail around at Raphael, but then both he and Manfried turned their attentions to the possessed yeoman. Heinrich fell into the arms of his acolytes as Manfried's ax cleaved into his shoulder and Raphael's sword slit open his belly. He cackled even as black slime bubbled from his wounds, his assailants returning to their task.

"Burn it!" Hegel told the two prisoners. "Oil the mecky fucker!"

"Don't let them!" Heinrich shrieked at Vittorio and Paolo, who still hung back.

Hegel had noticed Magnus's fresh wounds healed quicker

than new ones could be made. The severed rat-hand had melted into bubbling filth at their feet and a new, placenta-veiled bulge quickly grew from the stump. The Egyptian criminal helped the noble throw the rear paw off before it ate its way to his heart, but then the foot turned to ash and hooked toes burst from Magnus's gory ankle. Aghast, the younger prisoner had the sense slapped into him by his murderous countryman.

Without the two men working its legs, Magnus recovered sufficiently to leap away from the other four attackers, the fresh rat-hand uttering a snarling squeak at its rebirth. Manfried caught sight of something behind the great chops of its central stomach-mouth and charged. Hegel and Raphael were close after but Rodrigo slumped, his wounded leg leaking like a worn-out wineskin. Clumsily bandaging himself and taking up his crossbow, Rodrigo aimed at Magnus's face.

The abomination tried to stand on its hind legs but they were not yet whole and buckled, Magnus dropping to all fours to greet their charge. Raphael slashed across its nostril, popping the eyeball beside it and bringing the creature's focus upon him. Racing past the roaring arms, Hegel followed his brother until Manfried ducked under the creature's stomach and the beast lunged forward.

A thigh struck Hegel, teeth latching onto his arm and pulling him against Magnus's side. More mouths opened where Hegel had sworn there were none, pinning him flat as fangs rent his armor to get at his flesh. He tried to use his mace but a long, greasy tongue wrapped around it, pulling him closer. Immobile, Hegel saw a cloud growing around the wounded Heinrich, and, knowing what it presaged, began to pray as he struggled.

In the moonless shadow of the creature's belly, Manfried held his prybar in both hands and stood up—directly into the largest of Magnus's mouths. Blinded in the dank, plaque-ridden stink of its maw, Manfried held his prybar until the jaws closed on him and the metal tool embedded itself in the monster's gums. With a silent prayer, Manfried released his grip on the instrument that prevented the teeth from biting him in half, its muscles straining to snap the prybar keeping its mouth ajar. A warm, vinegar-sour mist boiled out of the hidden pit where all its mouths led, choking the Grossbart with its pungent exhalation. Reaching up into the blackness, Manfried tore with his bare hands through flesh and tissue, noxious blood burning his skin and eyes before the monster moved forward and the Grossbart held on to meat to keep from falling out. His boots dragging on the ground, Manfried dug through the back of the creature's gut-throat until several of Magnus's teeth popped and the prybar slipped, the beast's mouth snapping shut.

Firing his crossbow, Rodrigo saw Magnus's only human eye burst in Raphael's face before the rat-hand bit the brigand and began slinging him about by his shoulder. Hegel felt his helmet pulled free and heard it being rent in the mouth against his shoulder, then he felt another tongue wrapping around his neck and teeth chewing his beard, pulling his head in despite his efforts. Then Magnus collapsed, dragging Hegel to the ground and tossing Raphael through the air and onto Rodrigo.

The fight had taken them away from the campfires and the moon hid, but criminal eyes are always sharpest in darkness. Noble and misanthrope alike stood transfixed, weapons slipping from their shaky fingers. The beast lay motionless but none of the crusaders moved, two sprawled a dozen feet away, one half-chewed in the mouths peppering the abomination's flank, and the last swallowed whole. The two popes held up their priest, who vomited bile and smoke, the miasma coalescing around him into horrible shapes cavorting in the starlight. The odors and sounds his body released would have gagged a necromancer but his acolytes savored the vileness.

Then Magnus's neck bulged and the prisoners stared, wondering what new horror birthed from its gargantuan corpse. Fur split, its entire head suddenly rolled away from its body, and a man-shaped thing crawled forth.

"Mary!" the magenta man gasped, holding aloft Magnus's giant heart. "By the Virgin, we done it!"

At Manfried's invocation of Mary's name Hegel tore himself free of the cooling tongues and teeth, and Rodrigo and Raphael slowly untangled their sprained and bleeding limbs from one another. Manfried's beard resembling afterbirth and Hegel's chewed down to his cheeks, the Grossbarts embraced atop their fallen adversary, shouting amens that were taken up by the few survivors.

Over his brother's shoulder Hegel saw Heinrich erupt in a bloody mist, and a sinisterly familiar shape landed in the spray beside the yeoman's deflating body.

Heinrich did not see the grotesque demon vacate his largest bubo, his stolen melancholic humour coursing through the parasitic monster in place of blood. Instead he saw Brennen as the boy had first appeared in the midwife's arms, chubby, yawning, and terribly put out to be brought into such a cold world. His chest heaving with the pulse of festering corruption instead of life, Heinrich heard the Grossbarts shouting and realized he could search for eternity and never find a devil as evil as they. His son's name bubbled on his rancid lips as he slipped beyond pain and joy alike.

"Circles!" Hegel shouted, shoving the mace into Manfried's arms and sprinting toward his fallen pick. "Draw circles bout you in the dirt! Now!"

"Ah fuck it all," Manfried groaned, seeing what his brother was on about. "Not all this again."

"Grossbarts!" The high-pitched squeal shook their bowels. "Thought you had me! Thought you had me in those hills, in that hog!" The carapaced, miasma-wreathed thing bounded in ten-foot strides toward Hegel but he snatched his pick and knelt on the ground. The demon saw what he intended and sped at him, its victorious rant turning to a horrified wail. Completing the circle in the sand, Hegel looked up to see the cloud of pestilential, stinking fog surround him, the demon bouncing before him on its rearmost legs. Hegel started back but caught himself before he fell outside the ring he had scratched in the sand.

Without further hesitation the demon spun and made for Manfried, but the crimson Grossbart had completed his own circle, being mindful not to drip onto the band that encircled him. The foul thing hopped toward Rodrigo and Raphael but the men had made a wide ring around both of them. Without understanding the language the prisoners saw enough to imitate the crusaders, and again the demon was denied.

With a final agonized screech the demon leaped high into the night and vanished, all going silent upon the desert. The young noble began shouting and jumping in the air, praising the name Grossbart. Hegel and Manfried both yelled at him to calm his foolish ass but he could not understand, and as his foot landed straddling the edge of the circle a stinking comet plummeted into his face.

The noble rolled in the sand and they saw the suddenly shrunken demon squirming down his bulging throat, pus oozing around his split lips. The other Egyptian turned away after making sure his own circle remained unbroken. Rodrigo and Raphael stared in shock but the Grossbarts knew at once how to handle this dire turn.

"Shoot'em!" Manfried shouted, realizing his crossbow had fallen somewhere during the battle. "With the quickness!"

"Rigo!" Hegel yelled at finding his own broken. "Shoot, Rigo, shoot!"

Rodrigo stared blankly at the possession taking place while Raphael clumsily tried to cock the bow. With one hand this proved impossible given the model of weapon and Raphael shook Rodrigo, yelling in his face. The younger man blinked at him, and vomited all over them both.

"Rigo!" Manfried bellowed. "Listen, fuckwit, that's what happened to Ennis!"

"Ennio!" Hegel shouted. "That same demon did that same thing to your brother Ennio!"

This captured Rodrigo's attention, and he notched the only bolt left in his quiver. The possessed noble gained his feet, ropes of bile swinging from his chin. The cackling demoniac snatched up a dropped sword and swayed toward the closest Grossbart— Manfried. As he swiped the weapon down to smudge Manfried's circle, Rodrigo's last quarrel penetrated the noble's chest and skewered his heart. The man collapsed, screeching and spraying biles from every hole.

"Grossbarts," it lamented as it clawed out around the bolt. Pulling itself free in a welter of gore, it had diminished to the size of a cat. "Break their wards! Help me, brothers, as I helped you!"

Paolo and Vittorio appeared through the gloom but made no move to rush the Brothers Grossbart. The brains of the two boys had long since baked from fever and sun to little more than paste but they strode forward nevertheless, their putrescent hearts pumping pus and biles through bodies long ripe for the grave.

"Something the matter?" asked Paolo.

"Something troublesome?" asked Vittorio.

"Kick their circles!" the demon howled, dancing around them. "Please, brothers!"

"No," said Vittorio.

"No," agreed Paolo.

"Why?!" The demon jumped onto Paolo's shoulder and howled in his ear, "They've done you as wrong as I!"

"Wrong." Paolo stroked the fiend's thorax before it hopped

back down to the sand. "They have done you wrong, and these mounts of ours, but what have they done to us?"

"What?" asked Vittorio, "save reprimand your folly? Many chances to spread the gift you have wasted, leading us here."

"What?" asked Paolo, "save deliver us our freedom from your yoke? What have they done to *us*?"

"This!" Manfried shouted, hurling a dagger with expert precision. The long knife disappeared in the rotten robe, the handle marking where Paolo's heart lay. The barber's son pitched onto his face, farting, belching, and smoking.

"And you!" Hegel's pick spun through the air, the point sinking in Vittorio's stomach. He was knocked to the ground, and several more Grossbart-born missiles struck him before he could rise. A dagger once used by Captain Barousse to end his own life flew from Hegel's fingers and sunk into the Road Pope's chest.

"Ain't suffer no demons to live!" Manfried shouted at the pincushioned corpse.

"Witches neither!" Hegel hollered. "When yous get to Hell tell'em Saint Hegel put you there!"

The first demon shook with laughter, bouncing atop the corpses and chastising its fellows as they burst from their hosts' buboes. These two were smaller but equally vile, and they at once skipped to the first, their sharp digits, pointy horns, and hooked feet scratching at skin and plating that strained to contain the greasy fluids within. The first continued to reprimand the others, easily evading them with its longer legs as the organ crowning its posterior fired spurt after chunky spurt of rank discharge into the air.

Nothing stirred on the sands for leagues and leagues save the encircled men, all living things fleeing at the first whiff of Heinrich's rank retinue—even the maggots had abandoned their rotting hosts as the demons wreaked the full extent of their evils upon the flesh of their human mounts. The demons sprang toward the Grossbarts, bringing their stinking miasma with them. Even this could not penetrate their circles, and the Grossbarts heckled the demons and spat upon them until they realized this pleased the creatures. As the darkness dwindled and light began to creep over the sands a strange transformation in attitude took place, all three demons piling against each other and frantically bartering with the Grossbarts to leave their circles.

"I know where riches beyond counting lie," the first demon squealed.

"I know where there are more," the second countered, "and I'll leave you intact as soon as we find another body for me!"

"Please," the third whined, "if you break the circles of your fellows we shan't touch you, and may part in peace!"

"Balls," snorted Hegel. "Cockcrow's at hand, so yous best set to prayin. To me."

"It's gonna hurt," Manfried said excitedly, "ain't it? It's gonna hurt worse than I can imagine, bein sent back down!"

Rodrigo and Raphael were barely awake but dared not rest until the fiends departed for good. The last prisoner shifted from foot to foot, ineffectively trying to banish the cramps that plagued him. Like the Grossbarts, he had drawn a narrow circle that did not afford him enough room to safely sit within its boundary. The demons also hassled him, Raphael, and Rodrigo but none would bargain.

The sunlight crested a dune and the demons groaned, clumsily hurling themselves away from the glow, too weak to move with more than staggering bounces. Then they ceased their moaning and all turned toward the light. The Grossbarts perked up, for all three snuffled the anteneae-ringed weeping sores they had in place of mouths and pushed themselves toward the rising sun.

Tears of pus dribbled as the sunlight descended upon them, two curling their legs underneath themselves and covering their eyes with their skeletal paws, but the original demon forced itself forward. Then a beam touched its loathsome body mid-hop and its exoskeleton shattered with a thousand fissures. The swirling miasma became a black cloud of smoke issuing forth as it shriveled to nothing in the sand, only a scorch mark on the earth denoting its passing. Manfried felt the sunlight envelop him and stepped out of the ring to better taunt the last two demons.

One mustered its strength and flew at him, howling his name as it entered the sunlight and burst, rancid liquids staining the sand at his feet. The last gave a final desperate push into the shadows and then was overtaken, belching pestilential fumes as it deflated and spun in the sand. Then they were alone in the desert, the demons forced back into their pit to scheme and moan and curse the Grossbart name.

XXXI
The Final Heresy

Of Raphael and Rodrigo little more is recounted here, for the men parted ways with the Grossbarts after their battle with the demons. Rodrigo sought to liberate Barousse's bones from the Hospitallers' cemetery on Rhodes, wishing that he might rest in a holier place—a goal the Grossbarts heartily approved. Raphael wanted only to leave the miserable country that had shaken his spirit and stolen his fist, and so he accompanied Rodrigo on the long, limping trek north to the Holy Land and beyond. Mary willing, their fresh wounds did not fester and their path remained clear, but the Grossbarts did not know, for they turned south as they always did.

The sole surviving prisoner, a hardened killer named Hassan, led them to Cairo, and while the sun scalded and the sand chafed and Hegel's three-fingered hand itched and Manfried's punctured gut throbbed they at last stood on the dunes overlooking the great tombs of Gyptland. They could not verbally communicate with Hassan, referring to him as Arab in Al-Gassur's stead, yet through pantomime and prayer he had brought them to their destination. No tears of joy or shouts of triumph passed through their beards, only smug mutters of satisfaction.

They spent several days scouting the stone monoliths, choosy as nobles about their grapes. All the pyramids appeared too exposed to still hold riches, but eventually they stumbled across a stone arch half-buried in the sand. They spent all night clearing out the entrance and bickering.

"This Arab done us better than the last," Hegel panted.

"Least he don't talk all that rubbish. Be nice if he talked proper though, so we could explain why his share'll be less than ours." Manfried dumped another helmet of sand out of their excavation.

"He'll get the point in one fashion or another." Hegel spit on his hands. "Think we's bout ready."

"Yeah." Manfried removed his prybar. "Let's crack it."

"Wonder what befell our Arab. The other one, I mean." Hegel jammed his tool into the slight seam in the stone.

"Sandy-eared fuck." Manfried strained. "Told you. Got carried off long with that other monster. Seen it myself."

"Yeah, I mean after that, though," Hegel grunted.

"Well it was either demon or angel, so Heaven or Hell."

"But which?"

"You's the damn saint." Manfried felt the block shift slightly. "Ask Mary."

"It's there!" said Hegel.

It actually took them the rest of the night to wedge it open enough to slip through. Before they entered they called Hassan down from his sentry position on top of the dune to have a drink. While the three laughed and rubbed their hands in anticipation light crept up the side of their dune, and the Grossbarts ate the last of the camel they had stolen from a Bedouin several days before. The beast had struck Hegel as even more suspect than a horse.

"What you reckon's inside?" asked Hegel.

"Witch's gold," Manfried belched. "If we's lucky, regular gold if we ain't."

"Why'd I want some gold touched by a witch?" Hegel demanded.

"Cause then we'd never be able to spend it all."

"But if a witch grubbed it up—"

"Then you bless it pure, thickhead, I swear, you's..." Manfried trailed off, his eyes trained on the beams of sunlight brushing the top of the arch.

"I's what, bath-mouth?" Hegel asked. "Answer up, son, and lose your holy station."

"Shut it." Manfried dropped his meat and slowly stood, brushing the weathered stone. "Brother," his voice shaking along with his shoulders, "what you make a this?"

Hegel set down his wine but before he could reprimand Manfried he saw it too, and slumped back in the sand. "What the shit?"

"It's it, ain't it?!" Manfried turned away from the rough G chiseled in the stone, the symbol clearly fresher than the worn bas-reliefs. "That's our goddamn mark!"

"Yeah." Hegel felt sick. "Damn if it ain't."

"What in Hell!?" Manfried kicked the sand and threw his prybar down. "Lousy old fucker! All the goddamn tombs in Gyptland!"

Hassan stood and gestured to the engraving, shrugging his shoulders. Manfried sucker punched him and when the man fell he booted him again. For several minutes Manfried raged and swore and Hegel drank.

"Our grandad," Hegel explained to the contorted guide. "Truth finally be laid bare, I'd kind a doubted he ever made it."

"Pack it up," Manfried said. "Let's get movin to the next one."

"Hold a tic." Hegel held up his hand.

"Why? Why the fuck—"

"Cause I said so!" Hegel jumped up. "You know that feelin I get when somethin don't wash, or we's liable to get some ill our way?"

"Yeah?"

"Well, I ain't got it." Hegel scratched his beard. "Anythin, I feel, I dunno, good bout this here crypt."

"Eh?"

"Yeah!" Hegel picked up the prybar and offered it to his brother. "I mean, he might a carved it fore he went in, and dropped dead at the sight a all the loot. Or he couldn't carry it all, meant to come back for it but didn't want our cunty da slippin in fore he could get back."

"Suppose the possibility exists." Manfried stroked the end of his beard to remind his brother that with half of Hegel's in a monster's gullet, there could be no denying the superiority of Manfried's silver bush.

"Can't hurt nuthin." Hegel stood up. "Get with it, Arab."

Hefting their gear, Hegel lit an oil lamp taken from the same unfortunate traveler whose camel they had killed and squirmed inside. Manfried followed with Hassan close behind, only his fear of the saint preventing him from knifing Manfried in the back. Stone stairs led down into midnight, and with each step Hegel felt more confident. Then the stair underfoot gave a soft click as he put his weight on it, and even without the goosepimples exploding on his neck he would have known to run for it. A thunderous crashing echoed after them, and reaching an opening Hegel ducked around the corner followed by Manfried. As they looked back for Hassan an explosion of dust and rock shards exited the stairwell, snuffing out their lamp.

"Feel *good* bout it?!" Manfried punched at his brother but in the black vault he only hurt his hand on the wall. "Mecky fuckin asshole!"

"Stow it," said Hegel, "I's relightin the lamp so's we can find a way out."

When Hegel finally got it lit they saw the entire stairway was choked with fallen blocks from the ceiling. They stood in a massive stone chamber far exceeding any sepulcher they had previously pilfered. Amidst grumblings they agreed there must be another stairway or exit somewhere in the vault. They were wrong.

There lived Grossbarts before Hegel and Manfried, and, unfortunately for this happy world, there have lived Grossbarts since. A complete chronicle of that benighted clan would fill more volumes than every holy text of every people of every land, and so rejoice that there is little more recorded here. The Brothers Grossbart received exactly what they deserved down in that hallowed desert tomb, and it is easy to assume they lived only as long as their water and air held out. Thus, their end may have been more merciful to humanity than the tragedy that was their birth.

Before their eradication, preachers of the Grossbart Heresy alleged that Saint Hegel gave his own life a second time to save his brother, but the tales of madmen and heretics are just that. Far, far to the east, however, there lies a chain of islands with curious beliefs. The people of that land have long held that eating the flesh of a sea maiden grants immortality; perhaps, then, the Brothers Grossbart still dwell in that lightless tomb long buried in sand, tugging their beards for all time.

Bibliography

Only through scholarship is the writer capable of realistically rendering the historical world. Some of the books below were consulted prior to beginning this work in order to inspire and inform, others were read after its completion to check specific details. Most were extremely useful, and all offered something, even if their tokens wound up excised with cruel snips of the drafting process. This lamentably brief—to some, doubtlessly overlong to others—bibliography reflects of course only the specific books consulted immediately before, during, or after the drafting of the novel; many more titles I can no longer recall laid the groundwork for my understanding of the era and its beliefs.

As for the study of the Grossbarts in particular, I am strongly indebted to several esteemed specialists in the history of that ignoble line: Señor Ardanuy, Heer Dunn, Monsieur Rahimi, and Kyria Tanzer. In addition to their help with this adaptation, their previous works on the subject have been a great boon and are cited accordingly. Finally, while their works are not to be found below, the tutelage of many a non-Grossbartian historian and teacher helped me immeasurably—Steve Armstrong, Bruce Boehrer, Margaret Burkley, Roy Campbell, Ken Foster, Doug Fowler, Don Howarth, Marlow Matherne, Rod Moorer, Paul

Reifenheiser, Mike Rychlik, Bawa Singh, Paul Strait, and Trisha
Stapleton, to name but a few.

Allen, S.J. and Amt, Emile. *The Crusades: A Reader*. Canada:
Broadview Press, 2003.

Ardanuy, David. *Saint Hegel: The Self-Idolatry of the Righteous in
Medieval Europe*. Florida: Goat Head Walking, 1989.

Arikha, Noga. *Passions and Tempers: A History of the Humours*.
New York: Ecco, 2007.

Atwood, Margaret. *The Handmaid's Tale*. New York: Hough-
ton Mifflin, 1986.

Barber, Richard (ed.). *Bestiary: Being an English Version of the
Bodleian Library, Oxford M.S. Bodley 764 with all the Original Minia-
tures Produced in Facsimile. Translated and Introduced by Richard Barber*.
Great Britain: The Boydell Press, 1993.

Benton, Janetta Rebold. *The Medieval Menagerie: Animals in the
Art of the Middle Ages*. New York: Abbeville Press, 1992.

Borges, Jorge Luis with Margarita Guerrero. *The Book of Imaginary Beings*. Translated by Andrew Hurley, illustrated by Peter
Sis. New York: Viking Penguin, 1967.

Budge, E. A. Wallis. *Babylonian Life and History*. New York:
Barnes and Noble Books, 2005.

Caciola, Nancy. *Discerning Spirits: Divine and Demonic Possession
in the Middle Ages*. New York: Cornell University Press, 2003.

Campbell, Michael D. "Behind the Name—the Etymology
and History of First Names" (1996). http://behindthename
.com.

Cantor, Norman F. *The Encyclopedia of the Middle Ages*. New
York: Viking, 1999.

Cantor, Norman F. *In the Wake of the Plague: The Black Death and
the World It Made*. New York: Harper Perennial, 2002.

Cavendish, Richard. *The Black Arts*. New York: The Putnam
Publishing Group, 1983.

Collins, Robert O. *The Nile*. Connecticut: Yale University Press, 2002.

Constable, Giles. "The Financing of the Crusades in the Twelfth Century." In *Outremer*: 68–88. Jerusalem: Yad Izhak Ben-Zvi Institute, 1982.

Contamine, Phillipe. *War in the Middle Ages*. Translated by Michael Jones. New York: Basil Blackwell Inc., 1984.

Curryer, Betty Nelson. *Anchors: The Illustrated History*. U.S. Naval Institute Press, 1999.

Dean, Trevor. *Crime in Medieval Europe: 1200–1550*. Great Britain: Pearson Education, 2001.

Duffy, Eamon. *Saints and Sinners: A History of the Popes*. Yale University Press, 1997.

Dunn, Travis. *Holy Beard, Holy Grail*. Italy: Garamond, 1982.

Ekirch, A. Roger. *At Day's Close: Night in Times Past*. New York: W. W. Norton and Company, 2005.

Gies, Frances and Joseph. *Life in a Medieval Village*. New York: Harper and Row, Publishers, 1990.

Goldschmidt, Arthur. *A Concise History of the Middle East*. Colorado: Westview Press, 1999.

Hamilton, Bernard. *The Medieval Inquisition*. New York: Holmes and Meier Publishers, Inc., 1989.

Henisch, Bridget Ann. *Fast and Feast: Food in Medieval Society*. Pennsylvania: Pennsylvania State University Press, 1976.

Hirst, Anthony and Silk, Michael (eds.). *Alexandria, Real and Imagined*. Great Britain: MPG Books, Limited, 2004.

Housley, Norman. *The Avignon Papacy and the Crusades 1305–1378*. Great Britain: Clarendon Press, 1986.

Houston, Mary G. *Medieval Costume in England and France: The Thirteenth, Fourteenth and Fifteenth Centuries*. New York: Dover Publications, Inc., 1996.

Hughes, Pennethorne. *Witchcraft*. Great Britain: Longmans, Green, 1952.

Hume, Edgar Erskine. *Medical Works of the Knights Hospitallers of St. John of Jerusalem*. Baltimore: The Johns Hopkins Press, 1940.

Irwin, Robert. *The Middle East in the Middle Ages: The Early Ages of the Mamluk Sultanate 1250–1382*. Great Britain: Croom Helm, 1986.

Kagay, Donald J. and Villalon, L. J. Andrew. *The Circle of War in the Middle Ages*. Great Britain: The Boydell Press, 1999.

Kelly, John. *The Great Mortality: An Intimate History of the Black Death, the Most Devastating Plague of All Time*. New York: Harper Collins Publishers, Inc., 2005.

Kottenkamp, F. *The History of Chivalry and Armor*. New York: Portland House, 1988.

Lecouteux, Claude. *Witches, Werewolves, and Fairies: Shapeshifters and Astral Doubles in the Middle Ages*. Vermont: Inner Traditions, 2003.

Longrigg, James. *Greek Rational Medicine: Philosophy and Medicine from Alcmaeon to the Alexandrians*. Great Britain: Routledge, 1993.

Lynch, Joseph H. *The Medieval Church: A Brief History*. Great Britain: Longman Group UK Limited, 1992.

Maalouf, Amin. *The Crusades Through Arab Eyes*. Translated by Jon Rothschild. New York: Schocken Books, 1984.

Madden, Thomas F. *A Concise History of the Crusades*. New York: Rowman and Littlefield Publishers, Inc., 1999.

Manley, Deborah, Editor. *The Nile: A Traveler's Anthology*. Great Britain: Cassell, 1991.

Marozzi, Justin. *Tamerlane: Sword of Islam, Conqueror of the World*. Massachusetts: Da Capo Press, 2004.

Morris, Jan. *A Venetian Bestiary*. Great Britain: Thames and Hudson, 1982.

Peters, Edward. *The Magician, the Witch, and the Law*. Pennsylvania: University of Pennsylvania Press, 1978.

Rahimi, Jonathan. *Eight Centuries of Exotic Easterners in Western*

Storytelling, from Al-Gassur to Fo Qi Shu Kai Li. Florida: Calliope Press, 1999.

Riley-Smith, Jonathan. *The Oxford Illustrated History of the Crusades.* New York: Oxford University Press, 2001.

Russell, Jeffrey Burton and Lumsden, Douglas W. *A History of Medieval Christianity: Prophecy and Order.* New York: Peter Lang Publishing, Inc., 2000.

Santosuosso, Antonio. *Barbarians, Marauders, and Infidels: The Ways of Medieval Warfare.* Perseus Books Group, 2004.

Sayce, A. H. *Lectures on the Origin and Growth of Religion as Illustrated by the Religion of the Ancient Babylonians.* Great Britain: Williams and Norgate, 1888.

Schulz, Juergen. *The New Palaces of Medieval Venice.* Pennsylvania: Pennsylvania State University Press, 1927.

Scott, Walter. *Demonology and Witchcraft: Letters Addressed to J. G. Lockhart, Esq.* New York: Bell Publishing Company, 1970.

Singman, Jeffrey L. *Daily Life in Medieval Europe.* Greenwood Press, 1999.

Smith, Joseph Lindon. *Tombs, Temples, and Ancient Art.* Norman: University of Oklahoma Press, 1956.

Tanzer, E. M. *The Mad Woman in the Hut: Gender in the Große Bärte Texts.* Paris: Du Peltier Publishing, 2001.

Thompson, C. J. S. *Mysteries and Secrets of Magic.* Montana: Kessinger Publishing, LLC, 2003.

Tuchman, Barbara W. *A Distant Mirror: The Calamitous Fourteenth Century.* New York: Ballantine Books, 1978.

Unknown. *Die Tragödie der Brüder Große Bärte.* Germany: Golddämmerung, 1882.

Vauchez, Andre. *The Laity in the Middle Ages: Religious Beliefs and Devotional Practices.* Indiana: University of Notre Dame Press, 1993.

Venit, Marjorie Susan. *Monumental Tombs of Ancient Alexandria.* Great Britain: Cambridge University Press, 2002.

Walker, Trevor Caleb. *Black Monolith, Enter the Nexus: The Ballad of the Grossbarts.* Berkeley: Dappled Unicorn Press, 1967.

Wills, Garry. *Venice: Lion City: The Religion of Empire.* New York: Simon and Schuster, Inc., 2001.

Wolff, Robert Lee and Hazard, Harry W. *A History of the Crusades, Volume II: The Later Crusades, 1189–1311.* Madison: University of Wisconsin Press, 1969.

Acknowledgments

If only for chronological purposes, any sort of gratitude must first be directed toward my family. My parents, Bruce and Lisa, have been indispensably helpful and patient over the years of our acquaintance, and my brother Aaron and sister Tessa have shown me a sibling's understanding of a sort markedly different from that of the Grossbarts. The entire multitude of my rabbit-like extended families are likewise deserving of mention, and of course my grandparents—particularly my grandmothers Mary and Ulamae for instilling me with a love of speculative fiction and folklore, respectively.

My wife, Raechel, inspired and encouraged me through every step of the writing process, and my partner-in-skulduggery Molly provided invaluable assistance with the novel's various incarnations—without Raechel this project would never have gotten off the ground, and without Molly it might have exploded in a fireball rather than landing gently and safely, and a sight better than when it started. John, husband of Molly and so much more, helped maintain perspective as matters progressed, and offered the sagacity of a Buddha in all regards. Andrew Katkin and his father, Dan, both aided in ways they may never comprehend.

The coming recitation of names, of equal import to the catalog of ships in *The Iliad*, must wait a moment longer as I salute five fair folk who helped with this project and are therefore deserving of a heavy-handed metaphor and an awful pun. Trevor, you are my thumb, conqueror of all comers and gladiatorial judge. Caleb, you are the index finger that points the way to enlightenment. Pat, you are both defender and avenger of my honor, the middle digit. Selena, you are that penultimate finger without which hands are but paws. Jonathan, you are the pinky to be bitten when only the fanciest of giggles will suffice. To you five I say huzzah, and thank you.

Many others have inspired and encouraged me over the years, and while my mind is not what it once was, a handful of names float like cream to the top of my memory mug: Lauryn, Patrick, Jimmy, Becky, Daniel, Tracy, Don, Luke, Robbie, Willem, Joyce, Chad, Lara, Monique, Edgar, Greg, Carrie, Reinhardt, Barbara, Sean, Jeff, Rayford, Victor, Terry, Bobbie, Daylan, Nate, Mary, Allison, Kat, Stephanie, Bill, Angelo, Debbie, Paul, Eddie, Walt, Julie, Eric, Jen, Richard, Albert, Jon, Brenna, Ross, Meg, Ben, Shawn, Erica, Jeremy, Kido, Tom, Brooke, Sheri, Hunter, Ari, Jim, Twyla, Nick, J. T., Orrin, Clint, Music, Holly, Mike, Marlena, and Martin; Phil, Shirley and Olivia; the Zoltens; the Family and Brothers Johnson, the Mother and Brothers Capellari; the Maier-Katkins; the Katkins; the Maiers; the Browns; the Mastrofskis; the Greenbergs; the Reeses; the Lowells; the Jacobsons; the Flemings; the Reeves; the Rambalskis; the Schmidts; the Kenneys; the Hoovers, the Knudson; SAIL; the baristas of All Saints Café; the customers of Video 21; my website designer James Childress; and the memories of Alex and Jeff.

Then there are three standup fellows without whose humor and inspiration this novel would not be the work that it is. David, your beard is as spiritual as it is physical, and I quail before its majesty and the witty portal it gilds. Travis, never before have I encountered a tongue and brain in such harmony, each a razor of Occam's and yet so often nice in more than the sharp meaning of the word. Jonathan, the pinky analogy stands now and forever. I am fortunate to know them, and you are ill-fated not to.

None of this touches on the countless writers, artists, musicians, filmmakers, game designers, actors, historical figures, and everyone else who inspires and inspired me, but such a list would be prohibitively lengthy. A single name that demands inclusion, however, is that of Istvan Orosz, whose art graces the cover of this very tome. Let me close by heartily praising those who are directly responsible for this book being held before your eyes: my peerless agent Sally Harding, as well as Suzanne Brandreth, Mary Hu, and everyone else at the Cooke Agency; my amazing editor, Tim Holman, and everyone at Orbit, particularly Dong-Won Song, Jennifer Flax, S. B. Kleinman, Keith Hayes, Alex Lencicki, Lauren Panepinto, and Mari Okuda; and the inimitable VanderMeers, Jeff and Ann, for their counsel, and for Jeff's guidance to the Promised Land. Thank you one and all for your faith in this project.

extras

about the author

Jesse Bullington's formative years were spent primarily in rural Pennsylvania, the Netherlands and Tallahassee, Florida. He is a folklore enthusiast who holds a bachelor's degree in history and English from Florida State University. He currently resides in Colorado, and can be found online at www.jessebullington.com

Find out more about Jesse Bullington and other Orbit authors by registering for the free monthly newsletter at www.orbitbooks.net

interview

Have you always known that you wanted to be a writer?

To the best of my memory I've always wanted to be a story-teller but I wasn't always sure in what medium I would most prefer to work. I was writing short stories as soon as I could spell, and my first rejection letter was from *Highlights* or *Cricket*, one of those children's magazines, when I was maybe seven or eight years old. At first it was just an innate desire to tell tall tales, and as I grew up I vacillated amongst ambitions of working in film, television, comic books, theater, and fiction proper, if there is such a thing. In the end I lacked the social-herding abilities required to realize your vision onstage or in front of a camera, and comics were likewise out as I was never able to either render the imagery myself or con a skilled friend into illustrating my stories. This is not to say that I became a novelist by default, but rather that for these flippant reasons combined with a strong literary inclination I found novels to be the ideal medium to transmit my stories.

How did you get your big break into publishing?

By striking up a conversation with a stranger when I was working in a video store. That stranger wound up being the brilliant and generous author Jeff VanderMeer, who offered me greater advice and assistance than we mortals are accustomed to since our oracles fell silent. After checking out my novel Jeff blogged about it and posted an excerpt on his website, which was seen by a very talented agent who offered to read the manuscript. That agent, Sally Harding, loved the novel and things progressed rapidly. The moral here is obvious, I think.

When you aren't writing, what do you like to do in your spare time?

Hiking is one of my favorite activities. I love few things more than a vigorous walk, regardless of the setting, season, time, or weather. Nocturnal hikes are preferable, as starlight and shadow render mundane landscapes far more interesting, and the increased risk of an animal mauling or a twisted ankle imbues such sport with the heady cologne of menace.

Who/what would you consider to be your influences?

All the usual sources — history, folklore, musicians, artists, filmmakers, actors, my friends, my family, my dreams, my experiences, cultures both foreign and domestic, the world around us, and other writers. In general I wear my influences on my page but, that said, I am never one to pass up the opportunity to promote my favorites. Confining myself to a baker's dozen of all sorts of creative collectives and individuals and resigning myself to thinking up an even better list as soon as I'm finished, my influences include the Tiger Lillies, Vincent Price, Angela Carter, Roald Dahl, Alan Moore, Edward Gorey, Clive Barker, Kentaro Miura, Irvine Welsh, the Coen Brothers, Italo Calvino, Nick Cave, and the Weird Tales triumvirate.

The Sad Tale of the Brothers Grossbart is an amazing novel that's truly like nothing else out there. How did you derive the idea for this novel?

A question I find every bit as tough as its reputation. I wanted to write a novel set in medieval Europe containing as many of my favorite aspects of fiction as was feasible that also satirized dull literary devices and archetypes. That and I wanted to take the romance out of grave robbing. A different sort of protagonist was mandatory, and once I had the Brothers themselves sussed everything progressed naturally.

As per your studies, are Hegel and Manfried based upon any real characters in history?

The Brothers Grossbart are not based on any particular individuals but history is rife with their ilk. Modern society as well, for that matter.

Do you think the novel is controversial? If so, why?

I think most things worth talking about are controversial if one asks around enough, but I didn't give much thought to whether or not my novel would qualify as such when I was writing it. I did intend to subvert some of the conventions of mainstream fantasy fiction, so it may well end up being divisive anyway. Much of what I love about fantasy, horror, adventure, and historical fiction seems at odds with what is currently popular in those genres, and this novel probably reflects that.

Now that The Sad Tale of the Brothers Grossbart has been published, what will be next for you?

I have several projects percolating at any given time and anticipate completing two more novels in the next couple of years.

Finally, as a first-time author, what has been your favorite part of the publishing process?

Meeting individuals at Orbit and the Cooke Agency whose humor and friendliness are surpassed only by their wisdom and keen insight. Also, having such a stunning artist as Istvan Orosz create a beautiful cover to house my humble words has made me a very happy fellow indeed.

if you enjoyed
THE SAD TALE OF THE BROTHERS GROSSBART

look out for

MR SHIVERS

by

Robert Jackson Bennett

Chapter One

By the time the number nineteen crossed the Missouri state line the sun had crawled low in the sky and afternoon was fading into evening. The train had built up a wild head of steam over the last few miles. As Tennessee fell behind it began picking up speed, the wheels chanting and chuckling, the fields blurring into jaundice- yellow streaks by the track. A fresh gout of black smoke unfurled from the train's crown and folded back to clutch the cars like a great black cloak.

Connelly shut his eyes as the wave of smoke flew toward him and held on tighter to the side of the cattle car. He wasn't sure how long he had been hanging there. Maybe a half hour. Maybe more. The crook of his arm was curled around one splintered slat of wood and he had wedged his boots into the cracks below. Every joint in his body ached.

He squinted through the tumble of trainsmoke at the other three men. They hung on, faces impassive. One of them called to the oldest, asking if it was soon. He grinned and shook his head and laughed.

Ten miles on Connelly felt the train begin to slow and the countryside started to take shape around him. The fields all seemed the same, nothing but cracked red earth and crooked fencing. Sometimes there were men working in the fields, overalled and with faces as beaten as the land. They watched the train's furious procession with a country boy's awe. Some laughed and called to them. Most did not and watched their coming and going with almost no acknowledgment at all.

The old man before him hitched himself low on the train, eyes watching the wheels as one would a predator. He held up three fingers, waved. Then two. Then one, and he dropped from the side of the train.

Connelly followed suit and as he rolled he saw the churning wheels no more than three feet from him, hissing and cackling. He slid away until he came to rest in a ditch with the others. They stood and beat the dust and grit and soot from their faces. Then they crouched low in the weeds and waited until the train's passage was marked only by a ribbon of black smoke and a roar hovering in the sky.

"Think they coming back?" whispered one of the young ones. "Coming back to look for us?"

"Boy, what are you, an idiot?" said the old man. "No train man is going to double back looking for trouble. If we're off then we're off. Done."

"Done?"

"Yeah. Count your limbs and teeth and start using your feet. Maybe your head, too, if you feel like it." He scratched his gray hair and grinned, flashing a crooked mouthful of yellowed teeth.

They shouldered their packs and began heading west, following the tracks.

"Should have held on longer," said one of the men.

"Ha," said the grayhair. "If you did that then I guarantee you wouldn't be looking so hale and hearty right now. Don't want to get caught, caught by the freight boss. He'd whale you raw."

"Not with him, I'd reckon," the man said, nodding toward Connelly, who was a head taller than the others. "What's your name?"

"Connelly," he said.

"You got any tobacco?"

Connelly shook his head.

"You sure?"

"Yeah."

"Hm," he said, and spat. "Still think we should've held on longer."

They took up upon an old county road. As they walked they kicked up a cloud of dust that rose to their faces, turning their soot- gray clothes to raw red. The land on either side was patched like a stray's coat, the hills dotted with corn lying flat as though it had been laid low by some blast. Roots lay half submerged in the loose soil, fine curling tendrils grasping at nothing. In some places growth still clung to the earth and men grouped around these spots to pump life into their crop. As Connelly passed they looked up with frightened, brittle eyes and he knew it would not last.

The two younger men paced ahead and one said, "Why don't these dumb sons of bitches leave?"

"Where they going to go?" asked the other.

"Anywhere's better than here."

"Looks like home to me. This seems to be my anywhere and it ain't much better."

"Things'll turn different in Rennah," the other said. "You just watch."

The grayhair dropped back beside Connelly. "You headed to the same place? Rennah, you headed there?"

Connelly nodded.

The grayhair shook his head, swatted the back of his neck with his hat. "Your funeral. Nothing going to be there, you know that?" He leaned closer to confide a whisper. "These fellas is just suckers. They flipped that ride 'cause they heard there's work here, but there ain't. Further down the line, I say. Maybe south, maybe west. Eh?"

"Not going for work," said Connelly.

"What? What the hell you going for, then?"

Connelly bowed his head and pulled his cap low. The old man let him be.

The sun turned a deep, sick red as it sank toward the earth. Even the sky had a faint tinge of red. It made a strange, hellish sight. It was the drought, everyone said. Threw dirt up into the sky. Touched the heavens with it. Connelly was not so sure but could not say why. Perhaps it was something else. Some superficial symptom of a greater disease.

He counted the days as he walked and guessed it had been more than two weeks since he had left Memphis. Then he counted his dollars and reckoned he had spent a little over three. He was spending at far too high of a rate if he wanted to go much farther. And he would have to go farther. The man had a week's head start on him at least. It was unlikely that he'd even be in Rennah. But he had been there once and that was all Connelly needed.

Closer, he said to himself. I'm close. I'm very close now.

"Town's up that way," said one of the men, pointing to a few lines of smoke on the horizon.

The old man eyed the spindle- like lines twisting across the sunset. "That ain't the town," he said.

"No?"

"No. Those are campfires."

The men looked at each other again, this time worried. Connelly was not surprised. He knew they had expected it, whether they said so or not. For many it was the same as the town they had just left.

Connelly caught its scent before he saw it. He smelled rotten kindling and greasy fires and cigarette smoke, excrement and foul water. It was a plague- stink, a battlefield- reek. Then he heard the cacophony of dogs barking and children crying, a junkyard song of pots and pans and old engine parts and drunken melodies. Then finally it came into view. They shaded their eyes and looked at the encampment before them, saw jalopies lurching between canyons of shuddering tents, people small as dots milling beside them. A wide smear of gray and black among the white- gold of the fields. There had to be at least a hundred people there. At least.

"Jesus," said one of the men.

"Yeah," said another.

"Can't see there being much work here."

"I reckon not, no."

"Told you so," said the grayhair softly. "Told you so."

Connelly and the men parted ways as they approached. The men walked on and came to the camp's ragged border. Some of the people had tents and some had cars and some had nothing at all but still mingled around these tattered constructs like refuse caught washing downstream. They watched the new strangers approach, too tired to hold any real resentment. The men split up and wandered in and were caught among the webs of the encampment, filtering through the grubby people to find some spot to sit in or a fire to stand by. They sat and made talk and waited for night and the following dawn. By now it was routine.

Connelly did not join them. He walked around the camp and into town.

Chapter Two

The town couldn't have been more than five hundred people, at most. Yet the essentials were there: a main street, a post office, a general store, and finally a saloon at the end of the street.

Connelly peered through the yellowed windows of the bar. Dusty bottles were lined up behind an old wooden countertop. Men sat in sweat-soaked shirts with their hats pulled low, staring into their drinks with eyes like muddy ice.

He walked in carefully, stepping like the floor could collapse at any moment. All the men looked at him, for his size caught the eye. He removed his cap and stuffed it in his pocket and sat down at the bar. The others relaxed as he did, seeing that underneath all the miles of travel he was still a man, though no doubt one who had been roughing it for the past months. His hair had grown long and a beard crawled at the edges of his jaw. He could have been thirty, or forty, or even fifty, as his skin was tanned and dark and bore deep lines from the sun.

"What can I get you?" asked the bartender.

"Whisky," Connelly said.

"Ten cents."

"All right."

Neither one moved.

"You don't have whisky?" asked Connelly.

"We have whisky. You have ten cents?"

Connelly reached into his satchel and took out a thin wallet and a dime and slid it over.

"Sorry," said the bartender, taking it. "Got to do that. Lots of folks come in here, order, then run out."

"Wasn't anything."

The bartender poured and placed the glass in front of him. Connelly took the glass and drank it in a single swallow.

"Long time getting here?" asked the bartender.

"Here is just another stop on the road," he said.

An ancient old man stood up and came and sat beside Connelly. He ordered as well, hands trembling. Then he turned to Connelly and studied him, his face fixed in a terrible awe.

"What you doing there, grampa?" asked the bartender cautiously.

The old man did not answer. Instead he said, "West."

"What?" said Connelly.

"West. You're going west, ain't you?"

"If that's where I'm going, yeah," said Connelly.

"You are," he said. "You are. I can tell. I seen enough people heading west to know when one's going that way. And you are."

"Okay."

"You shouldn't, you know. You shouldn't."

"I could go back south or north right after you get done talking to me."

"No. You won't. Certain men, the way they look at things and the way they walk, they're drawn to the west, to the far

countries. Even if they turn aside and walk for days on end, soon enough they'll find themselves facing sunset again."

"A lot of people are moving west right now."

"True. That's true. But they should not go."

Connelly fiddled with his glass, ignoring him.

The old man said, "They say the sun kisses the land out there, like a lover. That may be so. I been out there. For years, I been out there. And if that's so then the sun's love is a terrible, harsh thing. Where it's placed its kiss nothing grows, all is burned away, everything is scorched and nothing lives and your heart is the only one of its kind that beats for miles and miles. And all is red. Where the sun and the horizon and the sands meet, all is red."

"Is it?"

"Yes," said the old man. "You should not go. You should turn around. Stop looking. And go."

"You leave me the hell alone," Connelly said.

"Listen," the old man pleaded. "Listen to me. I been out there. I seen the great, red hunger, and where it walks everything aches. From the stones to the skies, everything aches. It's broken land, there. It is broken and lost, like those who live there, and they cannot go back. You should not go out there.

You should not."

The bartender scowled. "Get out of here, you damn crazy fool. Stop worrying my customers and get the hell out of here."

"Go back to your home," said the old man.

"I don't have a home," said Connelly. "Not anymore."

"But you still could have another," said the old man. "In the west there is no hope of that. Such things are forfeit there."

"Get out. Now," said the bartender. "I won't ask you again.

If you stay here for one more second I'm going to whale you, I don't care how old you are."

The old man stepped down from the seat and staggered out onto the sidewalk. He mumbled to himself, played with the buttons on his overalls, and shambled away.

"I apologize for that," said the bartender. "Damn old coot.

He's always causing trouble. I don't think he even lives here. He just drinks when he can and sleeps in whatever alley he finds.

There's more and more of them. They're almost like dogs."

"Another whisky," said Connelly.

The bartender poured, gave him the glass, and watched again as Connelly drank in one swallow.

"Well, you don't spend like an Okie and you don't drink much like an Okie, either," said the bartender.

"Probably 'cause I'm not an Okie."

"Oh?"

"No."

"Where you from?"

"Back east."

"Ha. People who're east ought to stay east, I'd say."

"You going to give me another earful like the old man?"